He was bent over
so close she could
rustle of wool agai
own clothing, the heat of his
breath upon her lips.
And those eyes, so very dark—
dark as a moonless night!—
never wavered from her own...

In Praise of the Novels of
SAMANTHA JAMES

"Powerful. Tender. A beautiful love story."
Stella Cameron on *A Promise Given*

"A passionate and intensely
emotional experience."
Lisa Kleypas, author of *Stranger in My Arms*,
on *Every Wish Fulfilled*

"A marvelous book that tugs
on the heartstrings."
Catherine Anderson, author of *Cherish*,
on *Every Wish Fulfilled*

"A spectacular roller coaster ride
of emotions. Be sure not to miss it!"
Romantic Times on *Just One Kiss*

"An enthralling historical full of
sensuality and excitement."
Rendezvous on *My Lord Conqueror*

Avon Books are available at special quantity discounts for bulk
purchases for sales promotions, premiums, fund raising or educa-
tional use. Special books, or book excerpts, can also be created to
fit specific needs.

For details write or telephone the office of the Director of Special
Markets, Avon Books, Inc., Dept. FP, 1350 Avenue of the Americas, New York, New York 10019, 1-800-238-0658.

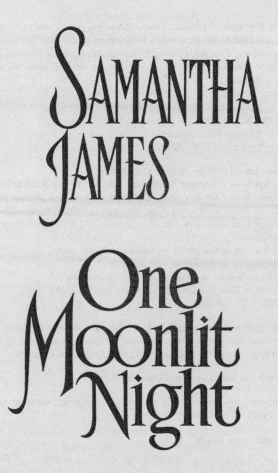

SAMANTHA JAMES

One Moonlit Night

AVON BOOKS  NEW YORK

This is a work of fiction. Names, characters, places, and incidents either are the product of the author's imagination or are used fictitiously. Any resemblance to actual events, locales, organizations, or persons, living or dead, is entirely coincidental and beyond the intent of either the author or the publisher.

AVON BOOKS, INC.
1350 Avenue of the Americas
New York, New York 10019

Copyright © 1998 by Sandra Kleinschmit
Excerpt from *Christmas Knight* copyright © 1998 by Roberta Helmer
Excerpt from *Cherish* copyright © 1998 by Adeline Catherine Anderson
Excerpt from *One Moonlit Night* copyright © 1998 by Sandra Kleinschmit
Excerpt from *Anywhere You Are* copyright © 1999 by Constance O'Day-Flannery
Inside cover author photo by Steimonts Photography
Published by arrangement with the author
Visit our website at **http://www.AvonBooks.com**
Library of Congress Catalog Card Number: 98-93164
ISBN: 0-380-78609-5

First Avon Books Printing: December 1998

AVON TRADEMARK REG. U.S. PAT. OFF. AND IN OTHER COUNTRIES, MARCA REGISTRADA, HECHO EN U.S.A.

Printed in the U.S.A.

WCD   10 9 8 7 6 5 4 3 2 1

Prologue

"I have something to tell you," *she whispered*.

She was a beauty, with long, gleaming black hair that fell to her hips, slanted dark eyes and skin that was sleek and golden. But Madeleine was scarcely aware of her charms, though many a man had been struck by the vibrancy of her beauty, the radiance of her smile and laughter. And only one man had ever truly captured her eye. Her very soul.

This one.

"James?" she whispered again. "I—I have something to tell you."

This time, the slightly husky undertone—the remnants of lovemaking—had vanished from her voice, which carried a slight accent. But the hint of shyness remained, the . . . uncertainty.

The covers shifted. James St. Bride, Earl of Ravenwood, propped himself on an elbow. A dark brow cocked high.

"What is it, *petite?*" As he spoke, he ran a fingertip up and down the length of her bare arm.

Madeleine could not suppress her shiver of delight. God help her, but he was a handsome man!

He waited, his expression faintly detached. As he

1

caught her gaze, one corner of his mouth lifted slightly.

Madeleine took a deep breath. There was no help for it. She must simply say it and be done with it.

"I am with child," she said softly.

His finger stilled. His smile withered. The room grew very silent, a hush she felt to the marrow of her bones. It was difficult to believe only moments before his heated cry of ecstasy had filled the chamber.

He snatched his hand from her and rolled from the bed. One lithe fluid motion and he was on his feet.

Madeleine swallowed as he turned away. She stared at the back of his head. Rich brown hair the color of mahogany glistened shiny and bright in the light from the fire. The muscles of his shoulders flexed and rolled as he reached for his robe. His movements jerky, he slid his arms into the sleeves.

Slowly he turned to face her. To her dismay, his features reflected nothing of his thoughts. His eyes, the deep blue color of sapphires, were cool and remote. His mouth was a thin straight line.

An awful feeling coiled deep in her middle.

"Surely you must know a potion."

"A potion?" Her brows drew together over her eyes. She was confused.

"Yes, a potion! To get rid of the brat!"

Never before had he spoken to her so brusquely. He could barely restrain his agitation. She had to stop herself from cringing at his impatience.

"Come now, Madeleine! You are a Gypsy! Surely you know of a potion!"

Madeleine eased to a sitting position, clutching the coverlet to her breast. She was stunned to the depths of her being that he would suggest she would kill her own child . . .

"James," she said haltingly. "*James*." She blinked back tears, tears that burned her very soul. She could only shake her head, over and over.

"What! Did you think I would be pleased?"

With her eyes she mutely pleaded with him. "I thought that you . . . that we . . . that we might be . . ."

He made a sound of disgust. "Good God! What are you saying . . . that you would have me marry you?"

Madeleine had gone very still. In truth, she had scarcely dared to hope . . . But she had prayed. Prayed nightly that he would marry her—oh, it mattered not if it was the Christian way. Even if it were only words, words that pledged their hearts together forever . . .

And so her answer lay in her eyes, huge and wide and dark as midnight skies, fixed mutely upon his. He remained where he was. So very distant. So very aloof. Everything within her cried out in pain. She'd given him everything. Her body. And her heart as well.

His lip curled. "I am the Earl of Ravenwood, *petite*. And you are a Gypsy."

He taunted her—oh, most cruelly! Yet even as Madeleine longed to wither away and die, pride brought her head up high. "If I were one of you, you would not treat me like this!"

His tone was faintly bored. "But you are not, are you?"

No, she echoed silently. She was not. She was a Gypsy. And of course, that was something he would never forget . . .

But *she* had. In her dreams, in her hopes, she had blinded herself . . .

They had met the summer past. She'd first noticed him one night. He'd allowed her people to camp on one of his estates. She'd been dancing, swaying in time to the soulful pitch of a lonely violin, a haunting tune that vibrated deep within her body. But there was a story to be told, a story as old as time. A story that echoed the pangs of heartache yet soon brought the promise of tomorrow— the promise of brightness and gaiety. And as the chords of the music escalated, her feet echoed the beat, atune with the rhythm of her heart. On and on it went, until she was laughing, her arms raised high, her skirts flying up to reveal a tantalizing glimpse of lithe, slender legs. And it was while she was still caught in the aftermath of a whirling excitement that he had approached her . . .

Lovely, he had called her. The most lovely creature he'd ever seen.

He'd returned yet again the next night. And for the following six thereafter. Ah, but he was a most splendid specimen of a man! Oh, the others had warned her. That he was a *gadjo* who wanted nothing from her. But she had not listened. And on one starry, moonlit night he had made her forever his.

Contrary to what most of the *gadje* believed, she was not a wanton; Madeleine had guarded her virtue well. James had been surprised—but oh, so very pleased—to discover he was her first lover.

And so when he left . . . she went with him.

For nearly six months she had lived here in the country with him. Waiting as he conducted his business in London and at his other estates. But though he had oft spoken of passion, of the pounding need that burned his blood and thrilled her to the core of her being, not once had he spoken of love.

Madeleine could not help it. A single tear leaked from her eye.

"What is this?" he demanded. "Tears?" he scoffed. "From a Gypsy whore?"

Gazing at him now, his face scored with contempt, it was hard to believe he had ever been tender. That he had been kind. Yet now there was a darkness in him, a blackness she could not reach . . . could never reach.

Perhaps it had always been there.

Her hands were shaking—and so would her voice if she let it. She stilled both by sheer determination. Boldly she met his cold blue gaze.

"I am no whore, James. I gave you everything . . . everything! I've lain with no other man save you and you know it as well as I."

"What does that matter?" he demanded. "I fed you and took you from that dirty Gypsy camp. You knew what I wanted from the very beginning, Madeleine. And you wanted it too. Dear God, you were as insatiable as I!"

Her fingers curled into the coverlet. She said nothing.

"You see!" he taunted. "You know I am right. I gave you satin and lace and furs. You ate from the finest china. I gave you things you'd never have had without me. You took it all, knowing I promised nothing in return."

For the first time she knew shame. Shame at what she had done. Oh, but how rash she had been! She had thought she could change him. That she could make him love her. Love her as she loved him.

Ah, yes, she had loved . . . while he had lusted.

Slowly Madeleine raised her chin. "You call me whore. But I am no whore. I am . . . what you made me."

A tight smile curled his lips. "You were well paid for your services, *petite*. And you are what you are. A Gypsy whore."

Her chest rose and fell. Each breath burned like fire. "And what about my babe?" she cried. "*Your* babe?"

"And how do I know there *is* a babe? This could be naught but a trick for me to marry you. But 'twill do no good, *petite*, for you see, I'll never marry you. When I marry, it will be a woman with impeccable bloodlines, not a common Gypsy waif."

Raw pain crowded her chest. She was a fool. A fool to love a man such as he . . . For he was right. A man such as he could never marry her.

His tone should have served as a warning. "Let us not quibble. The time has come for you to leave, *petite*. Let us not part in anger." He strode to the highboy across the chamber, opened it and reached within. There was a satin, tasseled pouch in his hands when he turned.

"Here." He tossed the pouch on the bed. There was a jangle of coins as it landed near her feet. "You Gypsies are fond of gold, are you not? I trust that is ample compensation."

Let us not part in anger.

But Madeleine *was* angry. A bitter blackness fired her blood, searing away her heartache. He would never know, she vowed. He would never know she loved him.

Her gaze traveled from the pouch to his face.

"I do not want your gold. I will not take it," she said levelly. "And I promise you, James, you will regret this."

"Will I?" He gave a bored shrug. "I think not. There are other women in the world, Madeleine, women just as beautiful as you."

"I carry a son. The only son you will ever have."

"You carry a bastard."

His tone was scalding, yet his eyes were cold as ice. Dear God, did he possess not a shred of feeling?

Madeleine wet her lips. With one hand she swept aside the coverlet and rose from the bed. Heedless of her nakedness, she walked to him and stood before him.

Her hands lifted to his face. But she did not touch him. Instead, her native Romany flowed from her lips, as she let loose the storm in her heart.

James was disconcerted. She could see it in the way his eyes flickered uneasily.

Her words gained strength and volume. Hands beckoned. Fingers pointed accusingly.

The tension in the room grew ever more powerful.

Finally, as her voice rose to a crescendo, his hands shot out. Strong fingers curled almost violently into her narrow shoulders.

He shook her. He shook her until she was silent, until her head fell back like a broken flower on its stem.

Madeleine didn't retreat from his fury but met his countenance with glittering eyes.

"What is this?" he demanded. "A Gypsy curse?"

Madeleine allowed a faint smile to grace her lips.

"So you believe . . . then so it will be."

He released her with a scowl. "You're mad," he said baldly. "As mad as that Gypsy fortune-teller Adriana."

A secret smile touched Madeleine's lips. The old woman Adriana had told James that he was destined to a life of unhappiness. She'd said his wealth would buy him no joy in life.

"Perhaps I am," Madeline said quietly, "but Adriana was right. You will never be happy, James." Deliberately she touched her belly with both hands. "Behold your son, James, for you will father no more children, neither sons nor daughters . . ."

His expression turned to one of utter disgust. "Your Gypsy curse doesn't frighten me, Madeleine. When I return this evening, I want you out. Go back to the streets. Go back to your Gypsies. I care not where you go. Do you hear, Madeleine? I care not where you go."

He whirled and started toward the door.

But Madeleine had seen a glimpse of that which he feared, in the way only her people could see . . . and now it was her turn to taunt him.

"Remember, James. I take your son with me, your only son. So you believe, then so it is."

The door slammed.

Her strident cry resounded through the room. "Damn you, James. Damn you to hell!"

Even as the words spilled from her lips, while the fires of hatred spilled through her veins, she could not deny the truth of her own heart . . .

Her strength failed her. She slumped to the floor. Tears ran unchecked down her cheeks, until there were no more tears left.

All was silent when at last she raised her head.

She touched her belly anew, but it was different now—her touch was light and reverent, almost worshipful. And all at once Madeleine knew . . .

It would be just as the music foretold the night they had met . . . From grief would come joy. From heartache would come happiness. Her people would welcome her back. This she did not doubt. She would bear her babe. Her son. *Her son.*

But James must never know. He would never know . . . For she was aware with a certainty that defied all belief . . . that just as she carried his son . . .

It was her own curse to love him . . . James St. Bride . . . always.

One

Ravenwood Hall, 1821

"He's a Gypsy, you know, Olivia." There was an elbow in her ribs. "The devil's own."

The Gypsy.

In her own mind, Olivia had begun to call him that the very day she'd been hired on at Ravenwood Hall. No doubt the others here in the household did too, for that was what he was. The old earl's bastard son . . .

The Gypsy.

Dominic St. Bride.

Olivia smiled politely, reaching for the yeasty chunk of bread that was her meal. As a man of God, her dearest papa—God rest his soul—had always regarded gossip as a grievous sin. No doubt Papa would have chastised her for even listening. Still, Olivia could not help it. Lord knew she harbored no affection for the Gypsies—nay, not after what had happened to Papa—yet she could not help it. She was intensely curious about the new master of Ravenwood.

A number of the servants had clustered together in the kitchen to take their noonday meal.

Franklin, the butler, raised bushy gray brows. "Langston—he's the butler at the London town house, y' know—said he's a brooding sort. And he sleeps with his window open, even in the dead of winter!"

"Oh, he'll be a cruel master, no doubt." This came from Mrs. Thompson, the pastry cook. From the look of her, she often indulged in that at which she excelled. Her belly was round as her bottom, but Olivia had heard Franklin say there was no finer pastry cook outside of London.

Charlotte, a young girl who'd just recently come from Ireland, made the sign of the cross. Doe-soft brown eyes were as wide as a full moon.

"No different than the other, the old earl," chimed in another with a grimace. "How I wish he would remain in London!"

Franklin shook his head. "I still cannot believe the old earl fathered no other sons. Can you imagine? Three wives and all barren."

"P'rhaps it was him, and not his wives. Did ye ever think o' that?" This came from the cook.

"He did take to his wine rather fondly his last years—"

"His last years? Why, the last decade, I daresay! Mildred, who's cousin to his London stable master, said he was in his cups from the day he went and fetched the boy from his Gypsy mother!"

Franklin nodded. "They say he could barely stand to look upon the boy. Why, it wasn't until his will was read that anyone realized he'd legitimized the boy's birth years ago."

"Aye," said the gardener. "It was only after he buried his last wife that he went after the boy. But the earl had to legitimize the little Gypsy's birth, for who else would inherit? Other than the Gypsy, a far-distant cousin was his only blood relative—and she is nearly as old as he was."

"But the title wouldn't have passed to her anyway. Besides," said Glory, one of the upstairs maids, "the old earl wasn't particularly fond of her."

"The old earl was not particularly fond of anyone!"

This last was followed by a rowdy burst of laughter from the group assembled.

Cook placed stout hands on her hips. Her gaze traveled from one to the other. "How can ye laugh?" she demanded. "A Gypsy now carries the title! And we'd best pay him the proper respect, else he'll likely cast a spell on us the way his mother did to his father!"

The laughter abruptly ceased.

"Oh, come now. That's rubbish!"

" 'Tis not. Why, I heard the earl ravin' about it meself as he lay dying! The Gypsy witch cursed him. She said he'd have no children save the one she carried in her belly!"

" 'E's a handsome enough devil, or so I've heard," said Enid, one of the chambermaids. Enid was rather pretty, with round blue eyes and curling blonde hair.

"Oh, but 'e's a wild one. Why, he was from the moment the old earl laid hands on 'im. Refused to stay in school, as I recall. The little wretch persisted in running away—I remember quite distinctly. And now that he's grown, it seems all he's interested in is gambling and whor—" The man hastily revised his words. "—and women. He's always taken a particular likin' to the ladies, if ye know wot I mean. Why, the women he's left behind . . . a duchess and a countess, I've heard. And at least two opera singers. I hear of late he's been taken with the actress Maureen Miller. Oh, yes, he's quite notorious, for he's trampled many a female heart."

Olivia's mouth turned down. Already she disliked him—not only was he a Gypsy, he was a profligate scoundrel—the veriest womanizer!

"That's certainly nothing wot's changed," added another chambermaid. "Why, he did that long before the old earl died! My mum, she lives in London—she used to send me the dailies. Why, no doubt 'tis what sent the earl into apoplexy!"

"His father threatened to cut him off many a time, but 'tis said the Gypsy cared not a whit!" came the rejoinder.

"Yes, but now he's coming here and I daresay we'd best be prepared." Franklin rose to his feet. "We've dallied long enough, ladies and gents. Let us return to our work."

Franklin, an austere-looking presence with his gaunt frame and immense height, was a mellow, gentle soul—though he *did* harbor a tendency to gossip. But he didn't let his position in the household sway him from associating with the rest of the staff; he was always ready with a smile and a greeting, for even the lowliest scullery maid. Olivia liked him; she liked that he didn't consider himself above the rest of them.

But the housekeeper, Mrs. Templeton, was another matter altogether. Her manner was brittle, as brittle as her features. Olivia was convinced that if she deigned to smile, her face would surely shatter into a hundred pieces. Nor did she look at one. She glowered. She did not ask. She demanded. Nor did she tell. She snapped, like the lash of a whip.

Rising to her feet, Olivia brushed the crumbs from the starched white apron which covered her drab black gown. These last days had been a flurry of activity . . . and all because of the imminent arrival of the Gypsy.

Olivia had lived all her life in the village of Stonebridge. She'd never met James St. Bride, the old earl, though she'd seen him occasionally, riding down the lane or trotting his horse through the village. He bestowed neither smile nor greeting but rarely. As vicar, Papa had naturally had dealings with him occasionally. One of the few times that Olivia remembered Papa being angry was just after he'd come from Ravenwood Hall; he'd asked the earl for monetary assistance in repairing the church roof, which had begun to leak most abominably.

The earl had refused. So it was that Olivia's only impression of him was scarcely flattering; in her mind, he had been a cold, selfish man who guarded both his money and his privacy with an iron fist.

Ravenwood Hall sat high upon a hill north of the village, a lofty, majestic sentinel of stone and brick and mullioned windows. Since the old earl had not spent much time at Ravenwood the last five years, much of the hall had been closed up; only a handful of servants had remained during that time. Even when the old earl had taken ill nearly two years ago, he hadn't returned to his ancestral home. He'd spent his last days at his London town house.

But Olivia had dallied a moment too long. She was one of the last to rise from the long oaken worktable; it was at precisely that moment that Mrs. Templeton entered the kitchen.

Her icy gaze lit straight upon Olivia. "Oh, but I should have known!" The older woman made no attempt to disguise the rancor in her tone. "I knew I'd not get a day's work out of you, young miss! Unfortunately, I had no choice but to hire you!"

Oivia was well aware what she referred to. Nearly a month ago, the Gypsy had sent word that he would reopen Ravenwood Hall. The village had been all abuzz with the news, but few were interested in hiring on at the Hall. Stonebridge residents were wary of the new master of Ravenwood Hall. To them he was an outsider . . . a Gypsy.

But the wages offered were too good for Olivia to ignore. Papa had never been terribly good at managing his affairs, but there had been some money left after his death, enough to last almost half a year, thank heaven. It had been a difficult time; Papa's death—the way he had died—had been a blow. Not only that, there was Emily's affliction to contend with . . . But now the time had come when funds were scarce, and she must make a living for them both. So it was that she needed the money a position at Ravenwood offered . . . needed it desperately.

Mrs. Templeton was still in a tirade. "No doubt you think that you, a gentlewoman, are above the rest of us. But I'm warning you, Miss Olivia Sherwood, do not make me regret it!"

Two bright spots of color stained Olivia's cheeks. Her face was burning, for several of the servants had paused in the doorway. They watched, their mouths all agog. She was only barely able to hold her tongue, yet she shuddered to think what would happen if she were without employment.

Instead she held her head high. Calmly she said,

"I regret that you feel that way, Mrs. Templeton. I assure you, I am well aware of my place in the household. Indeed, I am fully prepared to do as you wish."

Her quiet dignity only seemed to infuriate Mrs. Templeton further. Her lips barely moved as she said, " 'Tis good that you feel that way, Miss Sherwood, for I should like you to clean and polish the grand staircase. And you'll not be dismissed until it is done to my satisfaction."

The grand staircase was immense. Midway, it divided in two, leading upward to each wing of the house . . . Why, no doubt it would take her hours to finish . . . Her heart sank. Bravely she resisted the temptation to glare at her tormentor. Instead she inclined her head and left. From the beginning, Mrs. Templeton hadn't liked her. Olivia had seen it in her eyes. Indeed, she was surprised she hadn't been made a scullery maid.

Charlotte was waiting just around the next corner. She lightly touched her arm. "Don't worry, Olivia. She's always been like that, or so I'm told. She's at odds with the world, and all in it."

Olivia gave her a weak smile. "And I thought it was me."

Moments later, she carried a generous supply of cloths and beeswax into the entrance hall. Determinedly she began the herculean task. On the other side of the staircase the yellow orb of the sun could be seen. Olivia tried to ignore the sun's reflection as it slipped beyond the horizon.

Time dragged. The clock below tolled the hour of ten. Olivia had just reached the landing where the staircase separated when a shadow fell over her. Pushing a stray wisp of golden-russet hair from her cheek, she glanced up.

Thankfully, it was only Charlotte. "I've come to 'elp ye," Charlotte said promptly.

Olivia got to her feet with a shake of her head. "Charlotte, no! Mrs. Templeton will be angry if she finds you here."

"And if she does, I'll 'ave to tell 'er that what I does on me own time is my business and none o' hers."

Reaching out, Olivia straightened Charlotte's cap, for it was ever askew.

"I'm touched that you should offer, but this is my work, not yours, Charlotte."

"Come now," Charlotte said crisply. "Ye've your sister to attend to at home. Indeed, ye should be on your way 'ome to 'er this very instant."

Olivia arched a slender brow. "And you should be at home with your son." Charlotte was three and twenty, not so much older than she, but she had a seven-year-old little boy, Colin. Colin's father had died, and times were hard in Ireland. For that reason, Charlotte and her mother had moved to England—and Yorkshire.

"And me mum can take care of 'im as well as I. Indeed, p'rhaps better, for she raised fourteen of her own!" Charlotte gave her a lopsided grin.

Olivia sighed. There would be no arguing with Charlotte—that was very clear. Handing her a rag, she whispered her thanks.

And indeed, it proceeded much faster with Charlotte's help. An hour later, she gently touched Charlotte's shoulder. "You've done enough, Charlotte. Please, I beg of you, go home to your little one." Charlotte opened her mouth to argue, but

Olivia was quicker. She pointed to the last ten-foot section. "Look, that's all that remains. I can have that done in no time. Besides, if you stay and Mrs. Templeton finds you here, she'll have both our hides, and I don't want that on my conscience."

Charlotte bit her lip, then got to her feet. Olivia gave her a hasty embrace. "I can't thank you enough, Charlotte. Should you ever need anything, you have only to ask."

Charlotte's departure was well-timed. Olivia had scarcely finished the last stroke than Mrs. Templeton climbed the grand staircase. She ran a finger along the polished cherrywood and held it high before her nose, looking for dust; those small brown eyes missed nary a thing. Olivia held her breath anxiously, until at last Mrs. Templeton reached her.

The woman delivered neither praise nor reprimand. When she spoke, her tone was as sour as her disposition. "You may go," was all she said.

Olivia muttered a hurried thank you. Only when she had fled around the corner did she release a pent-up sigh of relief.

The house was dark as a tomb. In Olivia's mind, the name "Ravenwood" had always conjured up images that were dark and sinister. But that was before she had ever set foot inside the Hall. It had been a pleasant surprise to discover that Ravenwood Hall was lovely beyond measure. There were windows everywhere, filling the spacious rooms with light and a golden warmth that seemed wholly at odds with its name. Even as she shivered, curiously the house seemed almost hauntingly lonely.

Her footsteps echoed on the polished floor as she hurried toward the rear entrance near the kitchen.

No one else was about. Many of the servants had beds in the servants' quarters, one floor below. A few, like her and Charlotte, lived in the village.

She winced a little as her hand closed around the doorknob. She'd spent all day yesterday scrubbing floors, hauling bucket after bucket to the third floor. Her shoulders and back still ached abominably, and half a dozen blisters had formed on each palm. Her fingers felt stiff and swollen from clutching the polishing cloth.

She trudged down the long, curving lane that led to the road. She knew there would be no extra wages for her efforts this night—oh, to be so blessed!

A melancholy sadness seeped into her heart. She blinked back the foolish tears which threatened to come, for the time to weep was long past. There was a part of her that still could not believe Papa was gone—and Mama, too. Yet she had only to stare into Emily's vague, sightless eyes to know it was true.

A chill breeze caught her full in the face, rousing her from her doleful mood. She drew her cloak more tightly around her shoulders. The hour was late, near midnight, she suspected.

A low mist had begun to cling to the ground. Here the forest nearly trespassed upon the roadway. Gnarled branches twisted and turned overhead, mingling with one another in a dance that was somehow almost macabre.

She chided herself. The dark was playing havoc with her mind. Stonebridge was a small, quiet community. There was naught to fear here. Indeed, the most shocking event of the decade had been the murder of her father—and the guilty man had been quickly apprehended and punished.

Still she could not banish the twinge of uneasiness that seized her. She moved to the center of the rutted roadway. Once she'd gained the next curve, the village was just over the next rise.

She felt it first . . . the rumble of the earth beneath her feet. Her head came up. A strangled cry caught in her throat. A coach and four had just rounded the corner. It lumbered toward her, coming closer . . . ever closer. The jangle of the harness reached her ears. She fancied she could hear the labored breathing of the massive beasts. Panic rose. Didn't the coachman see her?

It would seem not. Olivia dove to the side of the road just as the coach thundered by.

Branches scraped against her cheek. She landed hard upon her shoulder, jarring the breath from her lungs, and skidded across uneven ground until she rolled to a halt. Though her head was reeling, she was dimly aware of a shout. Stunned, she lay there, trying desperately to recover her breath. She was only half-aware that the coach had stopped. Struggling to her knees, she passed a hand across her eyes.

It was then that she saw it . . . a huge beast hurtling toward her. She gave a strangled cry and flung up a hand, but it was no use. A tremendous force crashed into her chest. She was knocked to her back once again. For the second time in as many moments, the breath was knocked from her. Too stunned to move, to even scream, she stared straight into the gaping jaws of certain death.

There was no help for it. Fear wrapped a stranglehold around her. She squeezed her eyes shut and let loose of a scream then, certain she would be this monster's next meal . . .

There was the crunch of gravel beneath booted feet.

"He's harmless," a disembodied male voice assured her, even as a warm, wet tongue lapped her cheek, "utterly harmless."

Her scream died in her throat. Olivia opened her eyes. From out of the shadows a towering form had appeared. It appeared he was dressed entirely in black.

A shiver touched her spine. Infinitely more frightening than this—this beastly mongrel was its master . . .

She stared into eyes as black as the devil's soul. Numbly she realized that it was he . . .

The Gypsy.

Two

Her first thought was that he didn't look like any Gypsy she'd ever seen. Where was the bright cloth-ing? The kerchief around his neck?

But of course he wouldn't, goose, she chided herself. The fall must have rattled her senses; he'd been living the life of a gentleman for quite some time now.

"Miss? Miss, are you hurt? Can you speak?"

So this was Dominic St. Bride, Earl of Raven-wood. His voice was low and deep, smooth as a well-oiled clock. Beside him stood the mongrel beast.

"Miss! Can you hear me? If you are able, please answer!"

A touch of irritation underscored the words. Only then did Olivia realize she was still staring. Why, no doubt he thought she was daft!

"Young woman! Can you move?"

His brow was pleated with lines, there beneath the fall of dark hair. Strong hands curled around her arms. He was bent over her, so close she could feel the rustle of wool against her own clothing, the moist heat of his breath upon her lips. Curiously, it was not at all unpleasant . . .

Heavens, what was the matter with her?

"I would be quite happy to, sir, if only you would release me."

Something flickered in his eyes. His lips twitched ever so slightly . . . a smile?

Nay. Nay, it could not be! The rest of the servants were convinced, as was she . . . the Gypsy would be a cruel master.

He released her. Cautiously Olivia tested her limbs. He stood above her now, offering a gloved hand to assist her. She took it, letting go as soon as she was on her feet. "Careful now. Not too swiftly."

There were more footsteps. A stout man appeared, a lantern swaying in his hand.

"My lord. Is all well? Dear God, I swear I didn't see the chit until it was too late! I tried to veer away but—"

"All is under control now, Higgins. You may return to the carriage."

Those eyes, so very dark—dark as a moonless night!—never wavered from her own.

All at once Olivia felt decidedly foolish, awkward and clumsy.

" 'Tis midnight," he said softly. "You should not be about at this hour."

Olivia bristled. He might be her employer—though he was not yet aware of it—but he was not her keeper.

"I'm well aware of the hour, sir, and I assure you, I'm quite safe."

"You were not, else we would not be having this discussion."

Olivia blinked. What arrogance! Why, he was insufferable! Her spine straightened. At two and twenty, she was her own woman. Papa had never dictated to her, but had always urged her and Emily to make decisions on their own, to be independent thinkers.

"I am not a sniveling, helpless female, sir."

It appeared as if he'd not heard at all. His only response was to pull a handkerchief from deep in his trouser pocket. Olivia stiffened in shock when he pressed it to her right cheekbone.

"You're bleeding," he said by way of explanation. "I saw it when Higgins came over with the lantern."

Her reaction was instinctive. She gasped and one hand went to her cheek.

"It's only a scratch." Even as he spoke, he let his hand drop. "It will soon stop."

All at once Olivia felt chastened and subdued. Lord, but he was tall! Why, she barely reached his chin. She didn't need the light of day to know that beneath his jacket, his shoulders were wide as the seas.

Her pulse was racing, in a way she liked not at all—in a way that was wholly unfamiliar. Quickly she wrenched her eyes from his form. Most assuredly, she did not wish to be caught staring again.

Her gaze lit upon the dog, who now stood close at his side. From the look of him, he was a mongrel—surely the ugliest creature she had ever seen! His head was immense, his coat black and rather longish. But he was powerfully muscled, his ears erect and pointing.

Her rescuer had seen where her attention now lay.

"This is Lucifer."

"Lucifer! Why, that is the name of the devil!"

Apparently he found her shock amusing; he threw back his head and laughed. "I assure you, Lucifer is a veritable pussycat."

"A veritable beast," she stated unthinkingly. She eyed the mongrel dubiously. Though the animal displayed no sign of aggression, merely stood docile at his master's side, she was apprehensive. "I much prefer cats," she heard herself say.

"Ah, but cats have claws."

"So do some women, or so 'tis said."

"Ah." The moon had slid behind a cloud, obscuring her vision. She could no longer see his features clearly, but he sounded amused. "And what about you, Miss . . ."

Olivia hesitated, oddly reluctant to share her identity. Yet what did it matter?

"Sherwood," she said at last. "Olivia Sherwood."

To her surprise, he stripped off one glove and tucked it beneath his arm. He then proceeded to take her hand.

Two things ran through her mind in that instant . . . For some strange reason she thought his skin would be cold as death; instead it seemed hot as fire. The second was that her hand was completely swallowed by his.

"Allow me take you home, Miss Sherwood."

Her gaze flew to his. She tried to remove her hand from within his grasp. His grip tightened ever so slightly.

"Y-you're holding my hand, sir." To her shame, her voice came out airy and breathless.

"So I am, Miss Sherwood. So I am." He glanced down at his hand, clasped in his palm, then back up to her face. A slight smile curled his lips . . . oh, a devil's smile surely, for she sensed he was making light of her. "And I would ask again . . . may I take you home?"

"Nay, sir!" A shake of her head accompanied her denial. " 'Tis not necessary," she hastened to add. "Truly. I live there, just over the hill."

"In the village?"

"Y-yes." It wasn't entirely true, for she lived nearly a mile past the far side of the village.

He persisted. "You may well have injuries of which you are unaware."

"Nay." She was adamant, or at least she prayed she sounded that way! "I would know it."

He gazed down at her, so long and so intently she could have sworn he knew she'd lied.

He released her hand just when she feared he never would.

"Very well then."

His tone was decidedly cool. Had she offended him? A sliver of guilt shot through her.

"Thank you for stopping, sir," she said quickly. "And please, tell your coachman 'twas not his fault."

He inclined his head, then spoke very quietly. "I'm very glad you came to no harm, Miss Sherwood."

Three steps and he'd disappeared into the shadows. Though she strained to see, she could not. She could only hear the jangle of the harness as the coach rolled off.

She released a long, pent-up breath. *Ravenwood*, she thought shakily. 'Twas a fitting name, for a fitting master. For there was something dark and mysterious about Dominic St. Bride . . .

Or did the midnight hour—and his Gypsy soul—but fuel her foolish fancies?

Her heart was still beating hard by the time Olivia arrived at the small cottage she and Emily now called home.

Should she tell Emily of the encounter? No. Emily would worry—for the first time she gave thanks that Emily was blind, that she could not see the cut upon her cheek.

She threw open the back door, calling out a gay greeting that shielded her turmoil.

"Emily? I'm home. Where are you, love?"

"I'm here."

Emily's voice sounded from the parlor. Olivia's footsteps took her through the kitchen. The parlor was filled with shadows, but she managed to make out the shape of her sister's form sitting in the rocker by the window. Briskly she set about lighting the candles. "My, but it's frightfully da—" Hurriedly she revised what she'd been about to say.

Emily now lived in a world of darkness.

"It's frightfully cool for a summer night. Why, I thought I should freeze to death on the walk home."

"It's only June, and still early, at that." Emily's fingers twitched at the fabric of her skirt. Her lovely brow was pleated with a frown. "Olivia, you're rather late, aren't you?"

"I am, and I'm terribly sorry, love. I fear it couldn't be helped." She gave a quick laugh. "You must be feeling neglected, I suspect. Have you eaten yet?"

"I had bread and cheese some hours ago." Emily

turned her head in the direction of her voice. "Olivia, you sound . . . different."

"Of course I don't. I simply feel the wretch for having to leave you alone so long."

"You needn't feel guilty, Olivia. Esther stopped by and we went for a walk earlier." When Olivia had begun working at Ravenwood, she'd hired a woman from the village—Esther—to help out with Emily's meals and take her out for a bit each day.

"It was his fault that you were late, wasn't it? The new Gypsy master." There was no denying the disapproval in Emily's tone.

Olivia sighed. The less she talked about the new Gypsy master of Ravenwood, the better. Emily had had nightmares, reliving the day Papa had been murdered, for weeks afterward. Yet she would not speak of it to anyone—not even Olivia. So it was that Olivia had no wish to stir that kettle anew.

"No, love, it wasn't. I fear I was a bit of a sluggard today, and Mrs. Templeton made me polish the grand staircase. 'Tis my own fault, and I've no one to blame but myself."

"I dislike you working for a Gypsy, Olivia. If only you could have been a governess—or a seamstress."

If only . . . But there were no rich households with young children for whom she might hire on as governess, not in Stonebridge. With a seamstress already well established in the village, it wouldn't have been fair to take business from her. They could have gone to Cornwall, where Mama's youngest brother Ambrose had lived. But Uncle Ambrose was gone, too, and his widow Paulina had her own dire straits to contend with—four young children to raise. Olivia would not even think of burdening her further. Nor would she take charity. Nay, she would not let pride be her folly.

And so she'd had no choice. Money was in short supply, but they had to eat. There was rent to pay. It didn't matter how menial the task; she was strong and she would do what she must so that she and Emily could survive. And somehow, if it took a hundred years, she would find the money to take Emily to a physician in London. It was so strange . . . the way she'd lost her vision, so suddenly, but a single day after Papa had been killed.

Olivia's heart squeezed. She would remember it always—the stricken cry when Emily had awoken the next morning, the way she'd flung out her hands. *"I cannot see. I cannot see!"* she'd cried, over and over.

The physician merely shook his head, at a loss for explanations. There had been no sign at all that Emily had been losing her sight, though she *had* hit her head when she fell from Papa's horse . . .

The remembrance made her ache inside.

Emily was but little more than a year younger than Olivia. She had once been a lively, vivacious girl, full of laughter and hope. Of course she'd always been a bit shy. Papa had thought it was because Mama had died when Emily was at an awkward stage—no longer a girl, not yet a woman. But when their father had died—and she'd lost her sight—it was as if a light had been extinguished inside her. Her blindness had made her even more shy and timid. She sat in her chair, a spectator of life, no longer a part of it . . .

It nearly broke Olivia's heart to think her sister might be destined forever for such a life.

Kneeling before her sister, she folded her hands

around Emily's where they rested in her lap. "We'll be all right, love. We've managed well enough thus far, haven't we? Besides, you've always had far more talent with the needle than I." She swallowed the ache in her throat. "We'll be all right," she said again. "I promise."

"But I feel so guilty, with you out working for— for that Gypsy! It isn't right that you should spend your days in drudgery. Oh, if only I could see . . . if only I could help!"

Olivia sought to reassure her. " 'Tis not so bad, really. I don't mind working at Ravenwood. Why, I've spent many a backbreaking day working in the garden!" She strived for a light tone but wasn't convinced she had succeeded.

She knew it for certain when Emily's lovely blue eyes filled with tears. "First Mama died in that horrible fall. And then the way Papa died . . . Why are we being punished like this, Olivia . . . why?"

Olivia's mind traveled back as well. Mama had always had a fondness for animals, especially horses; Mama's father had been a stable master for a duke, and Mama had often helped him in her youth. For her birthday one year, Papa had presented Mama with a dappled gray mare named Bonnie that he'd gotten from a nearby farmer. A wistful remembrance went through Olivia. Mama had been so thrilled! Indeed, the swaybacked mare might have been the finest steed in all of England, for Mama had adored Bonnie.

Olivia had always been nervous around horses; Papa had tried to teach her to ride, to no avail. In an attempt to ease her trepidation, one day Mama had taken Olivia up behind her. Olivia remembered the day well. Mama had eased Bonnie into a slow canter around the field near the house. Olivia had just begun to think that everyone was right—that perhaps riding was great fun after all. She'd even gathered the courage to grip the mare with her knees. She'd raised her arms. She remembered the feel of the breeze against her face, whipping her hair. 'Twas as if she were flying . . . Then all at once Bonnie faltered. She came to an abrupt halt. Unprepared, Olivia had toppled to the ground. But Mama . . .

Mama was flung headlong over Bonnie's head. Bruised and aching, Olivia remembered crawling to Mama. *"Mama!"* she'd cried. *"Mama, get up!"*

But Mama didn't. She couldn't.

Mama was dead.

Olivia's heart squeezed in aching remembrance. So much had changed since that carefree day. Papa, though he'd tried not to show it to his daughters, had never been quite the same. His smile was never quite so bright as it had been before that tragic day . . .

Olivia swallowed the tightness in her throat.

"Shhh, love. You know what Papa always said—that the Lord works in ways we cannot always understand. We must trust in Him, trust that better days lie ahead." She squeezed Emily's fingers. "Please, love, don't lose faith."

Emily sniffed. "You're right, of course. You're always right."

Olivia smoothed a golden strand of hair from Emily's brow. "Now. Would you like some warm milk before bed?"

Emily nodded. Her lips formed a tremulous smile. "That would be lovely, Olivia."

"Good. You go change, and I'll bring it to you in bed."

Olivia went into the kitchen to prepare it. Before long, she heard a loud thump in the bedroom they shared. Already clad in a long white night rail, Emily was bent over rubbing her shin. She must have heard the rustle of skirts for she glanced up.

"Sorry. I ran into something. I'm ever so clumsy these days."

Olivia's heart went out to her. "It was the chair," she said gently. "Remember, love, it's to the left of the bureau, not the right." It had taken some while for another vicar to be appointed after Papa's death; during that time they'd been allowed to stay in the quaint little house next to the church.

Emily had just learned to comfortably find her way around the house when a new vicar had been appointed—they'd been forced to leave the only home they'd ever known, for it was now occupied by Reverend Holden, the new vicar. Olivia knew it wouldn't have been so bad had Emily not lost her sight. But the move to the cottage where they now dwelled had been extremely traumatic for Emily; she'd cried and cried and spent many a day in her bed. That was yet another reason Olivia had decided to remain in Stonebridge. No doubt there would have been far more opportunity for a post in London, but Emily's state of well-being was far too fragile for her even to consider it. Perhaps later it would be possible . . .

She shivered a little, for even though the day had been warm, here in the cottage it was decidedly cool. She must have made some small sound, for Emily's head turned toward her.

"What, Olivia? What is it?"

" 'Tis nothing," she said cheerfully. "I'm just a bit chilled, that's all. This cottage is rather drafty, don't you think, even in summer?" She gave a little laugh. "Why, I fear in winter, should anyone come to call, we'll likely be so bundled up no one will recognize us."

To her relief, Emily smiled faintly.

While Emily drank her milk, Olivia changed into her night rail. Together the sisters slipped into bed. It wasn't long before Emily's breathing grew deep and even. She slept.

Not so with Olivia, who lay wide awake. Perhaps it was inevitable . . . her mind traveled to him. The Gypsy.

How on earth was she to face him again? Faith, but she'd made a fool of herself, being so frightened of his dog, Lucifer. Why, she had practically suffered a fit of the vapors, a feminine weakness she'd often denounced as silly!

But it was not entirely her fault. If his coach hadn't been traveling so fast, and at such an ungodly hour . . . The corners of her mouth turned down. Lucifer. What kind of name was that for an animal? But her problem remained . . . What if she should see *him* again? She reminded herself that she was but a maid, a lowly one at that. With luck, their paths would never cross . . . Even if they did, no doubt he would not recognize her.

Or so she hoped.

The black coach bounced along the narrow roadway, sleek and highly polished, its well-oiled springs such that the man within barely felt the bumps and potholes. The interior was richly sumptuous, the windows covered by the finest damask, the crimson velvet cushions soft and deep.

But of course, the man reflected with more than a touch of cynicism, it could have been nothing else, for it had belonged to his father.

After all, James St. Bride had settled for no less than the very best, the most costly and beautiful.

His mind no longer taken with the girl he'd left behind, he crossed his arms and stared out into the encroaching darkness. Odd, the man within the coach reflected, that James St. Bride had ever taken up with his mother. But then, his mother had been a beauty . . . No, it wasn't just a son's adoration that deemed her so, for Dominic had known at a very young age that his mother stood out above the ordinary, a jewel that shone bright and dazzling. From a very early age, he'd seen the way men gazed at the dark, exotic beauty, their eyes glittering and covetous. *Gadjo* eyes. Gypsy eyes as well.

But Madeleine had paid no heed, for though she spoke of it but seldom, her heart was forever chained by one man. The man Dominic had hated since the day he had first learned he was an earl's bastard.

He did not understand it, the love she held deep in her heart. Though seldom had she spoken of it, he knew she felt it to her core, so he had learned to accept it. Just as she had accepted his father's demand that he must live the life of a *gadjo* . . .

Their life is much easier, my son. There are far more comforts to be found.

He'd been so angry at her for allowing his father to take him from her—from the Gypsies. Yet in time, he had found himself swayed . . . as she had once found herself swayed. By riches. By pleasure.

Often he had posed the question to himself . . .

What was it that had drawn his father to his mother? Her beauty? Or because she was a Gypsy—a touch of the forbidden . . . ?

Whatever the reason, he was the result.

It had taken him years to begin to reconcile that fact.

In truth, reminded an insidious little voice within him, he still had yet to come to terms with it. Was he Gypsy? Or was he *gadjo?*

No matter. He was no longer a bastard—and yet he would always be one.

He was . . . who he was. *What* he was . . . and that was something that would never change.

When his father had died, it had been tempting . . . so very tempting to turn his back, to shun his father's title and fortune, to show the same disdain his father had always shown him. *"Little Gypsy rat,"* his father had often sneered.

His father had thought him wild and heathen.

His father had been convinced he could not change.

There were things his father had never known, that no one knew. They thought he was a wild, uneducated Gypsy . . .

But he could be . . . what his father had thought he could never be. A gentleman. Welcome upon society's most privileged doorsteps. It hadn't been easy, but he'd managed to accomplish it. He'd waltzed at Almack's. Gambled at White's. Placed bets at the Jockey Club while sitting elbow-to-elbow with the Duke of Worthington.

But deep inside was a longing for something else. A longing for something more. Something . . . he didn't fully understand.

It was his solicitor's innocent inquiry that had

spurred him on. Less than a month ago, Renfrews had asked, *"Will you be seeing personally to your interests at Ravenwood, my lord?"*

Ravenwood. Dominic had often sworn he would never set foot there, for it was his father's birthplace, his ancestral home ... and the place where his mother had lived with James St. Bride.

James St. Bride had never taken him to Ravenwood. *Never.* Dominic was under no illusions as to the reason why. It was his home, his father's—to take him there would have been to accept him, and in truth, though his father had acknowledged Dominic as his offspring, he had never accepted him as his son.

But the seed had taken hold, and now it flowered and grew.

He had claimed his inheritance, and now he would claim Ravenwood as well ... He would make his father's home *his* home.

Oh, but it was the sweetest revenge on the man who had fathered him ...

Moments later the tall, powerful figure alighted from the carriage. Several footmen scrambled to assist him. They were waved aside, for Dominic St. Bride was not a man who stood on formality.

The butler Franklin was notably nervous. He ran down the wide stone steps, his nightshirt rumpled. "Forgive me, my lord, but if we'd known you would arrive tonight, I'd have had the staff assembled and all in readiness—"

"I did not send word of the exact time of my arrival, Franklin. Rest assured, I expected no ceremonial greeting. You may introduce the staff in the morning."

Franklin's jaw dropped, clearly anticipating an outburst.

Dominic had given the brick-fronted manse but a cursory glance.

Instead he stood on the last step, eyeing the storm clouds brewing on the horizon. Where before the moon had cast its gilded veil of light, a dark haze all but obscured it. The air had grown heavy and damp. Dominic was not surprised, for the countryside they had passed was wild, the weather unpredictable. He'd felt stifled in London. Here there was room to breathe.

This would suit, he thought. Ah, yes, this would suit quite well.

Three

*"There was a terrible storm last night," said Char-*lotte. "The thunder was so fierce, why, it nearly shook me from my bed!"

Olivia smiled slightly. "We're often given to such storms in summer, I'm afraid. My father used to say it was the angels clapping in time to the Lord's music."

"Angels clapping in time to the Lord's music," Charlotte repeated. Her eyes lit up. "Why, I think I'll tell that to Colin, so he won't be so frightened again!"

"Charlotte! Olivia!" The whisper came from Fanny, another of the maids. "Hurry! We're all to assemble in the entrance hall to greet the new master."

Olivia's heart sank like a weighted stone. The moment she had dreaded had arrived.

As luck would have it, she and Charlotte were among the last to fall in line. Under Mrs. Templeton's watchful eye, she stood smartly alert.

From the corner of her eye she saw him. Faith, but he was tall! He towered over Franklin, who was certainly not small in stature. Her stomach churning, she waited, praying this would all be over as quickly as possible. But Providence was not smiling on her today, for he stopped before each and every servant, calling each by name and exchanging some pleasantry.

Her nerves were screaming as he came near. She longed to sink through the floor to the depths below. At last he stood before her, his hands behind his back, looking so relaxed and at ease she longed to scream.

"My lord, Olivia Sherwood, one of the maids."

Olivia searched deep for the courage to meet his gaze—oh, a mistake, surely! His regard, though ever so brief, was intensely penetrating. No sign of a smile broke the plane of his lips. No hint of recognition flickered in his eyes, which she was stunned to discover were not dark at all, but a piercing shade of blue.

He inclined his head. "Miss Sherwood, I'm exceedingly pleased to have you here at Ravenwood."

He moved on to Fanny.

Olivia blinked. 'Twould seem he didn't remember her! Was she insulted . . . or relieved? She decided most heartily in favor of the latter.

At last it was over. They were dismissed, free to go back to their duties.

The other maids were all atwitter.

"Did ye see him? No wonder all the fine ladies of London were fallin' all over 'im!"

"He has his father's eyes. Blue as sapphires, I tell ye!"

"He deigned to smile at me. Did ye see it? He smiled at me!"

"He took my hand. Why, it nearly made me swoon!"

Meeting Charlotte's gaze, Olivia smiled and shook her head.

Charlotte leaned over and whispered, "Oh, come now, luv. Well, ye have to admit it, 'e is a handsome devil!"

All of a sudden a hush fell over the group. Olivia soon saw the reason.

Mrs. Templeton had appeared—and she was marching straight toward her!

Olivia's heart sank. What had she done that the housekeeper looked so disapproving?

Mrs. Templeton stopped before her. But first her biting gaze swept toward the others. "Do none of you have duties to attend?" she snapped.

The group dispersed in a heartbeat. Olivia started to leave as well, but the housekeeper's hand on her arm forestalled her.

"He's asked for you," the woman said tersely.

Olivia was confused. "Ma'am? I beg your pardon?"

"He's asked for you. The master." Mrs. Templeton's lips were thin. "He wishes to see you in the library."

Olivia swallowed. She didn't like the sound of that, nay, not at all! "Very well," she murmured.

Olivia turned to leave. Mrs. Templeton's voice stopped her. "One more thing, Miss Sherwood."

She glanced back.

"A good servant is neither seen nor heard, young woman. In future, you'd do well to bear that in mind."

Her stomach felt as if it were tied up in knots.

But so was his.

He stood near the marble fireplace, his hands behind his back, his mind still reeling. Never had he thought to find her at Ravenwood. He'd thought of her last night—and again this morning when he woke. He'd been faintly irritated that their encounter had taken place in the dead of night; he'd wanted to see her in the full, stark light of day, to see if she was as fair as she'd appeared in the moonlight.

Now he knew.

She was exquisite, as exquisite as he'd somehow known she would be.

Her face was oval, her skin smooth and the color of Devonshire cream. Her eyes were the color of jade, wide and thickly lashed; the arch of her brows was slightly piquant. The sun streamed through the window, gleaming on her hair—it was part gold, part russet. Oh, she'd not have been considered a beauty by London standards—her hair was not pale and blonde, and she was far too slender.

"You wished to see me, my lord?"

Direct and to the point. Dominic liked that, just as he liked her quiet dignity. She stood with her hands folded primly before her, her narrow shoulders squarely set. She was nervous, he decided, but determined not to show it. That made her rather brave . . .

"Mrs. Templeton tells me you have been employed here only a short time, Miss Sherwood."

"Yes," she said quickly. "Much of the staff has been employed but a short time. The house has been closed up since the earl—I mean the old earl . . . I mean, your father—"

"I take your meaning quite well, Miss Sherwood."

A faint coolness had crept into his tone. Olivia fell silent; she couldn't help but take note of it. Her fingers curled into her palms. She couldn't have taken her eyes from him, even if she'd wanted to.

She would not have called him swarthy, for his hair was not black—but rather like darkest chocolate—and a trifle longer than was the fashion. And his skin looked as if it had been kissed golden brown by the sun.

It struck her anew ... he did not look like a Gypsy. Yet neither did he look like any gentleman she'd ever seen. He was dressed in a snowy-white shirt and cravat, tight doeskin breeches and shining knee-high boots. Yet he possessed a curious roughness that was almost at odds with his elegant clothing. But there was no denying it ...

He was almost sinfully handsome.

It was he who broke the silence. "Finished?" he said quietly.

The thoroughness of her perusal had not gone unnoticed. Never in her life had she been so embarrassed!

She shifted uncomfortably. "Sir, I—"

"Look as long as you like. I'm sure you find me quite the oddity."

His tone was ever so pleasant. Olivia flushed. "I'm sorry."

"No need to apologize. I've grown accustomed to it."

He hadn't; there was an edge in his tone that told her so.

She clasped her hands before her. "Sir," she began, her voice very low, "if you've no further need of me—"

"I would like for you to show me about the house."

Her lips parted. "But ... I've only been here a

scant week. May I suggest that someone else—"

"No. I want you, Miss Sherwood."

I want you. She had an uneasy feeling he meant something else entirely.

She inclined her head. "Very well then." She gestured toward the door. "Shall we proceed?"

"Indeed we may."

Olivia stiffened. Was he making light of her? She could have sworn a faint mockery dwelled in his voice.

It didn't make the next half hour any easier. As they moved through the house, she prayed he would not discern her nervousness.

In the study, she dared to breathe a little easier. They were almost done. There was a portrait of his father there, hanging over the mantel. He stood before it for the longest time, his hands behind his back, the set of his shoulders rigidly square. Though James St. Bride had hair of mahogany brown, there was a marked resemblance between father and son. Both possessed the same square chin, the same high cheekbones . . . the same intense blue eyes.

Dominic St. Bride had yet to move. He stood as if frozen in place, his gaze locked on the portrait of his father.

There was a protracted silence. "You favor him," she said awkwardly, not knowing what else to say.

"I have his eyes, but I should like to think I am *not* like him." His voice was clipped and abrupt.

He had yet to look away from the portrait. An odd prickle crept down her spine. He hated him, she realized. He hated his father. Olivia sensed it with every ounce of her being. Yet when at last he turned toward her, his manner was as easy as ever.

"Pray let us continue, Miss Sherwood."

All that was left was the conservatory. To her surprise, Olivia was curiously reluctant to rush, for in her mind, the conservatory was the loveliest room in the house. It was immense, with an extraordinary sense of light and grandeur. On the far wall, double doors opened onto a stone verandah. Just beyond was a little garden crammed full of roses.

A feeling of wistfulness welled up inside her. She sighed, for it reminded her of the house she'd grown up in, the house that the new vicar, Reverend Holden, now lived in. She and Mama had spent many a happy hour tending the tiny rose garden outside the back door. Lord, but she missed it!

"Do you live alone, Miss Sherwood?"

A deep male voice jarred her from her reverie. It gave her a start to realize Dominic St. Bride stood directly behind her.

She turned that she might see him—and retreated a step in the bargain. "No," she murmured.

"I see. You've a husband then?"

"No. I—I live with my sister Emily."

He continued. "You are extremely well-spoken, Miss Sherwood."

Her chin came up a notch. "Thank you, my lord."

"And I assume well-bred."

"My mother, God rest her soul, would like to think so."

"And well-educated, I presume?"

"My father saw to it that I was well-schooled, yes." Olivia was uneasy. What was he about?

"Then I must say, I find it odd that a woman

such as you would take a position in my household."

Olivia stiffened. She knew what he meant now—that she was out of place. Taking a deep breath, she chose her words carefully. "My father always said that hard work was good for a man's soul, and, I daresay, a woman's as well. But if you must know, 'tis a case of needs must. I have no family other than my sister, so 'tis up to me to care for her."

His eyes flickered. "I didn't mean to offend you, Miss Sherwood."

Only then did she realize she'd been a trifle defensive. "You did not, my lord."

For the longest time, he said nothing. His gaze roved over her face, making her pulse quicken. Then, before she had a chance to think, he raised a hand and brushed his knuckles across the scratch on her cheek. "It's scarcely noticeable," he murmured.

Her heart lurched. She felt a rush of heat in her cheeks. "Yes," she said breathlessly. " 'Tis hardly serious."

But he was not finished. He took her hands within his and turned them palm up. With his thumb he traced the blisters that had risen there. Olivia flushed. Her heart stood still. What was he thinking? she wondered frantically. That she was unsuited for the work here? Nay. She couldn't even contemplate such a thing. If she were without employment, how would she and Emily survive?

Their eyes met. A lazy half-smile curled his mouth. "I thank you for your time, Miss Sherwood," he murmured, "and I trust we'll meet again soon."

With that he carried one small hand to his lips. To her utter shock, he kissed the back of each hand in turn, a fleeting brush of his mouth upon her flesh.

He turned and strode away. Olivia was left standing there, her pulse hammering wildly.

It was quite improper, the way he'd touched her cheek. The way he'd kissed her hands . . .

But he was no gentleman.

And she was no lady—not a *proper* lady, like those in London . . .

If Charlotte was to be believed, he was a rake of the highest order—a profligate rogue, no doubt! She could not approve. She *did* not approve.

Yet all she could think was that Charlotte was right. He *was* a handsome devil.

It was earlier tonight when Olivia prepared to leave Ravenwood. She was just departing when Charlotte caught up with her.

"Do ye mind if I walk with ye, Olivia?"

Olivia smiled at her. "Of course not. I'm glad of the company."

They hadn't gone far before Charlotte cleared her throat. Olivia glanced at her. A frown marred the smoothness of Charlotte's brow. She opened her mouth, then looked away, only to glance back once more.

Olivia took her elbow and came to a halt. "Come now, Charlotte. You've something to say, so out with it."

Charlotte's manner was unusually reticent. "All right then, Olivia. But feel free to refuse, for I've no wish to be a bother—"

"Charlotte!" Olivia chuckled. "Out with it!"

"All right then." Charlotte took a deep breath, then plunged ahead. "Ye know how ye said if I wanted anything, I had only to ask?"

"Indeed I do. I meant it, too, Charlotte."

Charlotte was wringing her hands. "I've heard that ye've been teaching some of the village children to read and write."

"I do," Olivia said promptly. "Sunday afternoons in the village square, and evenings when I'm able."

"I don't mean to burden ye, but I'd like for ye to teach my boy, Colin, to read and write, too. I never learned, and I—I want him to be clever and learned—like you."

Olivia started to protest.

"Oh, but ye are," Charlotte said earnestly. "Ye shouldn't be here slaving away with the rest of us. Ye're a lady—a truer lady than them wot calls themselves ladies."

Olivia was touched beyond words. "That's all you want? For me to teach Colin to read and write?"

Charlotte's head bobbed up and down.

Olivia had a lump in her throat. After her mother had died, she'd taken on the task of teaching the village children as her mother had done. Now that she was employed, of course, the time spent with them was less, but she'd vowed to continue.

"Of course I will, Charlotte. I'd be happy to. And don't worry about it being a burden. I've only a dozen or so that come regularly, so one more won't be a problem."

Charlotte searched her face. "Ye're sure?"

Olivia reached out and hugged Charlotte warmly. "Of course I am. Besides, that way Colin will have a chance to get to know some of the other children."

Charlotte's face was wreathed in smiles. "Oh, ye're a saint, Olivia. Bless ye, luv, bless ye."

They made arrangements for Olivia to stop by Charlotte's home the following evening. They parted near the duck pond in the village. Olivia waved good-bye and trudged onward. A short while later, she turned down the dirt pathway that led to their cottage.

She called out to her sister as she grasped the doorknob and opened the door. "Emily? I'm home, love."

"In here, Olivia."

Emily's voice came to her from the parlor. Olivia stepped briskly toward the parlor only to stop short.

Emily was not alone. She was perched on the edge of her seat. Across from her sat William Dunsport. William was the son of a minor baronet, and a retired military officer.

William had risen to his feet, his hat in his hands. Tall and blond, he smiled at her warmly. "Miss Olivia, forgive my calling on you unannounced. I'm having my horse shoed at the livery, so I thought I would stop by. Emily said she wasn't certain when to expect you, so I hope you don't mind that I waited."

Her smile wavered but an instant. "Not at all, William. Would you like tea?"

"Tea would be delightful."

"Good. I'll be back in just a moment."

Olivia busied herself in the kitchen. In the parlor she could hear William's low baritone and Emily's soft, shy tones. Returning, she slid the tray onto the small table before the settee where Emily was sitting.

Olivia eased down next to her. "Emily," she said calmly, "will you pour?"

Emily's head turned sharply in her direction. Olivia was well aware of her sharp intake of breath.

"Olivia—" she began waveringly.

"You can do it, love," Olivia prompted softly. "Here, I'll help you." She guided Emily's fingers to the tall white teapot. "The teapot is at three o'clock, the cups at twelve, six and nine o'clock."

Emily's fingers curled hesitantly around the handle. Olivia held her breath. For an instant, she thought Emily would snatch her hand away—she looked ready to cry. Olivia sent a silent prayer heavenward. This was something they'd practiced over and over. While she was confident Emily could do it, she suspected Emily was certain she could *not*. In the meantime, William looked on with a combination of doubt and skepticism.

Emily had found the first teacup. She slid it carefully toward the teapot. The gentle clink of china against china sounded; Olivia could tell she was listening intently for the sound. Very slowly Emily tipped the spout forward, even as she slipped the tip of a finger just inside the cup. When the hot liquid touched her nail, she stopped pouring.

Her sigh of relief was audible, her smile tremulous. Olivia felt like shouting her sister's triumph. "William," she said gaily, "cream and sugar?"

An expression of incredulity had passed over his face. "Cream," he managed. "Just a tad."

By the time Olivia had poured in the cream, Emily had already filled the second cup and reached for the third.

She spilled not a drop.

The victory was a small one, perhaps, but Olivia felt as if her chest would burst with pride. Emily was becoming most self-sufficient.

They spent the next half hour drinking tea and chatting. Emily even laughed several times as William related some of his experiences on the Continent during his stint in the military. When they'd finished, Olivia gathered up the tray and headed into the kitchen.

A moment later there was a touch at her elbow. Startled, she turned to find that William had followed her.

"Olivia, I know 'tis none of my affair, but I cannot help but wonder why you allowed Emily to pour tea as she did just now."

Olivia's chin came up a notch. "You're right," she said quietly, " 'tis not your affair."

He was taken aback by such bluntness. She could see it in his expression.

It came to her then . . . William seemed . . . different, somehow. Different from the jovial youth she'd known for so long. He was far more serious—and far less patient—than he'd been before he'd left to fight against Napoleon's army. At times—like now—she'd glimpsed a harshness in him that was totally at odds with the boy he'd once been. At other times he was insufferably arrogant!

She attempted to explain. "I cannot allow Emily to sit and do nothing for herself. She may be blind," she told him evenly, "but she is not helpless. And she must feel that she is still able to do things for herself."

Color rose high and bright on his cheekbones.

"Nonetheless, I cannot say I approve. Why, she could injure herself."

Olivia was faintly vexed. She *was* right, and he simply refused to admit it. Why was he being so stubborn? The William she'd once known had never been so imperious.

Quietly she spoke. "I do not need your approval where Emily is concerned, William. As her sister, I will do what I feel is right for her."

"I cannot agree, Olivia. I fear I must tell you that I believe you are quite wrong. Your sister is an invalid. Why you persist in treating her as if she were not, I do not know."

Olivia's lips tightened ever so slightly. "Say what you must, William, but so must I. Emily is blind, but she is not helpless. There are many things she can do for herself. 'Tis only a matter of learning how."

He stiffened visibly. "You are quite impertinent, Olivia."

"And you, William, are quite imperious," she returned.

"I think not, Olivia. Indeed, I am given to wonder what has come over you. Perhaps 'tis because of your mother's death. Yes, that must be it. You've had no guidance in matters of social decorum, else you would know that you must learn to curb your tongue, for a lady does not argue."

"I am in my own home, William," she stated levelly, "therefore, I see no need to curb my tongue. And if we are arguing, 'tis because you engaged the argument."

"And you who continue it!"

Olivia sighed. Indeed, it was becoming difficult

to keep her temper in check. "Perhaps you forget, William, but I was never a mouse."

"I've forgotten nothing, Olivia. Indeed, I remember a time when you were quite adoring of me." The sting had left his tone. In its stead was a hint of sadness. She knew it for certain when he gave her a long, slow look. "You've changed, Olivia," he said quietly.

"And so have you, William." There was neither spite nor malice in the statement. In truth, she'd only now begun to realize how very true it was.

For a fleeting instant he looked as if he might disagree. Then suddenly he ran his fingers through his hair, the gesture so boyish it tugged at her heart and reminded her of all that had once been . . .

Of all that would never be.

"Perhaps I have," he murmured. "I've seen atrocities that you cannot imagine—nor would I ever speak of them to a lady." His lips curved in a faint smile, but it was a smile which held no mirth. "I suppose one might say that war made a man of me."

And life had made a woman of her, she thought with a painful twist of her insides.

William looked at her. "Do you remember your eighth birthday?"

The merest hint of a smile curled her lips. "Yes. You pressed a bouquet of beautiful violets into my hand. I took them inside to show Mama but she began to sneeze so frightfully I had to leave them outside."

His tone turned husky. "You cried because it rained that night and they were ruined." He paused, then said softly, "You cried the night I left to fight against Napolean."

Indeed she had. Faith, but it all seemed so very long ago! So much had happened. Time and distance had separated them . . .

"I remember those days well, Olivia. One thing that has never changed are my feelings for you." His eyes bored into hers. "I regret that we argued. Indeed, that is the last thing I wanted, for I meant to speak with you about something far different."

Before she could say a word, he'd grasped both her hands. "Olivia," he began.

It was inevitable, perhaps, but all at once she was reminded of another pair of hands, hands that were lean and strong and brown; her own had seemed quite lost within his . . .

". . . I've known for quite some time now what I want. I can only hope that you want it as well. Olivia—" There was the veriest pause. "—'twould please me greatly if you would consent to be my wife."

His wife.

Those words brought her back to the moment at hand in a flash. He was asking her to marry him, she thought numbly. Mutely she gazed at him, at the blond hair brushed neatly back from his forehead, grappling for an answer.

Oh, but she should have known this was coming. He'd hinted now and again that he would like to expand their relationship beyond friendship. He'd even deigned to kiss her the very last time she'd seen him, but while his cheeks had been flushed with color when he'd lifted his head, she was curiously unaffected by his kiss. His lips had been dry, and there was no answering spark within her breast. She'd expected fire and heat and passion and all the things she yearned for deep in her heart.

Instead she'd felt . . . empty. And most of all a yawning disappointment.

Marriage. When she thought of marriage to William, she felt nothing—no fevered desire, no excitement. How could she marry him?

She didn't love him, nor did she want his pity.

It would have been the easy way out—but it was not the only way out. With hard work and perseverance, she could make it on her own . . . *they* could make it, the two of them, she and Emily. But she was not so desperate as to marry a man she did not love.

"William . . . At present I cannot even think of marriage. I—I must think of Emily. This past year has been difficult . . . for both of us." She was hedging, but she had no choice. "I pray you will understand, but . . . 'tis too soon."

William was silent for a moment. "I see," he said quietly. Then: "May I come to call tomorrow afternoon?"

"I'm teaching the village children then," she reminded him. Sunday was the only day she didn't work at Ravenwood.

A faint coldness crept into his manner. He disapproved of her teaching the village children—he was convinced it was useless, that there was no need for them to learn such things. They'd had several discussions over it, but Olivia was not about to stop her lessons simply because he disapproved.

"Perhaps another day then." William's countenance was unsmiling.

Olivia inclined her head. "Perhaps," she agreed.

With that he gave a low bow and was gone. Olivia gave a silent prayer of thanks that he hadn't kissed her again. He'd said his feelings had not changed. But Olivia knew they could never go back, just as she knew her feelings for him would never be the same. She didn't mean to hurt him, but she had no choice—just as she had no choice but to take care of herself and Emily, to go on as they had been.

Emily turned her head when Olivia returned. "Has William gone?"

"Yes." Olivia was anxious to change the subject. "What is that you have in your lap, love?"

Emily bit her lip. "Oh, 'tis nothing. Really." Olivia could see she was embarrassed. "Just a scrap of lace."

But Olivia was intrigued. She knelt by Emily's side. "May I see?"

"Well," Emily said tentatively, "if you insist . . ."

Olivia took the small square of lace from Emily's hands and held it before her. It was then she spied the needles in Emily's lap, half-hidden by a fold in her skirt.

She exclaimed in wonder, for the lace was fine and dainty, quite lovely indeed—and so she said, "You did this today? Emily, it's exquisite!"

Emily flushed. "Today, yes. But really, Olivia, 'tis nothing. I was just trying to see if—if I remembered . . ."

Olivia shook her head in awe.

"I counted the stitches." There was a small pause. "I'm quite surprised I remembered. 'Twas quite odd, really, for my fingers just seemed to know what to do . . ."

Olivia's eyes softened. "You've Mama's skill with a needle. Why—" She laughed. "—I can hardly sew a straight seam. You see why I had no desire to be a seamstress. You'll finish it, won't you? It would be quite lovely on the table against the dark wood."

Emily's pale face glowed with pleasure. Making the lace today had been a whim. But in truth, she'd enjoyed it immensely, for it kept her mind occupied, and far from . . . other matters.

She heard the rustle of clothing and knew that Olivia had arisen. Her footsteps carried her toward the kitchen. Emily could hear her bustling about there.

Her fingertips stole to her eyes. At times she had wanted to gouge them out, for what use were they? She would never grow used to being blind—never. She hated being blind, just as she hated the thieving Gypsy who had murdered Papa.

A shudder tore through her. She'd had a nightmare again last night. She'd seen his face again . . . that horrible Gypsy, with his club raised high to strike Papa once more . . . She shuddered. She knew Olivia had been hurt that she'd never spoken of what she'd seen that terrible night, but it was bad enough that she—Emily—must relive that horrible scene in her nightmares. She would not put Olivia through the same torment. Yes, it was better this way, to never speak of it.

She fingered the small square of lace anew. She felt so helpless just sitting here. But this afternoon when she'd been working on the lace, the time had passed so quickly. It was amazing how well she'd remembered the stitches. An idea took hold then . . . Excitement gathered in her breast. She could make doilies and table runners . . . and if she could manage to sell them . . . Oh, Olivia was such a dear! She'd taken care of her these many months, and . . . if she could lighten the burden, she wouldn't feel so—so useless!

But she wanted it to be a surprise. She wouldn't tell Olivia, not just yet. Olivia would think 'twas just a way to pass the time.

Before she knew it, she was humming a merry little tune in time with the rocking of her chair. Her mood was much more lighthearted than it had been in ever so long . . .

Four

Sunday dawned clear and bright and warm. Sunlight glinted off the duck pond near the market square. Just across from the square was a small Norman church that had been there for centuries; the entrance was marked by a carved Saxon cross. Tangled, leafy vines climbed one side of the rustic stone.

William had stopped by the village green just after Olivia arrived there. Olivia wondered if he did it solely so that she wouldn't continue her lessons with the children. When she reminded him of it, he looked a bit sullen.

He glanced at his pocket watch. "I must be off then," he said. "Mother is waiting tea." With that he leaned over and pressed his mouth to hers.

It was over in but an instant. Still, Olivia was aghast. How dared he do so before others! It wasn't as if they were engaged, and if little Emory hadn't appeared at her side just then, she would have told him so.

Olivia didn't know that other eyes saw as well—eyes that keenly surveyed the two of them . . .

An hour later she was sitting on the grass in the village green, slippered feet tucked under her, her skirts spread out around her. A dozen or so children clustered before her. Among them was Colin, Charlotte's little boy. He was bright-eyed but a trifle shy, with curling hair as flame-red as his mother's. He'd nodded eagerly when Olivia asked if he wanted to learn to read, but he had yet to speak a word though the lesson was almost over.

She moved her chalk swiftly over the small board she cradled in her lap and held it high for the children to see.

"Can anyone tell me what this word is?"

"It says 'Colin'." This came from Jane, whose father was a farmer. At thirteen, Jane was the eldest among the children. She attended every Sunday, along with her two sisters and three brothers.

"Excellent, Jane. It says 'Colin'." She smiled at Colin, whose eyes had brightened at the sound of his name. "Colin, do you see this?"

The lad nodded vigorously.

"Well, Colin, this is your name. Soon you'll be able to read it yourself—and write it as well, won't you?"

His head bobbed up and down.

"Very good. Now then, if you will all—"

She broke off suddenly, for every one of the children had lifted their eyes to a spot behind her. Lucinda ducked behind her sister Jane. Even Jonny, who'd been whispering to his neighbor, fell silent.

The skin on the back of her neck seemed to prickle curiously. Even before she turned, she had the strangest sensation it was him . . .

The Gypsy.

And indeed, she was right. Directly behind her was Dominic St. Bride. He was mounted atop a massive stallion, his mane and coat like blackest midnight. On horseback, he seemed as tall as the heavens . . .

Olivia opened her mouth to greet him. She had no desire to appear either discourteous or frightened before the children.

Before she could say a word, Jonny Craven's voice rang out. "I know who you are. You're the Gypsy, the Gypsy earl."

Olivia could have gladly disappeared. Jonny knew not when to mind his tongue—never had she been so certain of it! She longed to clamp her hand over the boy's mouth lest he choose to deliver another disparaging remark.

Yet curiously, it appeared Dominic St. Bride was not angry. Olivia was stunned, for he merely looked amused.

"Is it true?" someone else called out. "Are you the Gypsy?"

"I am."

To Olivia's surprise—but mostly her dismay— he showed no signs of leaving. Instead he dismounted, holding the reins easily between gloved hands.

"He doesn't dress like a Gypsy." This observation came from Lucinda, who peered out from behind her sister. The child flushed when she realized she'd been overheard by the others.

"That's because he's only half-Gypsy." Jane frowned at her sister. "His father was the old earl who had no sons because of his mother's curse. So he took him from his Gypsy camp to learn to be his heir—and a gentleman."

Olivia found herself holding her breath. Of course she'd heard the rumor many a time, yet now she wondered if he would deny it. Or if he would confirm it as truth?

"You're right. My . . . father—" There was the faintest hesitation, as if the word was distasteful to him. "—did take me from the Gypsies." His tone grew dry. "I dress as I do because I hardly think London would approve of the Earl of Ravenwood dressing in his Gypsy clothes."

"So which are you? A Gypsy? Or an earl?"

"He's both—a Gypsy and an earl!" one of the children proclaimed.

"How old were you when your father snatched you away?" Thomas leaped to his feet.

Dominic's gaze rested upon him. "I was twelve."

"Twelve. That's how old I am," Thomas boasted.

"You are not, Thomas Shelton," Jane argued with him. "You won't be twelve until after harvest."

Thomas stuck out his tongue at Jane. Olivia cast a warning glance toward the pair.

"Why do the Gypsies wander from place to place?" the boy asked, dropping the issue of his age.

"They are beholden to no one this way. They are free, at one with the world and with nature, free to wander where they wish. And there is a saying . . . 'God knows what tomorrow will bring.' Thus they are free of concern over the future and do as they please, whenever they please."

"My papa says they wander because no one wants them near." Thomas tipped his head to the side and regarded Dominic.

There was the slightest darkening of his features . . . yet it was gone so quickly Olivia wondered if she merely imagined it.

"That's what many people think, but they are mistaken," he said at last. "They wander because it is their way, as it has been their way for centuries."

"They don't have houses." Lucinda had crept out and now sat next to Jane. "They live in tents and carts."

"They are called caravans," he corrected. "*Vardo* by the Gypsies. For those not wealthy enough to own a *vardo*, the sky is the roof over their heads."

"But what do they do when it rains?" someone asked.

One corner of his mouth went up. "They get wet," he said promptly.

The children erupted into laughter. He had gone down on one knee to speak. Only then did Olivia glimpse a faint spark of laughter in those incredibly blue eyes.

"They talk strangely," one boy chimed in.

"That's because they often speak to each other in the language of the Gypsies. It's called Romany."

"Heathens, my da calls 'em."

He shook his head. "They believe in the same God as all of you. Their ways are merely different, that is all."

Olivia cringed inside. The children's questions were both blatant and bold. Somehow she thought he would be harsh and unrelenting. Yet Dominic St. Bride appeared both patient and tolerant of their curiosity.

"My papa says he once lived in a town where signs were posted that said 'No Gypsies,' yet still the Gypsies came."

"That's because they cannot read."

Colin finally broke his silence. "I cannot read," he said in a small voice.

"Ah, but with Miss Sherwood's guidance, you'll soon be able to." Dominic laid a hand on the boy's red curls, a gesture that she found wholly unexpected . . . and utterly endearing. Indeed, she had to remind herself that he was a Gypsy . . .

And a Gypsy had murdered her father.

At that very instant, he chanced to glance up and their eyes meshed for the longest time. Olivia could not help it. She had the strangest sensation he knew her very thoughts . . . But that could not be. It could not!

She had to tear her gaze away. "All right, children." Deliberately she chose not to look at him. "Remember your lesson and practice your reading and writing whenever you are able." With that the children were dismissed. They scattered in all directions. Rising, she got to her feet, twitching her skirts into place as she did so.

Only Colin remained, and he was whispering to Dominic, who, in the very next instant, swung Colin up and onto the back of his horse. Taking the reins, he led the horse in a circle around the square.

Colin beamed. His smile was as radiant as a thousand suns. Finally Dominic lifted the lad off and gently set him on his feet. "There you are, m' boy," he said lightly. "Run along home now."

Colin dashed off toward his cottage. Olivia had no doubt the child would sing endless praises of the Gypsy earl. Why, she could almost see Charlotte's mouth gaping open in sheer disbelief.

Once they were left alone, he turned to regard her.

An awkward silence ensued . . . awkward, at

least, for Olivia. To her consternation, Dominic St. Bride appeared completely at ease.

"That was . . . sweet of you," she said slowly. "To let Colin ride your horse that way."

A dark brow arose. "Sweet?" His tone held a trace of cynicism. "I suspect that's a word never before ascribed to me, Miss Sherwood."

She elected to make no further comment on his observation. Instead she said, "He's Charlotte's son, you know."

"Charlotte?" His expression was blank.

"Yes, Charlotte. One of the maids at Ravenwood. She has hair exactly like Colin's. If you see her, you'll know."

"No doubt I will."

Olivia took a deep breath. "You—you have a way with Colin. I must thank you. I could not get him to speak at all today."

"Ah. And you're surprised, aren't you, Miss Sherwood." It was not a question, it was a blunt statement.

A tide of color rose to her cheeks. "Frankly, I am."

"And why is that, Miss Sherwood?" There was a glint in his eyes. It flitted through her mind that he was displeased . . . "Did you think the children would cower away from the Gypsy earl?"

Olivia blanched. Her mind tripped. In truth, she *had* thought the children would be frightened to death. From the corner of her eye, she'd noticed how many of the villagers had stared at him when he arrived, only to retreat quickly toward their homes. Yet what could she say?

Salvation came in a most unexpected way. Just then the dog Lucifer appeared across the square, bounding toward her. He came directly up to her and thrust his huge head beneath her hand.

Only a heartbeat before, she'd very nearly screamed in fear. Now she could only stare in amazement, for his tail was swinging vigorously. A huge wet tongue lapped the back of her hand. Olivia blinked, and tentatively touched his head. Encouraged now, he bumped against her legs, his behind wiggling madly.

Olivia very nearly toppled over. She was saved only by two strong hands settling on her waist and holding her upright.

"Lucifer!" came the earl's voice. "Sit!"

The hound immediately sat. He gazed up at his master with doleful brown eyes.

It was a moment before Olivia could speak. The warmth of his hands seemed to burn right through her clothing. With a gasp she looked up at him. "Good heavens! Why, surely he weighs at least five stone."

"Six, more likely." Dominic's tone was dry. "It appears he likes you."

Her laugh was shaky. "Yes. It seems so, doesn't it?"

Lucifer had shifted his eyes to her. The hound seemed to gaze at her longingly. Olivia held out her hand, an invitation for Lucifer to come. The mongrel whined, looking at his master, as if for permission.

Dominic gave a slight nod. The dog immediately rose and once again thrust his head beneath her hand. Olivia bent slightly, stroking his head lightly.

She shook her head. "When I first saw him," she murmured, "I was terrified he would bite my hand off. But he's really quite tame for such a large beast, isn't he?" She gave him one last pat.

"Careful, Miss Sherwood. He doesn't care to be called a beast."

Olivia straightened, her eyes wide. "Why, surely he doesn't underst—"

Only then did she glimpse the faint twinkle in his eyes. Why, he was teasing her!

He cocked his head toward his stallion. "Come. I'll take you home."

Olivia blinked. "What?" she said blankly. "You expect me to ride with you?"

"Of course." He sounded as if it were the most natural thing in the world.

A shiver went down her spine. Her mouth grew dry at the very thought. Mama's fall had only increased her fear of horses.

She shook her head adamantly. "I think not, my lord."

"Why? There's no one about to see."

It was true. The market square was deserted except for several ducklings waddling behind their mother.

A feeling of dread curled down her spine. She suppressed a shudder. His stallion was a powerful animal, sleek and well-muscled.

She glanced away. " 'Tis not that," she said, her voice very low.

"What then?"

Olivia fell silent. She couldn't simply say she was afraid—that would sound childish. Nor could she tell him about Mama, for that was somehow too . . . intimate.

His sigh was audible. "Are you always so stubborn, Miss Sherwood? If you ride with me you'll be home twice as quickly. I know it's a long walk from here."

Her eyes meshed with his in a flash. "How would you know?"

"You left Ravenwood past dark the past two days. I followed you home."

Olivia was aghast—and, for perhaps the first time in her life, at an utter loss for words. He'd followed her? Her mind began racing. She was stunned. She was indignant . . . and there was a part of her that wondered if perchance there were some other reason he'd followed her . . .

"Why?" she asked shakily. "Why would you do such a thing?"

His eyes flickered. "To make certain that you arrived home safely."

"My safety, my lord, is none of your concern."

"I beg to differ with you. You are in my employ, and as such, it is."

So that was why he'd followed her. Why, it had been ridiculous to think it was anything else.

He swept a hand toward his horse. "Shall we?" he murmured.

She cleared her throat. "My lord, I'm hardly in need of—"

"Careful not to raise your voice," he murmured. "If you do, you'll make a spectacle of us both."

For the second time in as many moments, she was speechless. But he was right, she realized. No longer were they alone. Just across the square, Mr. Hobson strolled toward the churchyard.

"Very well then. This way I can return the handkerchief you loaned me the other night. But I'll walk—not ride." She relented as gracefully as she could. Her head held high, she turned toward home. Dominic fell into step beside her, leading his horse behind. Lucifer trotted along beside her.

They soon left the village behind. Olivia wished desperately that she could be unaware of him, yet heaven help her, she was overwhelmingly conscious of everything about him. Every so often, his elbow brushed her sleeve, making her pulse jump wildly. She was nervous as a schoolgirl, and she could not understand it!

Seeking to attain some semblance of normalcy, she broke the silence.

"May I ask you something?"

"Of course." He glanced over at her.

Faith, but in the sunlight his eyes were so very blue! In all her days, she'd never seen eyes so beautiful . . .

"The other day, you said you found it odd that a woman like me would take a position in your household. May I ask why?"

He regarded her, the merest hint of a smile lurking about his mouth. "The truth, Miss Sherwood?"

There was a faint note of something she couldn't decipher in his tone. "Of course. I respect the truth more than anything else."

"Nonetheless, I don't think you're prepared to hear it."

"I'm hardly averse to the truth, my lord."

"Don't call me that." He sounded most annoyed.

Olivia frowned. "What?"

"My lord. Don't call me 'my lord'."

Olivia was at a loss to comprehend his irritation. "Then what am I to call you?"

"You could begin with my name—Dominic."

"My lor—" She caught herself just in time. "Sir,

I can hardly do that. As you've already reminded me, I am in your employ."

By now they'd reached the small grassy area around her cottage. He stopped near the pathway that led to the doorway.

"Very well then, Miss Sherwood. I'll answer your question. Frankly, I'm surprised to find someone as lovely as you tucked away here in the northern wilds. I'm surprised you aren't someone's wife. If you were in London, you'd have been snatched up long ago by some rich gentleman and taken as his mistress."

He was right. She *wasn't* prepared for the truth—for such bluntness. Her mind was reeling. Did he truly think her lovely . . . ? All she could think to say was, "I—I've never been to London."

"I've shocked you by daring to speak of mistresses, haven't I, Miss Sherwood? Such things do exist, you know."

He was right yet again. She *was* shocked, but already it was beginning to fade. "Oh, I don't doubt that's something *you* know a great deal about." She couldn't quite keep the sting from her voice.

"There. Now I *have* offended you. Are you as innocent as you look, Miss Sherwood?" The arch of his brow was utterly wicked. "Why, I'll wager you've never even been kissed."

Olivia didn't understand him. One moment he was kind, even gentle. The next he mocked her most outrageously.

Her eyes flashed. "You are quite forward, sir. And—not that it's any of your concern—I *have* been kissed."

"Have you? I don't mean a mere peck on the lips, mind you. I mean really . . . *thoroughly* kissed . . . a kiss that makes the very earth move beneath your feet . . ."

Despite all, her mind veered straight to William—his peremptory kiss this afternoon and the other time he'd kissed her; the contact was hardly stirring.

"I *have*," she repeated yet again . . . but with far less confidence.

"You need not expound, Miss Sherwood. Your countenance says it all, especially your eyes. They're really quite expressive." He was laughing at her, the wretch! Laughing . . .

"Olivia? Olivia, is that you?"

It was Emily. Over her shoulder, Olivia saw that Emily stood near the cottage door, one hand poised on the door handle.

"I'm here, Emily!" she called. "I'll be inside in just a moment."

She turned back to the earl. "It's my sister," she said quickly. "No doubt she's wondering what's taken me so long." She paused awkwardly. "I would ask you in for tea, but . . ." Her voice trailed off lamely, for what could she say? That she could not, for her sister would despise him for his Gypsy blood? So much for the truth, she chided herself. Never before had she felt like a hypocrite, until now.

"Oh, you need not explain, Miss Sherwood. I quite understand." His laughter was wiped clean, as if it had never been. She had the oddest sensation she'd wounded him. But no. That couldn't be . . .

She watched in silence as he mounted his stallion. He turned the animal toward the roadway . . .

and galloped off, leaving in his wake a cloud of dust.

He'd said she was lovely. Had he meant it . . . ?

It was much, much later that Olivia remembered his handkerchief. She pulled it from the bureau drawer where she'd kept it. A fingertip traced the initials in the corner—DSB. She really should take it with her to Ravenwood tomorrow . . .

Instead she returned it to its nesting place deep within her drawer.

Five

A cold wet nose nudged beneath her hand.

Olivia glanced up from where she knelt, cleaning the floor-to-ceiling windows in the dining room.

"Lucifer!" she exclaimed softly. "Whatever are you doing here?"

Annie, the maid with whom she'd been working this afternoon, gave a most unladylike snort. "That wretched beast! Vicious, he is! Why, he growled and bared his teeth at me the other day when I tried to get him to move from the carpet in the library. Frightened me half to death, 'e did!"

Olivia dropped her rag into the bucket, then ran her fingers over his rough fur. She knew the other servants heartily disapproved of the way the hound had the run of the house. "Lucifer," she scolded gently, "you mustn't do such things. Now sit."

The dog immediately dropped his hindquarters to the floor. He gazed at her, his ears pricked forward, as if awaiting her next command.

Annie first gaped, then rolled her eyes. "Oh, fer pity's sake. No doubt ye'll next be charmin' the birds from the treetops!" She dropped her rag into the bucket and got to her feet. "You can finish up here, can't ye, Olivia?" Without waiting for an answer, she turned and marched off.

Olivia dropped her head, hiding a smile. "You really should reconsider, Lucifer," she whispered. "She's not half as disagreeable as Mrs. Templeton."

Lucifer's tail swished to and fro on the polished floor. Olivia chuckled and scratched behind his ears. Getting to her feet, she squeezed the water from her rag and folded it neatly, laying it across the sides of the bucket before she picked it up and headed toward the kitchen.

A quarter hour later, Olivia untied her apron and hung it on a hook in the storeroom. She'd finished her duties early, and she had only to let Mrs. Templeton know she was leaving. She'd spent the day on tenterhooks, afraid she would encounter the earl around every corner. He made her feel nervous and girlish and immensely uneasy, and the less she saw of him, the better. But thus far today, there had been no sign of him.

"Olivia!" A voice hailed her near the entrance hall.

She turned to find the butler Franklin hurtling toward her. "Olivia, do be a dear and take this letter to his lordship. It's just arrived." He thrust a small silver tray at her. "I believe he's in his study."

Olivia grabbed the tray before it clattered to the floor. She had no chance to say a word, for Franklin had already passed. Wherever he was going, he was certainly in a hurry.

Wonderful, she thought dryly, and just when she thought she'd managed to escape the day unscathed. With resolve, she marched toward the study. She would promptly deliver the letter and be on her way.

The door to the study was closed. Olivia knocked, but there was no answer. Frowning, she knocked again. A hollow voice from within bade her enter—a voice that didn't sound particularly pleased.

The earl was seated in one of two chairs before the window, gazing outside. He gave no sign that he'd heard her entrance. His profile was solemn and unsmiling, his gaze fixed on some faraway place only he could see. He'd discarded his jacket. His white shirt was rumpled, and his hair was slightly disheveled. A faint shadow darkened his jaw; she noted distantly that he needed to shave. His pose was indolent, one long leg extended negligently before him. A pungent aroma permeated the air. For a moment she was puzzled . . . Her pulse leaped as she spotted the source. A brandy decanter sat on a small parquet table at his elbow.

It was nearly empty.

Olivia cleared her throat. She approached him, steadying her heart—and her nerve. "I'm sorry to disturb you, my lord, but a letter just arrived for you." As she spoke, she offered the silver tray.

He made no move to take it. Indeed, he didn't even look at it. Instead, his eyes were fixed on her face.

"Open it."

His intense regard was unnerving. Surely he didn't mean for her to . . . She stole a hasty glance at the letter. His name was written across the front in a flowing, decidedly feminine hand.

"I believe it's private, my lord."

"No matter. Sit down and read it to me." With

a shrug he waved her to the other chair.

Two steps took her to the chair. She lowered herself slowly to the edge of the chair, then broke open the seal with the tip of her nail. Taking a deep breath, she began to read.

My dearest Dominic,

It's with utmost regret that I write to you. We both knew it would come to this, but still you chose to bury yourself in the country. You are a lover of superb skill, Dominic. Never will I forget those wild moments spent in your bed, but I refuse to spend my nights alone—and there are many men in London eager to take your place.

With fondest memories,
Maureen

Olivia's cheeks flamed scarlet by the time she'd finished. The letter was from the woman the other servants had spoken of—the actress Maureen Miller, his mistress! Olivia ducked her head, at a complete loss for words. She'd been well schooled in manners, but this was certainly a situation that had never been broached! What did one say to a man who'd just lost his mistress? Did decorum dictate that she should tell him she was sorry? Heaven help her, she had no idea!

"Your reaction is quite precious, Miss Sherwood. Are you shocked that I have . . . pray excuse me . . . *had* a mistress?" he stressed. "Or shocked that she's found a replacement for me?"

"Both." Her answer emerged before she could stop it. Heaven help her, but she still could not look at him!

"Well then. It seems I shall have to find another to warm my bed." There was a brief pause. "What about you, Miss Sherwood? You claim you've been kissed. But I wonder . . . have you ever had a lover?"

That brought her head up in a flash. Her wide eyes reflected her shock. He gave a short, harsh laugh. "Yes, I quite agree. It's a ridiculous question. Frankly, I'm skeptical that you've even been kissed."

Odd, but he seemed to harbor no remorse for a man who'd just lost his mistress. Indeed, he seemed almost amused. No doubt affairs of the heart meant nothing to him . . . Oh, assuredly the other servants were right. Women meant nothing to him. Why, a woman might be cast aside as . . . as easily as he might shed his jacket!

"I am not a liar," she said stiffly. "And I do not appreciate the way you make sport of me."

He paid no heed. "Who was it who kissed you? Your blond young suitor from the village square the other day?"

Olivia gaped. "You saw him?"

His gaze never left hers. "I did. But tell me, did you like it?"

Her mind skipped backward. What was it Dominic had said? *I don't mean a mere peck on the lips, mind you. I mean really . . . thoroughly kissed . . . a kiss that makes the very earth move beneath your feet . . .*

That would hardly describe William's kiss. Yet that was what she'd wanted. That was how she'd yearned to feel.

"You didn't, did you?"

Her gaze slid away. " 'Twas not what I expected," she said, her voice very low. "I expected a . . . a kiss—especially my first—would be a momentous occasion, a moment that would live on in my heart forever." The admission slipped out before she could stop it. Dear God, was she mad? Why was she confiding in him like this?

"So you were disappointed, eh?"

Drat him, why did he sound so pleased? She squared her shoulders and shored up her resolve. "I'll say no more on the matter, my lord. Indeed, I must ask you to refrain from such questions, for 'tis really none of your affair."

"I stand duly chastised." He mocked her openly. "But tell me—you don't approve of me, do you, Miss Sherwood?"

Unbidden, her gaze cut to the crystal glass atop the table next to him. He saw where her eyes resided so briefly, and picked up the glass.

"What, Miss Sherwood? Is it this? You disapprove of spirits?"

A scant half inch of brandy remained in the glass. He swirled the ruby liquid and downed it. All the while his eyes locked with hers.

Olivia's lips compressed. She said nothing. She didn't know why, but she had the strangest sense he was goading her.

"Come now, Miss Sherwood. Feel free to speak your mind. Despite what you think, I'll not hold it against you."

Olivia raised her chin. "I do not disapprove of spirits. Indeed, my father was rather fond of ale. I simply think that perhaps you've had far too much to drink this afternoon."

"That I have." His agreement surprised her.

"Nonetheless," he went on, "I think you dislike me."

A ready denial sprang to her lips. "Nay, sir. Indeed, I think 'tis you who dislikes me. The way you stare at me so . . ."

He who disliked her? Lord, but that was rich. He stared at her, for when she was near he could scarcely take his eyes from her. Even now, his gaze moved hungrily over her face, down the white column of her throat. He had the feeling that neither guile nor artifice was in her nature. No, she had no idea what a beauty she was . . .

And that only made him want her all the more.

He was also immensely pleased by the fact that she hadn't liked it when her suitor kissed her . . .

He shook his head slowly. "I assure you, Miss Sherwood, that is hardly the case. No," he went on, "it's you who dislikes me."

He was doing it again, Olivia noted wildly. She grew uneasy. "I cannot think why you should say such a thing."

"You avert your eyes when I'm near, and I don't think it's fear—I think it's distaste." He studied her from beneath half-closed lids.

She slid away her gaze, only to return it to him. She raised her chin, feigning a coolness she was far from feeling. "Why are you so convinced I dislike you, sir? I hardly know you."

"But what you know, you dislike."

He would not let the matter rest, damn him! Olivia folded her hands in her lap. Very well. If it was honesty he wanted, then it was honesty he would get!

"I cannot lie, sir. Though I assure you I am not a gossip, there has been . . . talk."

"Oh, but I don't doubt that! Come now, Olivia, don't be shy. Tell me what sort of talk you've heard."

The conversation had taken a direction she'd not anticipated. Still, she had no choice but to tell him.

"'Tis said you are very fond of women, my lord."

A roguish brow arched high. "I daresay I'm not the only man in England fond of women."

"That is true," she allowed. "Indeed, we would be a nation of the elderly were that not the case."

One corner of his mouth curled upward. "I'm glad we agree."

"However, 'tis said that you've trampled many a female heart, my lord."

He was darkly amused. "And so you're convinced I'm a rake. A libertine."

"Do you deny it, sir?" Olivia prayed he'd not remember this conversation. Had he not been foxed, she'd not have been able to summon the daring to speak to him of this!

"Allow me to say this, Miss Sherwood. My heritage being what it is, the dailies in London rather like me. Indeed, when I first saw you here at Ravenwood, I wondered if you hadn't been planted here by some rag in order to spy on me. If I may be so bold, let me impart a lesson in today's society—not half of what is printed is true."

"Nonetheless, sir, I simply cannot abide men who use women for their own purposes."

He gave a short bark of laughter. "Another lesson, Miss Sherwood. There are just as many women who use men for their own purposes. They marry to gain a fortune and possessions. To raise their place in society. To gain a title."

Olivia was not convinced. "Then why do so many gentlemen have mistresses? I do not understand why a gentleman cannot be satisfied with just one woman! And I despise men who discard women like—like a worn shoe!"

"And that is what you believe I've done."

"Haven't you, my lord?" Olivia was righteously indignant.

My lord.

Dominic gritted his teeth. The voice of a child tolled through his mind. *"So which are you? A Gypsy? Or an earl?"* He was not the earl. In his heart, his father was the earl—would always be the earl. But others thought of him—Dominic—as the Earl of Ravenwood. Lord, but it was still so hard to grasp. And he was now . . . what? A Gypsy? An earl?

He was neither. He was caught between two worlds . . .

He was on his feet in a heartbeat, and standing before her—tall and utterly commanding. Olivia was stunned to see that he'd grown abruptly sober.

"My mother was easily discarded, Miss Sherwood, and I would never do that to a woman—never," he emphasized. His gaze seemed to burn right through her. "Oh, I won't deny I've parted ways with many a woman—but the parting has always been mutually agreeable. And in the case of Maureen, I would remind you that I did not discard her. She discarded me. You have the proof right there." He indicated the letter she'd set aside. "And just so you know, Miss Sherwood, I *could* be happy with one woman. I simply haven't found her yet."

His tone had grown very quiet. Olivia was

shocked to her very core. He was utterly serious—this was not brandy talking. Could it be she'd misjudged him after all? That the gossip was not true?

She watched as he moved to the mullioned window that looked out upon the rose garden. He stood with his hands behind his back, booted feet braced slightly apart.

Olivia got to her feet. She stared at the proud, rigid lines of his shoulders. "I'm sorry," she said quietly. "I didn't mean to make you angry."

For the longest time she thought he hadn't heard. Finally he turned to face her. His expression was sober and unsmiling. "I am not angry," he stated curtly. "I am simply tired of being judged by those with little to judge by—those who cannot even bother to learn the truth."

He meant her. Shame washed over her, the shame of being petty and small.

He turned aside. "You'd better go, Miss Sherwood. It will soon be dark."

His tone was heavy, almost . . . resigned.

Olivia gave a quick curtsy. "Good evening, my lord." She left him standing there before the window, shadowed and silent and still, as if he were etched in granite.

She hurried down the hall and made her way outside, almost running from the house. So eager was she to be away from Ravenwood—and its master—that her steps never slackened until a stitch in her side nearly wrung the breath from her. Only then did she slow her pace.

'Twas then that she heard it . . . the swishing of leaves behind her.

She swung around. "Who's there?" she called

sharply. Her eyes strained as she sought to see into the deepening gloom.

For long moments there was no answer. An icy fear prickled her spine, and then she heard the sound again. Her heart leaped as a small form approached and took shape . . .

It was Lucifer.

"Lucifer!" The hound reached her side. Olivia gave a shaky laugh. Bending low she hugged him fiercely around the neck, for until then she hadn't realized just how frightened she'd been.

Lucifer's tail bobbed around and around.

She straightened and pointed toward Ravenwood. "Lucifer," she said sternly, "go home."

The mongrel wagged his tail and thrust his head beneath her hand. Olivia sighed and tried again.

"Lucifer, go home!"

Four more tries and Olivia was forced to admit the hound had a mind of his own. She renewed her steps and now he trotted along beside her. Curiously, though Lucifer was but a four-legged companion, she felt far less alone. It appeared she'd gained the hound's approval . . . but what about his master's?

Upon arriving at the cottage, she raised a finger toward the hound. "Lucifer, sit!" The hound sat. "Now wait," she commanded, and hurried inside. When she returned, he was still where she'd left him, his ears pricked forward as he waited. Holding her breath, she offered a small wedge of cheese she held in her palm.

Lucifer wolfed it down, then looked up eagerly. Olivia chuckled. "That's all, Lucifer. Now you must go home." She pointed in the direction of Ravenwood. Amazingly, the dog rose and retraced their steps, loping toward Ravenwood. Not until then did the realization come to her . . .

He'd sent the hound—Dominic. He'd sent Lucifer to escort her safely home . . .

An odd feeling knotted her heart. Despite the fact that she'd wounded him anew, Olivia was certain of it—as certain as she was that her heart beat strongly within her breast.

Six

"There are Gypsies camped near the stream."

Olivia paused in the midst of setting a steaming kidney pie on the table. She drew a sharp breath, her gaze resting on her sister. "Are you certain?"

Emily nodded. "Someone saw their carts travel through the village this afternoon. And Esther told me as well. They were setting up camp near the bend in the stream, she said."

Olivia peered closely at her sister. Emily seemed amazingly calm. Could it be that the memory of that horrible day their father had been murdered no longer haunted her? *Please, yes*, she prayed fervently.

Aloud she said, "Perhaps they're just staying the day and will be gone in the morning." Though the Gypsy who had murdered their father had not been part of a band, it wasn't unusual for Gypsies to camp nearby to tell fortunes, mend pots and pans and trade horses. Olivia was not afraid for herself, but the thought that they were near made her generally wary.

"That's what Esther said."

"Well," Olivia said lightly, "let us hope she is right." She slid a slice of pie onto Emily's plate.

"Do you think they came because of him?"

There was no question she referred to Dominic. "There are countless bands of Gypsies roaming through England," Olivia reminded her. "If they're camped near the stream, that's a fair distance away from Ravenwood land." She paused to consider. "I'm only guessing, mind you, but I should think not."

The sisters lapsed into silence, each seemingly absorbed by their meal. Olivia was about to rise from the table when the window behind her rattled. A shriek rose to a crescendo, then abruptly stilled.

Olivia frowned. "What on earth is that?"

Emily tipped her head to the side. "It's the wind. There's a storm on the way. I can smell it."

For just an instant, Olivia closed her eyes. She listened, her every sense attuned to the sounds around her, as Emily's were. It came again then, a low moan from without the cottage, a sound that rose and fell, fading to nothingness.

And in the quiet, she thought of him. Dominic. Tonight she'd glimpsed a side of him she'd never expected—oh, it wasn't that he'd been foxed. He was stern and harsh on the outside, but within was a man who could hurt and bleed the same as any other. As she'd watched him there before the window, she'd been stung by the sensation that here was a man who was lonely . . . as lonely as the wind outside. Yet Olivia could not lie to herself . . . there was a part of her that was wary of his Gypsy blood.

The last thing she expected was to be called to his study the next day. Her stomach roiled as she knocked on the door. She'd been too outspoken last

eve—too bold, too brash, and now she was going
to lose her position . . .

He was standing behind the desk when she entered. He was splendidly dressed in a dark gray
jacket and pantaloons. Freshly bathed and clean-
shaven, his dark hair still wet and sleek, he looked
so very handsome he stole the very breath from her
lungs.

"You wished to see me, my lord?" Thank
heaven, her voice reflected none of her inner turmoil.

"Yes, Miss Sherwood." He gestured to the chair
before the desk. "Please sit down."

Olivia wet her lips. "I'll stand, if you don't mind,
sir." The notion chased through her mind that
there was little point in sitting. She'd be on her way
in just a few short moments anyway.

Their eyes met; his quickly slid away. Oh, but
she'd been right to be nervous!

He cleared his throat. "Please understand, Miss
Sherwood, this is a difficult moment for me . . . for
both of us, I suspect."

Olivia's heart plummeted.

"But I fear this must be addressed—"

She blinked back the burning rush of tears. She
was right. He was going to dismiss her. Dear
heaven, how would she and Emily get by? And
their rent was due in just a matter of days . . .

"I must ask you to forgive my behavior last
night. While it may appear otherwise to you, I'm
usually not so inclined to tip the bottle—"

Olivia stared at him numbly. There was a curious
buzzing in her head. This was not what she expected, nay, not at all . . .

"—and so I offer my apologies."

She couldn't say a word. She could only regard him blankly. Had she heard wrong?

"Miss Sherwood?" He frowned. "Did you hear me?"

Stupid, foolish tears stung her eyes. "I heard," she said at last.

"Miss Sherwood, what the devil is wrong? You look ready to cry."

Perhaps because she was, she thought shakily. "I'm sorry, my lord—" She sat, because she could no longer stand. "—it's just that I'm so—so very relieved."

"Miss Sherwood, your reaction is most perplexing."

"I know, my lord," she said quickly. "It's just that I . . . I was convinced you intended to send me packing."

"Why on earth would I do that? Unless you've been doing something quite untoward—like stealing the silver."

She offered a watery smile. "No, no, it's nothing of the sort. It's just that I . . . well, I was quite outspoken when we talked last night . . . and I thought you might be angry . . ."

"Thank you, Miss Sherwood." His expression was grim. "Obviously you think me quite the tyrant. I'm gratified that you continue to hold such an esteemed opinion of my character."

Olivia was dismayed. She'd offended him again—a feat at which it appeared she was quite accomplished!

"My lord, you mistake my meaning. 'Tis just that I don't know what I should do if I lost this position. My sister is blind, you see, and I provide our only income." She prayed she didn't sound like a hopeless twit. "And about last eve, please rest assured I do not think less of you for . . . for . . ." She floundered helplessly. How could she put this delicately? "For being . . ."

He quirked a brow. "Foxed?" he supplied dryly.

"Precisely," she said in an embarrassed rush. "We are all of us given to excess now and then."

"Nonetheless, I hope you'll keep the contents of our conversation between the two of us."

She inclined her head, aware of the heat of a blush staining her cheeks. The oddest thing burned through her mind in those seconds. *And just so you know, Miss Sherwood, I could be happy with one woman. I simply haven't found her yet.* He'd been so quietly intent. Why, she could almost swear he meant every word.

"Of course," she murmured.

He'd taken his chair behind the massive mahogany desk. "There's another matter I'd like to discuss." His regard was steady on her face. "You said you'd been well-educated. Are you good with figures?"

"I used to help my father keep the books for the parish." If she sounded tentative, she couldn't help it. What was he getting at?

"You've knowledge of letter-writing as well, that sort of thing?"

"I also helped my father with such things."

He leaned back in his chair. "Then I wonder if you might be interested in taking on some additional duties. I need someone to keep track of the household accounts, update my business ledgers and write the occasional letter. I expect it would take several evenings a week." He named a wage that was more than generous.

Olivia sucked in a breath. The occasional letter. A vague nagging suspicion returned. She was reminded how he'd had her read the letter from his former mistress. Of course she'd heard how he'd run away from school and back to the Gypsies. She did not look down on him, but could it possibly be that he could not read or write? Her mind was off and running. But no matter; certainly she and Emily could use the extra wages.

" 'Tis tempting," she said slowly. "As I mentioned, my sister is blind, and I—I've been wanting to take her to London to see a physician there, one who might examine her eyes."

"Then the additional wage would be helpful."

"Most certainly," she admitted. "But frankly, sir, I wouldn't want Mrs. Templeton to feel that I'm usurping her position, for doesn't she keep track of the household expenses?" Oddly, Mrs. Templeton's abrasive nature had lessened somewhat these past few weeks.

He shook his head. A half-smile curled his lips. "You need not worry on that score. Mrs. Templeton has already informed me that the household accounts have never been a part of her duties."

So. That was why he'd asked her. Olivia was conscious of a vague disappointment, yet why it was so, she couldn't imagine. Still, a faint smile lifted her lips, for only Mrs. Templeton would have the courage to stand up to him. Olivia was well aware that half the servants were terrified of their new master.

Quickly she made up her mind. "I'd be more than happy to assist you, sir."

"Good. You may start tomorrow evening if you wish."

"I shall be here, sir." Her heart was singing—even if she only worked two evenings a week, her wages would be increased by more than half—and to think she'd been afraid he was going to dismiss her!

She started to rise; his voice stopped her. "One more thing, Miss Sherwood. If it should happen to be dark when you finish, I want you to make use of the carriage."

"Oh, but I couldn't do that." Olivia was adamant.

His eyes narrowed. "Why not?"

"Because 'tis not right that you should show such favoritism toward me. I would feel I'm being accorded a privilege not given to the others."

Her answer displeased him. She could see it in the tightening of his lips. "I thought we had agreed that your safety was my concern."

Olivia drew a deep breath and shook her head. "No, sir. You stated it was so, but I did not agree— I do not agree," she emphasized.

"You walk a very long distance home, Miss Sherwood."

It appeared he was as stubborn as she. "So does Charlotte, my lord."

"But not as late as you."

Her denial was quelled, for it was true. Charlotte usually departed earlier than she.

"Sir, I am well able to take care of myself."

"You leave me no choice then but to escort you myself. From now on when you finish—"

"Nay!" she cried. "You cannot."

"Why?" he said baldly.

"You are my employer, sir. 'Twould not be proper."

"I'm half-Gypsy." His smile did not quite reach his eyes. "Why would anyone expect me to be proper?" She was startled when he rounded the desk and proceeded to reach for her hand, pulling her up from her chair.

"The matter is not yet settled, Miss Sherwood. But for the moment, let us put it aside."

There was little point in arguing. "Fine," she said slowly, "but first I must know . . . You sent Lucifer after me last evening, didn't you?"

"He is a hound, Miss Sherwood. He goes where he pleases."

"And where you tell him." His mild tone didn't fool her. But she was startled to discover a faintly teasing gleam in his eyes.

He neither agreed nor disagreed. Instead he retained his grip on her hand. Turning it palm up, he traced the calluses there. Olivia flushed. She strained away slightly, but his grip didn't lessen. And indeed, his touch was doing strange things to her. Her heart vaulted high into her throat one moment, then fluttered crazily the next. The feeling was strange, something she'd never before felt. She wanted to dislike him, she realized. But she could not . . . She *did* not. And she could only look on as he raised her fingers to his lips.

"Until tomorrow then, Miss Sherwood."

Speech was beyond her. Olivia could only nod as at last he released her. She bobbed a quick curtsy and fled as if the devil himself were at her heels.

As for Dominic, he remained where he was long after she'd departed, his gaze on the door through which she'd passed. She was a beauty, though he suspected she knew it not. He had the feeling he'd rattled her, and he suspected she was usually quite unflappable. But he'd liked seeing her like this—flustered, a bit unsure. Oh, he knew what she thought of him—that he was a rogue. A bounder. His recollection of last night was almost painfully acute. He wondered what she'd have said if she knew that all the while she'd stood here, he admired the way the last embers of light cast golden streamers rippling through her hair. He'd longed to touch it, to feel for himself if it was as soft as it looked. And when she spoke, it was all he could do to tear his gaze from her lips, to not succumb to the masculine urges running rampant through his body. He'd wanted to seize her in his arms, taste her mouth and plumb the depths within with the eager glide of his tongue . . .

He was abruptly disgusted with himself. Christ, he was acting like a lovesick schoolboy. A fool, that's what he was, a damned fool. He'd come to Ravenwood for a number of reasons, one of which was to find some peace within himself and with the world.

In truth, he hadn't known a moment's peace since the night he'd first laid eyes on her.

His mouth twisted bitterly. She would never want him, never in a thousand years. Despite his trappings of wealth—his title—despite her position in his household, to her he was just a lowly Gypsy.

Oh, yes, he knew. He'd glimpsed it in her eyes a dozen times already. Oh, she'd tried to hide it . . .

But Dominic knew better, for he'd seen it far too often in his lifetime to know he wasn't mistaken . . . It was something she could not forget . . .

Nor could he.

*   *   *

"Oh, look, we're near the alehouse!" Esther exclaimed. A hand on Emily's elbow, she guided the younger woman to a bench. "Just sit tight here in the square for a wee bit, sweetings. I'm just goin' to dash in the alehouse and share a dram with me 'usband. I'll be back long before dark."

Emily stretched out a hand. "But Esther—"

There was no answer. Emily's hand fell to her lap. Left alone now, she had no choice but to remain where she was.

The minutes dragged. She heard the occasional footsteps of passersby, but no one approached. The sun beat down upon her head, for she'd forgotten her bonnet. Esther hadn't wanted to return to the cottage for it.

She'd been feeling lonely, with Olivia working so late and all. Olivia had been so excited, filled with plans for visiting London and a physician with the money she'd earn keeping the Gypsy's books. Emily hadn't the heart to tell her it would do no good.

She would never regain her sight. Never. She'd resigned herself to a lifetime of blindness months ago.

Still, she felt badly, with Olivia working so hard. She spent her days making lace, hiding it from Olivia before she came home. She'd had it in her mind to try to sell it somehow, to surprise Olivia with the money she could earn. But she knew of no one who would want to buy it—and so, in the end, 'twas just another way to pass the time.

Still Esther didn't return. She squirmed uncomfortably, wondering if anyone was watching her, thinking how odd it was that she sat all alone here in the village square. Before long, the air began to cool. Emily knew the sun had begun to wane and a feeling of panic wedged in her breast. Tears sprang to her eyes, but she brushed them away and bravely continued to wait.

There was a touch on her shoulder. "Miss?" said a strong male voice.

Emily turned. "Yes? Who is it? Who's there?"

Andre couldn't help but notice the beauteous young blonde waiting on the stone bench in the square. He'd been out to the camp and back, and still she was there. Now, as he stood directly before her, her gaze darting back and forth, he was struck by the realization that she was blind.

Well, he thought, *perhaps that was best.*

"I'm sorry, miss, but I couldn't help but notice how long you've been sitting here. Are you alone?"

"Yes . . . no." She was half-crying. "Oh, sir, can you please help me? Please?" She stretched out a hand and turned her face upward.

Andre sucked in a harsh breath. Unthinkingly he captured her fingers in his. Her eyes were blue as a morning sky, her skin the color of cream. Hair like golden summer wheat was caught in a ribbon at her nape, trailing down her back. In all his days, he'd never seen a creature quite so lovely.

"Tell me what's wrong."

"I came with Esther, but then she wanted to dash into the alehouse to share a cup with her husband. I—I've never told Olivia, but Esther is awfully fond of her ale . . . and now she hasn't returned, and I cannot see to go find her . . ."

Emily knew she was babbling, but she couldn't seem to stop. Oh, but she hated herself! She hadn't always been like this, afraid of anything and everything.

She gripped his hand more tightly. "Please, I—
I've been waiting dreadfully long and I—I want to
go home. Could you find Esther for me?"

The tearful waver in her voice went straight to
Andre's heart.

"Miss, I would be glad to, but I'm afraid I don't
know Esther. I'm—" He hesitated. "—new to Stonebridge. My . . . family has only been here a short
time." He paused again. "What does she look
like?" Too late he realized his mistake.

But Emily's response was telling—apparently
she hadn't always been blind. "It's been ages since
I've seen her, but as I recall, she has straw-colored
hair, and her bum is quite wide. I know, because
she always bumps the doorway at our cottage—
that never happens with Olivia and I. Oh, and Esther always wears a pink bonnet—Olivia always
laughs because it clashes terribly with her hair."

He squeezed her fingers. "I'll see if she's inside."

Emily smoothed a fold of her skirt. Her tears had
dried; indeed they seemed rather foolish. Who was
her rescuer? she wondered. Newcomers to Stonebridge were rare. Instinct told her he was young.

Andre wasn't particularly eager to venture into
the alehouse, but he'd promised the young lady he
would, and so he did.

It took a moment for his eyes to adjust once he
was inside. The interior was dark and rather
gloomy. Perhaps a dozen or so patrons were clustered at various tables. He ignored the sudden silence when those within saw him—he'd expected
that, for the *gadjo* who was friendly was rare.

He strode straight to the barkeep. "I'm looking
for a woman named Esther."

"Esther left with her husband quite some time

ago," the man said grudgingly. Andre gave a nod of thanks and left.

The young woman turned slightly when she heard his footsteps. "Sir? Did you find her?"

Andre squatted down beside her. "I'm sorry, miss, but the barkeep said Esther had already left." He paused. "If you'd like, I can take you home. That is, if you can tell me where you live."

Emily took a deep breath. A stranger had just offered to take her home. She knew nothing of him, nothing at all. Should she be afraid? *Most certainly*, warned a voice inside. Yet she was not . . .

"I do believe I can," she said breathlessly. "But I'm afraid I couldn't possibly let a stranger escort me home." She held out her hand. "I am Emily. Emily Sherwood."

Andre looked slowly from her hand to her face. She was smiling warmly, a smile that was utterly breathtaking. Not until then did he realize what she was about.

He took her hand and lightly shook it, a trifle uncomfortable. *Gadjo* ways were not Gypsy ways, as he well knew.

"I am Andre," he said.

"I'm very pleased to meet you, Andre." If anything, her smile brightened further. "Now we're no longer strangers." She rose to her feet. "May I take your elbow?"

Andre was at her side in an instant. He tucked her hand firmly into his elbow, unable to withhold a smile as his hand covered her fingers. He liked this far better than shaking hands . . .

"Now then. We must turn so that we face the church before we begin walking. Once we've passed the east side, there's a lane which veers to the left . . ."

He was tall, Emily noticed almost at once. She turned her head once, and her cheek brushed his shoulder. And his hand hovering just above hers seemed to encompass her own. She loved his name . . . Andre. Granted, 'twas unusual, but so much better than ordinary John or Paul.

He asked about Olivia, and she told him Olivia was her sister. She explained that Olivia worked for the new earl. Yes, he'd seen the stately brick manor from the road . . .

They were back at the cottage almost before she knew it. She experienced a smidgen of disappointment—nay, more than a smidgen.

"I must thank you again for escorting me home, Andre." She took a deep breath, afraid that she was being distinctly unladylike. Later there might be regrets, but she didn't want to think about that just now. "I hope you'll feel free to visit. It—it's very lonely during the day without Olivia here."

"I'm only pleased that I was able to help," came his deep voice. A moment's pause, and then, "Good-bye, Emily."

"Good-bye," she whispered, wishing desperately that she could see him.

There was the faintest brush of fingertips coasting down her cheek . . . or was it just a fanciful yearning?

She would not tell Olivia of her mishap, Emily decided, nor the fact that a strange young man had brought her home. Not just yet . . .

Seven

Several days passed. Olivia was in a quandary.
Nearly every waking thought was consumed by
Dominic. It seemed every time she glanced around,
he was there—behind her in the hallway. Coming
in from riding. Peering over her shoulder as she
made entries in the ledger.

Oh, if only she *could* dislike him! After all, he was
half-Gypsy, yet he was not the heathen she'd somehow thought he would be.

Yet neither was he a proper gentleman. Very often he dressed in riding breeches, boots and shirt.
He bared his arms and his throat and even part of
his chest! On such occasions, 'twas all she could do
not to stare, for she was aware of Dominic in a way
that made her not the least comfortable.

Certainly a way that had never happened with
William.

Lucifer continued to follow her home every evening. The second night it happened, she scolded
him fiercely and tried to shoo him off. He merely
wagged his tail and remained at her heels. From
that night forward, Lucifer remained throughout
the night, sleeping on the doorstep; in the morning,
he returned to Ravenwood with her. In truth, she

did feel safer when he was near. Nor could she deny she'd grown rather fond of him. Lucifer had also taken to Emily. He spent most evenings with them inside the cottage. Olivia didn't broach the subject again with Dominic.

She had the feeling he knew precisely where Lucifer spent his nights.

What she didn't know was that Dominic was in much the same dilemma.

Even when he had business to attend to, he found himself lingering in the house when he knew Olivia was about. He made excuses to go to his study those evenings she spent working on his accounts. Christ, he was acting like an animal in heat!

That was exactly how he felt. His blood fairly burned when she was near. Why it was so, he didn't know. She was wholly unlike the type of woman he tended to favor. They were worldly and sophisticated, while she was an innocent—that, too, was an enigma. He'd always preferred a woman with experience. He had no patience with tender wooing.

But Olivia . . . He suspected she had no idea what effect she had on him. He longed to frame her face in his hands, and mold his mouth against hers. He longed to kiss her long and thoroughly— and show her what her disappointing young suitor had not. He longed to arouse her as the other man could not.

A self-derisive smile curved his lips. He wanted far more than a kiss. At the thought, his loins tightened almost painfully. On more than one occasion, her very presence near him stirred his manhood to a rock-hard arousal. He hadn't dared rise for fear of embarrassing them both. He ached with the need to lay her down, strip away every last vestige of her clothing and discover the delights that lay beneath. He longed to chip away her quiet, dignified exterior and discover the woman beneath.

He wanted to possess her, possess her as no other man had done.

And yet it was more than that. He liked her inner grace, her calm serenity, her quiet intensity as she diligently worked over his books.

He knew he did not imagine the way she avoided touching him in any way. That night in his study when he'd taken her hand, he'd felt her resistance, felt her straining to pull away. Oh, he knew why—she was a lady, and he was half-Gypsy. No doubt she didn't want to soil herself, he thought blackly. He was both piqued and impressed by her prim, proper manner. With him, she was ever vigilant, ever reticent. Yet he'd seen her with the village children, laughing and sweet-natured. Ah, yes, he was both intrigued . . . and irresistibly fascinated. Perhaps his year in London had made him arrogant, but . . . he wanted her. And someday . . . someday he would have her.

On this particular evening Olivia was recording the household expenditures for the previous week. Mrs. Templeton and Franklin were charged with making such necessary purchases and leaving the receipts in his study.

The light in the study was dim, so dim that she had to light a lamp in order to be able to see. There was a small worktable in the corner, and it was there that she directed her steps. Glancing outside, she saw that the horizon was a seething mass of dark, churning clouds. With a sigh, she noted that a heavy drizzle had begun to fall from the leaden sky.

She'd barely sat down and opened the ledger when Dominic walked in. Olivia's heart immediately sprinted forward. Apparently he'd just come in from riding. Fawn-colored breeches clung lovingly to his thighs, outlining the powerful muscles of his legs. From the corner of her eye she saw him toss his jacket over the back of the velvet wing chair near the fireplace.

"Good evening, Miss Sherwood."

Olivia raised her head, the quill poised in her hand above the thick, leather-bound ledger. Her eyes ran over him. An unruly lock of hair tumbled over his forehead in a boyish fashion—yet there was nothing boyish about the man! An undeniably masculine aura surrounded him, an aura that made her feel wholly ill-equipped to deal with such virility.

"Hello," she murmured.

He regarded her with arms crossed over his chest. He'd rolled up the sleeves of his shirt, as he was often wont to do; dark, silky-looking hair liberally coated his forearms. As always when she saw him dressed like this, an odd feeling knotted her belly.

"May I ask you something, Olivia?"

Her heart leaped. *Olivia.* The sound of her name on his lips startled her. He'd always called her "Miss Sherwood," and now the use of her given name implied a kind of intimacy ... But no. She was being silly. Making something out of nothing ...

"Certainly." She deposited the quill in its holder and gave him her attention.

"You're rather young to be taking care of your sister as you do. Have you no other relatives?"

She smiled faintly. "I'm two and twenty, not so young as you think. And I'm afraid I have no other relatives, other than an aunt—my uncle's widow—in Cornwall. And I fear she has her own weight to bear."

"Your parents are dead?"

She nodded. "Mama died when I was twelve. Papa died—" The fact that he had been killed trembled on her lips. "—a little over a year ago." She paused. "What of you, my lord? Is your mother still with the Gypsies?"

His expression seemed to freeze. "My mother is dead," he stated flatly.

Olivia wet her lips and dared to ask the question that had long plagued her. Slowly she asked, "Is that why your father came to take you—"

"No." He cut her off abruptly. "Did you know the Gypsies consider it bad luck to speak of the dead, just as seeing a wolf or a fox is a sign of bad luck?"

A shiver went through her. "I saw a fox this morning."

"Then perhaps you're doomed." His smile didn't quite reach his eyes. "Have you heard of the curse? That it's the reason James St. Bride fathered no other children?"

She knew what he meant—the curse his mother had supposedly put on his father. "Y-yes," she admitted.

"And what do you think of it?"

"I don't believe in such things."

"What would you call it then? Chance? Providence?"

"I—I suppose."

"And do you believe in a force over which we have no control? Do you believe in God?"

"Of course I do."

"And would you say it was fate that brought us together that night you were nearly run over by my carriage?" As he spoke, he came to sit on the edge of the table, one long, booted leg stretched out before him. One lean hand toyed with an ivory letter opener. Olivia swallowed, staring at the black hair curling across the back of his hand. His fingers were lean and brown and strong.

His nearness was disconcerting. She had the feeling he'd placed himself next to her deliberately, aware that it would rattle her.

Indeed, it did. She didn't understand the rush of feeling whenever he was near. She knew only that he made her heart tremble.

Words seemed to dry up in her throat. "I don't know."

"Well, I do. I believe it was destiny. Fate's design, if you will."

Before she could say a word, a knock sounded on the door and Franklin stepped inside.

"Excuse me, my lord, but Mr. Gilmore is here, asking if he might see you. He's the solicitor in Stonebridge."

Dominic pushed himself to his feet and turned. "Certainly, Franklin. Show him in."

The words were barely out when a presumptuous hand pushed the door aside.

"Is he in there? Let me in then."

Franklin squared his shoulders. "Now see here—"

Dominic cut him off. "It's all right, Franklin. Please, leave us alone."

Franklin quietly withdrew, closing the door behind him.

Dominic waved a hand toward the fireplace and the two chairs grouped before it. "Mr. Gilmore," he said easily. "Please sit down."

Robert Gilmore stalked to the nearest chair. He sat his considerable bulk down on the edge.

"I'm not here to socialize. I've come about the Gypsies."

"Indeed." Dominic took the opposite chair, his voice cool.

Olivia bowed her head low. She'd never particularly liked Robert Gilmore, the only solicitor in Stonebridge; she'd always thought him a bit of a stuffed shirt. Though she tried not to listen, 'twas impossible not to hear.

"Are they here because of you?" Gilmore demanded.

Dominic's eyes flickered. "I'm not certain I know what you mean." His tone was ever so pleasant, but Olivia had the awful sensation he was seething.

"Oh, I think you do." Gilmore's hands balled into fists on his knees.

"Mr. Gilmore, there are numerous bands of Gypsies traveling throughout England. I can assure you that they are not here because of me; however, even if they were, I fail to see why that should concern you."

Gilmore made a sound of disgust.

There was a stifling silence before Dominic spoke again. "Perhaps, Mr. Gilmore, you should tell me precisely why you've come, and what it is you want."

"What the devil do you think I want?" Gilmore

was fairly shouting. "I want you to tell them they must leave!"

"Tell them they *must?*" Low as his voice was, there was an almost deadly note therein.

Gilmore was either too obtuse to notice, or else he didn't care. Olivia held her breath; it seemed her presence had been forgotten.

Gilmore swore. "They're dirty, thieving—"

"Have they stolen from you? From anyone?"

Olivia dared to glance at the two men. Dominic was regarding the other man coolly, his features a mask of stone. Gilmore's face had turned a fiery red.

"No, but—"

Dominic's eyes narrowed. A storm was brewing, not just outside . . . but within him as well. She sensed it instinctively. "Then they are not thieves, are they?"

"Now see here—"

"No, Mr. Gilmore. *You* see here. From your own lips, the Gypsies have done nothing unlawful. Therefore, I will not ask them to leave. Indeed, as long as they mind their own business, I suggest you do the same."

Gilmore jumped to his feet. "Oh, but I should have known. I daresay I speak for all of us, everyone in Stonebridge. We don't want the damn Gypsies here any more than we want you here!"

Dominic was on his feet as well, his smile tight. "A pity. As you've noticed, I've taken up residence here at Ravenwood—and it's here I intend to stay."

"You'll be sorry you came here. I'll make certain of it."

Dominic arched a black brow. "A threat, Mr. Gilmore? I must warn you, I don't take kindly to being threatened." He strode to the door. Pointedly he opened it. "Good evening, Mr. Gilmore."

Gilmore jammed his hat on his head and marched forward. As he passed Dominic, he said scathingly, "It's not a threat, but a promise! You won't last the summer. By God, I'll see to it!"

An instant later, the door clicked quietly shut.

Long moments of complete and utter silence passed. It was as if a sudden pall had been cast over the room. Not knowing what else to do, Olivia rose and moved to fetch her shawl from the hook near the door.

"What about you? Does he speak for you, too?"

His voice, quiet as the night, came from directly behind her. Olivia froze, then slowly turned. Determinedly she ignored the question.

"If you don't mind," she said levelly, "it's rather late. I think I shall finish tomorrow."

The excuse was ill-contrived, and he knew it. He smiled tightly. "That's right. Run away, Miss Sherwood. I must warn you, it does no good. I used to run away from school."

He was right. She *was* running, but she sensed his mood was dangerous.

"I'm quite sure I don't know what you mean." Bravely she lifted her chin.

"And I'm quite sure you do." His eyes were glittering pinpoints of light. "I'm surprised you can stomach working for me, that you aren't afraid you'll be tainted by my Gypsy blood. Did you know when I go to the village some of the shopkeepers pull their shades? Women hide their children behind their skirts and scurry indoors."

Her skin prickled. She hadn't been afraid of him

before. Yet she was now, for she was overwhelmingly conscious of his size and strength—
and his anger. He towered over her, broad and tall.
Olivia was not given to thinking herself feeble and
weak . . . yet next to him like this, that was exactly
how she felt.

And he knew it. She saw it in his features. Was
he deliberately trying to frighten her?

"Why are you doing this?" Her voice was very
low. "Why?"

His voice jabbed at her, like the point of a knife.
"You haven't answered, Miss Sherwood."

Her temper began to crackle. "Please let me go,"
she stated levelly.

"All I ask is an answer to my question. Somehow
I thought you valued the truth above all else. After
all, you're a vicar's daughter, or so I'm told. So tell
me, do you despise the Gypsies as well? Would
you be happier if they were gone?"

Her temper snapped. She took a ragged breath,
unable to break the hold of his eyes. "Yes," she said
wildly, the first thing that vaulted through her
head. "Yes, if you must know! I wish the Gypsies
had never come here—never! I wish *you* had never
come!"

Olivia knew as soon as the words were out that
she'd made a horrible, dreadful mistake. It wasn't
like her to be so—so small and mean-spirited.

His entire body seemed to stiffen. "So," he said
coolly, "at last we know your true feelings about
me, Miss Sherwood. After all, I'm half-Gypsy. Certainly we can't deny it. But do you know what?
I'm tired of narrow, close-minded people like you—
people who think they're better than the rest of the
world. Now. I believe you're right. I believe you

should leave, before I say something we both might regret. Oh, and you needn't worry. You still have your precious position here at Ravenwood. Despite your opinion of me, I'm not the inconsiderate bastard you think I am."

Olivia gave a tiny shake of her head. She could only watch as he moved to stare out the window at the encroaching darkness. The lines of his back were rigidly immobile.

A stinging rush of tears pushed to the surface. She blinked them back. Never in her life had she felt so low, so utterly miserable! Her mouth opened, but the words she sought just wouldn't seem to come. "Please," she said faintly. Quaveringly. "You don't under—"

He whirled on her. "Dammit, didn't you hear?" His tone was as blistering as his glare. "Get out, Miss Sherwood . . . Get out!"

Olivia waited no longer.

With a jagged sound she snatched her shawl from the hook and ran out. Out of the house. Out into the storm which had begun to rage. She didn't care where she went, as long as it was away . . .

Away from him.

His eyes squeezed shut. The world revolved in a crimson haze all around him. He was fiercely, bitterly angry. Damn her, he thought. *Damn her*. He knew what they all thought of him . . . Gilmore. The rest of the villagers. He knew what *she* thought of him . . . Olivia.

He couldn't help it. A deep, potent rage shook him. He felt betrayed. Bewildered. Christ, he'd even dreamed of her, for pity's sake, only to awake rock-hard and throbbing.

His eyes opened. His feet moved, without conscious volition. He found himself staring at the portrait on the wall, the portrait of James St. Bride.

His thoughts drifted. He remembered that long-ago day when he was but a lad of twelve, no longer a boy, not yet a man—the day James St. Bride had ridden into the Gypsy camp to see him.

Most of the others had gone into town to barter at the market. Only he, his mother, and a group of children remained. Dominic had only to glimpse his mother's paleness, her wild, panicked expression to realize the identity of this tall, mahogany-haired stranger atop a sleek-limbed, shiny black stallion. Instinct provided all the answer he needed.

Madeleine rose slowly from where she'd been sitting near the fire. Her hand had climbed to her throat, yet she faced him bravely.

"Why are you here?" she asked, her voice very low. She spoke in English, so the other children didn't understand.

But Dominic did. She'd taught it to him at a very early age.

James St. Bride swung to the ground. Dominic could see he carried himself with the arrogance of one accustomed to giving orders—and being obeyed instantly.

It was then that the fire of hatred began burning even more deeply in his soul.

"I've come to see for myself if you spoke the truth. To see if the bastard you carried is mine."

Madeleine said nothing.

James St. Bride's hard gaze encompassed the straggly ring of children lined around the fire, gawking at the stranger. He slapped his riding crop against his thigh. *"He's here, Madeleine. I know he is. I've heard of him. The Gypsy with blue eyes."*

Dominic longed to hide. He'd always known he was different. Gypsies from other bands whispered about the boy with pale eyes; *gadje* pointed in disbelief. Once, at a market fair, curiosity had gotten the better of him. Catching sight of a mirror in one of the stands, he stood before it and stared at his reflection, stared endlessly at eyes the color of a warm summer sky . . .

He'd shattered the glass with his fist.

And now, once again Dominic knew shame, the bitter shame of his heritage . . . the shame of his *gadjo* blood.

Deliberately he averted his face.

But James St. Bride had seen him. He advanced upon him, grabbing him by the shoulder and wrenching his chin upward.

Never in his life would he forget that moment. It was etched into his being as surely as a brand . . . the look of shock, of black resignation that traveled fleetingly across James St. Bride's countenance. Oh, he'd wanted to deny that this man was his father, just as James St. Bride had longed to deny that he was his son. But each of them had only to look into the other's eyes and know the truth . . . he was born from the seed of James St. Bride.

Dominic spit in his face.

A harsh smile twisted St. Bride's lips. His gaze locked with Dominic's as he wiped away the spittle.

"The boy has no manners, Madeleine. I think it's time he learned some."

Madeleine's lips parted. *"What! You—you would take him with you?"*

St. Bride released him. His lip curled as he moved toward Madeline. *"Does it make you happy to know that your curse worked, Madeleine?"*

Her eyes widened.

"Do not pretend ignorance!" St. Bride's expression turned brooding. *"I have no other children, save this one. No matter that I wish it otherwise, he is my son— my only heir."*

Madeline lifted her chin. Though she was still pale as winter snow, she was calm. *"A word with you in private,"* was all she said.

Dominic leaped to his feet. Madeleine whirled on him. *"Dominic, no!"* she said in Romany. *"Leave us alone."*

The two of them retreated to a secluded spot near the stream. Dominic watched them, saw his mother's head dip low for the longest time. Slowly she raised it, then gave a slight nod.

They turned and walked back. Dominic watched their approach with a sick feeling of dread winding all through him. His mother didn't look at him but went straight to their *vardo*. She emerged in but a few moments. In her hand was a small bundle.

Tucked within were his belongings.

He fell to his knees in the dirt, crying out. *"Mother, no! Don't let him take me!"*

"You will do as I say!" She spoke with rare sharpness. *"You will go with him, and you will learn the* gadjo *ways."*

Her gaze slid toward James St. Bride. He knew then, for he saw it in her eyes. She loved him. She loved him still.

"He is your father. I have had you with me these many years, Dominic. Now it is his turn."

A storm of rage swirled inside him. *"I don't want to—"*

"It must be," was all she would say. *"It must be. Now rise and be strong, my son."*

He could have done it. He could have been strong, if only her voice hadn't cracked. If only he hadn't seen the heart-wrenching sheen of tears in her dark Gypsy eyes.

It took two of James St. Bride's men to restrain him.

At last he stood tired and subdued between the two burly men. His chest burned with the effort it took to hold his pain inside. But he wouldn't shed a tear, not before James St. Bride.

Madeleine approached. She kissed each cheek in turn.

"Grow and learn, my son. And remember that a part of you is Gypsy, and a part of you is gadjo. Be true to them both, and to yourself."

She was wrong. He could not be both Gypsy and *gadjo.*

Oh, he'd tried to return to the Gypsies, to his people. But it wasn't the same. It would never be the same. And then his mother had died . . . and there was no reason to return.

Yet he would never forget what she'd told him. *Remember that a part of you is Gypsy, and a part of you is gadjo. Be true to them both, and to yourself.*

But he'd discovered he could never go back to the Gypsies. He enjoyed the comforts that money could buy . . . a roof over his head, shelter from the rain and wind. A soft bed beneath him at night. No, he could never go back . . . yet he could never be free. And so he found himself lost, trapped between two worlds.

All this he remembered. All this . . . and more.

And then he thought of her . . . Olivia.

A bitter storm of emotion caught hold of him. He'd lived under a veil of suspicion his entire life. He'd wanted her to be different, but she was just like everyone else. She knew nothing about the Gypsies, yet she hated them . . .

Did she hate him too?

Little by little his anger receded. What madness had come over him? He couldn't explain what had seized him. He'd been angry at Gilmore, yet it was Olivia who paid the price. He'd taunted her, taunted her into answering a question that should never have been put to her.

His insides twisted into a sick, hard knot. He remembered her expression as she'd rushed from the room. She'd looked shattered, as shattered as he felt inside.

His jaw clamped tight. He had to go after her. He had no choice. He couldn't let her go, not like this.

In less than a minute, he reached the stable and called for Storm, his horse.

The night was a wild one. Rain fell in drenching sheets from a steely sky. Wind snatched at tree branches, lifting his cloak from his shoulders. His hat shielded him from the rain. Eyes narrowed, he scanned the muddied roadway. It wasn't long before he spotted a small, bedraggled figure.

He bent low and called to her. "Olivia."

She ignored him and kept on walking. She stepped in a puddle. His ears picked up the sound of the splash but her pace never wavered. If anything, she walked faster. An unexpected smile caught at Dominic's mouth. Stubborn, he thought. Stubborn and full of pride.

"Olivia, please stop."

Her pace quickened even more.

Dominic wasted no more time but pressed his heel to Storm's flank. In no mood to cajole patiently, he wheeled the animal so that her path was blocked, then swung down from the saddle. Reaching out, he caught her shoulders just as she would have stepped aside to skirt him.

"You didn't take Lucifer." He cursed himself; that wasn't what he'd meant to say at all.

She refused to look at him. Beneath his hands, her body was rigid as stone.

"I don't need you or Lucifer to protect me," she announced.

Her expression was mutinous, but there were wet streaks upon her pale cheeks. His heart stopped. Rain . . . or tears? Before she could stop him, he snared her chin between his fingers and tilted her face up to his.

"Leave me be!" she cried, and then again: "Please just—just leave me be!"

Her voice wobbled traitorously; it wrenched at his insides. He condemned himself to the devil and beyond. Christ, he'd made her cry!

Without further thought, he scooped her up in his arms and placed her in the saddle. With a gasp her eyes flew wide. She lurched forward as if to launch herself from the saddle, but Dominic was already up and behind her. A hard arm about her waist, he caught her close and held her tight against the plane of his chest.

He bent his mouth to her ear. "Pray don't argue

with me, Olivia. I'm taking you home and I'll hear no more arguments from you."

To his everlasting surprise, she didn't challenge him further. She shivered, a tremor that shook the whole of her body. Indeed, she shocked him by winding her fingers in the front of his shirt and holding on for dear life. In his arrogance, he attributed her sudden acquiescence to gratitude. Not once did he consider it might have been something far different.

Storm was sleek and powerful, and quickly covered the distance to the cottage. He bent his head low, for Olivia had buried her head in the hollow just below his chin. "We're here, Olivia."

Without waiting for an answer, he leaped to the ground, then turned to reach for her. He pulled her from the saddle.

Only then did she raise her head. Her eyes were half-wild, her mouth tremulous. Dominic's hands tightened on her shoulders. Jesus, she was shaking so that she could hardly stand.

An oath stung the air. "Dammit, why are you trembling? Why are you so afraid? Is it me? My Gypsy blood? Or is it this?"

Powerful arms swept around her, drawing her close. Oh, but so very, very close . . . !

And then his mouth closed over hers.

Eight

*The world seemed to stand on end. All around thun-*der cracked. Lightning split open the sky.

But all she could hear was the pounding of her heart echoing in her ears. *No,* Olivia thought numbly. Shock and disbelief warred within her. This could not be happening. It could not . . .

Yet it was . . . *it was.* She was being kissed by the Gypsy earl. God above, the Gypsy earl!

All thought but one fled the confines of her mind. His kiss was nothing at all like William's, neither sweet nor worshipful nor brief. Alas, from the very instant his mouth closed over hers, 'twas as if she'd been caught in the rampage of the wind. Deep in some corner of her mind, she knew she should pull away—and was appalled that she didn't! It was as someone else had taken over her body, as if she'd been flung into a world where nothing else existed, nothing but the branding heat of his mouth on hers.

A shiver coursed the length of her, but this time it was not one of fright, nor of cold. She felt as if she were floating in a warm pool of darkness. All she could do was cling to him blindly. His mouth was warm, insidiously demanding . . . and utterly persuasive.

All at once she recalled the day he'd asked if she'd been kissed. *I don't mean a mere peck on the lips, mind you. I mean really . . . thoroughly kissed . . . a kiss that makes the very earth move beneath your feet . . .*

On and on he kissed her. In the driving rain. In the dark of night. God help her, it was just as he'd said . . . as if the very earth moved beneath her feet. His kiss was everything . . . everything William's was not.

Even as that realization tolled all through her, he raised his head. His arms fell away.

"There," he said roughly. "It's done. That's all you have to fear from me."

Reality caved in all around her. Olivia tried desperately to still the frantic thunder of her heart. Was that why he was angry? Because he thought she was afraid of him?

"Dear God," she said faintly, "it's not you I'm afraid of—" She pointed over his shoulder at the stallion. "—it's . . . it's *him*."

"You're afraid of Storm?" Dominic cursed himself. He should have known! That day in the town square when he'd first seen her teaching the children. He'd wanted her to ride atop Storm. She had vehemently declined.

She nodded. All at once she was laughing. She was crying, tears running unchecked down her cheeks. Her emotions lay scattered worlds apart.

Through a misty haze of tears, she saw him lift a hand toward her. "Olivia—"

"Go," she choked out. "Please . . . just go." She could say no more, for she could stand it no longer.

If she stayed—if *he* stayed—she was certain she would splinter apart. Picking up her sopping skirts, she whirled and rushed inside.

Emily was sitting in the parlor. "Olivia? Is that you?"

Olivia leaned back against the door. She pressed cold hands to her burning cheeks. "Yes, love. I'm here." She prayed she could disguise her tumult. Through some miracle, she managed to sound normal.

Or so she thought.

Emily tipped her head to the side. "Are you all right? I heard the rain. And the thunder—"

"I'm fine. I just need to—to catch my breath. And I fear I'm half-drowned. I must get out of these wet things." She hauled in a deep, fortifying breath. "It's been a long and tiring day, Emily. Would you mind terribly if I went straight to bed?"

"No. No, of course not." Emily frowned, faintly disturbed. She knew when something was amiss, and Olivia was most certainly not herself. "Was it that horrible Mrs. Templeton again?"

"Actually Mrs. Templeton has been quite tolerable lately."

The wet swish of skirts told Emily that Olivia had moved to the bedroom door. It was all Emily could do to hide her displeasure. If it was not Mrs. Templeton who caused her sister's troubles, then no doubt it was him—the Gypsy. Obviously Olivia didn't wish to talk, and she would not trouble her further, though she did wish Olivia would share her burden sometimes.

"Sleep well, Olivia," she said softly.

"And you, Emily."

In the bedroom, Olivia stripped quickly and

donned her nightgown. Slipping into bed, she pressed her cheek against her pillow. Her mind raced apace with her heart. Was he still out there? she wondered. Compelled by the need to know, she threw aside the covers and moved to the window. With one hand she parted the curtains and peered outside.

The darkness was like a thick fog. She couldn't see a thing.

Suddenly her spine seemed to shiver. All at once she could feel him, the force of his presence . . . and she knew . . .

He was still there.

Despite the night's fierce storm, the next day dawned bright and sunny. The afternoon turned so warm Emily opened the window against the heat.

It was just as she was turning around that she heard Esther's voice through the window.

"Emily! Emily, open the door, dear. 'Tis Esther!"

Emily obligingly moved to the door and opened it. "Hello, Esther," she murmured as Esther bustled inside.

"I've brought ye some bread just fresh from the oven. It's warm and yeasty, just the way ye like it."

"Thank you, Esther. That's very kind of you. I believe I'll save it for supper. Olivia rarely has time to bake anymore." Emily had a hard time holding back a smile. Esther had stopped by the day after she'd deserted her outside the alehouse, immensely contrite and full of apologies for having left her alone in the village. Yesterday she'd brought fresh berry tarts, and the day before, half a dozen buns— her way of making amends, Emily decided.

"I thought we might take a walk about," Esther

said brightly. "What do you say, Emily?"

Emily directed a smile her way. "Actually I'm feeling a bit tired today, Esther. Perhaps another day."

"Yes, of course." Esther didn't sound terribly disappointed. "Well, I'll just be off then. Oh, but it's a warm one outside today! I vow I'll have quite the thirst by the time I arrive home!"

A thirst which would no doubt entail a visit to the alehouse! Emily smothered a laugh as she bade the older woman good-by and closed the door. Despite her little habits, Esther really was a dear, generous soul. And if it hadn't been for Esther, she'd never have met Andre.

A sigh escaped her, for nearly four days had passed since her encounter with the young man Andre. She knew she'd been remarkably bold when she'd hinted he might visit; too bold, it seemed. Odd, but he hadn't seemed the sort of man to stand confined by the boundaries of propriety.

Strangely enough, it wasn't long before the crunch of gravel reached her ears. "Hello?" called a male voice.

Emily's heart bounded forward, then began to sing. *It's him—it's him!* She was on her feet and moving toward the door in an instant.

She groped for the handle, found it and slanted the door open. "Andre?"

"Here." He stepped within and closed the door behind him. His heart pounded as he drank in the sight of her. God, but she was a beauty. Her hair was like a shining golden waterfall. And she actually appeared glad to see him. He could hardly believe his good fortune, although not two months past, Irina had predicted that very soon a woman would come his way who would enchain his heart forever. As was his way, he'd laughed and boasted to his friends that there was not a woman alive who could accomplish such a feat.

This one could. He knew it. He knew it as surely as the sun had risen that very morn.

Her smile was warm and welcoming. Her fingers found his sleeve. "Here. Come into the parlor and sit."

In the parlor, she resumed her chair and indicated the small settee where Olivia usually sat. Nervous as a schoolgirl, she reached for the scrap of lace she'd been working on.

"I hope your sister wasn't angry that I escorted you here the other day."

"Not at all." Emily fidgeted slightly. That wasn't quite the truth. But then again, perhaps it was. Olivia hadn't been angry because she didn't know! Nor had she told Olivia about Esther deserting her. Esther had been extremely contrite the next day, vowing that it wouldn't happen again. Emily had assured her it was all right, that someone had found her and guided her home.

She simply hadn't divulged who that someone was.

Now, she heard the rustle of a movement. The next thing she knew there was a slight touch on her hands. "What are you doing?" she asked softly. Again she felt the slightest brush on the back of her hands. The lace she'd been clutching was pulled gently from her fingertips.

"Did you make this?"

She felt her cheeks heat up. "Yes. I—I count the stitches."

"It's quite exquisite."

"That's what Olivia said," Emily confided shyly. "I—I had this notion that—that I could sell it." The confession spilled out before she thought better of it. "Olivia labors hard and long at Ravenwood, while I sit here and—and do nothing. I thought if I could only sell it that I could help in some way . . ." She gave a half-laugh, a sound that was self-deprecating. "But of course the idea was quite foolish. I—I can hardly travel myself to sell it."

Andre took a deep breath. "I could sell it for you. Do you have more?"

"Yes, I—I have an entire basket full." She tipped her head to the side. "But . . . how would you sell it?"

"At market fairs perhaps. My—" There was the slightest hesitation. "—work often takes me to such places."

Emily bit her lip. Oh, but it was almost too much to hope for . . . "I hate to put you to such trouble—"

"It's no trouble." Andre gazed into her face. Lord, but he would travel the earth and back for her. Earnestly he said, "Let me try, Emily. If I cannot, then you've lost nothing."

Emily took a deep breath. "All right. I—I'd love it if you would try. But only if you keep a part of whatever proceeds you make."

"Oh, but I could not—"

"Otherwise I won't do it. Now," she said crisply, "do we have a bargain?" She lifted a hand toward him.

Andre took the hand she offered. He wanted to carry it to his lips, to pull her into his arms and smother her lips with his. Perhaps in time . . . "We do," he said huskily.

A slow smile spread across her face, a golden smile that made him feel he'd been punched in the belly. "I cannot tell you how happy I am that I met you," she said softly. "I hope that you'll be staying a long, long while in Stonebridge."

His own smile faded. "Most probably, throughout the summer." He prayed that he was right. Much depended on the *gadje*. If they were tolerant of the Gypsies' presence . . .

"Forgive me if I sound too forward, but I—I couldn't help but notice the scent of leather. Are you a tanner?"

"No, but I—" There was just the slightest hesitation. "—I work with horses." It wasn't a lie, but instinct warned him not to tell her he was a Gypsy.

Emily nodded. So. She'd been right. He was a working man. "Buying and selling?"

"Y-yes. And trading. I also break them in to the saddle. 'Tis said that my—" He caught himself just in time. "—that I have a way with them."

Emily listened intently as he spoke. He'd been moving around the parlor rather restlessly, she suspected, as if he were unable to sit still.

"Would you like to go outside?" she asked. "I believe 'tis a fine day—"

She never got the chance to finish. In the very next instant, she was scooped up and borne high in the air, snug within strong male arms. She was still gasping when he lowered her to the ground.

Slowly he released her. Emily found herself breathlessly wishing those hard arms would have stayed around her just a while longer.

"Princess," he announced gallantly, "your throne."

Beneath her was a soft bed of lush grass. Emily

tried to withhold a smile but failed utterly. "You, sir," she scolded good-naturedly, "are very brash."

"And you, princess, are very beautiful."

A tiny thrill went through her. He was smiling. Oh, she could not see it, but she could hear it in his voice and feel it in the very air around them.

Her mind was suddenly whirling. How old was he? Was he young? *Please*, she prayed. Was he married? Engaged to be married? *No. Please, no!*

Her smile faded. She hated being blind, hated it, for indeed, what man would want to burden himself with a woman who was blind? No doubt she was consigned to spinsterhood, forever and ever. She would grow old sitting in that horrid chair in the parlor. And poor Olivia would grow old with her, for she knew Olivia would be both honor- and duty-bound to remain with her. No, Olivia would never leave her alone. And poor Olivia's life would be ruined because of her—because of *her!*

Never had she hated being blind as much as she did at that moment.

"Emily," said a low male voice, "what are you thinking?" The laughter was gone from his voice as well.

She smiled faintly. "I can feel the heat of the sun, but it seems a lifetime since I've seen it." She couldn't tell him the truth.

He took her hand, enfolding it warmly between both of his own. "You weren't always blind, were you?"

It was a gesture of comfort, of friendship, and . . . oh, she was quite mad, but she hoped and prayed he stayed forever and ever in Stonebridge.

Wordlessly she shook her head.

"How did it happen?"

Emily's breath came fast, then slow. Memories flashed through her brain, one after the other. She felt herself tumbling from Bonnie's back; she saw Papa lying face-down on the ground, blood trickling from the corner of his mouth, that horrid Gypsy standing over him with a bloodied club in his hand . . .

A shudder tore through her.

Andre's hand tightened around hers. "You need not talk about it if you don't want to."

"I—I wish I could, but I . . . I cannot." Her voice was barely audible.

The calloused pad of his thumb ran across her knuckles. "I didn't mean to make you sad," he murmured. "It's a lovely day, too lovely for dark thoughts."

She took a deep breath and the scent of flowers teased her nostrils. The breeze whirled around her, cooling her from the warm air. Her blessings might not be many but she must be thankful for what she had. She was young and healthy, and . . . and the very best reason of all sat right beside her.

"You're right," she said softly. She summoned a smile. "Now, may we talk of something else?"

"We may," came his ready response. "Do you like roses, Emily?"

"I adore roses. My mother used to say there's no flower on earth fairer than the English rose."

"Did she now . . ."

The talk moved on to other things, silly things, mundane things. She marveled, for he seemed to know just how to make her laugh.

When at last he pulled her to her feet, she was stunned to discover the afternoon was nearly spent.

"Will you come visit again?" She couldn't disguise her disappointment—or her eagerness.

Andre gave a low chuckle. "Is tomorrow too soon?"

"Tomorrow is perfect," she murmured.

He chuckled again, and carried her fingers to his lips to press a fleeting kiss there. Emily thought her heart would surely stop in that instant. And when he was gone, she brought that very same hand to her own lips and smiled, there at the very place his lips had brushed. She felt absurdly happy . . .

Happier than she had been in a long, long time.

Returning to Ravenwood the next day was the hardest thing Olivia had ever done. She'd tossed and turned throughout the night, unable to stop thinking of Dominic—of what he'd done, the way he'd made her feel—so very unlike herself! Even with her eyes squeezed shut, she kept seeing him, dark as midnight, so handsome he stole the very breath from her lungs . . . as he had when he'd kissed her.

Little wonder that she dreaded the moment she might face him again. The day was interminably long. Mrs. Templeton had her and Charlotte cleaning downstairs. She feared every time she turned around that she might see him. Charlotte even commented on her edginess.

"What the devil is the matter with ye, Olivia? Ye jump at every little sound," Charlotte declared, jamming her hands on her hips and looking her up and down.

Olivia gave a tiny little laugh. "Of course I'm not."

Charlotte peered at her more closely. "Ye know, ye're lookin' rather pale. Are ye feelin' poorly?"

"I'm fine, Charlotte. Really."

Charlotte didn't look particularly convinced. Not until Olivia chanced to hear Franklin mention that Dominic had gone to York for the day did she begin to rest easy.

It was early evening when she started toward the study. She was anxious to finish the bookkeeping she'd begun last evening before Mr. Gilmore had arrived.

In some distant corner of her mind, she noted one of the double doors leading into the study was slightly ajar. Her hand reached out to pull it wide when a male voice reached her ears.

Olivia froze. It was Dominic, but there was someone with him.

"I hope you'll forgive my intrusion, m' lord."

"It's no bother, Mrs. Danbury. What brings you to Ravenwood?"

"Something awful has happened, m' lord. Charles, my husband, sent me to see ye—ye see, sir, he fell and broke his leg last week. The physician says he'll be confined to bed until early August. I—I've come because we cannot pay the rent due ye this month—and probably next as well. Ye see, until the harvest comes in, once a month Charles takes the sheep to market . . ."

Olivia blinked. The woman was Celeste Danbury. The Danburys lived on a farm just east of Ravenwood.

"So there is no one who might be able to take the sheep to market in your husband's stead?"

"No, m' lord. Our sons are but nine and ten, our girls even younger."

Olivia bit her lip. A sliver of guilt passed through

her. She really should leave. Yet she couldn't help but pause to listen.

"I see. So you're worried about payment of the rent."

"Yes, m' lord." Celeste's voice was shaking. She sounded terrified. Olivia could almost see her wringing her hands in dire fear for her life.

"Do you have geese on your farm, Mrs. Danbury?"

"Yes, m' lord." Celeste sounded puzzled. "We've several."

"Excellent. Have your boys deliver one to the kitchen tomorrow—I'm rather fond of roast goose. That's payment enough for this month's rent, and the next as well. By then, your husband should be back on his feet again."

"Yes, m' lord. I—I surely hope so." Celeste sounded stunned. "I'll send the boys right off in the morning. Oh, sir, I cannot thank ye enough. Charles and I were so afraid ye would turn us out . . ."

"Only a selfish tyrant would do such a thing, Mrs. Danbury. I should like to think I'm neither. And by the way, I'll see that someone is sent out to help with the farming chores."

The voices were coming nearer. "Oh, ye're a saint, m' lord, a saint!"

"I'm hardly that, Mrs. Danbury." Dominic's tone was dry. "Give my regards to your husband."

Olivia quickly stepped out of sight behind the door just before it swung open. Though she couldn't see Celeste, she heard her footsteps echo down the hall. Holding her breath, she prayed Dominic would either leave or return to the study.

"You may come out now, Olivia."

Drat! How long had he known she was there? Cringing inside, Olivia stepped out from behind the door.

He was dressed in a loose white shirt, buff trousers and boots. His gaze swept quickly over her from head to toe. "I'm glad to see you've suffered no ill effects from last night's storm."

Olivia envied him his calm, for inside she felt like a runaway fire.

"I didn't know you were back," she said weakly. "I came to work on the accounts . . . I didn't mean to eavesdrop."

He said nothing, merely regarded her with his hands behind his back, his expression decidedly cool. It was hard to believe she'd been in his arms last night. Looking at him now, it was hard to believe the kiss—that impossible, unforgettable kiss—had ever happened.

She swallowed. With a nod, she indicated the direction Celeste had taken. "That was good of you," she said slowly.

Black brows shot up. "What! Are you surprised? Did you think I would be totally insensitive to their plight? I may be half-Gypsy, but I have a heart that bleeds like any other."

Olivia drew a sharp breath. He sounded—so bitter! Their eyes locked. All at once an unbearable tension vibrated between them.

Her gaze was the first to falter. "My lord," she said very low, "I would like to apologize for what I said last night."

"What do you refer to, Miss Sherwood? I fear my memory is rather short."

Olivia fought a sizzle of anger. He was demanding his pound of flesh. "That I wished the Gypsies had never come here . . . that—" She summoned all her courage. "—that *you* had never come."

His jaw was implacable. "Did you mean it, Miss Sherwood?"

She took a deep breath. "At the time, but—"

"Then any apology you make is insincere."

He was curt and angry, and—and she shouldn't have cared, but she did. God help her, she did.

"I—I have good reason to feel as I do." With a lift of her chin, she defended herself.

"Oh, I don't doubt that. You and the rest of England—why, the rest of the world. They hate the Gypsies simply because they exist. They need no more reason than that." His tone was as cutting as his eyes.

"That's not true of me," she said levelly. "I tell you again, I have good reason to feel as I do."

"Do you now?" He was openly skeptical.

There was a heartbeat of silence. "Yes," she said quietly. "You see, my father was murdered by a Gypsy."

Nine

A ripple of shock went through him. Dominic went very still. He didn't know what he'd expected her to say . . . but it was not this. From the very beginning, he'd sensed her reticence—he'd thought it was merely disdain. But now that he knew . . . he was stunned that she had ever come to work for him.

Snaring her by the elbow, he pulled her into the study. The door clicked shut behind them. "What happened?" he asked, his expression grim.

Her eyes were downcast. "Just over a year ago, Papa was out visiting a woman who was ill. My sister was with him. They were on their way back to Stonebridge when it happened. The Gypsy tried to steal Papa's horse. There was a struggle . . . Emily suffered a bad fall . . . Papa was badly beaten. A farmer nearby heard shouts. But by the time he reached Papa, it was . . . too late."

"He was gone?" His probing question was very quiet. Olivia couldn't help but note that the hard edge had left his voice.

"Yes." She shuddered, her reply but a whisper. Clearly it was a subject that still pained her deeply.

Dominic said nothing for a moment, merely beheld her pale countenance. He almost wished he hadn't been so insistent. It would have been easier to remain ignorant. No, he could hardly disregard her response—nor damn her for feeling as she did. Still, one more question gnawed inside him, and he had to know.

"What happened to the Gypsy?"

"He was caught a few days later. He was not with his people—" She frowned, searching for the right word. "—not a part of his band . . ."

"*Marime.* An outcast."

"Yes." At last she raised her head. Her eyes grazed his, then quickly looked away. "There was a trial," she said, her tone very low. "He was . . . hanged."

Dominic said nothing. He did not question that the man had deserved his punishment—he had, for he'd taken another's life. Yet he couldn't withhold the thought that sprang to the fore. Had the man not been a Gypsy, his life might have been spared; he might have been locked away instead for the remainder of his days.

Carefully he chose his words. "I am sorry about your father's death, Olivia, and I understand why you feel as you do. But would you condemn all because of one man's cruelty? The Gypsies are hardly responsible for the ills of the world. I think those who inhabit England's prisons can well attest to that."

He was right. Deep inside, she knew it. But right now logic defied her feelings—and it wasn't his father who'd been killed.

"Look at me, Olivia."

She didn't want to. Then all at once he raised a

hand. A finger beneath her chin demanded that she look at him.

"What do you see?" He was quietly intent. "Do you see a Gypsy? Or do you see . . . something else?"

She drew a deep, uneven breath. "I see . . ." She broke off, for what could she say? She saw a devastatingly handsome man who disturbed her far more than he should. She saw a man who governed the very rhythm of her heart—and she knew not why. And indeed, all with naught but the stroke of his eyes! But she could hardly confide this to him.

"Have you no mercy, Olivia? No forgiveness?"

The weight of his stare was unnerving. Her lips parted. She gave a tiny shake of her head. " 'Tis not so—so easy."

His hand fell away. He gave her a long, slow look. "Apparently not. Well, we all have our demons to conquer, don't we?" He stepped toward the door. There he turned. His expression was guarded as he spoke.

"I'll leave you to your work."

Something painful caught at her heart, something she didn't understand. Left alone, she had the oddest sensation she'd somehow disappointed him. It was a notion that stayed with her throughout the next few days, and troubled her deeply. Why it mattered, she couldn't say.

She knew only that it did.

All her life she'd been suspicious—and yes, fearful—of the Gypsies who occasionally chanced to pass through Stonebridge. Everyone was, everyone she knew.

It was hard to dismiss the beliefs of a lifetime so easily.

Andre returned the next day. And the next and the next.

He picked flowers and brought them to her. Their scent filled the tiny cottage with their sweet, heady perfume. Emily was touched beyond measure, yet she was touched by a bittersweet poignancy—if only she could see their loveliness for herself.

She was thrilled when he told her he'd sold all the lace she'd made. She stowed the money away, hoping to surprise Olivia with it when the time was right. But she still hadn't told Olivia about his visits, for she was uncertain what Olivia would think. Meeting a man unchaperoned was hardly proper, but Emily didn't care. Since she'd awakened that horrible morning after Papa had been murdered, her life had never been the same, yet when Andre entered the cottage, something seemed to light up inside her. She wasn't strong and brave and stalwart like Olivia. Was it wrong that being with Andre should bring her pleasure?

He helped her make tea one afternoon. She started to return to the kitchen, only to bump headlong into a solid male form.

"I'm sorry!" he exclaimed. "How clumsy of me to get in your way."

It happened again that same afternoon, only this time he reached out and caught her elbows to steady her.

Emily put a hand on her hip. Though she tried, she somehow couldn't manage to act sternly. "I do believe you *want* me to bump into you."

"And if I did, would you mind?"

He was grinning, rather pleased with himself. She could hear it in his voice, and she sensed it in every pore of her body. "Of course I would!"

He just laughed.

It seemed she didn't fool him either.

Later they sat on the sofa in the parlor. "Andre," she murmured.

"Yes, princess?"

A thrill shot through her. He was teasing. 'Twas hardly an endearment, yet still she loved it when he called her "princess."

"No doubt you'll think me quite ridiculous—"

"Never," he vowed.

"I . . . I would really like to . . . to know what you look like." She rushed on before she lost her courage. "Are you . . . handsome?"

"Were it not for my two front teeth missing, I've no doubt I'd be quite handsome," he stated brashly.

Emily struggled not to laugh. "You don't!"

"You'll have to see for yourself, won't you?"

Her smile faded. "You know I can't."

"Yes, you can, princess."

"How?" She couldn't withhold a trace of bitterness.

"Like this." His voice had gone low and husky. Strong fingers encircled her wrist. He carried her palm to his cheek.

Emily drew in a sharp breath. Surely he didn't mean . . . or did he? Her other hand lifted very slowly, almost as if it pained her. Scarcely daring to breathe, her fingertips touched his face.

Her heart began to clamor. With the very tips of her fingers, she explored the hollows of his cheeks,

quiveringly aware of the faint raspiness of his skin.
He needed to shave, she thought distantly. She
trembled inside as she encountered the smoothness
of his mouth—he had a beautiful mouth, she just
knew it. It carried the slightest smile, his lower lip
slightly fuller. Though she longed to linger, she
dared not. He had full, bushy brows that nearly
met over his nose. A fingertip brushed the slight
bump just below the bridge of his nose.

"How did that happen?"

"Boxing." He spoke with unabashed candor.

"Boxing!"

"Yes. And I'm proud to say I won the bet."

"Oh, my. Perhaps you really do have two front
teeth missing!" She paused. "Your eyes. Are they
blue?"

He gave a slight shake of his head. "Sorry to
disappoint you, princess, but they're brown."

"And your hair? Is it brown as well?"

"Y-yes." Now Andre was the one who held his
breath.

"Light? Or dark?"

"Dark." He felt a pang of guilt, yet it wasn't precisely a lie. His hair was black as a raven's wing,
which made it dark, didn't it?

Emily swallowed, her mouth suddenly dry.

"How tall are you?"

He pulled her to her feet. "The top of your head
just touches my chin," he said softly.

Her hands were warmly clasped in his. They
stood so close she could feel every breath he took.

Her own had gone ragged. "I—I should say
you're quite tall then."

"Only because you're just a mite."

Never in her life had she been so conscious of

one man. His size. His strength. Did he feel it too? she wondered wildly, this—this sizzling awareness? If only she were able to look into his eyes, what would she see? She lowered her lashes, suddenly afraid of what her own might reveal.

"Emily," he said softly.

"Yes?" Her voice was but a wisp of sound.

"If you had one wish, what would it be?"

To see you, she nearly cried. "To see," she whispered, and suddenly there was a wealth of sadness in her voice.

Faintly calloused fingertips slid beneath her chin, gently turning her face upward.

There was a heartbeat of silence. "Mine, princess, would be for you to see *me*."

For one heart-stopping moment, she felt the brush of his lips across hers . . .

Then he was gone.

As usual, the following Sunday found Olivia in the village green, teaching the children. She was most pleased with the progress Colin had made in just a few short weeks. Charlotte was doubly pleased— that he was so anxious to learn, and that he was doing so well.

She was also pleased about Emily. Emily's mood had lightened considerably this last week. She had begun to laugh and tease again, much like the Emily of old. She'd even decided there was no need for Esther to stop by. Whatever the reason behind it, she was glad for Emily.

The children had just dispersed when she glanced up to find William standing before her.

"I just wanted to say good-bye before I left."

Olivia allowed him to help her up. "Where are you going?"

"To London on business. I'll be gone a week or so. I'd planned to leave this morning, but my horse turned a shoe."

He still held her hand. Olivia tried as best she could to gently disengage it. At last he let it go.

"I stopped by to visit several nights ago, but you weren't there. Emily said you hadn't yet returned from Ravenwood." His tone was laden thick with disapproval.

"I was doing the earl's bookkeeping," she murmured.

"He works you far too many hours."

"It was my choice, William." She felt compelled to defend herself—and Dominic.

William went on as if he hadn't heard. His mouth curled in a sneer. "The bastard should go back to London, or better yet, back with his own kind. Can you imagine, a Gypsy trying to pass himself off as a gentleman!" His tone turned sullen. "I dislike you working there. It will have to stop once we're married. Besides, there'll be no need."

Olivia stiffened. She was about to remind him that she had *not* consented to marry him, but before she could say a word, there was a touch on her elbow.

She turned to find a Gypsy woman standing there, holding a basket of onions. She was small but heavy in stature, her dark skin heavily lined. She wore a kerchief that covered all but an inch of dark hair streaked with gray. Bracelets jangled as she seized an onion and held it out.

"You want, yes?" the woman said in heavily accented English.

Olivia had no chance to reply. William stepped forward. "No," he said sharply, giving the woman a shove. Caught off guard, the woman lost her balance and fell heavily to the ground. The basket slipped from her arms. Onions tumbled out, rolling in every direction.

"God in heaven, will we never be free of them?" William cursed. "Filthy beggars, all of them."

Olivia gasped and turned to the woman. She helped her to her feet, then bent to gather the onions which had fallen. Behind her she heard William make a sound of disapproval.

"Good heavens, Olivia, let her do it!"

The delicate line of her jaw set tightly, Olivia ignored him.

At last they were finished. The woman gave a wordless nod of thanks, but her dark eyes flashed as she shook her finger at William, all the while spewing something in Romany. Finally she turned and waddled away.

William rolled his eyes. "God help me, she's probably cursed me."

Olivia felt like cursing him herself. Gypsy or no, his action had been unspeakably cruel.

Pointedly she lifted her chin. "You were just leaving for London, weren't you?"

William frowned. "For heaven's sake, Olivia, why are you in such a snit?" he complained. "She's just an old Gypsy hag."

Olivia would not debate the point just now. She was too angry. She glared at him mutely.

He shrugged. "You'll have forgotten all about it by the time I return," he predicted. "Stay well, Olivia." He bent and pressed a brief kiss on her lips.

Olivia's temper was still steaming as he mounted

his horse and rode off. It was all she could do not to scrub his kiss from her mouth.

She dusted her skirts and twitched them into place. As she raised her head, she spotted Dominic with Colin just a short distance away. Colin was atop Storm once again. He lifted the little boy from Storm and set him on the ground. Grinning, Colin said something and Dominic laughed, then he ruffled the lad's hair, and Colin ran off toward home.

Dominic turned.

Olivia's heart lurched. Dear heaven, he was coming toward her! Had he seen William?

She was about to find out.

He halted. "Charming fellow, your gentleman friend." His tone was easy, but his eyes were hard. "Rather lacking in social decorum, don't you think?"

Olivia's heart sank. So he'd seen William's cruel display with the Gypsy woman. That was unfortunate.

Dominic went on. "He appears to be rather free with you. Why, that's twice now I've seen him kiss you here in the village square."

Olivia could feel her face burning.

"Clearly he fancies himself in love with you."

Her chin came up a notch. "Is that so hard to believe?"

"Not in the least," he said smoothly, "but I'm curious. Are you in love with him?"

"No!" she gasped, before she thought better of it.

"So you haven't agreed to marry him?"

"No. I mean, he's offered, but—"

"You said no, didn't you?"

Olivia regarded him with no little amount of irritation. Damn him. Damn him for his smug certainty! He knew her not at all—and yet he knew her far too well!

"Not precisely." She took great pleasure in informing him he was wrong. "I told him I could not even think of marriage at present," she added stiffly, and then wondered why she'd bothered to answer.

Some of the hardness had left his features. "He's not the man for you, Olivia."

Olivia again. Her heart pounded. More and more he called her by her given name. It seemed he called her Miss Sherwood only when he was displeased.

A slender brow arose. "And I suppose you know who is?"

His slow-growing smile was maddening. "I do."

"Indeed," she said archly. "And who might that be?"

He smiled directly into her eyes. "You wouldn't be happy with him." He continued as if she hadn't spoken. "I think you would only be satisfied with a man who, when he kisses you, makes the very earth move beneath your feet."

A man like you. Olivia couldn't withhold the thought which sprang through her mind. Oh, but he was so utterly confident. Why, the very thought of them together was preposterous! And yet . . . she found his teasing wholly disarming.

"Perhaps I've yet to find that man," she informed him loftily.

He laughed, the sound low and deep. Olivia realized it was the first time she'd heard him laugh—really laugh in genuine amusement.

Something happened then, something she

couldn't decipher. But like a shadow, it was there. Though she couldn't touch it, she could feel it . . . it seemed to reach out and grab hold of her very heart.

In the sunlight, his eyes were so very blue, his teeth so white against the bronze of his skin. She couldn't withhold the spontaneous smile that curved her lips—nor did she wish to.

When next he spoke, it was not what she expected. "I've been asked to come to the Gypsy camp tonight. Will you accompany me?"

Her smile faded. "Why?"

His own was gone as well. "Because I want you to see that they are not all murderers, nor are they all thieves and beggars."

He paused, awaiting some reaction. Olivia floundered, unsure of her feelings, or what to do. A part of her welcomed the chance to—to be with him. But to go to the Gypsy camp . . .

"I won't deny there are some who do indeed steal," Dominic said quickly. He didn't say that for many Gypsies, stealing was not considered a crime—but an accomplishment. "But for the most part, it's not done out of malice. It's done out of necessity—grass for their horses, wood for the fire, fruit and chickens for food. As for begging, they often look dirty or sick so people give money just to be rid of them." He paused. "Well, Olivia? Will you come?"

Still she wavered.

A glint suddenly appeared in his eye. "How important is your position at Ravenwood?" he asked suddenly.

It took a moment before she understood . . . "That's unfair," she accused, her voice very low.

"It is," he agreed mildly.

Her distress lay vivid in her eyes. "You'll discharge me if I refuse?"

"Perhaps a better question is this—are you prepared to take that chance?"

"You know I'm not!" she said heatedly.

"Then it would seem the choice should be easy." A faint smile lingered upon his mouth. "Will you come?"

"You leave me no choice," she snapped. "Apparently, I must." Oh, but she longed to wipe that satisfied smile from his face!

"Excellent. I'll stop by your cottage before nightfall."

Ten

That evening, Olivia was of a very good mind to be absent when he called. Only the fear that he might indeed mean what he said kept her from doing so.

She dressed in a pale blue muslin gown that left her arms and throat bare, for the day had been rather hot. She brushed her hair till it shone, then left it loose and flowing, securing it away from her forehead with a ribbon that was slightly frayed at the ends. Smoothing her skirts, she critically examined her reflection in the mirror.

A dozen doubts suddenly crowded her mind. Would he think her gown dowdy and old? No doubt the women in London whom he'd favored had dressed in the height of fashion, she thought wistfully. No doubt they were sophisticated and worldly. All at once she felt wholly inadequate. Worldly she was not, nor was she sophisticated—she was far too practical. As if to prove it, she reminded herself that a new gown was an extravagance she could not afford. There were far more pressing matters to attend to—like food. And somehow, she must find a way to get Emily to London. Impatiently she chided herself. Why was she taking such pains with her appearance anyway?

She'd certainly never have done so for William!

But this wasn't William, a tiny little voice reminded her. This was Dominic—Dominic who made her feel as if she no longer knew herself . . .

There was a knock on the door. She had to consciously stop herself from rushing forward. Whatever was the matter with her! She opened it to find him standing there, looking enviably at ease! He was dressed in a loose white shirt and tight breeches that showed off the narrowness of his hips and muscled thighs almost shamelessly; gleaming black boots completed the picture. Her heart gave a strange little catch. His hair gleamed dark and damp. He appeared freshly bathed and shaved and smelled of some wonderful scent. When her eyes returned to his face, she discovered he was doing a rather thorough investigation of his own.

His gaze slid down her body and up again. Could it be he liked what he saw? But all he said was, "It's quite refreshing to see you garbed in something other than drab black."

She experienced a vague disappointment. Was that all?

"You may wish to tell your sister it may be quite late when we return."

"I—I already did." She hadn't told Emily she was going to the Gypsy camp. She'd told her she was needed at Ravenwood for the evening. Though she disliked deceiving her sister, Olivia was too uncertain of her reaction.

She called to Emily that she was leaving, then turned to him. "Shall we go?" she murmured.

He offered his arm. Olivia hesitated but an instant, then placed her fingertips on his elbow.

Outside, the evening air was still warm. A slight

breeze swirled around them, carrying with it the faint scent of roses. But Olivia stopped short when she saw a small cart and horse beneath the tree.

"You needn't look so alarmed, Olivia. I promise, I'll go slowly."

Her gaze flew to his face. She half-expected mockery to be written there. Instead she found him watching her, his expression very grave.

"It's rather far to walk," he said quietly, "especially in the dark."

Olivia drew a long, shaky breath, her mind working furiously. Then, with only the smallest hesitation, she walked to the cart. Dominic lifted her inside, his heart soaring. Did she know what she had done? She had just yielded a sign of trust . . .

Trust in *him*.

As he climbed into the cart and took his place beside her, he couldn't have been more pleased.

They were off. The seat was small and narrow, just barely wide enough for the two of them. Olivia tried to relax, but it was difficult. Nor was it because of fear of the horse. No, it was something far different. The muscled stretch of his thigh rode against her own, disturbingly warm and strong. Her gaze strayed again and again to his hands, lean and brown and so very masculine! Her mouth grew dry. What would it feel like, she wondered, to have those hands upon her body, sliding over her skin . . .

She inhaled sharply, shocked by the very audacity of her thoughts! It took a moment to realize Dominic was speaking.

"Has your sister always been blind?"

Olivia shook her head. "No. Only for the past year."

"The past year. But that's when your father . . . Wait. You said she took a bad fall, didn't you?"

Olivia's eyes darkened. "I'm convinced that's when it happened."

"Is that why you're afraid of horses?"

A tiny little pain speared her heart. "No," she said at last. "I was never very fond of horses, though my mother adored them—so much so that Papa bought an old mare for her one year. Her name was Bonnie. One day when I was twelve, Mama decided to show me there was nothing to fear. She took me up behind her on Bonnie's back." Olivia smiled faintly, but there was a wealth of sadness in her eyes. "We began to canter around the field. I'd begun to think that Mama was right, that riding was great fun after all. Then suddenly Bonnie halted. Perhaps something spooked her; indeed, we'll never know."

Dominic's eyes were on her face. "What happened then?"

Olivia took a deep breath. "I tumbled to the ground. I was sore but unhurt. But Mama pitched forward over Bonnie's head . . ."

Dominic frowned. "She was injured?"

"She was dead," Olivia said very quietly. "Her neck was broken."

So that's why she was so afraid . . . Dominic couldn't blame her, nay, not at all. Dear God, it wasn't just her father who had died tragically, but her mother as well! How, he wondered, could fate—and God—be so cruel to some, yet so generous to others?

He had no answer. He glanced at her. Her demeanor was one of utter calm, yet he sensed the pain the loss still caused her. It was then he realized . . . She'd lost her mother at the same age he'd been taken from his . . . True, Madeleine had not been dead, not then—but she had been gone from his life forever . . .

Fate. 'Twas fate that had brought them together. He was more certain of it than ever before.

"I'm sorry," he said, not knowing what else to say. She inclined her head in acknowledgment, but made no reply.

They traveled along in silence for some distance, bouncing along the lane. The evening sun hovered bright and golden, just above the roll of gentle hills to the west.

It was Olivia who broke the silence. "Were you acquainted with this band of Gypsies before they came here?"

"No," Dominic answered, "though I discovered one day while talking to Nikolos, their leader, that he knew my mother and a dozen others in her band."

Olivia tipped her head to the side. "Where is the camp?" she wondered aloud.

"Not far now," Dominic assured her. "The Gypsies usually camp near grazing lands for the horses, and near a stream for water—yet close enough to a town or village to mend pots and pans, and trade horses. Generally it's an out-of-the-way site. They prefer a place where they won't be observed by locals or chased away by authorities."

Or perhaps to elude authorities. Olivia couldn't help the thought that ran through her mind. At the same time, a pang of guilt went through her.

When she said nothing, Dominic glanced at her.

"You know you're in far more danger from me than from the Gypsies." His tone was light. "Indeed, an innocent girl shouldn't be out at night with a dangerous man."

"I am not a girl," she said promptly.

"Ah, but you are innocent, aren't you?"

Color bloomed on her cheeks. "That, sir, is none of your affair!"

He sighed. "Call me Dominic."

"I cannot."

"And why not?" His retort was as quick as hers.

" 'Twould not be proper."

"And do you always do what is proper, Olivia Sherwood? But of course. You're a vicar's daughter."

Were it not for the teasing quality of his rejoinder, she might have taken vehement exception to his statement.

"And what of you? I recall you told the village children that Gypsies are free, at one with the world and nature." She replied in kind. "Are you, sir?"

His smile ebbed. He was abruptly sober. It was a long time before he spoke. "I am no longer a Gypsy, nor am I one of you."

His response was cryptic. She wasn't quite certain what he meant. Yet all at once she longed to see him smile, just once more. "Ah," she said lightly, "but are you dangerous?"

Dangerous? *No*, he thought. She was the one who was dangerous, for she was right . . . She was no girl, but a woman—a woman who roused his senses and stirred all within him that was primal and male. His gaze roved over her face. Her lips, a tempting, innocent provocation, reminded him of a dew-misted rose, her eyes of fresh spring grass. He knew that were he to reach out and touch her cheek, her skin would be as soft as sun-warmed satin. His gaze dipped lower, falling to the generous swell of her breasts beneath her gown. Though she was slender, her body was delightfully ripe and full—were he to weigh her breasts in his palms, that delicious fullness would fill his hands. He found himself wondering if her nipples were pink or brown, small or large, pert and uptilted or . . .

On and on his thoughts tormented him. But it seemed she was completely oblivious to the frankly erotic bend of his mind—but perhaps that was best, he decided wryly. He had the feeling his imaginings would have shocked her to the core of her innocent heart.

As the cart topped the gentle rise of a hill, he spied the Gypsy camp, nestled in a small hollow. Just beyond were the woods.

Olivia saw it too. She couldn't waylay the sudden tension that gripped her body, every muscle contracted with it.

Beside her, Dominic reined the horse to a halt. He spoke, his tone very solemn. "It's a different way of life, Olivia. Not wrong, just . . . different. Will you bear that in mind?"

To refuse would have been petty and small. Taking a deep breath, Olivia nodded.

A plume of smoke drifted in the air. Just beyond a fire were a dozen vividly painted wagons. Some were bright yellow and green, some scarlet and gold. Here and there a number of tents had been erected. As they approached, two men came out to watch them. By the time they rolled to a halt, the men had been joined by several others. One of them, a heavyset man with an enormous belly, gave a shout and raised a hand high.

Dominic jumped lightly to the ground. He gave the man a quick embrace. The man said something in Romany and glanced at Olivia. Dominic gave a nod and replied in kind. His gaze sought Olivia's, and she was surprised to see laughter glimmering in the depths of his eyes. Wordlessly he beckoned to her.

Olivia rose to her feet, her legs none too steady. She was stunned to realize she was shaking. Dominic's eyes caught hers; before she could take a breath, a pair of strong hands settled on her waist. She was swung to the ground.

He pulled her close to his side. Olivia was in no frame of mind to object. Standing so near to him, she couldn't help but note that were they standing face-to-face, her head would fit neatly beneath his chin . . . Quickly she curbed the thought before it progressed any further.

"Nikolos," he said easily, "this is Olivia Sherwood. Olivia, this is Nikolos, leader of this particular band of Gypsies."

His face was lined and weathered, with white teeth showing beneath a black, drooping mustache. "Welcome," he said in English. His smile was so utterly engaging she couldn't help but smile in return.

For the next quarter hour, Nikolos led them through the encampment. Very soon her head was spinning with names and faces. She was shocked to see an old woman smoking a pipe; the woman watched them pass with dark, heavy-lidded eyes.

Oddly, Olivia didn't shrink away. Instead she smothered a smile.

A large-bosomed woman wearing a full, bright skirt beckoned them close. Bangles shook as she pointed at Olivia, then motioned them near. Bright hoops hung from her ears.

"*Tu serte*," she called to Olivia. "*Tu serte!*"

Olivia glanced up at Dominic questioningly. "What does she want?"

He wore an indulgent smile. "To tell your fortune."

Olivia took a deep breath. Her earlier anxious dread had begun to depart. She was rather surprised to admit she'd met no one who frightened her. On the contrary, they were lively and animated and eager to please. No doubt this was due to Dominic's presence at her side, but no matter. All at once she felt reckless and daring.

"All right," she announced. "I'll do it."

The woman beamed. "Good. Good! Remember all your life what this poor Gypsy Catriana tells you this day." Briskly she rubbed her hands, then took the palm Olivia proferred.

Long moments passed while Catriana frowned intently at her palm. A fleshy brown finger traced an arcing line that extended across her wrist.

"There has been much unhappiness in your life, no?"

Olivia hesitated. Without question the last ten years had seen much heartache. First Mama had died, then Papa.

Catriana patted her shoulder. "No need to answer. I see it—not only in your face but in your palm. Much unhappiness, indeed. But do not worry. Very soon all will be different."

Olivia smiled wistfully. If only it were so.

Catriana bowed her head once again. Finally she looked up with a gap-toothed smile. "Yes," she said in satisfaction. "I see it. There is luck in your palm, lovely lady. You will live a long and happy life with a handsome man," she pronounced.

Dominic bent low, so low his mouth grazed her ear. "Of course we know that couldn't be William," he murmured.

Olivia was possessed of an urge to deliver an elbow to his ribs. "His opinion of you is no less flattering," she said sweetly. Odd, but his insult bothered her less than William's of him.

"Now that I do not—"

"Shhh!" Catriana cast a pointed look at Dominic. "I tell the lady's fortune, not yours!"

His startled look made Olivia bite back a laugh. Effectively quelled, he stood silent while Catriana finished. Listening intently, Olivia was bewildered by the woman's knowledge that her parents were dead, and that she had one sister.

By the time she'd finished, Olivia was thoroughly amazed. But of course it was just coincidence—a lucky guess. When Dominic handed her a coin, she nodded her head in thanks and retreated into her caravan.

So. She would be happy, would she? Perhaps it was true. Perhaps not. Unbidden, a melancholy sadness seeped into her heart. But what of Emily? The thought pained her deeply. Tears pricked her eyelids. She dropped her head, but Dominic had already noticed the sudden glaze in her eyes.

"Tears?" he inquired softly.

Her smile was watery. "I'm sorry. It's not for me. It's just that I was thinking of—"

"Your sister."

Her eyes darkened. She nodded. "It's so unfair. Emily is so young! To endure the rest of her life in endless darkness . . . I cannot imagine it. And I could never be truly happy while Emily is *un*happy."

"You anticipate the worst, Olivia. You should listen to Catriana. I know it sounds strange, but the Gypsies have a way of knowing things, of making the impossible happen. I cannot say why. If Catriana believes you will be happy, do not doubt it." He paused. Very quietly he added, "My mother used to say, 'So you believe, then so it will be.'"

Olivia didn't dare believe, for to believe might only end in bitter disappointment. This she kept to herself, though. She had no wish to dampen Dominic's spirits. Indeed, he seemed much more at ease than she had ever seen him.

They had just turned away when another woman stepped before them. It was Irina, Nikolos's wife. In her hands was a lovely gold necklace. Attached was a small, round charm. The charm captured Olivia's attention instantly. It gleamed like sunlight on water. It seemed almost alive, reflecting every imaginable color. Her breath caught in awe. She reached out to touch it. "May I?" she asked.

Irina said something in Romany and gestured, as if for her to take it.

"The necklace is for you," Dominic told her.

Irina's head bobbed up and down as she slipped it over Olivia's head and around her neck.

"Oh, it's lovely!" she exclaimed. Her eyes sought Dominic's. "But really . . . I couldn't possibly accept it . . ."

"It's a gift, Olivia. You'll offend her if you don't accept it."

Olivia considered but an instant. Almost reverently she touched the charm. "Tell her I'll treasure it always." Impulsively she reached out and gave Irina a brief hug. "Thank you, Irina. Thank you."

As she drew back, she saw Irina wink at Dominic. Olivia didn't understand the meaning of that wink, but suddenly it didn't matter.

Darkness settled upon the land. A full moon began its slow ascent into the sky. The air carried the scent of some wonderful, spicy aroma. It hadn't cooled appreciably, but remained almost as warm as the day had been. They found a place between two caravans and sat upon the grass. A young girl, smiling shyly, brought a delicious, mouthwatering stew to them. Olivia savored every mouthful, surprised at how hungry she was. While they ate, they talked.

"The girl who brought this," Olivia said. "Why does she wear a kerchief when none of the other girls do?"

"Only the married women wear kerchiefs. Once they're married, they are never without it in public."

Olivia stole a glance at the girl, who couldn't have been more than fourteen or fifteen. "She's married?"

His chuckle was low and husky.

"But she's so young! Why, I feel quite ancient!"

Dominic laughed again.

She set aside her rough wooden plate. "Why do so many wear red?" she asked. She'd noticed earlier that many of the women wore full red skirts or blouses, and many of the men wore scarlet shirts as well.

Dominic was secretly pleased at her questions. She was curious, not demeaning, and that made all the difference. "Red is believed to bring good luck." He paused. "White is for funerals."

"I see." To Olivia it seemed a strange custom, for to her white was a symbol of purity and innocence. Still, she reminded herself it was just as Dominic had said . . . Their ways were not wrong . . . just different.

"Look there." Dominic pointed suddenly to the edge of the camp. Two young men were engaged in a boxing match. Boisterous shouts cheered the pair on. The taller of the two—his name was Andre as she recalled—took advantage of his slim physique. He twirled around and sidestepped several punches.

Olivia gasped and sat up straight. "Someone should stop them!"

"It's just a game." He shrugged. "They mean no harm to each other."

He was right. Few blows were landed, and those that were, were not intended to be vengeful. She shook her head. "Why men find such sport entertaining is beyond me."

"The Gypsy women say the same. They throw their hands in the air and walk away."

She knew what he was trying to say—that they weren't so very different after all. Olivia was uncertain how to respond, so she kept silent.

Dominic's eyes ran over her profile. Their shoulders were touching. She seemed oblivious to the contact. Her eyes were downcast, but she tipped her head ever so slightly, so that the silken length of her hair brushed his sleeve. He sucked in a sharp breath. He wanted to feel it, warm and soft and alive, against his bare skin. Trailing across his chest. The crease between his thigh and hip, with the velvet heat of her mouth following the path it took . . .

Christ! He shifted, for he was beginning to have a distinctly physical reaction to his wild imaginings. His shaft pounded with the pulse of his blood. With an effort he forced his mind far away from the swelling fullness in his loins—a feat that proved nearly impossible with her so close!

He gazed out where a hundred tiny stars had appeared in the sky. "Do you know," he began, his voice very low, "that there are places on the Continent where the Gypsies hide in their *vardos* at night and do not venture out until morning?"

"Why not?"

"Because they are afraid."

"Afraid?" A frown appeared between slender brows. Her eyes searched his.

"Oh, yes," he assured her gravely. "It's been like that for centuries, but it's only at night when they are in danger."

An eerie prickle ran up Olivia's spine. All at once she had no desire to venture home in the dark. "In danger from what?" she asked.

"Men who turn into creatures of the night."

Her tongue came out to moisten her lips. He nearly groaned. God, how would it feel in his mouth? Bravely she said, "An owl is a creature of the night. So are mice. Neither are dangerous."

He shook his head. "Not creatures like those. Demon creatures, with teeth that are this long—" He measured wide with his fingers. "—and rapier-sharp."

She listened in half-fear, half-fascination. "No," she said slowly. "That cannot be."

"I do not jest, Olivia. They are demon creatures, half-man, half-beast."

Her eyes were huge. She shivered, unconsciously nestling closer to him. "Truly?"

He turned slightly so that the hollow of her shoulder fit neatly beneath his arm. Stretching out his hand behind her, he touched the bare skin of her upper arm.

With a cry she nearly leaped into his lap.

He erupted into laughter. "Careful, Olivia, else I'll think you've begun to grow rather fond of me."

Olivia stared into twinkling blue eyes. "You tricked me! This was naught but a ploy to get me—"

"—into my arms?" He grinned hugely.

She pushed herself back from his chest. "You are the only beast of the night!"

Dominic experienced a fleeting regret. Perhaps he shouldn't have been so hasty. He liked the feel of her close against his side.

"You were only trying to frighten me," she accused.

"Not so," he denied. "Every word I spoke was true, I swear on the grave of my mother. I've heard tales of such creatures even here in England."

She darted a quick glance around, at the encroaching shadows of the forest beyond the camp. She no longer looked so smug. Then all at once she smiled. Her hand came to rest on the amulet from Irina. "If that is true," she said breezily, "then this will protect me."

Slowly he shook his head. "No, it will not."

Her expression fell. "It won't?" Her tone was so plaintive he very nearly laughed.

"No." His grin was devilish.

"It won't bring me good luck?"

"Hardly." A smile lurked on his lips.

She stared at him suspiciously. "What is it then?"

Again he chuckled. "I'm not certain you want to know."

"I do."

"You'll be angry with me."

"I promise, I won't."

"You're quite sure?"

"I am. Now tell me. Why won't this charm protect me?"

His smile widened slowly. "Because," he said softly, "it's a love charm."

Her stunned expression was precious. "Oh," she said weakly. "You mean to . . . to make me . . ."

"Yes. To make you fall in love. As long as you wear it, you're in danger of falling in love. I daresay in far more danger than from any creatures on the Continent."

Her eyes flared. "So that's why she winked at you—why you were so amused!"

"You promised you wouldn't be angry," he reminded her. "And you can't give it back. Irina would be—"

"Yes, yes, I know. She would be offended. So what the devil shall I do with it tonight if I cannot take it off?"

"I suppose you have no choice but to wear it."

She stared at him, exasperated. It couldn't possibly be true, could it? All of a sudden his voice tolled through her mind. *The Gypsies have a way of knowing things, of making the impossible happen.* She was reminded of his mother's curse. But that was coincidence. It had to be . . . it had to!

Yet suddenly there was an unfamiliar dryness in her throat. She stared at the place where his hair met the nape of his neck. She found herself possessed of a most curious urge to run her fingers there, just along his nape where his hair grew dark and lustrous.

A tall, slim Gypsy strode up and stopped before them. He gazed at Olivia for the longest time, then finally looked at Dominic. He said something in Romany.

Then suddenly Dominic's gaze dwelled long and hard upon her, too. He replied in Romany, his eyes never leaving her. Olivia's heart beat a rapid tattoo. They were talking about her. She sensed it instinctively. Dominic's mouth carried the faintest smile as he spoke. The Gypsy laughed.

"What did he say?"

"He said my woman is beautiful."

"But I'm not your wom—"

She broke off. A dark, forbidden thrill went through her. She *was* his woman, if only for tonight. A burning ache seared her heart. Just once, she longed to pretend she was not who she was . . . pretend *he* was not . . .

A tremor went through her. "What did you say?" she asked, her voice but a thread of sound.

His was low and husky. "I said he was right—" There was just the tiniest pause. "—that you are beautiful."

Did he truly think so? Olivia couldn't look at him—she just couldn't! She wasn't used to coy flirtations, not like the women of the *ton* . . . the women he had known.

"He also said that perhaps if I'm lucky, my bed will be warm tonight."

His voice carried a faint trace of amusement. She was almost unbearably conscious of his regard, and wished for one wild moment that she *were* a flirt—that some glib, facile comment would spring to her lips in this game of seduction.

But that wasn't what was happening here, was it . . . *Was it?*

Just when she thought it could get no worse, a young couple stopped almost directly in front of them. To Olivia's shock, they were soon wrapped in each other's arms, and the young man was availing himself of a long, deep kiss. The woman moaned softly . . . a sound of pleasure.

Olivia looked away. Up. Down. Anywhere but at the pair of young lovers. Beside her, Dominic laughed softly.

"You truly are an innocent, Olivia."

At last the pair moved on. "And you, sir, are quite jaded."

It was a moment before he replied. "Nay, I am not. If I were, I'd see the world as a dark and gloomy place where some use others." He paused. "I simply don't know my place in it."

Olivia looked at him sharply. He sounded strange, so somber. Though his lips still smiled, his eyes were no longer laughing. She was stunned to realize he was serious. There was no time to question him further, for the long, pure note of a violin filled the air.

"The celebration begins," Dominic murmured.

He was right. Flames leaped high and bright

from the fire in the center of the camp. A dozen Gypsies had already begun to dance around it. Others clapped and cheered.

"What are they celebrating?"

She thought he might say a betrothal, or some Gypsy holiday. Instead he said simply, "Life."

Another had joined the dancers, a young woman named Eyvette with long, curling black hair. A tall, sleek beauty, her shoulders were bare and her skirts flew up to reveal sleek, brown calves and a hint of bare thigh as she swirled and clapped in time to the music. She swayed to and fro, a wild, exotic tilt to her black eyes and full red lips. She was not partnered by anyone, but was alone.

Perhaps not for long. Seductive and graceful, she came to dance directly before Dominic, a lithe, sinuous dance of erotic provocation. Bathed in the glow of the fire, slender arms raised high, she whirled, then bowed low—so low she offered an uninhibited view of bounteous charms. Her breasts were clearly visible, round and voluptuous and unfettered.

Beside her, Dominic watched with apparent appreciation, a lazy smile on his lips. Olivia was hardly inclined to do the same. A slow curl of something very akin to jealousy coiled deep in her breast.

The music ended. Eyvette rose. She spoke to Dominic in Romany. Though he still smiled, his reply was brief. Eyvette shrugged and moved on.

Olivia leaned toward Dominic. "Let me guess— perhaps your bed *will* be warm tonight." She was secretly aghast that she dared to speak of such a thing—and to a man yet!

He merely laughed. "Eyvette is an attractive woman, is she not?"

"Quite," she returned baldly. "I must say, however, I found the young man called Andre quite handsome indeed." Her eyes scanned the group. Unfortunately, Andre was nowhere to be found.

But her ploy had worked. Dominic's smile vanished. Olivia's returned—perhaps he wasn't feeling quite so certain of himself now. Her victory proved to be short-lived, however. He was on his feet in a heartbeat. Before she knew what he was about, he seized her hands, pulled her to her feet and out among the dancers.

There was no time to protest—and indeed, soon she did not want to. It was as if she'd been caught in some strange Gypsy spell, as if some stranger had taken control of her body. Her feet were swift and agile and caught in the wild, pagan beat of the music, possessed of a rhythm never before known. His arms strong and hard about her waist, Dominic gazed at her, his eyes blue and bright and glowing. Then suddenly she was laughing, her head cast back, the arch of her neck and throat long and white and supple. The ribbon in her hair had come free. Her hair tumbled around her shoulders and down her back, a russet-gold waterfall.

One last primitive note, and he caught her up against him. Time stood still as she hung suspended in the air high above him; slowly he let her slide down his body. Another time, another place, and she would have been shocked to the core, but here in this wild Gypsy camp, it was entirely natural.

Together they retreated from the circle of dancers. He snatched up an eiderdown quilt and tossed it over his shoulder. His fingers woven tightly through hers, he led her to a tiny knoll that looked down upon the blazing fire in the center of the Gypsy camp. Olivia was still laughing as they sank down upon the quilt.

"Tell me," he said softly, "do you think it was fate that brought you here with me tonight?"

"Nay," she responded promptly, her eyes suddenly sparkling. " 'Twas your ultimatum!"

Dominic chuckled. "Why don't you believe in fate?"

A frown appeared between her brows. Her smile faded and her expression turned thoughtful. "Perhaps it's because I'm a vicar's daughter, but I believe that what happens to us is in God's hands, part of His plan for us, if you will."

Dominic had turned rather grave as well. "Even what happened to your father? Your sister? And your mother?"

Olivia's reply was very quiet. "Yes. I don't pretend to know His reasons. I know only that I must believe it else I risk losing my faith in God."

"So you don't believe it's possible to believe in both God and fate?"

She hesitated. "I'm not sure," she said slowly. Then: "Do you?"

"I do. Indeed, I often wonder if fate is simply just as you say—God's plan for us."

"It's . . . possible," she admitted cautiously.

"There! You see? You *do* believe in fate!" His tone reflected his triumph.

All at once Olivia felt happy and carefree as she hadn't felt in ever so long. She couldn't resist teasing him just a trifle more. "Ah," she proclaimed airily, "then I need not worry about this love charm making me fall in love, do I?'' She touched the charm with her fingertips.

He winked at her. "Oh, but I should not be so hasty if I were you, Olivia, for sometimes fate needs a helping hand."

Olivia heaved an exaggerated sigh of exasperation. He threw back his head and laughed. Her breath caught in her throat. Lord, but he was handsome! Why, she could almost believe she was halfway in love with him . . . Yet how many other women had fancied themselves in love with him? she wondered suddenly.

"You are incorrigible," she accused blandly.

"Hardly. You cannot believe everything you hear, you know."

"Indeed. But what I've heard is that you've indulged in many a dalliance."

He pulled a face. "And many a mistress, too, no doubt."

Olivia took a deep breath and gathered all her courage. "Were you in love with any of them? Or all of them?"

"Had I been in love, I'd not have indulged in many a dalliance—" His tone was jesting. "—or many a mistress, as you put it."

"Come now," Olivia protested. "I'm quite serious. Have you ever been in love?" She held her breath. Later, she might wonder what had come over her that she should be so bold. Later. But not now . . .

His answer was a long time in coming. "No," he said finally. "I've never been in love. I've been with a number of women—though not the multitude you seem to think—but I have no claim to ever being in love."

Now that it was out, Olivia wasn't sure if she should be pleased or not! The night he'd received the letter from Maureen Miller, he'd said he would never discard a woman as if it were nothing. He'd also claimed he could be happy with one woman, that he simply hadn't found her yet . . . Was she a fool for believing him?

"You're an earl now. Haven't you given some thought to marriage, to having children to carry on the title?"

"Ah, yes, duty and all that. While I've acknowledged the necessity of such, I've not begun to actively pursue a bride. I'm hardly in my dotage—" His tone was dry. "—so I daresay I have a few more years in which to produce an heir and a spare."

Before she could reply, a dark brow arose. "But what about you, Olivia? Why did you turn down William's offer?"

"Because I don't love him!" The answer emerged before she could stop it.

"So you would rather live your life alone than wed a man you don't love?"

"I—I would. Regardless, I've Emily to take care of. Besides the fact that there are few eligible men in Stonebridge of marriageable age, I doubt any man would be willing to provide for both me *and* my sister."

She didn't see the way his gaze moved hungrily over her face. "Oh, I think you're wrong," he said softly. "If you went to London, I suspect you'd have your pick of men willing to provide for both you and Emily. No, I can't see you spending the rest of your life alone."

Olivia flushed. "You forget, I would only marry

a man I loved. I could never settle for anything less."

Dominic looked amused. "You are a rarity, Miss Sherwood. You don't believe in fate, but you believe in love. Don't you know that marriages are seldom made for love?"

Olivia's eyes flashed. "That may be, but that would not be the case were I to marry! No, I cannot imagine how a woman could stand by and watch her husband go out and find his pleasure where he pleases."

Dominic's lips quirked. "You mean elsewhere?"

"I do indeed!" Olivia warmed to the subject. "Why, if I were the man's wife, I should heartily disapprove!"

"But there are many wives who do the very same."

Olivia's lips pressed together. Her opinion of such women was very clear.

Dominic gave a hearty chuckle. "On second thought, you'd better not go to London after all. You'd set out to reform all rakes and the *ton* would never be the same."

Olivia could hardly take offense. "No doubt that would be a good thing."

"No doubt it would," he assured her with an entirely straight face.

Olivia sighed. "You're making sport of me."

"Not at all. Why, I can't recall when I've been so highly entertained."

Olivia's lips twitched. His eyes were filled with a hundred tiny lights, and she could see him struggling not to smile.

She nodded toward Eyvette, who still swayed lithely before the fire. Every so often, Eyvette glanced toward the knoll where the two of them sat.

"Since we speak of dalliances, my lord, I suspect the lovely Eyvette would be glad of your attention."

He glanced toward the dark-haired beauty. "Yes," he said mildly, "I suppose she would."

"What! Such modesty, sir!" Olivia pretended to be indignant.

He grinned. "Are you jealous, Miss Sherwood?"

"Of course not!" It wasn't entirely true. Alas, it wasn't true at all! She thought of the way he'd kissed her and could have cheerfully strangled any one of the women on whom he'd lavished his attention—and his thorough, soul-stirring kisses!

He laughed softly. "That's good, because I'd much rather be with the woman at my side right now." His tone had turned husky. As he spoke, he reached for her hand, curling his fingers around her own.

His laughter had faded. A tremor went through her. Their eyes caught . . . and held . . . held endlessly.

It was a moment no less intense for Dominic. He could feel the fragile bones of the hand he held in his own, the narrow span of her wrists. Despite the callouses, they were the hands of a lady, through and through.

His thoughts were hardly gentlemanly. His blood was suddenly burning. His rod was half-erect, just looking at her. He could have her, a niggling little voice inside told him. He'd had many a lady in London. They were fascinated by the element of danger, the wildness they sensed in him. But Olivia was different. An innocent.

God, he thought. This was madness. He stared at the delicate line of her cheek and jaw, and thought about what she would taste like there, in the tiny hollow just below her ear. He ached with the need to tumble her down, wrap her arms around his neck and plant his shaft heavy and deep and thick inside her, so deep he couldn't move.

Her lips were slightly parted, her face turned to his. She smelled of rosewater, a scent that teased his nostrils. Just thinking of her mouth beneath his caused his belly to tighten, like a fist drawing closed. He recalled with stark, vivid intensity the last—the first—kiss that they had shared. Lord, he thought, he should never have brought her here . . .

Because he was about to do it again.

Eleven

Olivia had only to turn her head to encounter the sheer masculine power of his presence. *Oh, Lord,* she thought helplessly. *What is happening to me?*

His gaze had fallen to her lips. She quivered inside, for all at once she knew, with a certainty that defied all else, that he was going to kiss her.

Never in her life had she wanted anything more.

The moon hung full and bright in a night-dark sky. Moonlight cast a silvery, ethereal light over all. It was moondust. It was magic.

It was heaven. He pulled her to her knees so that they faced each other; his arms engulfed her. Her heart leaped the instant his mouth claimed hers, the sensation of it heady and compelling. In some faraway corner of her mind, she realized she wanted him to kiss her again and again.

God help her, he did.

He kissed her endlessly, his mouth hot and passionate and meltingly slow. Her arms slid around him. Her fingers traced the fluid line of his back. She thrilled to the feel of tightly muscled flesh beneath her fingertips. The music had changed. It was soulful and sweet, a melody at midnight. Time had no meaning. Lost in the fervor of his kiss, she feared the moment it would end.

The drumming beat of her heart clamored in her ears. A tiny jolt went through her as his tongue touched hers. A probe of pure flame, it curled far and deep, tasting the hidden depths within. Trapped in a haze of pleasure, she was scarcely aware of impatient fingers stealing beneath the neckline of her gown, loosening the strings which held it closed and sweeping it from her shoulders.

Only then did his mouth release hers. He raised his head. His eyes were smoldering—they spoke of a hunger, a hunger she was only beginning to comprehend. Olivia glanced down, stunned at the sight of her naked breasts, pale and gleaming in the moonlight. Her breath caught in her throat. Seized with an almost painful awareness, she could only watch as his gaze brazenly charted the swelling curves seen before by no other man.

Her lips parted. Some slight sound escaped. What she would have said, she would never know. He reached for her again, taking demanding possession of her mouth even as she felt the brand of his fingers on her naked flesh. He clasped the narrowness of her waist. The world seemed to hold its breath—and so did she—as those bold hands slid relentlessly upward. Heaven above, surely he would not touch her there . . .

His knuckles skimmed the underside of her breasts. They seemed to swell into his hands. Her nipples tingled, peaking hard and tight, and it was there he now worked his magic. She nearly cried out as his thumbs flicked across each aching summit, over and over, a tormenting caress. Searing pleasure licked along her veins. She felt alive in places she'd never known before—in ways she'd never known before.

A hard arm slid around her back. She felt herself borne down to the softness of the quilt. Rational thought seemed a forgotten skill, yet her mind climbed fuzzily through layers of pleasure. There was a reason this should not be happening . . . He was lying over her, the weight of his body heavy and unfamiliar. But it was that extra hardness, stiff and swollen, against the softness of her belly that triggered an alarm in her head. She was inexperienced, yes—but not so innocent as he would believe. Olivia was suddenly overwhelmingly conscious of the blatant intimacy of their embrace. Tearing her mouth away, she hauled in a deep ragged breath.

"Wait," she cried against his shoulder. "Wait!"

Above her, she felt his body freeze. For a heart-stopping moment she feared he hadn't heard. His mouth deserted hers. He bowed his head low, and Olivia stared at his face, where the strain was clearly visible in the tense line of his jaw. His arms were still taut around her, so very taut . . . Only when he exhaled, a rush of air that seemed to come from deep inside him, did the tension leave him.

He eased to his side, then propped himself on an elbow. Olivia slid her gown back up over her shoulders, grateful that the darkness hid her flaming cheeks. His expression was hidden in shadows as he regarded her.

"I didn't mean to frighten you," he said quietly.

She struggled to smile. "You didn't." Oddly enough, it was true. It wasn't him she was afraid of, but the strange way he made her feel—as if there were a side of her she didn't know existed.

He sighed and ran his fingers through his hair. Rising to his feet, he turned and helped her up. "I should take you home."

The ride back to the cottage was accomplished mostly in silence, yet it was not an uncomfortable silence. Once there, he lifted her to the ground. She felt the warm roughness of his palm as he reached for her. Together they walked to the cottage door.

He turned. "There's something I would very much like to do for you, Olivia."

His regard was unsmiling. He appeared very solemn, very intent. She searched his features. "What is it?"

"You said once that you wanted to have your sister's eyes examined by a physician in London."

Her eyes darkened. "I intend to, as soon as I have the funds necessary for the trip."

"I could help you with that."

She hesitated. "I appreciate the offer. Truly. But— you've been more than generous already. And this is something that I . . . that *we* . . . should do for ourselves."

For a time she thought he meant to argue. Then he nodded. Perhaps she was being stubborn. Perhaps she was too full of pride to accept charity. But it was just as she'd said—this was something she was determined to do herself.

His eyes rested once more on her lips. Anxious awareness gathered deep in the pit of her belly. Her pulse began to clamor. It struck her just how much she longed to feel his mouth on hers again.

"Good night, Olivia." He turned and strode away.

He didn't kiss her . . . but oh, how she wished he had.

* * *

Andre quietly slipped away from the camp. On horseback, the distance to Emily's cottage didn't take long to cover. He knew he was taking a risk, but he didn't care. All he could think of was Emily. All he cared about was Emily. His people might leave at any time. He would never see her again.

He couldn't bear the thought.

She was so enchantingly lovely. Her sweet shyness tugged at his heart, yet she was far more at ease with him than he'd dared believe possible when they'd first met. Still, she seemed so delicate and fragile—he was half-afraid to touch her for fear she would break apart.

The cottage was dark when he arrived. He frowned, but then he realized . . . why would it be otherwise? Emily lived in a world of darkness— what need was there of light? Just then a shrill cry shattered the air.

It came from inside the cottage.

Andre didn't think. He simply reacted, for his beloved was in danger. He leaped from his mount and grabbed the key he knew lay hidden beneath the pail near the door. He found it and thrust it into the lock, then thrust the door wide.

The cries came from the bedroom. Andre charged within. His feet braced wide, fists raised high to deliver a killing blow to an unknown assailant, his frantic gaze swept around the room.

There was no attacker. There was no one there . . . no one but Emily.

She lay twisting on the bed, stricken cries tearing from her throat. "Don't hurt him!" she screamed. "Please don't hurt him!" Suddenly her arms stretched high in the air.

"Papa!" Her shrill, desperate scream pierced the air. "Papa, no!" She began to sob. "Get up, Papa. *Get up!*"

Andre hurriedly lit the candle at the bedside, then dropped down beside her. He reached for her shoulders, giving her a gentle shake. "Emily, wake up. Wake up, love. Princess, please, open your eyes."

She stopped twisting beneath his hands. Her eyes opened. Her stare was wide-eyed and glazed, her breathing shallow and rasping. An eerie prickling went through him. He had the uneasy sensation she was still lost in the throes of her nightmare.

"Emily. Emily! Wake up, you're safe, love."

Her head turned. "Andre?" she whispered.

Strong brown fingers smoothed a damp lock of hair from her temple. "Yes, princess. 'Tis I."

She reached for him at the very moment he brought her close against his chest. Her arms stealing around his waist, she sagged against him. He felt the shudder that wracked her slender form.

His arms tightened. "What's wrong? Can you tell me?"

"It was nothing. Just a dream." Her reply was muffled against his shoulder.

It was clearly more than that. "Tell me about it," he invited, his lips against the tender skin of her temple.

He felt her stiffen. "Why?" she asked.

He stroked the tightness from her spine. "I don't know," he murmured. "But maybe it wouldn't be so frightening if you told me about it."

"It—it's always the same."

"So you've had it before?"

She nodded. In the beginning, it had come nightly, she almost confided. But no. *No.* Though the images no longer came each night, the memory was still too vivid, still too close. She couldn't bear to think about that horrible day, not now, not ever.

"You cried out to someone, Emily, not to hurt your father. You cried for him to get up—"

Her hands came up between them. "Don't!" she said with surprising force. "Don't say it! I can't stand to think of it again. Don't you see, I . . . I can't!"

Andre had drawn back so he could see her. She would have pushed away but he wouldn't let her.

"Emily—"

"Andre, I beg of you." Her mouth was tremulous. "I cannot speak of it . . . I cannot!"

Her voice verged on hysteria. Andre stared at her, his mind racing. He had the chilling sensation this dream was something she had experienced. Whatever it was, it remained locked within the prison of her mind . . . at least for now.

He urged her head onto his shoulder once more. "You don't have to tell me anything you don't want to," he soothed.

"You—you won't make me?"

She sounded so much like a hopeful little girl he almost laughed. "How could I make you tell me something you don't wish to?" He let his hand drift up and down her back, the motion soothing and monotonous.

She let out a deep sigh. After a moment, she murmured, "You're very kind. Like Olivia. She doesn't make me tell either."

Andre stowed this little piece of information away, for it only solidified the idea that this dream was something she'd truly experienced.

"I nearly forgot. I have something for you." He released her and reached inside his shirt. Taking her hand, he pressed something into her palm.

She tipped her head to the side. "What is it?" With her free hand she ran her fingertips over the smooth, cool surface.

"It's a crystal. Among many in my—" He caught himself just in time. "—my family, it's believed to have magical healing powers. My aunt always carries one in her pocket."

She tipped her head to the side. "Really? That almost sounds like something a Gypsy would do. She must be quite superstitious."

Andre could have kicked himself. Why hadn't he realized she would know? But wait . . . perhaps she didn't. Cautiously he spoke. "Yes, I suppose some might think so." He held his breath, carefully watching Emily's face for any sign that she'd guessed the truth. When she said nothing, he went on lightly, "It's really quite pretty. When held toward the sun, it catches every color of the rainbow."

Emily smiled faintly. "It's been so long since I've seen a rainbow, I can hardly even imagine it anymore."

Andre cursed himself. "I'm sorry. I thought it might bring you comfort and—keep you well. I didn't mean to make you sad."

"You didn't," she said quickly. She stretched out a hand and touched his arm. "Thank you, Andre. I'll carry it with me always. Will you set it on the bedside table for me?"

He did as she asked, then turned back to her.

"I'm surprised that you're here so late."

"I must confess, I saw your sister walking toward Ravenwood." A pang of guilt shot through him, but he could hardly tell her the truth—that he'd met her at the camp.

"Yes." Her lovely mouth turned down. "She had duties there this evening. The Gypsy earl pays her quite handsomely to tend to his books."

"At any rate, I knew you would be alone. I didn't realize you'd be asleep."

Emily colored slightly. "I—I wouldn't have if I'd known you were coming." Her hand came to her breast. Only now did she remember she wore only a thin cotton nightgown.

Andre nearly groaned, for now that his attention was drawn to it, knowing she wore nothing beneath it wreaked havoc with his insides.

He forced his attention elsewhere. "There's a market fair in Greenboro tomorrow. I wanted to ask if you would come with me."

Her hesitation was marginal. "I can't," she said, her voice very low. "It's not that I don't want to," she hastened to assure him. "I—I just can't."

His gaze was steady on her face. "Why not?" he asked in that direct, dauntless way that was so much a part of his charm.

Emily was not so inclined to think so at this moment. She took a deep quivering breath. "I-I would feel like everyone is staring at me."

"If they do, it's only because you are so beautiful."

"What about you? Do you think I'm beautiful?" The question slipped out before she could stop it.

In answer she felt his fingers beneath her chin. "There is no one more beautiful than you, princess."

"If that is true, then why have you never kissed me?"

Andre blinked. "I was trying to be a—" He fumbled for the right word. "—a gentleman."

"I would much rather that you were *not* a gentleman and—and kissed me instead." Emily cringed inside. Heavens, this was getting worse by the second!

"Princess—" There lurked in his tone just the faintest hint of laughter. "—you have only to say so."

And then it was done. His thumb beneath her chin, he guided her face to his. Her eyes fluttered shut as his mouth met hers. His kiss was infinitely long and sweet, so tender it almost brought tears to her eyes.

When it was over he rested his forehead against hers. "You make it difficult to leave, princess."

Her heart was surely flying among the clouds. "Then do not," she whispered recklessly, "though I fear this is hardly proper."

She could feel him smiling. "Do you care?"

"Not a whit." Though it was but a whisper, she was adamant.

"Nor do I."

"What if Olivia returns?"

"Then I'll have to jump out the window—and hope she doesn't carry a pistol."

Emily gave an unexpected chuckle. "I assure you, she does not." Her smile faded. She knew only that his presence drove away the chill of the darkness. "Will you stay until I sleep?"

His heart turned over. "I will," he promised.

He eased back upon the bed, pulling her tight

against his side. He could imagine no greater privilege or pleasure than holding her while she slept.

"Have you ever been kissed?"

Olivia glanced at Emily in startled surprise. The question came from nowhere. Only minutes before, the two of them had been discussing the week's bountiful yield from the garden.

"Kissed," Olivia repeated, still wondering if she'd heard correctly.

"Yes," Emily said solemnly. "*Kissed*. By a man."

Olivia's entire body went hot. Her mind veered straight to Dominic. She had indeed been thoroughly—rousingly—kissed . . . but she could hardly divulge that to her sister. Only the two of them knew . . . only the two of them would *ever* know.

She tried to force a laugh. "Emily, whyever would you ask such a thing?"

Emily lowered her teacup. "Do not make light of this, Olivia. I know that William is very fond of you. And I thought that perhaps . . . he *had* kissed you. So I—I would like to know what it was like for you. I want to know if it made you feel . . . oh, I'm not certain how to say it . . . as if—"

"As if the very earth moved beneath your feet." It slipped out before Olivia could stop it.

"Yes, yes! Olivia, is that how it was for you?"

Dear God, yes. *Yes*. But not with William . . .

A bittersweet smile touched Olivia's mouth. "Emily," she said gently, "I do not know how to tell you this, other than to come straight out with it. I do not love William. And, silly though it sounds, I would marry only . . . only for love."

"I don't think it sounds silly at all." A wistful

longing touched Emily's features. "That would be my wish for you as well."

Olivia reached for her hand and squeezed it. "And mine for you."

To her surprise, sudden tears filled Emily's eyes. Olivia was beside her in an instant.

"Emily!" She slid an arm around her shoulders. "Love, what is wrong?"

A single tear slid down her cheek. "I don't think I shall ever marry."

"Emily! Why would you say that? You are young and beautiful and—"

"And blind."

The catch in her sister's voice tore at Olivia's heart. "To the right man that will make not a whit of difference."

"I would be a burden." Emily clasped her hands in her lap and lowered her head.

"You are not a burden to me," Olivia said forcefully. "You would not be a burden to a man who loves you."

Emily gave a slight shake of her head. "You don't understand," she whispered. "It would hurt so much to . . . to love a man and . . . and never be able to *see* him."

The ache in Emily's voice pierced her to the quick. Her throat hot with the burning threat of tears, she reached out and hugged her sister. She had the oddest sensation there was something Emily was not telling her. She didn't pry, however, for if Emily wanted her to know, then she would tell her.

"I cannot pretend to know how you feel, Emily," she said gently. "I can only hope . . . pray . . . that when you find that man—or when he finds you—

that nothing else matters, as long as you are together.''

Emily clung to her almost desperately. At length
she drew back, dashing away her tears. ''You are
like Mama, Olivia. You always know what to say—
to make me feel better.'' She was quiet for a moment, immersed in thought before she broke the
silence.

''Do you know what I think?'' she murmured,
her expression pensive. ''If a kiss makes a woman
feel as you said . . . as if the very earth moved beneath her feet . . . then . . .''

Olivia frowned. ''Then what?''

''Then she could only be in love,'' Emily said quietly.

Olivia's smile froze. Her heart began to pound.
No, she thought dazedly, that could not be. She
wasn't in love with Dominic . . .

Or perhaps she was.

Twelve

Dominic had the awful feeling he'd frightened her — that he'd trespassed where he should not. Every time he closed his eyes, he saw her—exquisitely made, all pale, ivory flesh, gleaming and innocent before him, open to his gaze . . . his touch. He could still feel her breasts, trembling with each breath, ripe and warm and deliciously naked, filling his palm. The urge to taste those cherry-rose nipples had been overwhelming. Instinct warned he'd have shocked her to her very core. Yet he could not deny the hot possessiveness that surged in him. He knew no other man had ever touched her, and the knowledge only ignited the white-hot desire that boiled in him still.

Yet in the very next instant, he damned himself for a fool. Chiding himself bitterly, he realized that if he had any sense, he'd find a warm, willing woman and take her hard and fast. Anything to get Olivia out of his mind—out of his blood.

Yet all he could think of was her. All he *wanted* was her.

She bedeviled him, like . . . like a Gypsy curse! It was unwise, having her so close at hand—in his very home. Never in his life had a woman kindled such passion, a fire in his soul so heated and intense he felt scorched by it. She was a temptation, a thirst that refused to be quenched. Her presence in his household only sharpened the hunger to possess her. The voice of reason warned it would be best to remove temptation from his grasp, but he knew he wouldn't.

He couldn't.

As he had so often before, he felt torn, caught between two worlds. He almost hated his heritage—his Gypsy blood—for he couldn't help but wonder if that was why she held herself aloof. He reminded himself that despite the fact she was a servant in his home, she was a lady . . . a lady who would never lower herself to lay with a Gypsy.

The thought tormented him, tormented him endlessly.

It was several days later that he rode into Stonebridge. Storm had been favoring his right leg and needed to be reshod. There was a farrier at Ravenwood who could have done the job, but Dominic was determined to overcome the villagers' apprehension of him. By bringing the village tradesmen his business—improving their lot and livelihood—he hoped in turn their dislike of him would begin to lessen.

The ring of the hammer on the anvil echoed in his ears as he left the heat of the blacksmith's shop. The day was hot, almost sultry, and he sought a cool cup of ale to soothe his parched throat. On the way to the alehouse, a woman and a little girl emerged from the milliner's shop.

Dominic nodded his head in greeting. "Good day, mistress."

The woman grabbed the child's hand and bent

low. "Don't look at him," came her loud whisper, "lest he cast the evil eye upon you."

Dominic gritted his teeth. So much for pleasantries.

Not a single soul spoke to him as he walked to the opposite end of the village. By Jove, if looks could kill, he'd have been naught but a pile of cinders by the time he passed the village square.

In the alehouse he took a chair in the corner. The barkeep brought him his ale and still nary a word had been exchanged. A weary resignation washed over him. His thoughts grew bitter. Darkness stole through him, like an ominous cloud across the sun. Why had he ever come to Ravenwood? he wondered blackly. These people—their wary distrust— all were but a cruel reminder of his father, of all that tormented him, of all he longed to forget. But then he thought of *her* . . .

And he knew why he stayed.

The creak of the door announced the arrival of several other patrons. Dominic spared them nary a glance as they sat at a nearby table, for what was the use? He raised his glass and drank deeply of the pale amber liquid.

"Mark my word, William, there's a storm brewing. It'll be here within the week, or my name is not Jonas Arnold."

He paid no heed to their conversation. He sat alone and detached, wholly unmindful of their presence—that is until he heard a name.

Olivia.

Only then did he raise his head and glance to the side. Through narrowed eyes he saw a slender, slightly balding fellow. The other was younger and handsome . . .

William Dunsport.

Dominic's lips thinned. Every muscle in his body tightened. Dunsport was the one man he could not countenance just now.

". . . I admit, William, she's a handsome enough baggage."

Dunsport laughed. "So she is, Jonas, so she is. But mark my word—" He raised his glass high. "—before year's end, she'll carry my name."

"What! You've asked for her hand then?"

"I have." His confidence was unfaltering. "We've kept it to ourselves, so I must ask you to keep silent. We'll announce it soon enough. When we're wed, I was thinking of building a house of our own."

For an instant Dominic couldn't breathe. It was as if he'd been punched in the gut. That little cheat. That lying little cheat. Raw fury swam before his eyes.

"But what about the sister, Emily? My aunt is acquainted with Olivia. She was a friend of her mother's." Jonas Arnold shook his head. "You'll not get one without the other, old man."

A smug smile graced Dunsport's lips. He shrugged. "Ah, well, I daresay it will be worth it once she's in my bed."

The rest of his comment was lost in ribald laughter.

Dominic was scarcely aware of rising. There was a dead silence as he stopped by their table.

A hard smile curled his lips as he tipped his hat. "I do hope you'll invite me to the wedding." With that he was gone.

*   *   *

Olivia saw nothing of Dominic over the next few days. While a part of her was immensely disappointed, there was also a part of her which was vastly relieved. The most disturbing images spun through her mind again and again—images she had no business envisioning. His mouth on the side of her neck. His mouth on her breasts. His hand in places she dared not speak of . . .

His touch had opened a door that had never been opened. She was not a child who knew nothing of the ways of love—her mother had believed in the importance of understanding the physical intimacies between man and woman. Yet now her dreams were wanton and erotic. Only this morning she had wakened from a dream that remained vivid long into the day. She saw the two of them entwined in a lovers' embrace—only to her utter shock, she was sitting atop him—not just lying upon him, but . . . sitting! Was such a thing even possible? If only there were someone she could confide in, someone she could ask. She was too embarrassed to talk to Charlotte about such matters. She could think of no one who would know . . .

No one but him.

To make matters worse, Emily had asked about him only this morning. Lucifer had climbed upon Emily's lap, for he proved to be outrageously affectionate. Olivia was outside for a time and Lucifer refused to relinquish his perch. They had both dissolved into weak laughter before they were finally able to entice the hound from her lap.

It was then that Emily had said, " 'Tis odd, don't you think, that Lucifer ever followed you home— even more odd that he continues to do so."

Olivia hesitated. " 'Tis not odd at all," she said

slowly. "He simply did as he was told."

"By his master?"

"Y-yes."

"I cannot remember what you told me . . . Which of the Gypsy earl's staff is his master? The butler?"

"No. And I—I did not say."

"Then who is Lucifer's master?"

There was no help for it. "The Gypsy earl is his master," Olivia said quietly.

Emily's smile faded. "Then why did he tell Lucifer to accompany you?"

"You won't like the answer, Emily."

"Tell me anyway."

"So that I would not be alone when I returned home at night," she told her sister softly. "So that I would be safe."

It was a long time before Emily spoke. "Then perhaps he cannot be as terrible as I once thought. Indeed, if I should ever meet him, I—I shall have to thank him."

Strange, how wise Emily suddenly seemed. Her sister had grown up beneath her very eyes, and Olivia was suddenly so proud of her sister she felt she would burst inside.

"I'm curious," Emily went on. "What does he look like?"

"He's quite the handsomest man I've ever seen," Olivia replied—and so quickly they both laughed.

Then Emily's smile had faded. "Does he look like a Gypsy?" she asked quietly.

Olivia hesitated. "Yes—and no. He is tall, quite tall, I might add. His hair is dark, almost black. But his eyes—well, they are a startling shade of blue— his father's eyes, or so 'tis said. He cuts a fine fig- ure—his clothing is superbly tailored, but he looks most appealing when he wears a simple shirt, breeches and riding boots."

Only then did Olivia wonder if she'd divulged a shade too much. Luckily, Emily made no further observation and the subject was dropped.

It was early when Olivia finished her household duties that day. Franklin had told her that Dominic was planning a ball for some of the gentry in the area. He'd asked that she address the invitations over the next few days. Her step brisk, Olivia hurried to the study. She felt guilty for leaving Emily on her own so much lately, so she planned to work for perhaps an hour or so on the invitations, then go home.

She found the list in the middle of the wide mahogany desk. She was about to sit down when a tall form rose from one of the chairs before the fireplace.

"Well, well, if it isn't Miss Sherwood."

Dominic. Her heart began to hammer. The bite in his tone put her on guard immediately—and so did the way he called her Miss Sherwood. What on earth was wrong? she wondered wildly.

She cleared her throat. "Excuse me. I—I didn't know you were here."

He made no answer. Instead he moved across the floor and very deliberately closed the door. Crossing his arms over his chest, he regarded her coolly, a gaze that belied the seething emotions that simmered just beneath the surface

Olivia eyed him nervously. His mood was dangerous, his eyes like pale blue frost. It spun through her mind that he was a stranger. Looking at him now, so cold, almost forbidding, it was as if the carefree, tender man who'd kissed her so passionately at the Gypsy camp did not exist.

"It seems congratulations are in order."

Olivia blinked. "I beg your pardon?"

"Oh, come now, Olivia. You need not pretend any longer. Your intended was most forthcoming today."

Olivia squared her shoulders. She rallied her anger, for she'd done nothing to deserve this. "I have no idea what you mean," she said quietly.

He approached. Warily Olivia managed to hold her ground, though everything within her screamed to retreat. And then there was no chance, for strong hands laid claim to her shoulders. He turned her toward him. His eyes descended to the rounded swell of her breasts.

Olivia went utterly cold inside, for he stared as if he stripped her naked with naught but the touch of his eyes. His scrutiny was no less intense than it had been the other night, yet now it was scornfully brazen and made her feel small and ashamed.

His smile was as brittle as his manner. "Prudent. Practical. Proper and prim. I wonder, Olivia. Will you be so prim with the man you love . . . with William?"

She nearly faltered beneath his unrelenting regard. "William," she echoed. Was that what this was about? "You make no sense," she said unevenly. "What has this to do with William?"

He paid no heed. "I find I'm curious," he said suddenly. "Did you tell him? Did you tell him how I kissed you? Did you tell him how I touched your breasts?"

Deliberately he grazed the peak of her breast with his fingertips. Olivia inhaled sharply. To her horror, a jolt of sheer pleasure shot through her. Her nipples grew tight and tingly.

"Did you tell him how you lay naked before me? Why did you let me touch you as I did? You wanted me to, Olivia. You wanted it."

Her nails dug into her palms. She couldn't tear her eyes from his face. His expression was taut, his eyes filled with an icy, biting fury.

"Was it just a game? A game to taunt me? A game to torment the poor Gypsy—to remind him what can never be his?" His jaw locked hard and tight. "Did you plan it, you and William?"

"You speak of William, but you speak in riddles," she cried. "I—I don't know what you mean!"

"Then why did he tell Jonas Arnold that by Christmas you would carry his name? Why did he boast that soon you would be in his bed?"

Her breath caught. "No," she said faintly. "Surely he did not—"

"He did. I heard him this afternoon at the alehouse. He said the two of you had kept it to yourselves thus far, but soon you would announce it."

Olivia stared at him, unable to believe she'd heard right.

"Why, then, did you lie to me?" Dominic went on. "You told me he'd offered for you but you had refused."

"I did refuse!"

"Did you now? I feared you would be angry with me, that I had dared to touch your breasts." His lip curled. "Now I begin to think you played me for the world's biggest fool. I was so convinced you were chaste and virtuous and innocent—but I begin to think you are anything *but* innocent!"

Olivia gasped. Her temper unraveled. She reacted without thought, prompted by the sizzle of anger. Her hand shot out and dealt a stinging slap across the hardness of his cheek.

Too late she realized her mistake. Too late she realized what she had done. His expression went rigid. Before she could draw breath he dragged her against him.

Lean fingers slid through her hair, tilting her face up. His mouth trapped hers, holding her captive to the blazing fusion of his mouth upon hers. His kiss tasted of the wildness she'd always sensed in him, raw and untamed and greedy. His tongue dove swift and deep, blatantly bold and searing. It left no part of the honeyed cavern of her mouth uncharted. It was as if he were filled with a raging fever. She could feel the steely hardness of his thighs molded against her own . . . and the thick, rigid swell of all that lay between! Caught by the binding circle of his arms, she could do naught but cling to him feebly.

Caught in a raging swarm of emotions gone wild, he released her. He stared down at her in tight-lipped silence. His cheek still bore the mark of her hand. "No," he said in a terrible, grating voice. "No!"

Was it himself he denied—or her? Held only by the fiery vise of his eyes, Olivia didn't move. She couldn't. All at once she felt as if the world were toppling all around her.

She heard the harsh, indrawn breath he took. His jaw was inflexible, his features hard.

He swore. "Go, damn you! Just—go!"

His tone scalded her. Tears sprang to her eyes—and to think she had commended him to Emily only that morning! She didn't wait for him to tell her again. She whirled and ran from the room, her pulse hammering—and the imprint of his mouth burned into hers.

Thirteen

Olivia didn't go directly home. In the village she turned down the lane that led to the outskirts of town—and the genteel old house that belonged to the Dunsfords.

The Dunsford home was two stories high, easily several times over the size of the cottage she and Emily shared. The Dunsfords had lived there for well over a century. Gleaming tendrils of ivy climbed the stone fireplace at the side of the house.

She halted before the door, faintly vexed that Lucifer continued to trot alongside her. "Lucifer, go home!" she scolded sharply. The hound merely wagged his tail, his tongue lolling at the side of his mouth. He lay down on the top step and wagged his tail, as staunchly attached to her as ever.

She turned her attention to the matter at hand. Grasping the brass knocker, she knocked loudly on the front door.

From within came the sound of hollow footsteps. The door opened and William stood there.

"Olivia!" He hailed her warmly. "How wonderful to see you! Please, do come in." He motioned her inside and closed the door, then led her into the parlor, a comfortable room decorated in shades of brown and gold.

"Would you like tea? No? Are you certain?" He was ever the gentleman as he gestured her toward one of the wing chairs before the fireplace.

Olivia was too agitated to sit, but before she could say a word, William peered at her closely. "Why, love, your cheeks are as red as apples. Are you ill? Of course, it's this heat." He reached for her hands.

Olivia snatched them away. It was not the heat, but the fiery resentment burning inside her that accounted for her high color.

"I've something to say to you, William." She came straight to the point. "I'll thank you to stop spreading it about that we are to be wed."

His eyes flickered. "Why, Olivia, whatever do you mean? I cannot think what—"

She cut him off abruptly. "Spare me the denial, William. I know otherwise."

He stiffened visibly. "I dislike your tone, Olivia."

"And I dislike your presumption."

He stared at her hard, then seemed to relax. He even laughed. "I apologize. Perhaps I was indiscreet and spoke when I shouldn't have."

"Of that there is no doubt."

He gestured vaguely. "Come now, Olivia. What does it matter that it is not official?"

"It is neither official nor *un*official, William. I cannot imagine what possessed you to say such a thing!"

"What possessed me? Aren't you forgetting I asked for your hand?"

"And aren't you forgetting I did *not* give my consent?"

He pulled a face. "Look, I'm sorry if I misconstrued what you said—"

"You did indeed," she said curtly. "Never did I say I would marry you."

"You said not at the present time. Nonetheless, I thought it was understood that we would still—"

"It was not," Olivia informed him stiffly. "Perhaps it's best if we settle the matter here and now." She looked him straight in the eye. "Never did I consent to marry you, William. Indeed, I did the opposite!"

His hand dropped to his side. He eyed her coldly. "Who told you?" he demanded. "Who told you what I said?"

The edge in his tone was unmistakable. Before she had a chance to reply, he swore. "That bastard! It was him, wasn't it—the Gypsy earl! Of course, it had to be!" He raked her with a contemptuous glance. "Is that why you're angry? Because of him? What the devil has gotten into you, Olivia? It doesn't matter what he thinks, not to me or to you!"

But it did, an insistent little voice inside her whispered. When he would have reached for her elbow, she wrenched it away and tipped her chin high.

"What matters is that you would bandy it about that we are to wed when we are not! I will not marry you, William. Not now, not ever. And if you persist in spreading it about that we are engaged, I will have no choice but to announce to all that it is *not* true, that it was never true! And if that happens, you will surely look the fool."

His expression turned ugly. "You'll regret this,"

he said tightly. "And you'll be back, Olivia. You'll be back begging me to marry you and then we'll see who plays the fool!" He sneered. "Who else would have you and your invalid sister?"

Olivia picked up her skirts and headed for the door. "Good day, William." With a swish of her skirts, she was gone.

William's hands balled into fists at his sides. A vile curse erupted. By God, she would pay for this. She would pay dearly! And so would he...

The Gypsy earl.

Never had Emily been so utterly confused. She treasured the time spent with Andre, for he made her feel special and cherished in a way she'd never thought possible.

Yet it was painful to be with him, for being with him was but a wrenching reminder of all that was gone from her life... the vibrancy of color and light and movement. She wondered if she had changed. What she looked like... what *he* looked like.

An endless ache pierced her breast. Before she had met Andre, she had finally accepted that she would be blind for the rest of her days. The hurt had at last begun to lessen—but now the hurt was sheer, unending torture.

Yet deep within her, some frail thread of hope refused to die. The crystal Andre had given her... he'd said it had great healing powers... She kept it with her day and night. Hidden deep in her pocket. Beneath her pillow. She ran her fingers across the smooth surface often, praying as she'd never prayed before.

But was it merely fool's hope that nourished her?

She woke one morning after Olivia was gone. She knew the hour was late for she could feel the warmth of the summer sun slanting through the window. Her eyes opened. At first she thought she must still be asleep, for there came the flash of a sliver of light. She held her breath.

It came yet again.

She was half-afraid to breathe. She squeezed her eyes shut and began to count. One. Two. Three . . . But when her lashes lifted once more, there was nothing.

Nothing but the hated, oh-so-very-familiar blanket of darkness.

Dimly she heard herself cry out. She wanted so desperately to believe that she might someday see again . . . Was it simply her imagination? Had her longing somehow driven her to perceive something that was not there?

She curled up into a tight little ball, unable to summon the heart to rise. She must have dozed, for she began to dream—the horrible dream where she relived the terror of Papa's death. That horrid Gypsy leered, his black Gypsy eyes glinting as he raised his club high, though Papa begged for mercy . . . Then all was silent . . . a silence that was more terrible than all that had gone before. For she knew that Papa was dead . . .

She woke with a shudder, her palms clammy despite the heat of the day. Pushing the covers aside, she rose. Even when she was bathed and dressed, a shiver of dread shook her form.

Olivia had left bread and cheese in the kitchen, but she had little appetite. A short time later Andre knocked at the door and called a hello. She flung the door wide and hurtled straight into his arms.

"Now this is a welcome I'd not expected," he said with a husky laugh. A tender hand tucked a stray blonde hair behind her ear. "To what do I owe—" All at once he broke off, capturing her chin between thumb and forefinger.

"Emily, what is this? You've been crying!"

Emily tried to smile. The attempt was an abysmal failure.

Hands on her shoulders, he steered her into the parlor and onto the settee. "Emily, tell me what's wrong! Is it Olivia? Is she all right?"

"Olivia is fine." Despite her most stringent effort to the contrary, there was a slight catch in her voice. Andre said nothing, but she could feel his scrutiny.

"It's the dream. You had that blasted dream again, didn't you?"

There was little point in trying to deny it. She nodded.

He swore beneath his breath.

To her shame, hot tears pricked her eyelids. Though she despised her weakness, she couldn't control it. "Don't be angry with me, Andre! Please, I—I could not bear it if you were angry with me."

"Emily! I am not angry with you." The harshness in his voice had softened. He enfolded both her hands within his. "But this dream . . . it plagues you so much lately, I know it. Why, in this week alone, you've had it . . . what? Three times?"

"Four," she said in a small voice.

He gave an impatient exclamation. "This is not right. You hold too much inside, princess. I—I cannot help but feel it might help, if only you would tell me."

Emily wavered. To relive the day of her father's

murder again—the prospect made her cringe inside! Yet was it possible he was right? Oh, if only she knew! Instead she knew only that these last days, she dreaded the night for fear of sleeping . . . for fear of dreaming!

She exhaled, a long, uneven breath. "It's just so—so difficult," she confided. "I—I've never spoken of it, even to Olivia."

His hands tightened around hers. "I don't see that it can be any worse than it is now. Besides, sometimes remembering is the only way to heal," he said gravely. "Just try, will you, princess? You can always stop, I promise."

"You don't understand, Andre." Her mouth was tremulous. "This—this dream . . . 'tis not just a dream . . . It really happened."

His gaze was steady on her face. "I thought so," he murmured. He took a deep breath and prayed he was not making a mistake. "The other night, you called out to someone not to hurt your father."

Emily's shoulders slumped. The memory of that horrible day had festered inside so that the pain was almost a part of her. Was Andre right? Was remembrance the only way she could ever truly forget? She no longer knew. And indeed, how could it possibly be any worse?

It was this which finally made her decide. Yet she had to reach deep down inside to some secret part of her she hadn't known existed.

"Yes," she said woodenly. It was the only way she could speak of it. "Papa and I were riding through the woods. We were on our way back from visiting Mrs. Childress, who was ill. But suddenly there was a man in the road. He waved at us to stop. Of course Papa did, because he thought he might be injured. But the man—" A shiver shook her. "—he demanded that Papa give him his horse. Papa refused and—and tried to ride around him. But he grabbed the reins. He—he dragged both of us down . . . When I fell I—I hit my head on something. A boulder at the side of the road, I think."

She gave a slight shake of her head, her voice very low, so low he had to strain to hear. "I was dazed. My head throbbed unbearably. I—I think Papa tried to stop him from stealing the horse. Then I heard Papa cry out for help . . . pleading for mercy. My head was spinning . . . it—it was so difficult to see."

"Was that when you lost your sight?"

"No. When I woke up the next day, I—I couldn't see."

Andre frowned. How strange . . . "What happened then?" Gently he encouraged her.

Emily swallowed, steeling herself to go on. "All at once I saw them struggling. Papa fell to the ground. The man picked up a thick wooden branch." Her voice began to shake—and so did she. "He struck him, Andre. He struck him . . . countless times."

Andre felt sick inside. Dear God. She had seen it. She had seen her father murdered. No wonder these dreams haunted her still!

"I tried to reach him, but I—I couldn't move! There was blood on Papa's head . . ." She began to cry, heartrending sobs that wrenched at his insides. "He hit him, Andre, over and over and over, until . . . until Papa cried out no more."

Andre didn't hesitate. He brought her shaking body close and tucked her cheek against his shoulder, holding her until the storm of grief inside her was spent.

"The man who did this, Emily. Was he caught and punished?"

Soft blonde hair tickled his chin as she nodded. "He was hanged," she affirmed.

He sought to give what comfort he could. "Only a terrible man would do such a thing."

"I know. He was a Gypsy."

Andre froze. "A Gypsy?"

"Yes. They're all beggars and thieves, you know. And I—I hate them. I hate them all!" The bitter denouncement was torn from deep inside her.

There was no doubt she meant every word.

Andre reeled. It was as if she'd dealt a blow at the very center of his soul. He had no one to blame but himself. He'd persisted, wanting to know about her dreams—about her father.

Now he did, he acknowledged bitterly. God, but he wished he did not!

He continued to hold her, one hand absently stroking her hair, but his eyes were bleak, his heart torn. Emily so desperately longed to regain her sight—and he'd wanted it for her as well. Now. Before the Gypsies left this place. But if she did . . .

She would hate him—hate him forever.

Fourteen

The scene with Dominic was taking its toll. Olivia was not sleeping well. Not until the days that followed did the full import of what she had done that awful night take hold.

She should never have slapped him, for then he would never have kissed her—perhaps now the aftereffect of that turbulent encounter would not haunt her still. Was it her fault? Or his? If she hadn't provoked him, would he have reacted as he had? But he had insulted her most cruelly . . . Olivia was still shocked to the depths of her being that she had dared strike him. Such lack of control was so unlike her! Yet never in her life had she been so angry . . . but so quite obviously had he.

He wouldn't have been angry unless he cared. No. No, it wasn't possible. It wasn't as if he had a *tendre* for her. No doubt he'd sought out—and found comfort—in the arms of the Gypsy girl Eyvette. *You're blind*, whispered a voice. *He was jealous of William, wasn't he? Yes*, agreed another. 'Tis what precipitated the whole unpleasant incident . . . *Unpleasant*, scoffed the first. *'Twas hardly unpleasant during those mind-spinning moments when his lips lay hard and warm upon yours.*

On and on her mind roiled, first one way and then the other. Was it any wonder she avoided him? She knew not how she felt. She knew not what to say or what to do! She was lucky he hadn't dismissed her. Unfortunately, she hadn't the luxury of resigning her post. She was pleased with what she'd managed to put aside for a visit to a London physician, but it would hardly support her and Emily for long. Still, she had every reason to believe he was displeased with her. When she chanced to see him, he didn't speak. If anything, his jaw was harshly unyielding, his eyes dark and inscrutable. Yet she could feel his gaze dwell long and hard upon her though she didn't possess the courage to meet it. Indeed, she felt the effect of those ice-fire eyes long after he was gone, and his cold disdain pierced her to the quick.

Even the weather was a somber reflection of her mood. Gray, ominous clouds moved in from the north and east. A summer storm drenched the area with rain for nearly three days straight.

The household was in a frenzy preparing for the ball. Mrs. Templeton seemed to be everywhere, issuing orders, looking on. Even Franklin, usually so unflappable, seemed a bit harried. Olivia had not worked on Dominic's accounts for well over a week. It was Franklin who reminded her and asked that she stay late tonight. A sliver of guilt shot through her as she replied that of course, she would stay and see to it. It wasn't just the household duties that had kept her from the task. In truth, she was afraid Dominic might be there. But at least tonight, she would be alone. She'd heard Franklin mention that he'd been invited to dinner at the Beaumonts, a wealthy merchant family who lived some miles distant.

Throughout the week, the servants had been rife with speculation about the earl's invitation. It was rumored that John Beaumont sought a husband for his daughter Elizabeth, purported to be a blonde, irresistible beauty. When Olivia first heard, an odd little pang speared her heart. The servants were convinced the earl was his target. Gypsy or no, an earl would be an enviable match for his daughter—she already had an abundance of wealth, and if she were to marry an earl she would be assured of a place in society.

It was difficult to attend to her duties when all she could think of was Dominic—with Elizabeth Beaumont. She could not stop the wanderings of her wayward mind. Would Dominic find himself entranced with the lovely lady? The thought did little to hearten her.

All was quiet when Olivia slipped through the house, as most of the servants had retired for the night. The study was steeped in darkness when Olivia tiptoed inside. She lit the lamp on the desktop, then moved to close the door.

A blistering curse seared the air.

Olivia froze. She nearly cried out when, from out of the shadows, a towering male form suddenly loomed.

Dominic.

Her hand came up to cover her thundering heart. "I thought you were at the Beaumonts'."

"So you came because you thought I was gone. How flattering, Miss Sherwood. I hate to disappoint you, but John Beaumont sent word that his wife is ill. The evening has been postponed."

Olivia eyed him warily. He wore dusty boots and riding breeches. His loose white shirt was open nearly to the waist, revealing a startling wedge of wide, hair-roughened chest. Some little-known sense within her prickled in warning, for there was something alarmingly reckless about him just now.

And no wonder. There was a crystal glass in his hand—and the brandy decanter on the table next to the velvet wing chair was empty.

An unpleasant smile curled his mouth as her gaze traveled from his face to the decanter and back again. His eyes were bloodshot.

"You're foxed," she began, only to stop short. He'd turned to the side, and it was then she spied the portrait of his father.

It had been ripped from its berth above the mantel and now leaned precariously against the hearth—but that was not the worst. The canvas was tattered and torn—as if a knife had been plunged through it again and again.

"Dear God," she said faintly. "Who on earth . . ." The question was singularly ridiculous, a fact borne out by the glint in Dominic's eyes.

She took a deep, steadying breath, shaken to discover that he was capable of such violence. "You're foxed," she said again. "Otherwise, you'd never have done such a thing—"

"You're right. I've had quite a lot to drink. But contrary to what you think, when my drunken stupor clears, I won't regret it. Indeed, I find it much more palatable, for now I need not endure that bastard's prying eyes on me." His voice rang with false heartiness. "Ah, how remiss of me to forget. *I* am the bastard, am I not?"

Oh, but he was arrogant! Olivia was suddenly

angry. "How could you? How could you do such a thing? You have no respect for anything—for anyone! You care about nothing," she accused.

"Is that what you think? Is it?" His jaw hardened. He flung the glass aside; it shattered into a hundred pieces on the hearth. He crossed to stand before her, so close she could see the darker ring of blue around his eyes—eyes that seemed to burn clear inside her.

"You're wrong," he said fiercely. "I care about you."

She stared at him numbly.

His mouth twisted. "What! You don't believe me? It's true. I care about you. I care about you more than I should."

Her mouth grew dry, her breath unsteady. "What do you mean?"

"You know what I mean." His hot gaze fastened on her lips. For one fleeting instant, she was swept back into that magical moment when she was spun adrift in the fiery tempo of his kiss. But all too soon reality intervened.

She gave a tiny shake of her head. "I cannot believe it. I cannot believe that you are capable of any emotion, save one—hatred for your father."

"Believe it, Olivia, believe it. Oh, I know you will not, but he would never let me forget what I was . . . what I am . . . a Gypsy."

Her stomach clenched. He was tense, so very tense. The very air around him seemed to crackle and sizzle.

Her indignation faltered. "You say it as if it were a curse," she said slowly, then hesitated. "Why do you hate him? Why? Despite all, he was your father—"

"You would defend him? To me? To me?" He was outraged. "You stand in judgment of me," he said tightly, "when you know nothing of me— nothing of him. Let me tell you of him, of the man you call my father, of James St. Bride.

"From the time I was very young I'd heard the stories of how he refused to marry my mother when she discovered she carried a child, *his* child. When he came for me, she told me that I'd spent these many years with her, but now it was time to go with him, with James St. Bride."

In some distant part of her mind, Olivia noted that he never called him "Father" . . . it was always "James St. Bride."

"He sent me to school, a boarding school in Yorkshire where wealthy men like him sent their illegitimate offspring."

"But—you were his heir."

"Only because he was desperate. Only because he had no other choice. He had three wives, but no children. Nor did I know until he died that he had my birth legitimized even before he came for me. He didn't tell my mother because he knew it would have pleased her! He cared more about his title— his estates—than he cared for me. I ran away from school countless times, yet he always found me and dragged me back. Finally he had no choice but to engage a tutor, for he was determined to see that I was educated, to mold me into someone like him, a proper gentleman . . . his heir."

His tone was no less than bitter. "Not once, in all those years, did he touch me, *not once*. He let me know, in any way he could—in *every* way he could—that I was never as good, never as intelligent, as a *gadjo* boy. He was austere and harsh, while I was rebellious and troublesome. I savored the times when my tutor ran to him, bemoaning the fact that I could not read, that I refused to listen and learn. Oh, I suppose I should have been grateful he didn't beat me. Instead he had a far better means of punishment—Lord, but his tongue was vile! To him, I was just the little Gypsy rat—God knows he called me that often enough!"

Olivia listened in mounting horror. How could the old earl have treated his son so abominably? How could he have been so cruel to his own flesh and blood?

"Nor did he ever bring me here, to Ravenwood, to the home of his ancestors. Of course I knew why. To bring me here would have been a sign that he'd accepted me, when in truth, he'd acknowledged that I was born of his seed—but I wasn't his *son*. Not the way I should have been. I tried to go back to the Gypsies, but it wasn't the same. I discovered there were things I liked, comforts that the Gypsies didn't have. I—I felt as if I'd betrayed my people.

"When I was fifteen, my mother sent word that she was ill. He wouldn't let me go to her. He locked me in my room. I—I discovered later that she died alone, near the stream one day—" A shadow passed over his face, a fleeting pain that made her ache inside. "The Gypsies believe that no one should be alone when they die. I hated him for that, most of all."

Tears sprang to her eyes, tears she couldn't withhold. There could be no doubt that he had loved his mother deeply. Only now did she begin to understand the depth of his hatred against his father— and the reasons for it. Her chest ached with the force of the emotions scrambled in her breast. *Not once did he touch me, not once.* The life he had endured with his father had been so very, very cruel! She saw through the layers of pain . . . to the hurt beneath. The hurt of a boy, young and scorned and so very alone.

"When he died, I was tempted—oh, so tempted!—to turn my back on him, on my inheritance, to shun the life he was determined I live. But I'd already learned I couldn't go back. I couldn't have both, and so I had to make a choice. The solicitor in Stonebridge, Robert Gilmore, hates me for being one of them, a Gypsy. But I'm distrusted by the Gypsies because of my *gadjo* blood. And I'm despised by the *gadje* because of my Gypsy blood. I'm damned for what I am . . . what I am not. I asked you once to look at me, to tell me what you see. You had no answer, Olivia. Nor do I. Am I a Gypsy who's lost his way?" He gave a self-deprecating laugh. "Or a *gadjo* who's lost his way?"

He nodded toward the portrait. "I think you are like him, like James St. Bride. He would not let me forget who I am . . . what I am. Nor can you."

Her breath caught. Everything within her cried out in fevered denial. "No! That's not true—"

"Isn't it? Go ahead and say it, Olivia. You did it once before. You despise me. You despise me because I'm a Gypsy. Say it!" His features were a mask of stone. "Say it!"

An odd little pain knotted in her breast. Despite the tragedy of her father's murder and Emily's blindness, her childhood had been filled with many happy days of love and laughter. But for Dominic, those days had been all too few.

She gave a tiny shake of her head. "I cannot—" Her throat clogged painfully. "—for I *do* not."

He said nothing. His mouth thinned, a taut, straight line. The plane of his jaw was so grim, so very, very grim. What was he thinking? she wondered wildly. Her gaze took in the stiff, unyielding lines of his shoulders, his proud, rigid posture.

Unbidden, she reached out, her only thought to offer what comfort she could.

Fingers of iron shackled her wrist, thwarting her, stopping her cold. Slowly she raised her head, lifting tear-bright eyes to his.

He stared down at her, his features dark and forbidding. "Don't," he warned tautly. "Don't pity me. Don't cry for me."

There was a sharp, rending pain in the region of her heart. Why was he so cold, so distantly aloof?

Olivia didn't answer; she couldn't. All at once she was caught in a paralyzing uncertainty. Her rational mind urged her to flee. Yet she stood rooted in place, held by a compelling force more powerful than she—a force she didn't entirely understand.

Yet she couldn't deny it. She couldn't leave him alone. Not now. Not like this.

Her mouth was as dry as bone. "You're wrong if you think it's pity I feel for you," she whispered.

His eyes seemed to blaze. "You shouldn't be here," he said tautly. "Go back to your beloved William."

Realization dawned in a flash. Olivia was suddenly very aware of what he was doing—trying to drive her away. Something painful caught at a corner of her heart. She'd been given a glimpse into the dark, lonely side of his soul, a side she'd never dreamed existed. Despite his strength, despite his pride . . . he was vulnerable. James St. Bride had hurt him unbearably, a wound that the years had not erased . . . a wound that had never healed.

Perhaps it was time that it did.

Her heart in her throat, she shook her head. "I—I don't love William," she whispered.

Something flared in his eyes. He moved so quickly she nearly cried out, snatching her against him. "Swear it. *Swear it.*"

The tension stretched out endlessly. She stared at the hollow of his throat, covered by a wild tangle of dark, masculine hairs. All she could think was how much she longed for him to kiss her again.

The muscles in her throat ached so that it almost hurt to speak. But suddenly it tumbled out in a rush. "I swear it. I've never loved William—" Her eyes clung to his. "—and I never will."

Her fervent declaration seemed to let loose something inside him. He stared down at her. His eyes glittered, almost frighteningly intense. In that timeless void between one heartbeat and the next, something changed. Everything changed.

His arms engulfed her, almost crushing her. His mouth came down on hers, as if to seal the vow. His kiss was hard and plundering, as if to punish her, but it was himself he punished. His mind whirled in a brandy-induced fog. Dominic knew he was a bastard to do this to her. He should have made her leave. He could have, he knew. She was on the verge of tears. If he'd been cruel to her—if he'd taunted her—she'd have run away, as she had once before. But she would hate him, and he couldn't stand the thought. So instead, he was going to be greedy. He wanted her. He'd wanted her from the very instant he'd seen her crouching alongside the road, terrified that Lucifer was a demon-dog from hell. Her nearness was a temptation he couldn't withstand. He would take from her this night . . . take as much as she was willing to give.

And give she did. He felt an answering quiver in her lips, and he was lost. Her mouth yielded beneath the hungry demand in his, parting softly. Her tongue entwined with his, a tentative touch that made him shudder. With a groan he caught her head in his hands. Her hair tumbled down around his hands, over her shoulders and down her back, like warm, living silk.

Somehow he dragged his mouth from hers. He stared down at her. Her lips were pink and dewy and slightly swollen. Her lashes, thick and dark and spiked with tears, drifted open. He nearly groaned at the unguarded longing he glimpsed in her eyes. Did she know what she wanted? No, he decided. But *he* did.

His voice was ragged as he said, "Kiss me." God above, she did, framing his face with her hands and turning her mouth up to his. He made a sound deep in his throat. The sweet clinging of her mouth was more than he could stand. His mouth opened; the kiss turned hot and devouring. Then his hands were at her shoulders, tugging her gown down to her waist. He heard her swiftly indrawn breath as her chemise took the same path as her gown. Her chest rose and fell quickly, her breathing grew shallow. His eyes were dark and burning as he stared at her naked breasts. Her flesh gleamed ivory and pale in the lamplight, exquisitely round and full, and tipped by glorious rose nipples. He was dimly aware of her gaze shying away, of the pink stain which slowly spread upward to her cheeks.

With his palms he touched her nipples. She gasped as they sprang tight and eagerly erect into his hands. Clamping his jaw, he battled a rush of white-hot desire, but it was no use. His hands closed over her shoulders. He sank to the floor, pulling her along with him.

His breath came heavy and labored. There was a primitive pounding in his head. His blood was scalding. Desire churned in his gut like a raging storm from the sea. His shaft swelled thick and hard and full, straining to be free of its confinement.

His breath was harsh and scraping. He fumbled with the buttons of his breeches, freeing his manhood into his palm. His fingers closed around his burning shaft. His hand slid clear to the arching tip and back. Again, and yet again. It wasn't enough. Not nearly enough. Her nearness was too tempting, and he was too desperate. Too needy. The thought of possessing her, of driving deep within her clinging channel, made him swell still further. Tonight, he thought raggedly, tonight he would bury his pain in her tender body, find respite in her softness, until nothing else existed. No past. No future. Only now.

Olivia knew it too.

She felt his hand beneath her skirts, lifting, sliding along her thighs and baring her to the waist. Her heart tumbled to a standstill. She slid her hands beneath his shirt, relishing the smooth hardness of his skin. All at once she was trembling from head to toe. But she cared not that he would vent his suffering inside her, only that she was close to him . . . as close as she could possibly be.

With his knees he parted her wide. She felt him,

his velvet-tipped heat, throbbing and scorchingly hot at the entrance to her core. She felt him breach those first outer petals, parting tender flesh that surrendered beneath the stunning pressure of his entry. Her thighs tensed; she couldn't help it.

He must have felt it, for he kissed the base of her throat where her pulse beat wildly. "I won't hurt you, Olivia. I won't . . ." The words were a ragged whisper.

He raised his head. His eyes sheared straight into hers, hot and molten. With her hand she reached up to trace the rugged beauty of his mouth, an unconscious caress. Her thighs parted helplessly.

His eyes closed. His hands slid beneath her buttocks.

A single stroke of heated fire brought him deep inside her, clear to the gates of her womb.

Olivia's breath left her in a scalding rush. She couldn't withhold the startled cry that ripped from her throat. She clutched at his naked shoulders, her nails biting deep into his skin.

Dominic froze as he heard her cry. For one mindsplitting instant, he lay utterly still. But it was too late . . . too late. His blood surged hot and molten, there in the place he possessed so fully. *May God forgive me*, he prayed, for he couldn't stop. The feel of her melting heat around his thickened spear shattered what little control he had left. He could do naught but bow to the frenzied demands of his body. He plunged inside her satin heat, imbedding himself deep—ever deeper, his passion unchecked, spurring him toward the rapture he knew awaited him.

Olivia closed her eyes, praying that the rending pain would subside . . . and it did. Even as his rod claimed her again and again, so did his mouth, the pressure of his lips hotly fierce. He tasted of brandy . . . his torrid thrusts of a tormented hunger. She clung to him blindly, riding out the storm that swirled inside him.

In some faraway corner of his mind, Dominic knew he should have stopped. God, if only he could! But rational thought was impossible. It felt too good. *She* felt too good. The end was near. He could feel it building inside him. His thrusts quickened, until he was lunging almost wildly.

Then it happened. Everything inside him exploded. Wave after wave of scalding pleasure washed over him, through him. Arching his neck, he cried his ecstasy to the darkened room.

He shuddered, then collapsed against her. He felt her fingers sifting through the dark hair that grew low on his nape. Raising his head, his mouth sought hers. He tasted the saltiness of tears upon his lips . . . *Tears*.

That was his last awareness before he sank into oblivion.

Fifteen

Dominic awoke in his bedchamber lying facedown
on the bed. It was day, for a pale ribbon of light
trickled through the drapes. He turned his head,
only to regret it. Pain stabbed at his temples. He
lay very still and closed his eyes, willing sleep to
come again.

It was no use. A headache had begun to rage,
but far eclipsing the pain was the feeling that he'd
done something terrible, something regrettable.
With a groan he eased to his back, staring up at
the intricate pattern on the crimson bed hangings.

He had no recollection of coming to his bedchamber. The last he knew he'd been in his study.
Vague, tantalizing memories snatched at his brain,
memories of eager, willing lips and vital warmth,
of immense sexual satiation. Christ, he must have
been dreaming!

With a groan he pushed himself to a sitting position. This was a terrible way to awaken from such
a glorious dream. He staggered to his feet, thinking
that never again would he drink as he had last
night. Stripping off his clothes, he made his way to
the washbasin across the room.

An oval mirror hung above the washstand. As

he caught sight of his reflection, he noticed four distinct red lines scraped across the skin of his shoulder. It was then he chanced to glance down. His member was smeared with telltale traces of blood . . .

Blood that could only mean one thing.

His head jerked up. A stricken cry resounded in his brain. Olivia, he realized. Dear God, *Olivia*. It hadn't been a dream at all. It had been real. It had been *real*.

Memories assailed him. Small hands on his shoulders. A soft, trembling body in his arms. The salty warmth of tears trapped between their lips. Panic leaped in his breast. She'd been crying. *Crying* . . .

Fear wrapped its stranglehold around him. Christ, had he hurt her? She'd been so damnably small, her virgin passage so very tight. His mouth curled in self-derision. Immense sexual satiation indeed. He remembered lunging wildly into her, desperate to reach that pinnacle of pleasure.

Why the hell had she let him make love to her? Why hadn't she stopped him? *You fool!* he berated himself viciously. *The blame rests squarely on your shoulders. It wasn't her fault. You were drunk.* Self-disgust roiled in his belly. He'd shown her no tenderness, no care for her innocent state. He'd been too drunk—and too selfish—to care about anything but himself.

What the devil had he done? Christ, he'd taken her on the floor like—like a doxy!

The memory washed through him again, and with it a fresh wave of molten desire—and something else. A cold fear assailed him, unlike anything he'd ever felt before. Did she hate him for

what he'd done? Would she forever regard him
with loathing and disgust?

He couldn't bear the thought of either.

Another memory surfaced—that of a small hand,
tender and soothing, stroking the nape of his neck
as he lay spent and unmoving atop her body, his
head buried against the hollow of her throat.

He didn't understand it. He didn't understand
her.

He willed aside the pain in his head and called
for a bath, his mind churning. This was Sunday.
Olivia wouldn't be here. But this was the afternoon
she taught the children. If he could catch her either
before or after . . .

Christ! And if he did, what the hell was he to
say to her?

It was early afternoon when he rode toward Stonebridge. The storm that had plagued the skies these
last few days was gone. The air was comfortably
warm and pleasant. Fluffy white clouds skidded
across the sky.

Storm's hooves echoed loudly on the wooden
bridge that crossed the stream. Dominic noted idly
that only a few feet separated the water from the
bridge.

He'd just reached the outskirts of the village
when a shout rang out. Glancing over, he saw several people run toward the stream. A man had
stopped near several women outside the bakery
shop; they pointed in the direction the others had
taken. Here where the stream cut through the village, the waters were usually calm and placid;
now, swollen by rainfall, they were a muddied
brown, swirling and rushing.

Just then came another shout—and the unmistakable scream of a child. What the devil . . . A frown upon his brow, Dominic straightened in the saddle.

What he saw sent a chill down the length of him. Two small heads were bobbing in the stream. He caught just a glimpse of flailing arms.

He swore beneath his breath but waited no longer. Vaulting from the saddle, he ran toward the stream. Without a second thought he dove head-first into the water.

While Dominic could do nothing but remember the night just past, Olivia was determined to forget . . . a task far easier said than done, as she was discovering.

She couldn't stop thinking about what he'd said. *"Am I a Gypsy who's lost his way? Or a* gadjo *who's lost his way?"* Her heart bled as she thought of all he had endured at his father's hand . . . Oh, James St. Bride had not been physically cruel—he had not beaten his son, not with hands or fists. Instead he had done so with words, unspeakably cruel words that had wounded a young boy's soul. But now that boy had grown into manhood . . .

Yet still he suffered.

He knew not if he was Gypsy. Or *gadjo*. In truth, she reflected, he was just a man who'd lost his way . . .

She no longer wondered why he hated his father—James St. Bride. But that hatred was like a dreaded disease that spread throughout his being. He must put his hatred aside, or it would consume him forever . . .

And he would never find his way.

Olivia still could not explain what had possessed

her last evening, even to herself. She'd hated seeing him like that—so anguished, so alone.

If she was lucky, perhaps he wouldn't remember—certainly he'd been quite foxed.

It had happened, she told herself over and over. But it would never happen again. And so she must put it aside and forget . . .

A piercing ache rent her breast. If only she knew how!

There was no doubt her mind was not where it should be. When Jane twice posed a question, Olivia knew it for certain.

She closed the book she'd been reading from. She summoned a smile. "I'm afraid, children, that I've developed a bit of a headache. I thought we might stop early today. Besides—" Her gaze encompassed the half-dozen faces gathered around her. "—it doesn't appear as if I'll be missed. Where is everyone today?"

"Gwyneth's mother is ill and she's tending to her," Jane announced promptly. "Thomas went with his papa to York."

"Henry and Jonny built a raft," Colin piped up. "I helped," he added proudly.

Olivia stood. Her hand cupped the back of his head. Colin had gradually lost his shyness during these past weeks. Though she doubted he would ever be as outspoken as his mother, he was a bright, sweet child whose gap-toothed grin melted her heart. "Did you now? Well then, it must be a very fine raft indeed."

"Oh, it is," he said earnestly. "Jonny said 'twould surely sail to China and back."

Olivia smothered a smile. "No doubt," she said gravely. "Though I do hope they intend to make certain it floats before they set out on such a long journey."

"Oh, they do," Colin assured her. " 'Tis why they are gone today." The boy turned, then pointed. "Why, look! There they are!"

Olivia looked beyond the duck pond to the stream. Surely enough, Jonny and Henry were perched atop a small, square platform of wooden branches lashed together. Her heart leaped high into her throat, for the waters of the stream, normally so placid, churned treacherously.

Now it was a deadly torrent.

Even as they watched, the raft tipped precariously, dumping the pair into the raging current.

A cry broke from Olivia's lips. "Oh, sweet heaven!"

Dimly she heard a shout for help. The boys' heads bobbed up and down as they were carried along downstream. Midway to the opposite bank, a huge boulder jutted from the water; it was there the boys were headed. Through some miracle they managed to catch hold of a large root that grew across the surface. They clawed desperately to pull their heads free of the water. Olivia could only imagine the terror they felt, with the water churning madly, sucking at them, eager to drag them down into the murky depths.

It was reflected on their faces, the sheer, stark terror. She could see it from where she stood along the bank. Half a dozen others had joined her. Then, all at once, from the corner of her eyes there was a whir of movement. A man plunged headfirst into the stream.

Dominic.

Her heart in her throat, Olivia could only watch

as Dominic swam toward the rocks. Strong, even strokes took him toward the pair. Powerful legs kicking furiously, he reached them at last. With one hand anchored in a crevice, he shoved Jonny up and out of the water onto the flat, smooth slope of the rock. Jonny huddled there, wet and shivering as Dominic caught Henry beneath his arms. She could see him shouting instructions. He half-turned, and Henry flung his arms around his neck, shifting his weight to Dominic's back. Thus encumbered, Dominic began the awkward swim back to the shore.

At last they were there, yet even then Henry refused to relinquish his hold on Dominic—perhaps he was unable to. His fingers had to be pried from Dominic's throat.

Then it was back across the stream for Jonny, and the laborious task began anew. By the time they were halfway across, Jonny's father James had arrived. Pale and white-faced, he charged into the stream and reached for his son.

Just then a large branch rushed by. It struck Dominic squarely in the temple. He had no time to find his footing. He was swept onward with nary a pause.

Olivia whirled. "Help!" she screamed. "Someone help him." A wall of faces whirled before her. Robert Gilmore wore a telltale smirk upon his mouth. Gerald, who owned the alehouse, crossed his arms over his chest and stared. Even William refrained from moving.

It was to him she directed a dire plea. "Help him, please, William. Please help him!"

William regarded her in unremitting silence.

Olivia waited no longer. She stumbled along

downstream, trying desperately to keep him in sight.

Panic engulfed her as she saw him haul in a frantic rush of air before he was pulled under again. He was fighting the current . . . fighting to stay alive. Then a sudden rush of water began to carry him toward the bank. Everything within her leaped as he began to swim once more, but he was weak, his strength depleted. Yet somehow he made it. Near the bank, he staggered upright, only to collapse on the embankment.

He was lying on his back, just barely out of the water. Olivia reached him at last. With a cry she fell to her knees beside him. Her heart was pounding so hard it hurt. Yet the hurt wasn't nearly so intense as the pain that throbbed in her breast.

He was so still. There was a ragged cut on his temple. He was pale and white but for the blood that still flowed from the wound. His lashes were wet, dark crescents on his cheekbones. Olivia prayed as she'd never prayed before.

"Dominic? Dominic! Wake up! Dominic, please!"

She cradled his head in her lap, half-sobbing. "Can you hear me? Dominic, please, you can't die! Dominic!"

His lashes fluttered. He opened his eyes. The merest smile grazed his mouth as he gazed up at her.

"I didn't realize . . . I'd have to nearly drown . . . to hear you say my name."

To Olivia's shock, there was the veriest thread of unlikely laughter in his tone.

She ducked her head and wept.

* * *

It was James who loaned Dominic a set of dry clothing. Olivia took him back to the cottage, still furious that no one had come to his aid. Though he had made light of it, he might well have drowned!

Not until then did she realize how deep the bias against him ran.

Emily was standing in the parlor when they arrived. Olivia made a rather hurried introduction.

"Emily, I have with me the Earl of Ravenwood. My lord, this is my sister Emily."

Dominic still held a bloodied rag to his temple. With his free hand, he reached for Emily's. " 'Tis an honor to finally meet you, Miss Sherwood."

Emily murmured something; Olivia scarcely heard. All her attention was focused solely on Dominic. She was relieved to note some of the color had crept back into his skin. Quickly she ushered him into the kitchen to sit, then hurried to fetch clean cloths from the bedroom.

Emily followed her. "Olivia," she said in a hushed, disapproving whisper, "whatever is he doing here?"

Olivia whirled. Her sister's condemnation was the one thing she could not abide just now. "He's injured, Emily Sherwood, and don't you dare berate me for bringing him here." She relayed what had happened in the village. "No one would help him, Emily," she finished, her voice low and choked. "No one! They just stood by and—and watched! I—I cannot understand how they could be so—so cold! He's not a monster—he's no different than any of us! Why, it makes me ashamed to call Stonebridge my home!"

Emily's features were grave. Perhaps she sensed

her sister's distress, for she touched Olivia's sleeve. "Is he all right?"

"Other than the cut on his head, I think so. Excuse me, Emily, I must tend to it."

"I'll be out in the garden," Emily murmured.

Olivia nodded, took a deep, calming breath and retraced her steps to the kitchen.

Dominic glanced up when she reentered. She immediately set to work cleaning the wound, though she fretted that it had yet to cease bleeding.

"Perhaps you should see a physician."

"No," he said quickly. "There's no need."

She caught her lower lip between her teeth and glanced at him. "Are you certain?"

"Absolutely. Besides, I'd much rather have you tend me than some balding old man."

Her cheeks pinkened. He had the feeling she was embarrassed. Oh, no, he wouldn't stop her for the world. He liked the feel of her hands on him. He yearned to feel them elsewhere. Descending the ladder of his ribs, sliding lower. Lower still . . .

Her nearness—the clean, fresh scent of her—wreaked havoc on his senses. Her hair was caught in a knot on the back of her head. A tiny wisp curled against her nape. He had a sudden urge to plant his lips there, to taste her tender skin and see if it was as soft as it looked. As she dabbed at the cut on his temple, his hands settled on her waist—to steady her, should she ask. In truth it was but an excuse to touch her again. His eyes were level with the gentle thrust of her breasts.

Last night's encounter loomed high in his mind. Snatches of little things tormented him. The way her nipples had hardened beneath the eager lash of his tongue; how her hips had lifted, seeking his, just before he exploded inside her.

He had to glance away, lest his body betray him. He said the first thing that popped into his mind. "Your sister is quite lovely," he murmured, "almost as lovely as you."

Olivia burned, there where his hands laid claim to her waist. Her hand paused in its ministration. The color in her cheeks deepened. "You shouldn't say things like that."

Dominic paid no heed. His gaze returned, settling on the curve of her mouth. Her lips were the color of ripe summer berries—and just as sweet. He was tempted—oh, so very tempted!—to taste them once more.

Instead he heard himself say, "Why are you doing this?"

She dropped the cloth into the basin. "Because you've a nasty cut there."

"That's not what I mean."

There was something in his tone, something that drew her eyes to his in a flash. She found him watching her, his expression dark and inscrutable.

"What do you mean then?" The question emerged rather breathlessly.

"I'm surprised you bothered to help me—that you didn't leave me lying there. Why didn't you leave?"

Her eyes darkened. "I couldn't. I couldn't leave you like that." The confession emerged before she could stop it.

He swallowed. "I wouldn't blame you—" His voice came out sounding low and tight. "—after what I did last night." There was a heartbeat of silence. "Olivia . . . are you all right?"

There was an odd tightening deep in the pit of her belly. The subject was one that was best left undisturbed. She smoothed the edges of the plaster on the cut. "There. 'Tis done."

She tried to withdraw a step. He wouldn't let her. He rose, pushing the chair away with the back of his knee. He drew her near, so close her feet were squarely between his. A quiver shot through her. He looked totally rugged and masculine in the rough clothing, though the shirt was a trifle small. The muscles of his chest and shoulders strained at the worn material. The shirt was open at the throat, revealing a patch of bronze, hair-roughened skin.

"Tell me, Olivia. Are you . . . all right?"

His voice was gritty. Their eyes collided. She was the first to look away. "I'm . . . fine."

His hands on her waist tightened. He recalled how small and delicate she'd felt in his arms, how hot and tight was her silken channel.

He swallowed. "I didn't—" The words emerged with difficulty. "—hurt you?"

Heat rushed to her face, through her entire body. She closed her eyes. With a scalding rush she recalled the tremendous pressure of him planted snug and hard inside her. Deep—so very deep. Something strange had happened last night. Something strange and terrible and utterly wonderful.

Her breath wavered. Her eyes clung to his. "A little," she said faintly.

"I'm sorry." His heart lurched. "Are you ashamed?"

She floundered. "Yes . . . no . . . oh, I—I don't know!"

He stiffened. When he would have pulled away, she caught at his arms. "It's not what you think," she cried softly, "Not because you're . . ."

"A Gypsy?" His lips barely moved.

"Yes." His muscles were as rigid as stone beneath her fingertips. She wet her lips, floundering, praying she could find the right words. "It's just . . . I wasn't expecting it . . ."

"Nor was I."

Her lips smiled tremulously. "I—was hoping you wouldn't remember."

The tension began to seep from his limbs. "When I woke up this morning, I—thought it was a dream. A wonderful dream." His eyes seared into hers. "I didn't mean to hurt you," he said, his voice very low.

"I know." And she did. She didn't regret that it had been him. Indeed, she could imagine such intimacy with no other man. Just thinking about it made her pulse clamor wildly. "Dominic," she said helplessly, "I don't think we should . . . talk about it."

"That won't make it go away. We can't pretend it didn't happen."

He was right, she realized. What she didn't know was that he didn't want it to go away. He wanted to remember. He wanted it to happen again . . . and again. Only this time he wanted to be fully awake, fully cognizant of everything. To feel every breath she took. Every sweet, luscious curve of her body.

"Besides," he added, staring hard at her mouth, "how could I forget?"

A tremor went through her. She would never forget . . . never.

"The ball I'm having," he said suddenly. "It's very important to me, Olivia. All my life I've struggled for acceptance. I thought I belonged with the

Gypsies, only to find I did not—" He paused, and she sensed he was struggling for the right words. "—yet neither did I fit in to the *gadjo* world. But I am the Earl of Ravenwood, and if London can acknowledge me as such, it's time I was recognized here as well."

Comprehension washed over her. "By all," she said aloud, "both villagers and gentry alike."

"Yes—yes! Ravenwood is my rightful home and it's here I intend to stay."

Olivia nodded. Indeed, she'd addressed a goodly number of invitations—and acceptances had been steadily pouring in. Yet after the incident near the river today, she feared the villagers would not come around so quickly . . . She was frustrated and angry all over again. Why couldn't they see he was not a man to be feared and distrusted?

"I want you there, Olivia. At the ball. At my side."

Her breath caught painfully. This was something she hadn't expected . . . "Dominic, I—I am honored. Truly. But . . . I cannot."

His eyes narrowed. "Why not?"

She drew a deep breath. "You forget," she stated with quiet dignity, "I am but a maid—and you are my employer."

"To the devil with that!" His expression was suddenly as dark as a thundercloud.

" 'Tis easy for you to say. Oh, I wish I *could* be there as your guest! But it—it simply would not be right. What would I tell the others? Franklin and Charlotte. Mrs. Templeton—"

"You need not tell them anything. 'Tis none of their affair." He was every bit the imperious lord.

Wistfulness welled up inside her. In truth, she

would like nothing more than to attend as his equal; to wear a lovely gown, to dance and sip champagne in carefree abandon. But that would never be, and there was no point in wishing otherwise.

She was . . . who she was . . . and so was he.

Her smile faded. "I cannot," she said again. "I must ask that you show me no favoritism. Please do not try to persuade me—and please do not threaten me with dismissal, for I fear I would have to oblige."

He glared at her—she could tell he was sorely vexed. "You won't change your mind, will you?"

"Nay," she said simply.

His lips thinned. "You are stubborn."

"And you are every bit the fine lord, accustomed to having his way," she found herself teasing.

An odd expression flitted across his features. In the next instant an arrogant brow arched high.

"You deny me your presence at the ball . . . but will you deny me a kiss before I go?"

Even as he spoke, he drew her near. Excitement kindled within her as his head began to lower.

"Never, my lord," she whispered, even as his mouth claimed hers.

He kissed her long and deep, a demanding caress that spoke of passion and desire and left her weak and breathless, trembling both inside and out . . . He made her feel both terrified and exhilarated . . .

And so very, very hungry for more.

Robert Gilmore strode through the front door of his home on the outskirts of the village. Behind him, the door slammed so hard the windows rattled in their panes.

He went straight to the sideboard and the bottle of brandy he kept there. Seized fast in the hold of his dark, bitter mood, he did not bother with a glass, but tipped the bottle to his lips and drank deeply. The dark brew burned a path down his throat, burned as his anger burned.

An hour later, the bottle was nearly empty. The brandy had dulled his senses—but not the fire of his anger.

"Thieves and whores," he muttered. "Thieves and whores, every last one of them."

He thought of her, the Gypsy slut who had given birth to him—to Dominic St. Bride. And he thought of another . . .

The one who had bewitched his father.

His lip curled. A vicious curse erupted as he damned them all to the darkest, farthest reaches of hell, especially him . . . Dominic St. Bride. For Robert hated him with every fiber of his being, just as he hated all Gypsies who tainted the earth. His body vibrated with rage as he thought of the Gypsies camped on the other side of the village. No doubt the thieves had come because of *him* . . . No doubt they remained because of him!

He stumbled to the window and there stared out in the direction of Ravenwood Hall, bringing the bottle to his lips. He drank deeply, then slowly he lowered the bottle to his side. With the back of his hand he wiped his mouth.

Ravenwood Hall. To think the Gypsy earl was so arrogant to believe he could toss him, Robert Gilmore, out of his luxurious manor and be done with him. Well, it wasn't that easy, and soon the proud earl would be brought to his knees.

Robert Gilmore would see to it, and he knew he would be honored by the community for his feat.

There would be an end to Dominic St. Bride.

And with that promise, he drained the rest of the bottle.

Sixteen

There was much to be done in the final days before the ball. The ballroom in the east wing hadn't been used for many a year and was in abominable shape. According to Franklin, the last time the grand room had held guests was on the occasion of the old earl's anniversary to his third—and last— wife. Every inch had to be scrubbed from floor to ceiling, for there was dust everywhere. The window hangings were removed, and taken outdoors to be beaten and cleaned. Olivia, Charlotte and another maid spent two whole days cleaning the windows. Olivia fell into bed exhausted every night. In all honesty, she was grateful that the days were so full. They passed quickly, and left little time for thoughts of Dominic . . .

And the intimate encounter they had shared.

They hadn't spoken any further. Olivia saw him in the village several days after his heroic rescue of Henry and Jonny. To her shock, she chanced to glimpse several men who tipped their hats to him. From across the street, she'd held her breath as several women with children approached. But this time they didn't shield their children from his gaze. Indeed, they even deigned to speak to him! He re-

plied and the women laughed, then continued on
their way. Was it possible that the boys' rescue had
thawed the iciness from the villagers' hearts? For
his sake, she prayed it was so.

Shortly thereafter, he was gone for over a week,
traveling to London. Olivia hated the thought
which sprang to the front of her mind. Would he
seek out Maureen Miller, his former mistress? Or
perhaps he would find another. Perhaps he would
decide to remain after all . . .

On and on the turmoil inside her raged.

He didn't return until the day before the ball. She
saw him in the entryway as he strode in. At the
sight of him, her heart turned over. Travel-stained
and dusty as he was, she couldn't imagine a man
more handsome than he. Though he passed directly by, he spared no word for her, not even a
nod.

His coolness was like a slap in the face. Her joy
at seeing him again wilted. He had kissed her, and
held her tight against his heart. Was it possible she
meant nothing to him? *You forget*, a voice inside
reminded her, *you asked that he show you no favoritism*.

At last all was in readiness. Even Mrs. Templeton
could find no fault. The ballroom was dazzling,
alive with color. The floor positively gleamed, an
eye-catching pattern of black and white. Indeed, it
was the perfect foil for the huge, golden urns filled
with fresh flowers—their sweet scent was divine.

Most of the housemaids, like herself, had been
given other duties for the evening—helping to
serve dinner, and later, once the music began in the
ballroom, serving champagne and other tidbits. It
was anticipated the ball would go on quite late; for

those who usually returned to Stonebridge, like her and Charlotte, Franklin had made arrangements to stay the night. Because she didn't want Emily to be alone the entire night, she'd asked Esther to spend the night at the cottage with her.

Almost all of those who were extended an invitation were present. Olivia didn't recognize most of those who attended. Many were wealthy, upper-class gentry with country homes in the area. Olivia heard someone whisper that a viscount from London and the Earl of Wrenford were among those present. It was Glory the upstairs maid who pointed him out to Olivia. He was tall and blond, rather handsome, with a winsome smile and an exuberant manner. Not an hour later, he took a glass of champagne from her tray. His gaze ran over her from head to toe; he winked at her boldly, then beckoned her close. Olivia blushed to the roots of her hair, grateful when someone else called for champagne.

Every so often, she was certain she felt the weight of Dominic's eyes upon her. Yet when she found the courage to glance at him, she found she was wrong. She smothered a pang of disappointment—he had no more awareness of her than any of the other servants.

Oddly enough, she found herself caught up in a fanciful musing. What it would be like, she wondered, to attend a ball such as this? To wear a grand, magnificent gown and shed her drab black dress? A sigh escaped. How she wished Emily were here to see how lovely it looked—Emily so loved flowers. Her heart twisted suddenly. How she wished Emily could *see* . . .

Charlotte nudged her. "Look there," she whis-

pered excitedly. "That's Elizabeth Beaumont dancing with the earl. Don't they look striking
together—him so dark and her so fair?"

Her stomach tensed. It was with a sense of
dreaded inevitability that she followed the direction of Charlotte's eyes.

A hollow band of tightness crept around her
chest. Never had she seen Dominic dressed in evening clothes—oh, but he made a wondrous sight!
She couldn't blame Elizabeth Beaumont if she'd set
her cap for him. Nor could she look away as they
glided across the floor together—the two of them—
almost as if they were one. Elizabeth Beaumont
was stunningly beautiful, her hair caught up in
blonde ringlets atop her head. She was slender but
curvaceous; her white satin gown revealed the generous tops of pale, creamy breasts.

Olivia couldn't look away. Her very heart
seemed to hurt. She could imagine nothing more
painful than seeing them together. That night at the
Gypsy camp, Dominic had confided that, as the
Earl of Ravenwood, he had a duty to fulfill; he'd
acknowledged the need for an heir . . . and an heir
would require a wife.

Elizabeth Beaumont would fill that role quite
nicely.

Certainly Elizabeth Beaumont seemed entranced
with him. Was he as dazzled with her? She prayed
it wasn't so! They'd stopped dancing near the edge
of the floor. Elizabeth was smiling, coyly peeking
at him over the top of her lacy pink fan—and he
was smiling back, the cad! Elizabeth slid a white-
gloved hand into the crook of his elbow and nodded toward the terrace.

Olivia could not withhold the sharp bite of jealousy deep in her soul. She longed to follow them onto the terrace and hurl champagne in her lovely, heart-shaped face.

In the very next instant she was appalled at herself for daring to even *think* about doing such a thing! It wasn't like her to be so petty.

From that moment on, she stringently avoided looking at him—looking *for* him. She didn't notice when they returned from the terrace. They could stay there all night for all she cared!

It was after midnight before the last guest departed. She and Franklin were still in the ballroom when Dominic suddenly appeared. Olivia, who was sweeping in the corner, froze. But he paid her no heed and instead addressed himself to the butler.

"That will be all for tonight, Franklin. There's plenty of time to clean up tomorrow. Oh, and my heartiest appreciation—you and the staff did a splendid job."

"Thank you, my lord." Sounding rather pleased, Franklin bowed and retreated.

Olivia ducked her head and pretended she hadn't heard.

"You may stop now, Olivia."

The whisk of the broom stopped. Olivia raised her head and regarded him—he sounded immensely amused. And why was he smiling? He had such a beautifully masculine mouth . . . and when he smiled the way he was right now . . . which didn't happen often enough . . . he was utterly devastating.

A dozen steps brought him before her. "You avoided me," he said with preamble.

"Not so." She feigned a lightness she was suddenly far from feeling. "Indeed, I should say you appeared quite occupied with your guests." *And one in particular.*

"Not so." He borrowed her words of the moment before. "You were on my mind every second."

"Indeed," she said sweetly. "Even when you were dancing with Elizabeth Beaumont?"

He gave an unexpected chuckle. "Why, Olivia, I do believe you're jealous."

Her chin lifted. He hit dangerously close to the truth—oh, why was she being so stubborn! It *was* the truth! But she, too, had her pride. She would never admit to such a thing—it would have pleased him far too much!

"You make a handsome couple," she informed him—quite graciously, she was certain.

"I noticed the Earl of Wrenford appeared quite taken with you." So he hadn't been so unaware of her as she'd thought. She smiled suddenly.

"Was he?" she said lightly. "I hadn't noticed."

Again that low, husky chuckle. " 'Tis good we're not in London, Olivia. I do believe you're quite the coquette. No doubt I would have to fight my way through droves of admirers to catch even a glimpse of you."

Their eyes met and held—hers were aglow with pleasure, while his were faintly teasing.

"Seriously, though. Do you think the ball went well? Or was it an abysmal failure?"

Though his smile remained in place and his tone was matter-of-fact, Olivia sensed his anxiety. Oh, he pretended to be coolly indifferent, uncaring of what others thought of him, but Olivia knew the truth—deep inside he longed to be accepted by the world in which he lived. The ball was his way of announcing to the world that he intended to stay and take his place here at Ravenwood.

She smiled. "I think it went quite well—quite well indeed."

"Truly?"

It was her turn to chuckle. "Yes!"

But she had to know for sure . . . "You won't be returning to London?" Olivia held her breath and waited.

"Only on those occasions when it's necessary."

He wouldn't be returning to London. He was going to stay here—*here!* She felt absurdly happy.

He captured her hand and raised it to his lips. Olivia flushed, conscious of the calluses there. Her heart stood still as he kissed each knuckle in turn, his gaze holding hers all the while. His skin was warm, making her tremble inside.

"I wish you'd been at my side tonight," he murmured. "But since you couldn't—nay, *wouldn't*—"

Olivia gasped as she was suddenly swung high in his arms. To her shock, he turned and strode from the ballroom.

"Dominic! Wh-what are you doing? Where are you going?"

He was mounting the grand staircase. "I should think it would be obvious—though perhaps not." He gave an exaggerated sigh. "I do forget you are a prim little miss sometimes—"

"I am not a prim little miss!"

"Not after tonight you won't be." He stopped on the landing and grinned at her aghast expression. "What, Miss Sherwood! Have you never heard of a secret liaison? I'm abducting you—that we might share a secret liaison."

His mood was light, almost carefree. Never had she seen him like this. But she liked it—oh, most definitely.

A slow smile crept across her lips. "That sounds—deliciously forbidden."

"Delicious? Of that I have no doubt. Forbidden? Most likely. But I promise you . . . a night you'll always remember. A night you'll never forget."

The huskiness in his tone was thrilling. Her fingertips moved where they rested on the brown skin of his nape, the merest caress. Her eyes searched his. "But what about Charlotte? She'll be expecting me—"

"No, she won't. And you needn't worry that anyone will find out. I told Franklin you would be returning home for the night rather than staying. And I know that you've already arranged for someone to stay with Emily."

Olivia's heart pounded. There might never be another time like this—another night like this—a chance like this. Oh, and perhaps it was wrong, but she didn't care. Whatever the night brought, she would welcome it.

All that mattered was that they were together. All that mattered was *him*.

She tipped her head to the side. They were so close their lips nearly met. "Then I wonder, sir, what you are waiting for."

He needed no further encouragement. He took the remainder of the stairs two at a time. Within seconds they were striding through the dark-paneled double doors that led to his bedchamber. With the heel of his shoe he pushed the doors shut. They closed with a quiet click.

He lowered her to the floor, letting her slide

slowly down the length of his body before he stepped back. Olivia's gaze swept around the room curiously. She'd passed by his chamber on occasion, but the doors had always been closed. Glory and another maid were the ones who were charged with cleaning here in this wing.

The furniture was made of cherrywood, deep in color and undeniably masculine. The bed hangings were of crimson damask, rich and heavy. But she paid a cursory glance to the furniture, for the room was lit by the glow of dozens of candles. They were everywhere—upon the bureau and bedside tables, next to the inviting chairs pulled up before the fireplace. Flickering candlelight reflected from the windows and spilled across the carpet, filling the room with a golden glow. Olivia caught her breath in awe, unaware that Dominic watched the play of expression on her face.

What was it he'd said? *A secret liaison*. Her pulse began to beat faster.

Her gaze finally returned to him. "You planned this, didn't you?"

He stood with his arms folded across his chest, unable to hide his smugness—nor, she suspected, did he wish to.

One corner of his mouth slanted lazily upward. "Do you object, Miss Sherwood?"

In truth Olivia was flattered that he had gone to such lengths to please her.

"How could I? Dominic, it . . . I've never seen anything quite so lovely."

Her answer pleased him. She could see it in his face. He said nothing, but crossed to the huge bed that dominated the center of the room. Upon the coverlet was an enormous box she hadn't noticed until now—he gestured to it and beckoned her near.

"This is for you," was all he said.

Olivia blinked. "What is it?"

"Open it and see."

Taking a deep breath, she removed the lid. Peeking inside, she saw layer upon layer of gauzy tissue—and a glimpse of jade. Excitement brimmed within her. Unable to stop herself, she tore into the tissue like a child who'd been too long without a gift.

Gleaming jade silk came into view—it was the bodice of a gown—a ball gown, she realized. The material was fine and shiny and smooth, as if it possessed a life of its own; she was half-afraid to touch it, she decided, lifting it from the box. Tiny pleats fell from the Empire waistline. The sleeves were long and tightly fitted. There were spotless white gloves, and even a pair of matching slippers and a reticule.

He spoke from directly behind her. "I bought it in London. I thought it would bring out the green in your eyes."

Olivia shook her head, still a little dazed. "Dominic, I—I'm truly touched, but I cannot accept such an extravagant gift. It's far too costly. Besides, where would I wear it?"

His gaze captured hers. "Wear it for me," he said very quietly.

Imprisoned in the web of sapphire eyes, she felt her mouth go dry. She wanted to, she realized. She wanted to with an intensity never before experienced.

Talking suddenly seemed a forgotten art. "Now?" she whispered.

He nodded. The heat in his eyes seemed to pin her to the spot.

She swallowed. "Do you think you might . . . turn around?"

His gaze softened. Something flashed between them, a glimmer of understanding. Turning, he strode to the window and there looked out into the night.

Olivia stepped quickly from her drab black gown and slippers. Carefully she eased into the ball gown. It was so fine and fragile she was afraid she might tear it. She slipped her arms into the sleeves before she pulled up the bodice, only to stop in consternation. The bodice was so low she couldn't wear a thing beneath it! She paused but an instant, then slipped her chemise over her head. Directing a fervent glance heavenward, she prayed that God would forgive her this transgression.

"There," she said finally. "You may turn around now."

He turned. For the space of a heartbeat, Olivia held her breath. She wanted to be beautiful. Desirable. To be . . . oh, everything he had ever wanted in a woman . . . Yet never had she felt so inadequate!

His eyes made a slow, thorough journey from head to toe—they lingered visibly on the mounds of her breasts, pushed together by the bodice. Her reward came a scant instant later—the sudden blaze in his eyes made her go hot all over. The relief that swept through her made her feel giddy.

Wordlessly he extended his hand. Olivia crossed to him on shaky legs. He pushed her gently toward the mirror in the corner.

"Look," he urged softly.

Slowly Olivia raised her head. The neckline was low and deep, displaying the slope of her shoulders and long, slender neck. It dipped scandalously low, exposing the top half of her breasts; the rest molded to that rounded fullness like a sleek second skin. Never before had Olivia worn anything so revealing.

For the longest time all she could do was stare at her reflection. It was exactly as she'd said earlier—she felt deliciously forbidden, yet somehow alluring—just the tiniest bit wicked in a most outrageous way.

Dominic came up behind her. He'd removed his jacket and neckcloth, and loosened the buttons of his shirt. Beneath the whiteness of the cloth she could see the darker shadow of the hair on his chest.

"A perfect fit," he observed. "I had to guess as to your measurements, you know."

Olivia bit her lip. She turned slightly, first one way and then the other. "You don't think it's a trifle small in the bodice?" She glanced where her breasts swelled generously above the neckline.

And so did he.

A slow smile crept across his lips. "I repeat," he said softly, "a perfect fit."

Olivia flushed—more from pride than embarrassment, she was stunned to realize. He had poured a glass of wine, she saw, and when he offered it to her, she took it, sipping gratefully, for all at once she was at a loss for words—for what came next.

Dominic took the glass from her. He drank from the very same spot her lips had just deserted, then handed it back to her.

His eyes never left hers.

Olivia gave a shaky laugh. "Are you trying to seduce me?"

He countered with a question of his own. "Am I succeeding?"

She couldn't tear her gaze from his. "I'm afraid you are," she whispered helplessly.

The glass was plucked from her fingers and set aside.

Strong, warm hands settled upon her bare shoulders. "Don't be afraid, Olivia. I want this to be . . . everything that it wasn't before." He paused. "You look beautiful," he said softly.

Both the words and his regard were quietly intent. Her throat tightened. For the first time in her life, she felt beautiful. If indeed she harbored any doubts, they fled in that moment. She could no more stay the yearning in her heart than she could the raging of the stream.

"So do you." Her lips formed a tremulous smile.

The merest smile grazed his. "Men aren't beautiful."

"You are," she assured him solemnly. She surprised them both by reaching up to touch the sculpted beauty of his mouth.

His smile stilled. He kissed her fingertips. "Are you sorry it happened?"

Her heart leaped. They both knew what "it" meant. She shook her head and let her fist drop to the plane of his chest; its heat and hardness sent a tiny thrill through her. Courage blossomed. "Are you?" she whispered daringly.

His eyes darkened. "God, no."

His fingers came up to tangle in her hair. Slowly he pulled her head back. His gaze roamed her face, then dropped to her lips. Olivia knew then that he was going to kiss her. Never had she wanted anything more. Never had she dreamed she could want something so much . . .

His mouth met hers, tender and sweetly clinging, his breath blending with her own. At the touch of his lips, emotions that had been swirling just below the surface rushed to the fore. Passion. Desire. Need unchecked. His tongue touched hers, as if in question. She responded to the foray by indulging in an exploration of her own, tasting the ridge of his teeth, the hot, slick interior of his mouth. Her hands came up to clutch the warm skin of his neck. He made a sound low in his throat. She could feel the straining fullness of his manhood against the softness of her belly.

Her boldness seemed to stoke the fires within him. A steely arm clamped around her waist, bringing her so close her breasts were crushed against his chest. The pounding of his heart echoed against her own. His kiss turned sweetly fierce and hungry. His fingers worked the pins in her hair; it tumbled down around her shoulders, a wavy, silken mass.

Before she knew it, the ball gown lay puddled around her ankles and she was naked. Swinging her high in his arms, he laid her on the bed.

Olivia slipped beneath the sheet, still shy before him, for this was still so very new to her. Not so with Dominic. Swiftly he tugged his shirt over his head, leaving his torso bare. Her mouth went dry at the sight of him. The candlelight bathed him in a halo of gold. Darkly magnificent, he reminded her of some pagan god of old. Her fingertips tingled. She was possessed of the urge to run her fingers over the knotted hardness of his shoulders and arms, through the dark fur that matted his chest.

His hands were on the buttons of his trousers. She couldn't look away as he pushed them down his legs. Slowly he straightened.

The night in his study they had been partially undressed. Olivia saw what she had only felt that first time . . . She stared, her gaze riveted to his obvious arousal, for that which had only been hinted at was there in the flesh, rigid and brazenly erect between the columns of his thighs. She swallowed. No wonder she'd felt that sharp, stabbing pain, she thought hazily.

He bent over her, sweeping aside the sheet and leaving her bare. Modesty fled in the wake of his avid gaze. A tiny little thrill went through her at the possessive heat she glimpsed on his face. Slowly he stretched out beside her. She quivered as a blunted fingertip traced a flaming line from shoulder to hip. The need to touch him was suddenly overwhelming. Giving in to it, she cupped her palms around the taut strength of his shoulders.

It wasn't enough—not nearly enough. A rash boldness seized her then. She combed her fingers down the wiry pelt on his chest and abdomen, noticing for the first time that a finely crafted gold ring hung from a chain about his neck. She skimmed her fingers across the surface of his chest, even daring to trail her fingertips down across the ridge of his hips, clear to the muscled strength of his thighs.

It was on her upward trek that she chanced to brush the jutting hardness of his shaft. Her heart lurched. She snatched her hand back as if she'd been burned.

Dominic rested his forehead against hers. "Touch me," he said thickly. The pitch of his voice was low and rough, vibrating with need.

His eyes sheared straight into hers. Olivia floundered. "I—I don't know what you mean," she said faintly.

He showed her. His hand trapped hers, guiding it down to close around his throbbing rod.

"Oh, my," she said faintly. But she didn't retreat. Instead she uncurled her fingers. A tentative fingertip trailed slowly from his ultrasensitive crown clear to the root of him, and back along the ridged underside. His hips thrust forward, as if to show her what he wanted. Dainty fingers encircled him anew and suddenly there was no need to guide her further. The clasp of her hand, so small and soft, around that part of him that ached for her swelled still further. He gritted his teeth against a lightning bolt of sheer pleasure that shot through him from head to toe. Locked in exquisite torture, he resisted the urge to pump his hips, determined to allow her to explore on her own. And God above, she did. Her hand mimicked the motion that would take him to heaven and back, a motion not unlike the one which would come later . . .

Her pulse skittered wildly. His eyes were closed, his head arched back, the tendons in his neck taut. His size and breadth made her quiver—to know that he wanted her so—and she reveled in the shudder that racked his body. He was immense, rigid and thick. He was heat and fire, velvet and steel.

His eyes snapped open. "Dear God," he breathed,

"stop or I cannot promise this will not end here and now."

Her hand stilled. A tiny frown appeared between her brows. "What do you mean?"

He nearly groaned. "I mean that I will spill myself—and then I fear you'll find no pleasure."

"Oh," she said in a small voice, then smiled. "I take it you find this . . . pleasing?"

He gave an odd little laugh, aware that she'd discovered the power a woman might easily wield over a man.

His mouth took hungry possession of hers, hotly devouring, and now it was his turn to tease. He filled his hands with the upthrusting bounty of her breasts, rotating his palms against the jutting peaks, taunting her nipples until they sprang stiff and erect against his palms. Her breathing hastened and he experienced a swell of pure satisfaction. His mouth slid down the slender grace of her throat, until at last he took the deep coral center into his mouth. Her head fell back as he alternated between first one and then the other, his tongue curling and lapping and sucking deeply. With a breathy little sigh she arched shamelessly into the hot wet suction of his mouth.

His knuckles brushed the hollow of her belly. His fingers grazed the silken fleece between her thighs, tracing her furrowed cleft. Olivia bit back a low moan. There was a peculiar ache centered there, a pulse of feeling that seemed to spiral ever higher.

But he was not yet finished.

He slid down her body, further, ever further. She was stunned and confused as she felt his hands slip beneath her thighs, and then he was drawing her legs over his shoulders, leaving the most secret part of her open and vulnerable. Olivia raised her head from the pillow. She stared down past her breasts— her nipples were the color of rouge, still shiny and wet—only to reel at the sight of his dark head poised between the cradle of her thighs.

Her heart all but stopped beating. "Dominic," she said faintly. "What . . ."

She got no further. His head lowered. He kissed the tender flesh of her inner thighs, first one and then the other. With his thumb he stroked the very heart of her desire, a tiny nubbin of flesh hidden deep within damp, dew-bathed flesh. Her breath escaped in a scalding rush. But that was not the end. Indeed, 'twas just the beginning . . .

The rough velvet of his tongue was a divine ecstasy. With torrid, tormenting strokes of fire he teased her, driving her half-mad. When at last he claimed that swollen, distended kernel of flesh with the wanton glide of his tongue, a jolt of pure flame shot through her and she knew he had found it.

It was there he now worked his magic. Again and again he tasted her, taking her higher . . . ever higher. Awash in an agony of pleasure, her body seemed not her own. Her hands caught at his bare shoulders, tightening, as if to keep him there. A burning ache kindled inside her. Her body was screaming, screaming for something . . . she knew not what. Then suddenly she had found it, a piercing rapture that sent her soaring to the heavens and beyond. Dimly she heard a sharp, shivering cry. Belatedly she recognized it as her own.

She floated slowly back to earth. Her eyes opened, dazed and smoky. Dominic was on his knees between her thighs, his eyes fiercely aglow, his shaft still rigid and thick.

His features were tense and strained, a silent testimony to his iron control. "Take me inside you," he said tautly. "Take me now . . ." The words were heated and raw.

Without a word she reached down and guided him home.

This time there was no discomfort. She could feel herself stretching . . . stretching beneath the pressure of his invasion. Her arms crept around him and clung, wordlessly urging him deep—as deep as he could go, until there was no more of him to give. Imbedded to the hilt in her silken sheath, his chest rose and fell. He kissed her with greedy urgency, then braced himself above her. His arms were corded and bulging. Slowly he began to move, as if he sought to prolong the pleasure.

But there was no help for either of them. Fired by emotions held too long in check, his control shattered. His hips churned a frantic rhythm, driving and seeking. Olivia's blood seemed to shimmer with molten flame. Caught in the same wild frenzy, her nails dug into the binding tightness of his arms. She couldn't look away as he thrust inside her, again and again. Deep in the center of her being, a tempest twisted and swirled, rising with every plunge of his rod inside her.

It was no less intense for Dominic. The feel of her satin heat, clinging tight around his turgid flesh, melted him inside and out. And then he felt it . . . Tiny contractions milked his member, signaling the pinnacle of fulfillment. He caught her whimpers of rapture in his mouth, her spasms of release but spurring his own. His body stiffened. A ragged cry tore from his throat. His seed erupted, scalding and hot, flooding the gates of her womb.

Long moments passed before the throb of his heart slowed. He combed his fingers through the web of curls tangled about them both. Easing to his side, he cradled her close. A finger beneath her jaw, he guided her mouth to his and kissed her tenderly.

"Stay the night with me," he whispered. In answer she smiled against his lips and pillowed her head against his shoulder.

It wasn't long before her breathing was deep and even. A powerful tide of emotion swept over him as he watched her sleep. She was his, he thought possessively. He had been her first lover . . .

His arms tightened. He vowed he would be her *only* lover.

It was then he heard it . . . the hoot of an owl outside the window. An eerie chill sped down his spine . . .

To the Gypsies it was an omen of death.

Seventeen

Esther had come only an hour earlier, but Emily had explained that there was no need for her to stay the night after all—Olivia would be home, later than usual, perhaps, but she would still be home. Apparently there had been a mix-up, and Olivia had simply forgotten to tell her. She prayed she was right; that Esther hadn't been suspicious. She hadn't lied, she told herself, merely stretched the truth a bit. Olivia would indeed be home—tomorrow. And she wouldn't be alone . . .

Andre would be here soon.

Andre. She shifted a little where she lay on the bed, wrapped her arms around herself and smiled. Her entire body seemed to hum at the mere thought of him. She loved him—she loved him so much, and she was almost certain he was in love with her. He was sweet and attentive and considerate and—and she couldn't imagine life without him! She'd even begun to think of the future, and Andre was very much a part of that future. If all went as planned, he'd soon ask her to marry him. They would share a cottage—it didn't matter how big or small—as long as they were together. In time they would have children—a little dark-haired boy, perhaps . . . or a tiny little girl. Oh, but life would be so wonderful!

True, she didn't know what his family would think of her—or his marrying her. Would they like her? Accept her as his wife? A niggling little doubt surfaced. Yet in the very next instant, it struck her that she really knew very little about his family. His parents, or even if he had brothers and sisters.

She frowned suddenly. She'd asked several times about his family, but now that she considered it, he'd told her very little—only that there were times his family had not stayed long in one place. To Emily, who had rarely ventured further than the next county, it sounded like a grand, wonderful adventure, and she'd gone on to wistfully inquire about the places he'd been. Only now did it occur to her that he had seemed almost reluctant, rather vague, when she'd asked about his family . . . But no. She chided herself. Andre was not a man to harbor secrets, she felt it in her very heart and soul. He was warm and compassionate, so open and honest that she could not even begin to imagine that he would ever lie to her about anything.

As for Olivia, Emily knew that her sister only wanted her to be happy—and Andre made her happy. Of course, she should tell Olivia about him, and soon . . .

So intent on her musings was she that for once she failed to hear the door open. The next thing she knew she felt something incredibly soft run down the tip of her nose, circle around her cheek and finally come to rest against the center of her mouth.

She smiled. "You brought me a rose."

She heard soft, masculine laughter. "I did."

The mattress dipped as he sat beside her.

"What color is it?"

"A dark shade of red."

Her smile turned wistful. "That's always been my favorite."

Setting the rose aside, Andre reached for her. She came into his arms, nestling her cheek against his shoulder. A fierce swell of masculine pride welled within him when she turned her lips up to his. Lord, she was sweet.

It was a very long time before he released her lips. The curtains at the windows were open. Moonlight shimmered through the glass, making the room nearly as light as day.

He gave a playful tug at the lacy neckline of her nightgown. "I thought you were expecting me."

A tremor shot through her. "I was," she confided shyly. She twined her arms around his neck anew, and gathered every ounce of her courage. "Stay with me," she whispered. "*Stay.*"

The world seemed to turn upside-down. Andre went very still. *No*, he thought in amazement. She couldn't possibly mean what he thought . . .

His body had gone tense. "Are you certain Olivia won't be back?"

Emily nodded her head. "Not until late tomorrow. The Gypsy earl is having a ball. She's spending the night at Ravenwood."

In the back of his mind he noticed the way she said "Gypsy" . . . with a telltale disdain. He winced. Damn, but he felt so guilty for not telling her the truth.

Yet if he did, he was very much afraid he would not be here right now.

Time stretched between them, time where he wavered, first one way, then the other.

A frown marred the smoothness of her brow. She spoke his name. "Andre?"

Andre stared down at her, torn cleanly in two. Her lips hovered just beneath his, soft and full and tempting. His heart was pounding, thudding heavily in his chest. Desire flamed in his veins, yet his mind urged caution. He should say no. He should leave this instant. But she was so warm, so willing . . .

She touched his mouth in silent question.

Andre smothered a groan. His fingers slid into the golden waterfall of her hair, tilting her mouth to his. He kissed her with ravenous hunger. She arched against him, as if he were all she'd ever wanted. For Andre, it was both heaven and hell— the moist clinging of her mouth beneath his, the eager press of her body against his, knowing she wore nothing beneath her nightgown . . . He was half-mad with sheer need.

Suddenly he broke off the kiss. "Oh, God," he groaned. "This isn't right."

Emily stared at him in shock. The realization dawned slowly. She'd made a fool of herself, she realized. She'd thrown herself at him, but he didn't want her. *He didn't want her!*

She managed to swallow the burning ache in her throat. "Go then," she cried, "if that's what you want—"

The blur of tears in her voice was his undoing. Andre could no longer fight it. He'd wanted her since the moment he'd first seen her. He'd wanted her as he'd never wanted another woman—he would *never* want anyone the way he wanted her. He snared her by the waist when she would have turned away, bringing her flush against his chest.

"That's not what I want," he whispered, sounding raw inside.

Emily had to stop herself from pounding her fists against his chest in sheer frustration. "Then what *do* you want?" she cried softly.

His hands tightened around her waist. He could feel her trembling. "What I want is right here. What I want is *you*." His tone vibrated with need. "But I can't stop myself from wondering . . . what if you're sorry? What if you regret it?"

Emily blinked back tears. Love crowded her heart, almost more than she could contain. Lifting her hands, she framed his face between her palms.

"I won't be sorry. I won't regret it. And I can think of nothing that feels more right—" Her lips were tremulous, her lovely blue eyes abrim. "— than to be here with you."

Andre was lost. He turned her so that she was on her knees before him, taking her lips in a long, unbroken kiss, breathing into it all the fire of his longing. His hands at her shoulders, he whisked the gown from her body. Slowly he released her mouth and looked his fill.

She was perfect, her skin creamy-white and unblemished. Her breasts were small, tipped with cherry-rose nipples he ached to taste with lips and tongue. Her hips flared out from her narrow waist. Her belly was flat and smooth as satin.

"Andre?" She tipped her head to the side. "Wh-what are you doing?"

"I'm looking at you." Almost reverently he traced the incurve of her waist, the line of her hips.

Emily blushed, yet she wouldn't have traded this moment for the world. Desire spread its fiery wings all through her. Her hands crept up to his chest. "And do I . . . please you?"

He gave a low, husky laugh. "Princess," he whispered into the shell of her ear, "if you pleased me any more, I should surely die of it."

His mouth slid down the slender length of her neck. His hands drifted over her, discovering the ripe fullness of her breasts, the nip of her waist, the swell of her hips. She didn't stop him. She let him touch her wherever he wanted, *however* he wanted. Something hotly possessive welled up in him. To think that she wanted him . . . *him* . . .

Slowly he raised his head. His clothes were suddenly a barrier he could not tolerate. Swiftly he removed them, throwing them aside.

Emily's heart leaped when his hands again laid claim to her waist. Then his mouth was on hers and he was pulling her down beside him on the bed. A jolt ran through her as her legs brushed the hairy roughness of his. He was as naked as she . . .

Soon it didn't matter. His body threw out the heat of a fire. Never had she felt so warm, so safe— like the night he'd comforted her after her nightmare. His arms were a sheltering haven from all that could ever harm her.

She couldn't imagine being anywhere else. She couldn't imagine being *with* anyone else.

She ran her hands wildly over his chest and shoulders and arms, loving the steely strength of muscle sheathed in skin. Her shyness slipped away, like morning dew beneath a blazing sun. She gasped when he drew brazen circles around her nipples, then at last raked his thumbs across the straining peaks. Pure sensation seemed to leap from those twin peaks. *Please*, she thought dazedly, not quite certain what it was she was pleading for. *Oh, please . . .*

As if he knew exactly what she craved, his head slid down her body. When at last his mouth encompassed one deep pink center, a breathless sigh escaped. Her head fell back as he touched one delicate tip with his tongue. Then he was lightly sucking, tugging like a tide, all the way to her heart. Her hands slipped into the warm silk of his hair, as if to keep him there forever.

She quivered wherever he touched her—and he touched her all over, even there in the forbidden place between her thighs. Her head was spinning when at last he levered himself over her.

"I'll try not to hurt you, princess." The words were a hot mutter against the curve of her jaw. "Don't be afraid."

She caught his head in her hands and ran her thumbs over the fullness of his lower lip. She smiled, a smile of sweet serenity. "You won't hurt me," she whispered, "and I could never be afraid of you."

A groan broke from his chest. Even as he took her mouth in a deep, fervent kiss, he eased within her body, his penetration agonizingly slow.

A sharp sting was all Emily felt . . . It had scarcely registered before it began to fade. There was no pain, only a delicious sense of being filled as never before, a marvelous sense of oneness and completion.

At last he lay fully planted within her silken depths. She smiled anew. "You see," she chided gently, "I knew you wouldn't hurt me." A sigh escaped. "How could anyone be afraid of something so wonderful?"

He gave a half-laugh, half-groan. And then he kissed her, a kiss so sweetly tender she could have cried. A wellspring of emotion poured through her, every part of her. She wrapped her arms around him and clung, burying her face against the side of his neck.

"I love you," she said helplessly. "Oh, Andre, I love you so much . . ." The words were torn from deep inside her.

With a ragged moan Andre caught them with his lips. He abandoned all hope of restraint. He began to move, slowly at first, and then faster and faster as the tempest within rose to a crescendo. Their hips met again and again, a dance of primitive glory. It pushed them both toward the edge, bringing them to a shattering release.

It was a long time later that Andre eased to his side next to her. A possessive hand at her hip, he bent low and availed himself of a kiss. To his shock, he saw that her eyes were filled with tears . . .

Alarm skittered through him. "Emily," he cried, "what is it? Did I hurt you?"

She turned and reached for him. "No, Andre, no! It was—quite wonderful." Faith, but the word seemed so inadequate! "Indeed, I could ask for no more . . . except, perhaps . . ."

He peered into her face. "What, princess, what?"

"If only I'd been able to see you," she whispered.

Her heartache bled through to her voice. Andre drew her close, battling a feeling of weary helplessness. He could only imagine what it was like for her—to grow to womanhood with sight unimpaired, only to be robbed of it in little more than the blink of an eye.

His arms tightened. She lived in a world without color and light, he thought achingly. Were it only within his power, he would gladly give up his very soul, if only she could see again.

He kissed her temple, cradling her tight against his side. "Go to sleep," he urged softly. Miraculously, she did.

Instead it was Andre who lay awake long into the night.

Sunshine poured through the window the next morning, filling the bedroom with dappled splashes of light. A quick glance revealed Emily was still asleep. He eased out of bed, careful not to jar her.

As he pulled on his clothes, the sunlight caught the reflection of a small object that lay atop the bureau—it was the crystal he'd given her. He drew a sharp breath. His expression softened. So. She'd kept it.

His gaze swung back to her. She lay on her back, her hair spilling all around like the halo of an angel, her lips slightly parted. Unable to resist temptation's lure, he bent, just barely grazing her lips with his.

She stirred, rolling to her side. "Andre?" she murmured sleepily. Her eyelids fluttered, then opened. To his surprise, she squeezed them shut again. "The light!" he heard her say.

Andre went utterly still. Was it possible . . . ? He sucked in a breath. His head swiveled slowly. He stared at the crystal.

Emily seemed to share the same thought as well. An expression of sheer puzzlement flitted across her features. Her hands flitted to her eyes. "The light," she breathed, only now it was with a sense of wonder.

She was fully awake by now. "Andre!" she cried.

He was at her side in a heartbeat. "I'm here, princess." He forced down the excitement gathering in his chest. "Emily, did you see something? Anything?"

"I—I thought I did. I—I said nothing to you or Olivia, but it happened last week as well. Only now it seemed much . . ."

"What? Emily, *what?*"

Her hands had come up to shield her eyes. She was shaking. "Much brighter," she said faintly. She drew a deep, quivering breath. "My crystal," she said suddenly. "Where is it, Andre? I—I need it!"

What if it was true? What if she regained her sight? In truth, he'd never thought it would come to pass. For one mind-splitting instant, he was tempted to dissuade her, for if she saw him, she would know . . . An arrow of guilt sliced through him. No. *No.* If it were possible for her to see again, he could not take this from her . . . He *would* not.

He shook his head. "You don't need it, princess."

"But you said it had great healing powers—and it does! Now I know for certain!"

"No. No, princess. The crystal has no special powers. I told you that because I thought it might help if you had something to believe in . . . Oh, don't you see, it's you. This is happening because of you! You wanted to see and—and now you are." He coiled his fingers around her wrists. "Open your eyes, love."

Her fingers separated. She peered through them, only to screw her eyes closed again. "It hurts! Andre, it—it's too bright."

He rushed to close the curtains, then returned to her. "The curtains are closed. Please, Emily, try again."

She gave a stricken cry, a sound that tore into him like a blade. "I'm afraid. I'm afraid it's just another dream and—and when I wake, the world will be dark again."

His heart went out to her. "It's no dream, I promise you. You'll never know unless you try, princess. Open your eyes and—and look at me!"

She was trembling from head to toe.

"Oh, please, princess. This is what you wanted, remember?"

He was right, Emily realized achingly. This was what she'd longed for, almost from the very day they'd met. She was suddenly compelled by the need to see her beloved Andre, a yearning more powerful than anything she'd ever experienced before.

She lowered her hands and lifted her lids slowly. A pale gray haze danced before her.

"That's the way, princess. Now, look at me. What do you see?"

She was afraid even to breathe. "It's like looking through a dark curtain," she whispered. Her lids half-closed.

Andre groaned and settled his palms on each side of her face. Her lashes fluttered closed as he kissed her, a sweetly tender caress. She gave a breathy little sigh. Her lips parted beneath the warmth of his. "Once more," he murmured huskily, just before he raised his head. "Open your eyes just once more, love."

Love. Emily's heart contracted. He'd told her how much he loved her over and over again last night.

Holding her breath, she did as he asked.

There were shadows and light. They seemed to shift and blur . . . but wait! The outline of a face swam fuzzily before her. She blinked several times until at last she could focus.

Her pulse began to race. She saw eyes, so dark they were almost black. Hair tumbled over his forehead, as black as the wings of a raven. His skin was burned dark from the sun . . . She bit back a cry of sheer joy. Finally—finally!—she could see her beloved Andre . . .

The image sharpened. Her mind registered a shirt of bright red, and a kerchief tied loosely around his neck.

Her heart began to pound with thick, dull strokes. Her blood seemed to freeze. Shock made the world reel and tilt.

She cringed inside. It was impossible—impossible! Yet the proof was here before her. Her beloved Andre was a . . .

A Gypsy.

She hurtled from the bed, still staring. "No," she heard herself say, and then it was a cry of denial, a cry of agony: "*No!*"

He extended a hand. "Princess—"

She slapped it away. "Don't call me that! Don't ever call me that again!"

Her gaze scraped over him, contemptuous and accusing. He endured it as best he could. But before he could say a word she lashed out fiercely. "Damn you! Why didn't you tell me you're a—a Gypsy!" She nearly spat the word.

Andre steeled himself against the hurt, both inside and out. "I will not lie, Emily. I did not tell you because I was afraid you would refuse to see me again, and I could not bear the thought."

She paid no heed. "You talked about your family, how you didn't know how long they might stay . . . Oh, Lord . . . you meant the Gypsies!"

Andre raised his chin. "I did," he said levelly. "They are my family, as much my family as my parents who died long ago."

She made a sound that told how she felt only too well.

He took a deep, racking breath. She was right. He should have told her. But he would have lost her—he knew it now for certain. Yet perhaps it would have been better after all. It wouldn't have *hurt* the way it did now.

A hot tide of color seeped beneath the bronze of his skin. "Do you think this is easy for me? Do you think I haven't felt guilty each and every time I've been with you? Especially after you told me your father was killed by a Gypsy! I—I didn't know what to do!" With his eyes he begged for her understanding. "If I had told you, I would have risked losing you, and I couldn't do that!"

"Oh!" she cried. "So you were only thinking about yourself! Well, what about me? Did you ever think about how I might feel if I knew?"

"I admit it. I was selfish." His eyes bored into hers. "What about last night? Did it mean nothing to you?" He took a step forward. "Emily, I love you. Nothing has changed—"

Her eyes welled with tears. "Everything has changed!" she cried wildly. "I didn't know what you are . . . who you are!"

"I am the same as before," he said very quietly. "Emily, if you think about it, you'll realize it."

Sending a fervent pray heavenward, he reached for her.

She shrank away. "You are what you are. A dirty, thieving Gypsy and I—I hate you!"

She might as well have struck him. His hand fell to his side. His heart plummeted to the floor. There would be no reasoning with her, he decided wearily. There would be no changing her mind.

His gaze roved her face, as if to memorize each and every feature—as indeed he was.

"Good-bye, princess," he said very softly. With that he turned and was gone.

She stood there, trembling from head to toe. She could scarcely move for the torment that rent her insides. It was then she saw it . . .

The rose he'd given her. It had fallen from the bedside table.

A half-sob tore from her throat. She picked it up and stared at it. Only when the blood welled bright and crimson from her fingertip did she realize she'd been pricked by a thorn . . .

The hurt was nothing compared to the pain in her heart.

Eighteen

Dominic woke to the sound of a lone bird trilling outside the window. His gaze sped immediately to the spot next to him.

She was gone.

He couldn't stop the disappointment that flooded him as he saw empty space beside him. He ran a hand along the indentation left by her body. The sheets were still warm. He smiled slightly. She'd burrowed against him the night through, her arm draped across his belly, her nose buried in the cloud of hair on his chest. He remembered warm, moist breath pooling across his skin, the press of round, full breasts against his side.

He sighed. Both times when he'd lain with her he woke alone. He longed to nuzzle her awake, kiss her sleep-warm body to wakefulness while his own stirred to life! They'd spend a lazy morning in bed, just the two of them. They would share breakfast in bed . . . and each other. Perhaps even a long, leisurely bath, he decided wickedly . . .

It was a wild, erotic fantasy—one he hoped would come true. Still, he couldn't help but feel cheated somehow.

Not that he blamed Olivia. He knew why—knew

the gossip that would result if any one of the servants or villagers discovered their relationship. His mouth turned down. His day was full, since he'd scheduled visits with several of his tenants on the outskirts of his property. If not for that, he would . . .

What would he do? A voice inside chided him. He could hardly spirit her away as he had last night, not in the full light of day. It was so damned hard to pretend they were strangers—that there was nothing between them, when all he wanted was to drag her into his arms and keep her there . . . for a lifetime.

Belatedly he questioned his judgment, now when it was too late. By spiriting her away to his chamber, he had jeopardized her virtue, her good name. Perhaps she was right, and he *was* accustomed to getting his way. Yet never had he felt a passion so keenly, so deeply he could think of little else.

It was then he spied the jade ball gown. They'd left it in a heap on the floor; she must have picked it up and laid it upon the chair. Lord, but she'd looked enchantingly lovely! He wished she'd been able to take it. The next time . . .

The next time, he promised himself, would be far different.

The next time would be as his wife.

The curtains were drawn tightly closed when Olivia opened the door to the cottage late that afternoon. It struck her as odd as she stepped inside. She frowned. Was Emily ill?

She removed her bonnet and hung it on the hook near the door. "Emily," she called.

There was no reply.

Worried now, Olivia hurried into the parlor. Emily lay upon the settee, one arm thrown across her eyes.

"Emily! Heavens, you frightened the devil out of me! Why didn't you answer?"

"I—I didn't hear you." Emily pushed herself to a sitting position.

It was an excuse. Olivia knew it instantly. She sat beside her, laying a hand on her arm. "Love," she said gently, "what is it? Are you feeling poorly?"

Her answer was slow in coming. "I'm fine, Olivia."

Olivia's gaze sharpened. She sounded so odd! With the waning sunlight but a trickle through the window on the other side of the cottage, the light was dim. Not until now did she notice that Emily's lovely blue eyes were red-rimmed and swollen.

"Emily! You've been crying!" Olivia was immediately penitent. "Oh, love, I'm sorry to have left you alone for so long—"

" 'Tis not that." Emily clasped her hands together in her lap and stared at them.

"What then?" Olivia's stomach knotted. She tried not to be alarmed, but she couldn't help it. Emily had been so happy and gay these last weeks. But now . . . She was reminded of those days after Emily had gone blind—she'd had to plead and cajole to persuade Emily even to rise in the morning.

Something was horribly, horribly wrong.

She laid a hand atop Emily's. "Emily, please tell me what's wrong."

Slowly Emily raised her head and looked at her.

In that instant between one breath and the next, it struck her that something was different. Emily's gaze was no longer vague. She regarded her as if . . .

As if she could see her.

Olivia's heart was pounding so hard it hurt. "Emily—" Her voice sounded nothing like her own. "—you can see me, can't you?"

Her lips tremulous, Emily nodded.

Olivia was suddenly laughing and crying all at once. She hugged her sister fiercely. "You can see again," she cried over and over. "You can see again!"

Only when the euphoria began to fade did she realize there was no answering joy in her sister's manner. Emily returned her embrace, but it was a token response.

She retreated slightly, then reached for Emily's hand. Her fingers were ice-cold despite the warmth of the day. Worriedly she searched her sister's pale features.

"Emily, you should be delirious with happiness. Why, this is what you've longed for these many months—to see again."

To her shock Emily's eyes filled with tears.

"I thought it would be the most wondrous day of my life," she choked out. "Instead I fear it's the worst."

"But . . . how can that be?"

Emily shook her head. "I've done something terrible, Olivia." She couldn't withhold a half-sob. "I—I've fallen in love."

"But . . . that's not terrible at all. Why, 'tis a wondrous thing!"

"No." Her tone was as forlorn as her expression. "It is not."

"Why not? Doesn't he love you?"

"He—he said he does."

"Then why this melancholy? If he loves you, and you love him—"

Emily's eyes were two endless pools of pain. "Olivia," she whispered, "he is a Gypsy."

Olivia felt the blood drain from her face. "Dear God," she said faintly. Her mind swerved straight to Dominic. Of course that wasn't possible, yet who on earth could it be? A dozen questions spun through her. How had it happened? When? And where on earth had Emily encountered one of the Gypsies?

She clasped Emily's hand within hers. "Tell me what happened," she said quietly. "Where did you meet this Gypsy?"

"I met him in the village one day. Esther—oh, I know I should have told you earlier—but sometimes on our walks she would dart into the alehouse. Just for a drop, she would always say. But one day, it was growing dark and still she didn't return. I'd begun to grow quite frightened, wondering how I should get home, when he saw me sitting there in the village square."

"The Gypsy?"

Emily nodded. "His name is Andre."

Andre! Olivia very nearly gasped. She recalled the handsome young Gypsy she'd met at the camp with Dominic. Was it he? She had a very good idea it was.

"Olivia, he was so charming—so concerned! I know I should never have relied on a stranger, but I—I allowed him to escort me home. I could tell he was not a gentleman, that he was a workingman. A farmer, I thought, but he told me he worked with horses, buying and selling and trading."

A Gypsy trade, Olivia thought silently. With her sight impaired, she could see how Emily had never guessed he was a Gypsy.

Just as she could understand why Andre—taken with a lovely young woman who could not see him—would never have carelessly divulged the fact that he was a Gypsy.

Emily bit her lip guiltily. "I saw him many days when you were at Ravenwood," she confided in a small voice. "I know I should have told you. But I was afraid you might be angry—that you wouldn't allow me to see him again."

Olivia listened quietly while the story poured out. How Andre had sold the lace she'd been making. How it was not long before her feelings blossomed into something far beyond friendship. How he'd given her the crystal with healing powers. To think she'd felt so guilty about leaving Emily alone so many times! Olivia was secretly glad Emily hadn't been alone at all.

She could hardly deliver the chastisement Emily seemed to expect. For if Emily was guilty of loving a Gypsy . . .

Then so was she.

Olivia squeezed her hand. "Does he know how Papa died?"

"Yes. I told him several weeks ago that Papa was murdered by a Gypsy, yet still he didn't tell me! He deceived me, Olivia. He deceived me and I—I hate him! I—I told him I never wanted to see him again."

"So he won't be back then," Olivia said gently, "will he?"

Emily's eyes seemed to blaze, then suddenly her

face crumpled. "No," she whispered. Two large tears brimmed and overflowed.

Olivia slid an arm around her shoulders, while Emily wept her heart out. She held her, and offered what comfort she could. If Emily was confused, it was no wonder. To have watched their father die at the hands of a Gypsy, only to fall in love with one . . .

She said she hated Andre.

Olivia wasn't so certain.

After a while, Emily fell into an exhausted sleep on the settee. Olivia tenderly smoothed her sister's cheek, then rose. It was still difficult to comprehend that Emily had regained her sight—almost as difficult as it had been when she'd lost it. In some corner of herself, she wondered if that, too, was not because of Andre.

There was a knock on the door. Olivia hurried to open it. To her surprise it was Dominic. Before she could say a word he stepped inside and closed the door.

Without a word he pulled her into his arms. His mouth captured hers. Olivia struggled against an insidious pleasure. *No,* she thought vaguely. This was not right. She could not do this, not with Emily so near. How could she find pleasure in his kiss, when her sister lay brokenhearted in the next room?

It was she who broke off the kiss. She stepped back. "Dominic! I—I didn't know you were back." It was Charlotte who'd told her he'd gone to visit his tenants early that afternoon.

"I've only just returned."

There was a protracted silence. He regarded her

with eyes that saw everything, eyes that seemed to reach inside her very soul.

"What's the matter, Olivia?"

Olivia floundered. *Everything*, she wanted to shout. Her nerves were suddenly screaming. Last night had been . . . the most wondrous night of her life. But this morning, when she had crept from his bed, reality staked its claim once more. Doubt crept in, like a rising tide. She made love with him, not just once, but twice. *Twice*. What had she been thinking?

But it was Emily who commanded her attention just now. Emily's day had been traumatic, fraught with upheaval. This was hardly the time to confess to Emily her relationship with Dominic—if only he were not half-Gypsy! And indeed, she thought shakily, *she* was not precisely sure what that relationship was. She was not his mistress, though she had certainly behaved like one. So what was she then? His lover?

She winced inside. His mistress. His lover. Both sounded cheap and—and tawdry.

No, she decided. She darted a hasty glance over her shoulder, toward the parlor where Emily lay sleeping. She could not explain, not here. Not now. Emily's wound was still too fresh. Her sister needed no further reminders of Andre.

Dominic saw the direction of her gaze. His eyes narrowed. "What is it?" he demanded. "Who is inside? Someone besides Emily?"

Olivia lost her temper. "Of course not!" she snapped. "Now if you don't mind, I must ask you to leave."

His gaze was suddenly hard and glittering. "You don't want her to know I'm here, do you?"

Olivia straightened her spine. She spoke the only thing she dared. "I think you'd better leave."

The cast of his jaw was rigid. "Regrets already, eh, Miss Sherwood. I find I'm curious, however. Have you decided I'm too good for the poor vicar's daughter—or are you too good for a man who's half-Gypsy?"

Olivia's eyes widened. She didn't answer; she couldn't. She was stunned that such a thing would even cross his mind.

At her silence he made a sound of disgust and turned away. Four steps took him back to the door, which slammed in his wake. His posture was wooden, his expression taut. Only then did she realize he'd mistaken her silence for concurrence. She could only guess at the hurt he must have felt.

She couldn't stand the thought. He'd suffered enough at the hands of his father, and she wouldn't do the same.

She went after him. He was at Storm's side before she reached him. "Dominic!" she cried. "Dominic, wait, you don't understand—"

He'd already swung up onto Storm's back. His lip curled. "Oh, I understand, Miss Sherwood. I understand only too well." He whirled Storm around and was gone.

Olivia stared after him, a stark pain wedged in her chest. A tiny little voice inside refused to be silent. Perhaps it was better this way, it whispered. *How?* she wondered achingly. *How?*

Her spirit heavy, she retraced her steps back into the cottage. In the parlor Emily stirred, opening her eyes.

"Olivia? Was someone here? I thought I heard voices."

Olivia turned away so that Emily wouldn't see the single hot tear that scalded her cheek. "No one," she said sadly. "Go back to sleep, love."

Dominic sat in his study, watching the purple haze of twilight creep over the horizon. His mood was black as the devil's soul. *Damn her*, he thought viciously. *Damn her!*

He hadn't forced her to come to his chamber last night. Why had she bothered? Did she regret it? Did she feel she'd been tainted by his Gypsy blood? Only last night, he'd held her close to his heart, as close as two people could be. Yet this evening she'd been so very cool! She hadn't wanted to see him— 'twas so very obvious! Why did she hold him so distant?

He didn't understand it. He didn't understand *her*. He wanted her to share everything with him— her body. Her soul. Her every thought . . .

A voice within urged patience. *'Tis too soon. This thing between you is still so new, so tenuous . . . Or perhaps she is as uncertain of you as you are of her.*

His jaw locked hard and tight. No. No! It was disdain he'd glimpsed in those beautiful green eyes. Was she ashamed of what had happened between them—ashamed of laying with him? His mouth twisted. Certainly it would seem so.

There was only one way to know for certain.

He had no conscious recollection of striding into the stables and saddling Storm. The next thing he knew he was riding back to Stonebridge, to the small cottage on the far side of the village. But what he saw made his belly tighten and his jaw clench.

He recognized the bay gelding nibbling at the grass beneath the oak tree.

William Dunsport was there.

He reined Storm to a halt a short distance away. The dim glow of a lamp lit the interior with a hazy glow. Through the lace curtains he could make out the shadows of two figures on the settee. The minutes ticked by, one by one.

Still Dunsport didn't come out.

A slow burn had already begun to simmer along Dominic's veins. Then he saw it . . . The unmistakable silhouette of two figures rising, one much taller than the other . . . locked fast in each other's arms.

A vile curse blackened the air. His fingers clenched into fists on the reins. He had to leave— he had to, else he might very well charge into the cottage and tear the pair apart.

And he was suddenly very certain both would take vehement exception to such an interruption.

A heel at his flank, he wheeled Storm and urged him back the way they had come. By the time he arrived back at Ravenwood, he was seething.

He looked for solace in his best bottle of brandy, yet found little. Would Olivia give to William what she'd given to him only last night? The thought was like a thorn in his heart.

His mind turned fleetingly back to that long-ago night at the Gypsy camp. It was then that he'd begun to think they had something special, that she'd begun to comprehend that the Gypsies were not the terrible people everyone was so convinced they were . . . that *he* was not. Was it all just a lie? He meant nothing to her . . .

Perhaps he never had.

*   *   *

"You regained your sight only today?" William shook his head as he took a sip of tea. "It's really quite amazing."

"Yes." Emily smiled faintly. "It really is."

On the one hand Olivia could have almost thanked William for his unannounced visit—though Emily had been rather subdued, Olivia had the feeling William's presence was all that stopped her sister from breaking down in tears again. On the other hand, she'd been chafing since the moment he'd arrived. She had no desire to spend the evening in his company.

None of this showed as she reached for the teapot. "Emily? William? More tea?"

"None for me, Olivia," Emily said quickly. She got to her feet. "I know it's frightfully rude, but I—I'm really quite fatigued. Would you mind terribly if I retired for the night?" She directed the question to both William and Olivia.

William was on his feet already, taking her hand. "Not at all, Miss Sherwood. May I say again how delighted I am for you?"

Emily managed a slight smile. "Thank you, sir. You're very kind."

Olivia gave her an encouraging nod. "Good night, Emily," she said softly. "Sleep well."

For one horrible moment she feared she'd said the wrong thing—Emily looked ready to cry. But all she said was, "I shall try."

With that Olivia and William were left alone.

Olivia tensed. She'd dreaded this moment since she'd first opened the door and found him there. In truth, she'd never have opened it if she'd known it was William—the only reason she had answered his knock was because she'd thought it was Dominic.

There was a clink as William replaced his teacup in its saucer. He spread his hands wide, then settled them on his knees.

"Olivia," he murmured. "I don't know what to say other than . . . I owe you an apology. I behaved abominably at our last meeting."

So you did. Olivia had to bite back the reply. Oh, now he was oh-so-contrite. But she'd not forgotten the ugliness of his manner when they'd last met— nor would she.

Yet what was the point? In all honesty, she didn't care enough to remain angry.

She inclined her head and even managed a smile. "Thank you, William." She spoke very low so that they wouldn't disturb Emily. "I accept your apology."

William edged closer on the settee, so close their knees nearly touched.

Olivia stiffened. "Now, if you don't mind, I fear I've had a tiring day as well."

He extended a hand. "No," he said quickly. "Olivia, please wait. I—I have something I must say."

Olivia paused, though something within her prickled a warning. She brushed it aside. "What is it, William?"

He gazed at her steadily. "Olivia, nothing has changed. I still wish to marry you."

Well, I don't wish to marry you! she longed to screech. Instead she sighed, and gave a shake of her head. "William," she said earnestly, "please listen to me. I cannot marry you."

"Why not? You can no longer cite your sister's affliction. She is no longer blind. Oh, I know you're angry that I spoke of our wedding prematurely, and I regret that we had words over it. But it was naught but a lovers' tiff—"

"No, William, it was not. We are not lovers, nor will we *ever* be, for I will not marry you. Now, if you please, I must ask you to leave." She started to rise but he was quicker. All at once he seized her in a bruising grip.

"And I say again, it was just a lovers' tiff. Come now, Olivia, let us kiss and make up." Even as he spoke, he was aiming for her lips.

Olivia gasped. Wrenching her head aside, she managed to escape his kiss. Instead his mouth landed on the side of her neck, hot and wet. She pounded on his chest.

"Release me this instant," she warned as loudly as she dared. "If you don't, I'll scream for my sister."

Slowly he raised his head. Fear leaped in her breast. For one paralyzing instant, she glimpsed a depth of rage in those cold blue eyes that was frightening.

His lips drew back in a snarl. "It's him, isn't it? Your precious Gypsy. That's why you won't marry me. God, but I don't know what you see in him— he may have a title but he's still a Gypsy, and everyone knows they're beggars and thieves!"

"Dominic has nothing to do with this." As she spoke, she managed to slide her hands between their bodies.

He sneered. "Oh, so it's Dominic now, is it? I saw the two of you, you know, that day by the stream— the bastard should have drowned!"

Olivia finally managed to give a mighty shove against his chest. Caught off balance, his hold loosened. She broke free and grabbed the poker from the stand near the fireplace.

"I don't think he would be very pleased if he knew you were here, William," was all she said. "If you leave now, I won't tell him." It was bravado, sheer and simple. After today, she had no doubt Dominic would be the last one to defend her!

William pretended to dust off his sleeves. "There's no need for that, Olivia. I'll leave. But remember this. Your precious Gypsy lord may not be here forever, and then what will you do?" He gave an exaggerated bow. "Don't bother to see me out. I'll find my way."

In seconds he was gone. The door crashed in his wake. Olivia very nearly dropped the poker, stunned to discover she was shaking both inside and out.

The sound of the door had roused Emily, who suddenly appeared. "Olivia? Is William gone? I thought I heard shouting."

Olivia steadied herself. She didn't know whether to laugh or cry. "Yes, love, he's gone. Go back to sleep," she said for the second time that day.

Five minutes later she was rummaging through the bureau drawer in search of her nightgown. She pulled it out, but with it came a neatly embroidered square of linen.

Dominic's handkerchief, the handkerchief he'd pressed to her cheek the night they'd met.

Her knees were suddenly so weak she dropped to the floor. Her throat burned as she fought the urge not to cry. All this time she'd kept it. A dozen times she'd thought of giving it back . . . yet she hadn't. Why, she wondered, had she kept it?

She was all at once reminded of what William

had said. *They're beggars and thieves. Beggars and thieves* . . .

She crushed the handkerchief to her breast . . . as if it were Dominic's hand.

She was very much afraid he wouldn't be back. He was too proud to beg. As for being a thief, well, perhaps he was . . .

A thief who'd stolen her very heart.

Nineteen

Olivia was worried about Emily. Each day she grew ever more pale and wan. Her appetite was scant. She was clearly devastated that Andre was no longer a part of her life. Perhaps she was wrong, but Olivia reasoned that if Emily truly hated Andre, she could have put it aside—this state of despair would have long since passed. When Olivia tried to talk with her further, Emily refused.

"I don't want to think of him."

Ha! Olivia thought. Clearly he was *all* she thought of. She was more convinced than ever . . .

Emily still loved Andre.

Yet what could she do? Nothing. She reminded herself that Emily was no longer a child. This was something she could not do for her; even if she could, it was not her place. It was up to Emily to search out the furthest depths of her heart and find her answer.

As for Olivia, it seemed that she, too, must look to her heart for the truth.

She loved him. She loved him madly, yet it was a love that could only hurt. During those days when she was particularly distraught, she reached a bitter resolve. She couldn't take the chance that

Emily might find out—her state of mind was too fragile just now. If Emily should discover that her sister loved Dominic—to Emily it would not matter that he was only half-Gypsy—Olivia knew not what would happen. Nor would she take the chance.

What happened between them was over and done with.

Not that it seemed it could have been any other way. Olivia saw little of Dominic over the next several days. Charlotte was with her once—his nod of greeting encompassed them both. She saw him another time on the staircase. He looked straight at her, but did not speak. His coolness stabbed at her. Was he still angry? Or had he merely used her for his own pleasure and was now finished with her?

All the more reason to forget him . . . Ah, forget! Her heart twisted. How could she, when she dreamed of him nightly? Only last night she'd dreamed that she had kissed him in that brazenly erotic way he had kissed her—there, between the corded stretch of his thighs, her tongue tasting and swirling . . . As if that were not enough, the next thing she knew she was astride his hips, her hands braced on the taut plane of his chest. A teasing smile in place, she gazed down at him as she balanced herself on the very tip of his manhood . . .

The dream had awakened her from a sound sleep. Her pulse was pounding, echoing in her ears, and there was a damp heat gathered there in her secret cleft. She was aghast that her mind had even conceived of such audacious behavior. Faith, just thinking about it singed her every nerve ending. But she was given to wonder, did men and women *do* such things? The first particularly she was curious about—yet if he received even half as much pleasure as she had . . .

Odd, how it was on her mind that afternoon as she entered the library to dust. She thought the room was empty, but she was dismayed to find Dominic, reading in a velvet-covered chair near the window. A moment passed before it began to penetrate, and then she stood stock-still. *No*, she thought, *it could not be*. He was reading . . .

Reading.

He must have realized he was not alone, for he glanced up and saw her. He stood. The book clapped shut. He replaced it on the shelf behind him, then turned to face her.

"Miss Sherwood," he murmured, "the very person I wish to see."

Olivia was too incensed to notice. She took a deep breath and nodded at the book he placed on the shelf. "May I ask, sir, what you are doing?"

A brow arched high. " 'Tis not so difficult to see, Miss Sherwood. I was reading."

Olivia forgot her place in the household. She forgot everything but a fiery indignation that grew hotter with each moment. Within her glare smoldered an accusation.

"You said you couldn't read."

"No, Miss Sherwood. Never did I say that."

"No! You did. You said you ran away from school. You asked me to read that letter from—from your mistress!"

"As I recall, I'd had a cup too much and was feeling rather muddled."

"But . . . you said your father was angry because you couldn't read—that you relished the times your tutor ran to him, bemoaning the fact that you could not read, that you refused to listen and learn."

He merely looked amused. "And so you thought I could neither read nor write?"

"Can you?" she countered swiftly. "Can you read? Can you write?"

"Of course I can. How else could I conduct my business dealings?"

Olivia felt like a fool. Hot shame crept beneath her skin, because she had assumed—and wrongly so, it seemed!—that it was true, that he could neither read nor write.

"I did not belittle you," she said between lips that barely moved. "Must you belittle me?"

"I've done no such thing. Come now, Olivia. Can you deny you were always determined to think the worst of me?"

"But—you let me believe it!"

His eyes flickered. "As I recall, it was a matter never discussed between the two of us."

Olivia said nothing. Her mouth compressed, she spun around and headed for the door. Suddenly he was there before her—tall, virile and looking far too pleased with himself!

Her head came up. Her chin jutted forward. "Let me pass."

"Not while you're angry." A brittle smile on his lips, he reached behind and deliberately closed the door. Folding his arms over his chest, he regarded her. "If either of us deserves to be angry, 'tis I."

"You!" Her glare burned hotter. "I cannot think why!"

"You have a convenient memory, Olivia, but I don't forget quite so easily. I was not allowed to set foot within your cottage—yet you admitted him quite freely."

All at once the battle had shifted. Olivia paled a shade, for she was totally unprepared to defend herself. Her gaze slid away. "I don't know what you mean."

"And I'm quite sure you do. However, I'll refresh your memory if you insist." His smile had vanished. His mouth was a straight unyielding line. "You asked me to leave, while you welcomed William Dunsport with open arms. You turned me out, yet you had no qualms about admitting him into your home," he said again.

"Only because I thought it was you!" she cried before she thought better of it.

Dominic's eyes narrowed. His breath caught. His heart bounded. Perhaps he was wrong, and she *did* care . . .

"Then why did you ask me to leave?"

"Because I didn't know what else to do! Do you remember I told you a Gypsy killed my father?"

"Yes, but that has nothing to do with us."

"It has everything to do with us! When I arrived home, Emily was distraught." Suddenly it was all pouring out, how Emily had been seeing a young man, how she had regained her sight, only to discover that her suitor was a Gypsy.

Dominic looked startled, as startled as she surely had when she discovered Emily had been seeing Andre.

With her eyes she pleaded with him. "Don't you see, it wasn't *you*! I did not mean to hurt you, truly, but I feared that if she saw you, it would only remind her of Andre."

Dominic stroked his chin. "I can understand

your concern," he said slowly. He was silent for a moment. "Why have you been avoiding me?"

"I have not. I've been here in this very house!"

"And so have I. I'm hardly a stranger, you know, yet you refuse even to look at me. Even those times when you've been alone. *Especially* those times."

She looked at him now. He was dressed in a simple white shirt, dark breeches and boots. A lock of dark hair had fallen upon his forehead, lending him an almost boyishly handsome look.

An unexpected wave of despair washed over her. Olivia felt suddenly tired, tired beyond her years. There had been so much tumult. She longed simply to throw herself against him and forget all but the strength of his arms around her. Indeed, the temptation was almost more than she could withstand. Yet that would only complicate the matter far more than it was already!

His tone was very quiet. "I asked you a question, Olivia. Why have you avoided me?"

Olivia had a very good idea where this conversation was headed, and it was a road she would rather not take.

Her lashes fell, shielding her expression. She was deliberately vague. "I cannot think what you mean," she said faintly.

"Can't you?" He was as determined as ever. "Aren't you forgetting what happened between us—here in this very house? Not just once, but twice?"

His voice jabbed at her like the point of a knife. She winced. "I have not."

He stepped near, so near the hem of her skirts brushed his breeches. "Nor have I."

She quivered inside. She could feel the weight of

his regard, yet it was just as he'd said—she couldn't look at him. Instead she focused on the squareness of his jaw, dark with the day's growth of beard. He needed to shave, she thought vaguely.

She swallowed. "Must you remind me?" she asked, her voice very low.

He stiffened. "You were quite willing—"

"I know," she said quickly. "But I did not stop to think how I would feel . . . later. Oh, I do not know how to explain . . . ! I'm not like the women you knew in London. I cannot do . . . what we did . . . and treat it as if it were nothing—"

"And I have not asked you to." He studied her. A nagging suspicion began to dance in his head. "Did you think I would use you and cast you off?"

Olivia was certain her face was scarlet. "I—I did not know. I *do* not know." She drew a deep, shuddering breath. "I am not so naive as you think. I know that there are men who use women in their households for their own base needs and think nothing of it. Though I am not a lady, I—"

"Stop," he commanded softly. "Say no more." His knuckles beneath her chin, he guided her eyes to his. "You, Miss Olivia Sherwood, are the truest lady I have ever known—" The corner of his mouth turned up. "—quite possibly the *only* lady I have ever known."

Why was he doing this? His tone reached clear inside her, making her melt inside. "A lady would never have done . . . what I have done."

That made him smile. "You were hardly alone in this venture."

Her gaze skipped away, then returned. She gazed at him earnestly. " 'Tis different for a man."

"Not always." His smile deepened. He loved

seeing this side of her. Solemn. Sweet. Ever concerned with what was proper. The vicar's daughter to be sure . . .

"Oh, don't you see! I—I don't know what happens next. How I should feel!"

She sounded so miserable he almost laughed. "Perhaps we should leave that to chance. To fate, if you will. But I forget. You don't believe in that, do you?"

Even as he spoke, he drew her inexorably nearer. Her eyes clung to his. "Do not—mock me."

"I would never mock you," he whispered, and then his mouth claimed hers, warm and undemanding, a kiss that spoke more of consolation than passion. Her eyes drifted closed. Her hands uncurled on his chest. Her lips parted. She gave in to it, to him—and to herself.

His nearness was an irresistible lure. She felt a tingle in the tips of her breasts, a prelude to passion. A quickening heat stormed all through her. She knew he felt it, too, for his hands tightened on her waist. Like the flickering of a candle, she felt her resolve begin to waver.

She couldn't let it—she couldn't! The memory of the night in his arms was suddenly all too vivid. She'd felt—as if she belonged there! But Emily had been through so much . . .

With a low, jagged moan, she broke away. "I can't," she cried softly. "*I can't!*" Her eyes were suddenly swimming with tears. There was Emily to think of . . . and when he kissed her, she couldn't think at all!

Picking up her skirts, she rushed from the library, praying he wouldn't come after her.

He didn't.

She didn't trust him yet, he realized.

Bitterly he wondered if she ever would.

"Ye're very quiet tonight," Charlotte remarked as they departed Ravenwood the next day. "Are ye feelin' poorly?"

Olivia summoned a smile. "I'm fine, Charlotte. But thank you for asking." In truth, she was more confused than ever.

It didn't help when she glanced over to find Charlotte regarding her with a secret smile.

She sighed. "What? What is it? What are you thinking?"

"I don't want ye to be angry with me."

Olivia tweaked the end of Charlotte's curling red braid. "Have I ever been angry with you?"

Charlotte flashed a broad grin. "Come to think of it, ye haven't. Anyway, I saw the two of ye once in his study—ye and the earl—when you were workin' on his books. He was leaning over ye, and ye were lookin' up at 'im, and I couldn't help but think the two o' ye belonged together."

Olivia blinked. Surely she didn't *know* . . . "Why, that's ridiculous, Charlotte. Whyever would you think that?"

"Ye forget, I've already been in love. I know how the world wags."

Olivia couldn't help but chuckle. Charlotte was hardly older than herself. "And how is that?"

"Ye've only to watch 'im watch *ye* to know."

A pang swept through her. Oh, if only . . . "Nonsense," she said crisply. "He'll marry someone like Elizabeth Beaumont. Or a fine lady in London."

"Elizabeth Beaumont?" Charlotte gave an unladylike snort. "Never!"

"Oh, come now—"

"Mark my word, it'll never 'appen," Charlotte pronounced stoutly. "I watched him at the ball. *Ye* were the one his eyes followed, not her.

"I could tell the way he looked. Oh, he pretended to be polite, but every so often, his eyes would roam—lookin' for ye, no doubt. The twit, she didn't even notice! She still kept 'anging onto him like—like ivy to a tree!"

Olivia's heart pounded a ragged rhythm. Was it true? She didn't know. But she did know that Charlotte's observations were taking a direction that was best left well enough alone.

"I cannot believe I was so frightened of him before he came," Charlotte went on. "He's not at all as I expected. A bit stern-lookin' at times, and he speaks so quiet-like! Colin adores him. He says he wants to be an earl like the Gypsy earl, so he can ride a horse like Storm."

"There's no question Colin is fond of him," Olivia admitted, her eyes soft. Colin had lost his shyness long ago—one of his favorite things to talk about was Dominic—and of course, Storm. "And I know he's just as fond of Colin."

Their talk turned to other matters. Before long they reached the village. Olivia was just about to take the split in the road that led to the cottage, when she noticed a number of people gathered near the church. She frowned. Shouts and angry voices punctuated the air.

She and Charlotte exchanged glances. Charlotte glanced back toward the church. "Why, there's me mum," she said slowly. Olivia's gaze traveled over the group. Sure enough, she spotted Bridget, Charlotte's mother.

Their step hastened until they were almost running.

Just then a white-haired figure separated itself from the group. She gave a great cry when she saw the two women hurrying toward her.

"Charlotte!" she cried.

Charlotte reached her. "What is it, Mama? What's 'appened?"

Fat tears slid down Bridget's ample cheeks. "Someone took him," she wailed. "Someone took him!"

Charlotte's eyes were huge. "Who, Mama? *Who?*"

"Colin," Bridget sobbed. " 'Tis my fault, Charlotte. Ye can send me back to Ireland, but first, let us find him!"

Charlotte began to tremble from head to foot. Her mouth opened, but no sound came out. It was Olivia who said sharply, "What happened?"

"It was two hours past. He was sleepin' in his bed, the little lamb. I laid me head down, too ... just for an instant, I told myself. I must have fallen asleep—" Bridget's tone reflected her anguish. "— but then I heard the door creak. It took me but a minute—but by then he was gone!"

The woods crowded directly behind Charlotte's cottage. "Perhaps he wandered into the woods—"

"No." This came from Charlotte, who was white as snow. "He was terrified of the woods. He wouldn't even go behind the cottage unless Mama or I was with him."

"Someone took him," Bridget said, beginning to weep. "There were footsteps in the earth near the well. They led directly to the door. They weren't there earlier, for I swept there only this morning."

She began to weep. "Anyone could have looked through the window and seen the both of us sleepin' there. Someone came in and snatched him from his bed!"

Olivia ignored the voice that told her it would have been only too easy to sneak the little boy into the woods. "He has to be somewhere—"

"We've searched everywhere." This came from Reverend Holden. His thin face was shadowed. "As much as I hate to believe it, it appears young Colin was taken by someone—just like Lucinda."

Olivia's blood went chill. "Lucinda?" she whispered. Lucinda, so sweet and so shy, was the next oldest girl after her sister Jane.

It was then she saw Jane, who stepped up and wrapped her arms around Olivia. The girl's face was stained with tears. "Oh, Miss Sherwood!" she sobbed. "Lucinda is gone! She went out to the barn this morning to milk the cow. She never came back. Papa sent me out to fetch her, but I—I couldn't find her."

A wave of shock slammed through Olivia. *Dear God*, she thought numbly, *both Colin and Lucinda*. With two of them gone, it couldn't be coincidence. They couldn't *both* have wandered off . . .

She smoothed Jane's hair. "Try not to worry, Jane. She'll be found soon." She sought to comfort the girl, but it was an empty promise—never had she felt so useless!

Jane raised woeful eyes to hers. "What if she's not, Miss Sherwood? What if she's not?"

Olivia had no answer. She could only pray that such a thing would never come to pass.

From within the crowd came a shout. "It was the Gypsies! The Gypsies stole the children!"

An angry murmur swept through the assembled crowd.

"It must be!" yelled another. "Everyone knows they steal anything they can, even children!"

"Especially children!" claimed yet another.

A great hue and cry arose. "Let's go search the Gypsy camp!"

It was all the encouragement they needed. Fists punched high in the air. Voices rose, joining together in a roar. The very air seemed to sizzle with the thunder of angry emotions. A man broke apart from the others.

"Let's find the children!" he shouted.

Yet another man joined him, and still another and another fell into place beside him, until like a swarm they surged forward, marching together. Even the constable was among them.

They were headed toward the Gypsy camp.

"Miss Sherwood," cried Jane, "where are they going?"

"To make trouble," she said under her breath. She gave Jane a quick hug. "Go home, sweetheart, go home," she urged the girl.

Charlotte grasped her sleeve. "Olivia, do ye think it's true, that the Gypsies stole Colin and Lucinda?"

"Of course not, that's just an old tale!" she cried. "There's no truth to it, none at all!" She felt compelled to defend the Gypsies. Her eyes grew frantic. It might prove futile, but she had to at least try to stop them! "Oh, Charlotte, I cannot let them do this, I have to go after them! There are women and children there. Someone could be hurt!"

Charlotte swiped at her tears. "I'll go with ye—"

Olivia shook her head. "No, love, stay with your mother. You need each other right now." She gave her a fierce hug. "I'll be fine, I promise."

Olivia ran after them, crying out for them to stop, to listen to reason. The men paid no heed. She caught a glimpse of William—he'd been a soldier. Perhaps she could appeal to his sense of honor, but when she tried to reach him, someone reached out and shoved her viciously between the shoulder blades. She fell to the ground, scraping her palms and knees; the breath was jarred from her lungs. By the time she'd regained it, stumbling upright, the men had reached the Gypsy camp.

Olivia ran forward, pleading, cajoling, but her pleas fell on deaf ears. Tempers ran hot; emotions were strained to the breaking point. Half a dozen Gypsy men jumped up from around the fire. There was a barrage of furious words and then the villagers dispersed, knocking down anyone who got in their way. They climbed into the caravans, tearing them apart—the ground was soon littered with brightly colored clothing. There was little the Gypsies could do to stop them—they were outnumbered two to one by the villagers. The women clustered together, their children huddling behind their skirts, their eyes wide and dark and frightened. Battered by a sense of utter helplessness, Olivia could only watch in horror while they tore the camp apart searching for Colin and Lucinda. She was appalled, sick to the depths of her soul. Their judgment was colored by their hatred, their actions by scorn.

From the corner of her eye, there was a flash of movement. She turned to see Andre dart from within a tent. He was knocked to the ground by two men. One of them raised a stick of wood high, then swung it down . . . Dimly she heard herself cry out.

Suddenly there came a shout that rose above all. "What the devil is going on here?"

It was Dominic.

He rode in, looking like a savior from heaven, tall and proud and commanding upon Storm's back. The wind whipped at his shirt. The villagers stopped their looting, no doubt from the fierceness of his expression.

Nikolos, the Gypsy leader, walked toward him. His hands waving, he said something in Romany. Dominic scowled. His expression blackened further.

"Have you found what you were looking for?" His gaze swept over all those present. "Have you?" he demanded.

"No," someone answered sullenly.

"Then I suggest you leave—"

But someone else had other ideas. "What about you, m' lord earl? You're half-Gypsy! Perhaps it was you who stole the children."

"Yes," someone else shouted. "Where were you today?"

A murmur went up. Suddenly the attack was centered on him—on Dominic.

Olivia couldn't believe it. Why couldn't they see what was surely obvious if only they cared to look? When she looked at him she saw a bold strength tempered by the utmost gentleness. In her mind's eye, she envisioned Dominic and Colin, the sweep of his hand upon the boy's head as a laughing Colin was lifted from Storm's back. The boy idolized him—and Dominic was fond of Colin, she knew it for certain. Were Colin here, he could only attest to it himself.

Before he could say a word, she marched forward. Her eyes were sizzling, and her cheeks were bright with indignation.

"How can you condemn him?" she cried. "When Jonny and Henry were nearly swept away, no one else tried to rescue them—certainly none of you!" It was a stinging denouncement. "He alone was brave enough—courageous enough. What did all of you do? You stood and watched—you stood and watched while those two young boys nearly drowned! Yet you dare to accuse him of such a monstrous crime!"

A hush fell over all, but Olivia was not yet finished. She pointed at a man who leaned upon a cane. "And you, Charles Danbury! He's let you remain on his land rent-free while your leg healed. He sent some of his own people to help with the chores on your land!" Charles Danbury had the grace to look ashamed. "Would a man so fair and generous steal two children from their home and families? I think not!"

She was suddenly so furious she was shaking with it. Her chin high, she glared at all of them. "I know for a fact that he was at Ravenwood the entire day, so I suggest you look elsewhere for Colin and Lucinda!"

"She's right," shouted someone. "The earl had nothing to do with it! The children are not here, and we'd best look elsewhere if we hope to find them."

The shout was quickly taken up by someone else, and still another and another.

Dominic scarcely heard. He had gone very still.

He had listened intently to every word Olivia spoke. He listened . . . and he heard. But it was what lay beneath that revealed a far deeper truth . . . How, he asked himself, could she push him away, yet defend him so staunchly—and before all?

She loved him. *She loved him.*

She simply didn't know it yet.

Twenty

Somehow she had accomplished what no one else could.

One by one the villagers dropped back. Though a few appeared sullen, most were chastened and subdued and fell into a scraggly line. With no more protest, they headed back to Stonebridge.

Dominic had dismounted and stood talking to Nikolos. Olivia rushed to Andre, who lay sprawled in the dirt. With another young man's assistance, she turned him to his back. Her breath caught, for a massive, ugly bruise already swelled on his temple. Blood streamed down his face, over one eye. The woman Catriana, the one who had told her fortune, pressed a clean, wet rag into her hand. Gently Olivia wiped away the grime and the blood. A grimace of pain crossed his handsome face, but still he didn't awaken.

Dominic came and knelt by her side. "How is he?"

Olivia hesitated. "I can't be certain." The man who had done this—it happened so quickly she couldn't be certain—but for an instant she thought it was William. Witnessing such violence made her

309

want to retch. It was far too potent a reminder of how her father had died.

"The Gypsies are leaving," he told her.

Olivia's eyes darkened. "I think it's for the best." Already the Gypsies had begun to gather up their belongings. A quiet pall hung over the group.

Dominic glanced at Andre. That he hadn't regained consciousness yet was a bad sign. A chill went through him as he remembered hearing the hoot of an owl the night of the ball. He prayed this wasn't the consequence.

Olivia covered the wound with a clean strip of linen, carefully winding it around his head. "I'm hardly an expert, but I don't think he should travel."

"I know. I thought I would take him to Ravenwood. It's not far and he'll be safe there. The villagers may resent me, but I think it will pass." His eyes probed hers. "What about you? Do you want me to take you home?"

Olivia shook her head. "I'll be fine," she murmured.

He nodded, giving her shoulder a slight squeeze as he rose.

Emily was sitting in her chair, a square of lace in her lap. When she saw Olivia's disheveled state, she leaped up.

"Olivia! What on earth happened to you?"

Briefly Emily told her that Colin and Lucinda had disappeared—and the resulting fray with the Gypsies.

"The Gypsies are leaving," she finished. "I know you probably agree with those small-minded men who think the Gypsies are responsible—but please,

Emily, I'd prefer you keep it to yourself."

Emily felt very small. "I wasn't going to say that." She paused. "Is . . . everyone all right? Was anyone hurt?"

Their eyes tangled. An unspoken question hovered in the air between them. Olivia couldn't help but note her anxiety, but she was in no mood to coddle her—she was still too angry.

She raised a brow. "Anyone? Don't you mean Andre?" she asked calmly.

Emily looked at her oddly. "You sound as if you know him."

"I met him once, yes." It was time for Emily to know the truth as well. "I went to the Gypsy camp with Dominic one night. He wanted to show me that the Gypsies are not the scourge everyone believes." She paused a moment. "But I'm afraid Andre *was* hurt. Someone picked up a branch from the ground and hit him."

Emily seemed to struggle to speak. She grasped the top of the chair. "How badly was he hurt?"

Olivia gazed at her steadily. "Do you care, Emily?"

"I—I care not if I see him again, but I—I would never wish him ill!"

Olivia spoke quietly. "He was knocked unconscious. The blow left him bruised and bloodied." She hesitated. "But he is alive and in good hands."

Nearly every drop of color drained from Emily's face. "Oh, God, just like Papa," she breathed. "Is he with the Gypsies, Olivia? Is he?"

Olivia bit her lip. Should she tell her? Or would it but deepen her despair? When she said nothing, Emily made a choked sound and ran into the cottage. Olivia followed her. She'd thrown herself down upon the bed and stared up at the ceiling.

She sat next to her. "Would you go to him if you could?" Emily looked stricken; she made no reply. Olivia persisted. "Would you, love?"

Emily turned her head and gazed at her. "Why would you ask such a thing when you know I would not . . . *could* not! Why are you being so cruel, Olivia? Why?"

Her sister's wounded look stabbed at her. Olivia swept a stray hair from her temple. "I don't mean to be, Emily. I merely ask . . . what you perhaps should be asking yourself."

Her heart began to bleed when Emily's eyes glazed over, yet her whisper was almost fierce. "Sometimes I almost wish I'd never recovered my sight. Then it would be the same. I—I could love him without knowing he is a Gypsy. I never would have known . . ."

Olivia shook her head. "You'd have discovered it sometime, I think. Even if you didn't, the Gypsies were bound to leave soon anyway—and when he was gone you would have pined for him . . . Would that be better, to love someone knowing you'd never see him again? Or perhaps he would return, but only for a few days."

A tear slid from the corner of Emily's eye. "It hurts so much, Olivia. It hurts so much and yet— it makes me so angry!"

"But are you angry because he is a Gypsy? Or because he deceived you—that he didn't tell you he was a Gypsy?"

Emily pushed herself to a sitting position. "I'm angry at him because he didn't tell me—because he is who he is! And I am angry for allowing myself to fall in love with him! He is a Gypsy and that's something I can never forget!"

Olivia spoke almost whimsically. "Can't you?"

"I—I cannot love him!"

"Because he is a Gypsy." It was not a question, it was a statement.

Emily nodded.

"Is he kind?"

"Yes."

"Generous?"

"Yes, he is—"

"Considerate of you?"

"Yes, yes, yes!" Emily's tone was frustrated. "He is all of those things—"

"Then you love him for what he is—for who he is."

"I do, but—" She broke off as she realized what she'd just admitted.

"All of those things come from here," Olivia pointed out, touching her breast. "When you first saw him, if he had worn the clothing of a *gadjo*, a non-Gypsy, would you have known he was a Gypsy?"

"Do not ask me that," Emily cried. "Olivia, you wouldn't understand!"

Oh, yes, I would, Olivia thought silently. *Far more than you know . . .*

"Olivia . . . what you suggest . . .'tis impossible!"

"Is it?" Olivia paused a moment. "Do you know what I think?"

Emily hugged her knees to her breast. "I think you will tell me anyway!"

Olivia smiled slightly. Then her smile faded.

"What stands in your way has nothing to do with Andre," she said quietly. "You hate the

Gypsy who killed Papa because of what he did—but do not hate Andre because of what that one Gypsy did."

Reaching out, she smoothed Emily's hair, her eyes as tormented as were Emily's own. "Please understand that I do not mean to hurt you when I tell you this," she said gently. "I only want what's best for you, love. I want you to be happy, but clearly you are *not* happy. And if you refuse to see what your heart so clearly tells you, then perhaps . . . perhaps you are still blind."

Leaning forward, she kissed her sister's forehead. "I'll see to supper. Why don't you rest?"

Emily watched her leave, her expression troubled. *Rest?* her mind echoed in dismay. Ah, but there would be no rest. She laid her cheek on her knees. Her mind would not be still; it circled around Andre, ever and always!

If she could only find the courage to admit it, Olivia's words held more than a measure of truth. During this time without Andre, she'd been miserable—it was as if a piece of her soul was missing.

The morning she'd regained her sight came back in scorching remembrance. If not for Andre, she might never have tried . . . He had encouraged her, pushed her, urged her to try again and again. Only now did she consider that surely he must have anticipated her reaction when she discovered he was a Gypsy.

It hadn't stopped him.

There was a painful catch in the region of her heart. He'd said he loved her. *He loved her.* That was the one thing Emily did not question. He had risked her rejection—sacrificed all—knowing full well he might very well lose her.

It hadn't stopped him. He had thought only of her . . . only of her. Yet what had she done?

Dark shame washed through her. She didn't feel very proud of herself right now. Indeed, she felt small and close-minded.

Olivia was right, she thought with a pang. She was hiding from herself—hiding from the truth. Yet what was she to do about it?

The choice was hers.

She had only to make it.

Olivia saw Andre at Ravenwood the next day. He'd been given a room in the east wing, where she was cleaning today. In the afternoon when she had a bit of spare time, she peeked inside his room. He sat in a chair by the window, staring out at the forest. He was dressed in a clean shirt and breeches—Dominic's, she guessed. Other than a snowy-white bandage wound around his forehead, she was pleased to note he looked reasonably well. Clearly his condition was much improved.

She knocked lightly on the doorjamb. "Hello," she called.

He glanced up. A telltale red seeped beneath his skin as she stepped inside; she knew he'd recognized her.

"Hello," he murmured.

"Well," she said, "so we meet again."

Smiling slightly, he got to his feet. His expression was rather wary as he watched her approach.

Her eyes went to the bandage around his head. "How are you feeling?"

"Oh, I'm fine. The earl called in a physician, though I told him it wasn't needed." An engaging grin made a brief appearance. "I've had worse knocks than this while I was boxing."

"Nonetheless, you should probably stay quiet for a few days."

He made a face. "That's what the physician said."

An awkward silence reigned. Neither of them seemed to know what to say. Finally she decided there was no hope but to broach the subject on both their minds.

"I suppose you're wondering about Emily."

Something leaped in his eyes at the mention of her name—but then his features turned cautious.

"How is she? Can she still see?"

"Her vision is excellent. Her eyes are still a trifle sensitive to bright light, but other than that, it's as if she was never blind. It's really quite strange." She gave a tiny shake of her head.

"She's convinced it was the crystal I gave her that healed her."

"And I believe it was you."

He looked startled, but said nothing.

"I believe it was your love for her that allowed Emily to see again," she went on. "I didn't even know about you until several days ago, but . . . there was a change in her. I know now it was because of you." She paused, then said softly, "You love her, don't you?"

"With all that I am," he said simply, but then a fleeting despair crossed his features.

Olivia ached inside, knowing how hurt he must surely feel. She sought to reassure him.

"She loves you, Andre."

"No," he said flatly. "She hates me. She told me so."

"She's lost without you. Oh, I know 'tis none of my affair, but . . . don't leave just yet. Please, don't rejoin the Gypsies just yet." Lightly she laid her fingertips on his sleeve. "I—I do not mean to give you false hope, but give it some time," she urged. "Give *her* some time to accept her feelings . . . and you."

For the longest time he said nothing. "I'll try," he said at last, but his eyes were bleak.

With that she left him alone.

She chided herself as she walked down the hall. Who was she to dispense advice? She was feeling her own way just as carefully, wondering what would happen with her and Dominic. She'd lain with him twice—twice! Did it mean to him what it did to her? If only she knew!

It was early evening when she departed for home. She'd just closed the rear entrance to the hall when she heard someone call her name.

It was Dominic. He was striding toward her from the stables. Dusty and travel-stained, his dark hair was windblown and mussed. When she'd arrived at Ravenwood this morning, he was already gone. It was Mrs. Templeton who told her he'd been out since dawn. Despite herself, her pulse leaped apace with her heart. Lucifer trotted along beside him, his tongue lolling from the side of his mouth. When the hound spotted her, he bounded forward.

She patted his head absentmindedly as she awaited his master.

"Did you find them?" she asked the moment he was near.

Deep grooves appeared beside his mouth. His answer was written in the weary set of his shoulders. Olivia's spirits plummeted as he pulled her beneath a shady spot under the eaves of the stables.

"Most of the villagers were out looking as well," he said grimly. "No one found a thing."

"Did you see Charlotte?" Olivia had stopped by her cottage this morning, but her mother had told her she was still sleeping—that she'd spent most of the night crying. Not wanting to disturb her, Olivia had continued on to Ravenwood.

Dominic nodded.

"How is she?"

He grimaced. "As well as can be expected, I suppose."

She would stop by this evening, Olivia decided. Her eyes cloudy, she gazed up at Dominic. "Who would do this? And why? Why take two children from their homes and families?" She shivered as she recalled the horrible scene at the Gypsy camp. "Do you think it was done just so the Gypsies could be blamed?"

"It's occurred to me," he admitted. "Certainly it worked. The Gypsies were angry at being accused and moved on—they left last night." He was silent, his forehead creased. "Yet if that is the case, why weren't the children returned today?"

She suppressed a shudder. Colin and Lucinda must be terrified! Were they alone? Together? Were they still alive . . . no. *No!* She could not think like that. She *would* not.

Dominic's frown deepened. "Or perhaps someone was just as eager to blame me."

She glanced at him sharply. "It didn't work, did it? Were the villagers—"

"Everything was fine this morning," he assured her. "But the man last night—the man who shouted. Do you know who pointed the finger at me?"

"I couldn't tell who it was. Nor can I think of anyone who would wish you ill—" Suddenly she stopped.

Dominic's eyes narrowed. "What, Olivia? What is it?"

She bit her lip. "I was thinking of William," she said slowly. What was it he'd said? *Your precious Gypsy earl may not be here forever, and then what will you do?* At the time, she'd thought he meant Dominic might take up residence back in London, or elsewhere. But now . . .

Dominic gave a short bark of laughter. "What! Do not tell me he is not one of my staunchest admirers!"

She frowned at him. "Be serious."

"Oh, I'm quite serious, Olivia. He was among those searching for the children today, though we did not speak. Why would you think of him?"

"Because he—he dislikes you."

"Does he dislike me enough to go to such lengths?"

Olivia took a deep breath. "I don't know."

Dominic studied her. "Why does he dislike me? Because I'm half-Gypsy?"

" 'Tis not that." She brushed it aside. " 'Tis because—"

"Because what?"

Damn him! Why was he being so insistent? It was almost as if he sought to trap her into saying . . . into saying what? That she loved him?

"Olivia?" He stripped off his gloves and reached for her hands.

She tried to pull away, but he wouldn't let her.

His fingers tightened around hers, strong and hard and warm.

"Because—he knows about us," she blurted. "William knows about us!"

He tugged her closer, so close her small, slippered feet were planted squarely between his boots. Sapphire eyes moved warmly over her face, making her heart beat a little faster.

"I see," he murmured. "He knows that we are lovers?"

She was aghast. "No! Never did I tell him that!"

"What does he know about us then?"

She gazed at the squareness of his jaw, not quite able to summon the courage to meet his regard. "That I am . . . fond of you," she finished weakly.

"Ah, now this is good news indeed. *Are* you fond of me, Olivia?"

Her head came up and she glared at him—at least she tried to. His voice carried the faintest trace of amusement. Dear Lord, it would be just like him to ask her *how* fond . . .

Only now she couldn't tear her gaze from his. Their eyes clung. "You know I am," she said helplessly.

He did know, or at least he was beginning to; indeed, he prayed it was much, much more, for in his own way, he was just as uncertain as she was—just as vulnerable. And just now he needed the reassurance only her vow could give.

"Will you stay a little longer?"

"I would if I could. But I cannot. I must get back to Emily."

He nodded. Olivia was thankful he didn't press her further. But he was not yet ready to let her leave. A hand snared her waist. With the other he urged her mouth to his—and then there was no need to compel her further. Her mouth opened under his, like a flower beneath the blazing heat of the sun. It was everything a kiss should be—everything she wanted it to be—sweetly tender and wondrous, breath-stealingly thorough. He made a sound deep in his throat. With his hands he bound her hips against his . . .

There was a discreet cough behind them. "Forgive me, my lord, but your presence is required within the manor."

It was Franklin. Dominic smothered a groan. Reluctantly he released Olivia's mouth.

"I'll be there in a moment," he said without turning.

"Very good, my lord." Franklin departed as noiselessly as he'd come.

He ran the tip of his finger down her nose, his expression conveying his regret. "I must go."

Her troubled gaze sought his. "What about William?"

Blue eyes glinted, suddenly hard as steel. "I think I shall pay him a visit in the morning."

"Dominic, wait!" She caught at his arm. "Please, be careful."

He bent and availed himself of one last, fleeting kiss. "I will," he promised, and then was gone.

The long walk home seemed to take longer than ever tonight. Try though she might, she could not subdue the feeling that something was about to happen, something awful. She shivered, wishing Lucifer was at her side. She'd called for him, but he was nowhere about, and she was anxious to be home.

Her steps slowed. Her hand stole to her breast.

From her bodice she withdrew the handkerchief. Perhaps it was silly, but it gave her comfort to look at it. She smiled wistfully; since the day she'd pulled it from her drawer, she'd kept it with her, next to her heart every hour of the day.

Suddenly the sound of running footsteps reached her ears. She glimpsed a flash of movement from the encroaching forest, and then a hand grasped her sleeve. She whirled, so startled that she failed to notice the handkerchief fluttering to the ground at her feet.

It was Robert Gilmore.

He was short of breath, heaving from exertion. His expression was harried. "Miss Sherwood, thank heaven you're here! I've found the children!"

"You've found them! Oh, Mr. Gilmore, thank God!" She gave a cry of gladness. "Where are they?"

He pointed into the forest. "The little boy—he's injured. We must hurry, before it's too late!"

"Colin! Oh, no! How badly is he hurt?"

He shook his head. "I cannot say! I need your help to bring him out."

"Shouldn't we go to the village for help?"

"No, there's no time for that!"

Gilmore grabbed her elbow and began pulling her along into the bushes. "Hurry! It's this way!"

Refusal never crossed Olivia's mind. If Colin was hurt badly, time was of the essence. She would do whatever she could to help him. She hurried along beside Mr. Gilmore as he led the way deep into the woods. The brush was more dense here. A stone bit into the soles of her slippers as she stepped around a fallen branch. A shiver of apprehension slid down her spine, for it was dark and shadowed here; the last rays of evening scarcely penetrated the canopy of trees overhead.

She stopped to catch her breath. "Mr. Gilmore! How much further is it?"

"Not far. There is a hunting cottage, just beyond that tree there." He pointed to the east.

Olivia followed the direction of his finger. Sure enough, she glimpsed the side of a crumbling chimney.

Heartened, she hurried along behind him. Soon they stood at the door of a hunting lodge. It was old and shabby. Moss slanted across the roof. It appeared it hadn't been used in many a year.

Gilmore opened the door and gestured her inside. Olivia stepped within. The interior was filthy, devoid of any furniture.

Olivia frowned. "But wait! There is no one here . . ."

The door clicked shut. Gilmore stood directly behind her. His head was tipped to the side and he was smiling . . .

A smile that turned her blood to ice.

Her heart began to knock. Too late she realized . . . He'd been lying in wait for her. She'd warned Dominic to take care, never dreaming that she might be the one in danger. Oh, if only she could have taken Lucifer . . . !

But it was already too late. Her arm was seized and wrenched behind her. Crying out, she doubled over. There was a stunning blow to the back of her head.

She crumpled to the floor without a sound.

Twenty-one

Olivia regained consciousness slowly. The back of her head pounded without mercy. For a moment she couldn't remember where she was or why the floor was rough and hard beneath her cheek. Then memory came back in a rush; shock that she was still alive swept through her mind.

She tried to move, only to have pain shoot through her shoulders—her hands had been tied behind her back. She could feel the rough hemp digging into her tender skin. Her ankles had been bound as well.

"So, you're awake."

Gilmore again. She had to strain to see him, for there was a nightmarish cast to the gloomy interior. There was no glass in the windows. They had been covered with boards from the outside; the only light came from between the cracks. When her eyes adjusted to the dim light, she tilted her head back, uncaring that her eyes glowed her hatred. He eased to his haunches and stretched out a hand to caress her cheek.

Olivia jerked her head back, trying to elude his touch.

He laughed, a dark, sinister sound. "I suppose

you're wondering what I'm about, eh?"

"The thought had occurred to me," she snapped. "It was you who stole the children, wasn't it?"

His eyes glinted. "Smart girl."

She glared at him, her stomach knotted with loathing. "Why? Why would you do such a thing? They've done nothing to you! Why would you harm them?"

"They've not been harmed, nor will they be, as long as all goes as planned. As for why . . . well, they served their purpose well enough—they brought you here. And last night, oh, I almost thought there might be no need to take this further. I might have convinced the others that *he* was the one who stole the children."

"He?"

"The Gypsy earl!" Gilmore nearly spat the words.

Olivia's mouth grew dry. "So it was you who accused him."

"Yes, it was I. And I could have convinced them—if not for you!" His lips curled back over his teeth. "But no, you had to speak up and defend him! Why, they might have killed him then and there! He doesn't belong here, you know, the Gypsy bastard! Can you imagine? He fancies himself an earl yet! He thinks he's better than the rest of us, but he's a Gypsy, not fit to lick my boots!"

"Why?" was all she could say. "Why? Simply because he's half-Gypsy?"

"Because he doesn't belong here! None of them do! Oh, I warned him. I told him to get rid of them, that he'd be sorry if he didn't. But he didn't listen, so now he must pay the price!"

Olivia struggled for calm. "You forget, Mr. Gilmore, the Gypsies *did* leave."

"But *he* is still here!"

Olivia shook her head. "Why do you hate him so much? He's done nothing to you—the Gypsies have done nothing to you—"

"Haven't they? Well, let me enlighten you, Miss Sherwood. They ruined my life. They ruined my father's life—and they stole my mother's from her!"

Olivia stared at him numbly.

"Yes, Miss Sherwood, I can see you think I'm mad, but I'm not." He went on, "You've known me all your life, but I didn't always live here in Stonebridge. No, as a boy I lived in the south of England—in Dorset. It was there, one long-ago summer, that the Gypsies came and stayed. My father visited their camp often—he told my mother it was to try to get them to move on. But it wasn't true. No, it was because he was rutting between the thighs of a Gypsy whore!"

Olivia inhaled sharply.

"Yes, Miss Sherwood, I can see you're shocked. So was my mother when she found my father with the Gypsy slut! Shocked and shamed so much that she could not go on! So do you know what my mother did? She took a knife and ended her life. Oh, it wasn't a pretty sight, I can assure you! And do you know what my father did? He drank. He drowned his guilt in wine—why, he drank his way to his very grave! So do not dare to defend any of them to me. They're all alike, you see, they're all thieves and whores. Why, even your precious earl's mother was a whore, and he is the proof of it! We'll all be better off without him, you'll see!"

Olivia felt sick to her very soul. The tragedy he had endured as a child had twisted him into a man who no longer knew right from wrong.

She instinctively shrank back. The venom that blackened his features was terrible to behold. Numbly she realized this was naught but a scheme to be rid of Dominic. Colin and Lucinda had been the bait to lure her here, and she was the bait to bring Dominic.

"Dear God," she said faintly, "you mean to kill him."

His smile was but a twisted parody. "Oh, I will," he said almost gleefully. "Would you like to hear my plan?"

Olivia turned her face aside, but there was no shutting out the sound of his voice.

"It's really very simple, my dear girl. You came for the children—and he will come for you. Oh, I saw the way it was between the two of you the day you begged someone to help him from the river— he should have drowned, the cur! I might have spared you, Olivia, but then I saw the way it was between you . . . to think that you would lower yourself to him. Why, your dear parents would be appalled! And now he remains here because of you—because of you! You see why you must die, don't you?"

Raw fear clutched her insides as she realized he would murder her . . .

And Dominic as well.

"Tomorrow, I think—yes, tomorrow!—he will come for you, but I will be with him! Yes, I will be with him, and when the two of you are dead, I will tell the authorities how I sneaked after him, how I discovered that the two of you had spirited away the children, for God only knows what cruel purpose! And alas, I was forced to defend myself in order to save the children and me." His chortling laugh sent prickles up and down her spine. "Am I not brilliant?"

Olivia shook her head. "Why do you hate him so much? He has done nothing to you!"

His eyes were alight with the frenzy of sheer hatred. "I need no reason other than one—he is a Gypsy!"

Sickened by what he would do, she stared at him. "You will not get away with it. Colin and Lucinda will surely know who you are—"

"They do not! I was careful, you see. I covered their eyes. Never did they see me. And I brought them food and water in the dark."

"Where are they?"

For a moment she thought he would refuse to answer. "They are here. In another room." He rose to his feet and smiled nastily. "I must be off, Miss Sherwood. Scream all you like," he said pleasantly. "There's no one to hear."

With that she was left alone. She heard the sound of a bolt slide into place on the other side of the door. Desperation filled her chest. She had to find a way to free them before Gilmore could carry out his odious plan.

The light was dimming rapidly. Soon it would be dark. "Colin! Lucinda!" she shouted. Holding her breath, she strained to hear.

There was nothing.

She shouted again, and this time . . . this time she heard something. The sound was muffled, but there was no mistake—it was a child crying.

The room she was in was large and square. There

was a stairway opposite the crumbling stone fire-place. Though her head was propped at an angle, she could see a doorway at the far end. She tried to get to her knees, but with her arms bound be-hind her and her ankles bound as well, it was im-possible. She had no choice but to roll herself across the floor toward the sound. She gave a silent prayer of thanks that the children were not up-stairs. With her limbs thus encumbered, she'd never have been able to reach them.

Her progress was awkward and slow-going. The floor was filthy. Scraping along the floor, she felt something gouge into her hip, but she dared not speculate what it was. Her shoulders ached abom-inably every time she eased to her back. Soon her arms began to go numb. But she had nearly reached the first door.

Her eyes ran over it. Near the bottom corner there was a gap between the door and the door-jamb. The top hinge was missing as well. It looked decidedly rickety.

"Colin! Lucinda!" she called again. " 'Tis I, Miss Sherwood! Can you hear me?"

The crying stopped.

"Miss Sherwood?" called a quavering little voice. The voice came nearer—they weren't trussed up, thank heaven! "Miss Sherwood, where are you?"

Lucinda!

"I'm in the hallway, Lucinda. Lucinda, is the door locked?"

"Yes!" she cried piteously. "We can't get out!"

"I'm going to try to open it, Lucinda. Take Colin and move to the corner, as far away from the door as possible."

Through sheer dint of will, she managed to rise to her feet. She wobbled like a sapling in the wind. Taking a deep breath, she threw her shoulder at the door. All she could do was hope that the weight of her body would somehow manage to topple the door and break the catch of the lock.

There was an ear-splitting creak as one of the hinges separated. Then, as if in slow motion, the door gave way. Her cry of triumph turned to a gasp as she tumbled inside, atop the door.

She lay for a moment, stunned and breathless. Then all at once two small bodies hurtled themselves upon her.

"Miss Sherwood!"

"Miss Sherwood, how did you find us?"

Relief poured through her, for they appeared well and unharmed though their faces were streaked with tears.

"Lucinda, can you free my wrists?"

Lucinda nodded eagerly and set about untying her, her small fingers nimble and quick as they tugged on the knots.

The rope slipped away from her wrists.

She winced a little as hot needles seemed to go through her wrists. She rubbed the chafed, tender skin that had gone numb, then reached for the rope about her ankles. In seconds she was free. Her vision misty, she held out her arms toward the young pair, and then she was laughing and crying and fiercely hugging them both.

"Are you all right?" she asked again and again.

Lucinda's lower lip trembled. "We called and called but no one came."

Colin's little brows drew together, his expression woeful. "I'm hungry."

Olivia kissed his forehead. "I know, pet, but I'm afraid we'll have to wait a little longer before we eat. First we must find a way out of here."

Lucinda shivered. "Where are we?"

"At an abandoned hunting lodge deep in the woods." Olivia rose to her feet and held out her hands to the children. Together they returned to the main room of the lodge.

Colin grasped her skirt. "I don't like it here," he whispered.

Olivia squeezed his hand reassuringly. "With luck we'll soon be out." But alas, luck was not with them. Olivia tried the front door to no avail—it had been bolted from the outside. She threw her shoulder against it again and again, but it didn't budge. Abandoning the door, she slammed her hands against the boards which yawned across the windows, but they, too, held firm; inside was deserted, and there was nothing else she could use. By now, the interior was almost pitch black; she could see it was nearly dark outside.

She smothered a sob. She fooled no one, least of all herself. Even if she'd been able to find a way out of the lodge, it was dark outside—she feared she'd never be able to find her way out of the forest at night. Besides, there were the children to consider. If they should become lost, it might only frighten them further. Her mind skipped back to what Gilmore had told her. *Tomorrow*, he'd said, *tomorrow Dominic would come for her—and he, Gilmore, would be with him.*

She took a deep, fortifying breath. It was better to wait until morning, she told herself. At first light she would try again to find a way from the cottage, only this time she would succeed. When Gilmore arrived tomorrow, they would be gone.

With a sigh of resignation, she turned back to the children. Somehow she managed a semblance of a smile. "I'm afraid we'll have to wait until morning to get out. It's too dark for me to see what I'm doing."

She found a reasonably clean spot near the fireplace and settled down to spend the night. Easing to the floor, she rested her back against the wall and gathered the children beside her.

Lucinda's hand slipped into hers. "I'm glad you're here, Miss Sherwood. Colin and I—we didn't like being alone."

Olivia's heart turned over. "But you're not alone now, are you?"

Colin laid his head in her lap. "I want my mama," he whispered.

Olivia combed her fingers through his hair. "Tomorrow, love, tomorrow," she told him, praying it wasn't an idle promise.

Her shoulder ached terribly where she'd landed on it, and there was a sliver digging into her back, but if she moved it would disturb the children. Terror lay in a cold hard lump in the pit of her belly but she couldn't let the children see her fear. As they burrowed against her, tears of frustration mingled with the grime on her face and made her eyes burn. No doubt Emily would think she was working late at Ravenwood. And if she retired early as she sometimes did, she wouldn't even miss her until morning. Even if she did, no one would think to look for her here. Her expression bleak, she leaned her head back against the wall.

Like it or not, all they could do was wait.

*   *   *

Emily went to the door and peered out for the tenth time in the last hour alone. Olivia had been late before, but never quite *this* late. Her step agitated, she paced back and forth across the parlor. A strange unease gnawed within her. It was quite unlike anything she'd ever felt before. She couldn't suppress the notion that all was not right.

Finally she snatched up her shawl and tugged it around her shoulders. Concern for Olivia overrode all else. Squaring her shoulders, she marched out into the night. If she should encounter Olivia on her way home, Olivia would no doubt be extremely vexed that Emily had ventured out alone at night. But if they chanced to meet on the road to Ravenwood, so much the better—at least then she would know that Olivia was all right.

But Emily did not meet Olivia on the road. Indeed, with every step that took her closer to Ravenwood, the certainty increased that something was amiss.

Finally the sprawling brick manor came into view, dark against a midnight-blue sky lit by an ever-rising moon. Shivering against a chill that had little to do with the coolness of the night, she mounted the stone steps that led to the massive double doors. Her fingers curled around the brass knocker. Gathering her courage, she knocked loudly.

The sound echoed hollowly within. She shifted from one foot to the other and waited. It was late. There was every chance that all within were tucked snugly in their beds. Unable to curb her impatience, her fingers were already poised to reach for the knocker when the door swung wide. Emily looked up to find a white-haired gentleman peering down at her.

"Forgive the intrusion at such a late hour," she said quickly, "but I am Emily Sherwood. I—I wonder if my sister is here."

The man looked startled. "Olivia? You are Olivia's sister?"

"Yes, sir. You see, it's quite late and . . . she's usually home by now . . . and I—I thought perhaps she was still here—"

The old man shook his head. "I don't believe—"

He got no further. Another man had stepped up to the entryway. Tall, with dark hair and hawk-like features, there was such an air of mastery about him that Emily was instantly aware this was the earl.

"Olivia?" he said sharply. "You're looking for Olivia?"

She nodded. "Yes." Her voice quavered. "I—I expected her home ages ago."

An odd expression crossed his features. "She left here hours ago," he said in a strange voice.

Their eyes collided—each glimpsed in the other the same stark fear. It was Emily who expressed it aloud, barely able to speak past the sudden constriction in her throat: "Then where is she?"

"I don't know," he said grimly, "but I'm damn sure going to find her." The next thing she knew she was being swept inside the entrance hall and he was barking out orders. "Franklin, see that Miss Sherwood is given a room. Have someone alert the stables. I'll need to have Storm saddled and ready." He looked at her. "You'll stay, won't you? Of course you will. I'm not about to let you walk home again tonight."

His mind was elsewhere. Already he was walking away. Emily remained where she was, rather dazed. Olivia was missing. *Missing*. It was Franklin who took her arm and began to lead her gently away.

"This way, Miss Sherwood. We'll try to make you as comfortable as we can. If you should need anything, you have only to ring . . ."

They were mounting the stairs now. Her head was swirling. Everything seemed vaguely unreal. Dimly she heard another baritone added to the cacophony of voices.

"Let me go with you," someone was saying.

Emily froze. She knew that voice, knew it as well as her own. Driven by some force she couldn't control, she glanced back over her shoulder.

Framed against the backdrop of glittering candlelight was a black-haired man whose features would remain in her memory forever—the one man she'd thought she would never see again . . .

Andre.

Everything inside her came painfully alive. One look and the battle she fought was no more. But he was already striding away . . . It spun through her mind that if she let him walk out of her life now it would truly be for good . . .

"Andre, wait!"

Slowly he turned. Their eyes locked.

Emily was already flying down the stairs. She halted but a step away from him.

There was a heated rush of silence.

Neither of them noticed Franklin slip away. Emily longed to run her hands over his face and form, assure herself that it was really him and not some dreamlike image she'd conjured up out of the yearning in her soul.

"Andre, I—I didn't know you were here!" Her tongue nearly tripped over itself. "Are you . . . well?"

Time stretched endlessly, time in which he said nothing. Her lungs burned as she struggled not to cry.

Finally he spoke. "I'm fine," he said briefly.

His expression was wary and shuttered. Knowing she was responsible, knowing she had no one to blame but herself, everything collided within her breast. Regret welled up inside her, a world of it. She bit back a half-sob. Her eyes were swimming so that she could scarcely see.

Something flitted across his face. He raised a hand, only to let it fall to his side. "Don't worry about Olivia. We'll find her."

"It's not that," she said through a tear-choked voice. "Oh, don't you see? It's you." She could have kicked herself, for nothing was coming out the way it should have. "I—I'm so ashamed. I know I hurt you and I would take it back, if only I could! Oh, Andre, I—" Something inside twisted and broke free. "—I love you! Oh, I know the Gypsies like to wander. All I ask is that you give me what time you can . . . what you can . . . when you can . . ."

"Emily." Her name was a ragged sound. Suddenly she was in his arms, right where she wanted to be. "Emily," he whispered through the shining cloud of her hair, "I will be here always . . . if you want me."

Her heart surely stopped, then resumed beating

with thick, heavy strokes. She tipped her head back and gazed up at him. "What do you mean?"

"I love you, princess. I'll always love you."

A rush of emotion squeezed her chest, so intense it was painful. "You mean you're not leaving?" She was half-afraid to voice it for fear it might come true. "You're not going back to the Gypsies?"

The ghost of a smile rimmed his lips. "I'm not going anywhere," he said softly, "not without you. I would never take you away from your home, from your sister. I can never give you anything so grand as all this—" His gaze encompassed the room. "—but I'll give you what I can, if only you'll have me."

Emily stared. Happiness burst inside her. With a cry of gladness she brought his head down to hers for a sweet, endless kiss. Lost in a world of mindless pleasure, neither one surfaced until someone cleared his throat.

Emily blushed as she saw Dominic standing behind Andre. Andre turned, slipping his arm around Emily's waist and pulling her close.

One corner of Dominic's lips curled upward. "I understand if you wish to stay here," he said.

Andre was adamant. "You'll cover twice as much ground if I go with you." He turned to Emily. "Try to rest," he murmured.

Emily's eyes darkened. She gripped his hands, her gaze imploring. "Please, be careful—" Her eyes cut back to Dominic. "—both of you."

Andre bent and kissed her lips, and then they were off.

Luckily the moon was high, aiding greatly in their search. Between the two of them, they covered the area between Ravenwood and the cottage several times over, as well as a goodly portion of the woods.

There was no sign of Olivia.

The first faint light of dawn painted the eastern sky with a rosy glow when at last Dominic reined to a halt, midway between the village and Ravenwood. Andre brought his mount to a halt as well.

"She can't have simply disappeared," Andre said quietly.

"First the children, and now her." Dominic's jaw was tense. "Where the devil are they?" He cursed himself to hell and back. It had been daylight when she left, but he blamed himself. He should have seen to it that Lucifer accompanied her.

Andre looked at him. "Would the villagers help us look for her?"

Dominic's features were taut as he nodded. "I'll ride back and raise the alarm—" All at once he stopped. His gaze narrowed.

Lucifer had trotted ahead. Now he stood barking, a sharp, staccato sound, his hind legs apart and his tail high. His ears were pricked forward and he kept looking back at his master.

Dominic frowned. "What the blazes . . . ?" He nudged Storm forward.

Lucifer barked even more furiously, as if he were excited that at last he'd gained his master's attention. Dominic dismounted and strode forward. He laid his hand on the hound's back.

"What is it, Lucifer? What have you found?"

Lucifer whined and dropped to his belly; with his nose he pushed at something in the dirt.

Dominic squatted down. It was then that he saw it—a scrap of linen that had fallen into the ditch by the side of the road. He plucked it from its berth and held it high.

His brow furrowed. It was a handkerchief—*his* handkerchief, for it carried the initials DSB in the corner. In the dark, it hadn't been visible.

He inhaled, a hiss of sound. Something danced in his memory. This was the handkerchief he'd given her the night they'd met, near this very spot in the road. Raw pain spilled through him. *Olivia*, he cried silently. *Olivia, where are you?* His head bowed low, he crushed the scrap of linen to his nose and mouth and inhaled deeply. It carried the damp scent of earth and another scent . . . the scent of roses.

His head came up. Lucifer regarded him with wide, dark eyes. The hound whined, a doleful sound, his muzzle perched on outstretched paw.

Dominic held out the handkerchief. Lucifer sniffed, then bounded to his feet. He danced around in a circle, as if he already knew what would be asked of him . . .

Dominic rose. "Lucifer," he commanded, "find Olivia. Find Olivia!"

Lucifer barked once, then took off at a dead run. Dominic and Andre were right at his heels.

Twenty-two

It was the distant howl of a wolf that roused Olivia from her slumber. She wiggled a little, for her arms seemed curiously heavy. And never had her bed been so hard—it was most uncomfortable! The howl came again. She wondered crossly who would be hunting so close to the cottage. Only then did reality begin to seep in. She was not snug in her bed at the cottage, she was sitting on the cold damp floor of an abandoned hunting lodge. And that was no wolf. That was . . .

"Lucifer," she whispered. Her eyes snapped open, and then it was a whoop of joy. "Lucifer!

"Colin! Lucinda! He's found us!" She shook them awake.

Colin rubbed at his eyes with his fists. Lucinda blinked sleepily, regarding her as if she'd gone daft.

Olivia hugged them fiercely, filled with gladness. "Come, children, we must get up!"

She lifted Colin to his feet. Lucinda drew away with a mighty yawn. By the time the three of them were on their feet, the wrinkles tugged from their clothes as best they were able, the barking was louder.

Hoofbeats seemed to shake the very earth, then abruptly stopped. There was a murmur of male voices and then the bolt outside was wrenched back.

She squinted against the light that poured in. For the space of a heartbeat, a spare masculine form was outlined in the doorway, legs braced wide apart, shoulders broad as the seas.

"Olivia?"

It was Dominic. A galvanizing rush tore through her, propelling her blindly into his arms.

Strong arms closed around her. The hand that smoothed her hair was not entirely steady. "Christ, I thought I'd lost you." He slid a forefinger beneath her chin and lifted it. "Are you all right?" Anxiously he searched her face.

Her smile was tremulous. "I am now."

"And the children?"

Drawing back, she glanced around for the children. "Hungry and a bit cold, I suspect."

Colin, she saw, had already attached himself to Dominic's leg. Dominic lifted him high in his arms for a hug, then lowered him to the floor. Lucinda grinned at him shyly. Olivia spotted Andre just outside the doorway and gave a nod of greeting. Lucifer trotted into the lodge, his tail wagging madly.

"How did you find us?" Olivia asked.

"I have Lucifer to thank for that. He found your handkerchief by the roadside—" He flashed a disarming grin. "—or perhaps I should say *my* handkerchief."

By now they had all moved outside into the morning sunshine. Colin had spotted the horses and gave a squeal of delight.

Dominic's grin faded. "What happened, Olivia? Who did this?"

Olivia had no time to answer. Before she could say a word, there came a now-familiar voice.

"No need to answer, dear girl. I can speak for myself." Gilmore stepped out from around the corner of the lodge.

He had a pistol raised high in his hand, aimed directly at Dominic's chest.

Olivia paled.

Gilmore leered. "My, but you're friendly with these devils—not one but two rush to your aid! A poor choice, my dear Miss Sherwood." His mocking gaze flitted to Dominic. "As for you, my lord, you saved me the trouble of fetching you. However, your rescue is ill-timed, for now I fear I'll have to kill all of you instead of just you and the lady."

Dominic faced him boldly. "If it's me you want, then let the others go."

Gilmore's laugh was grating. "Oh, I think not, my fine and fancy lord, I think not! I'm not so stupid as you think—they'd run straight to the authorities! Besides, this way I'll be rid of the lot of you!" Pure menace blazed across his features.

On the other side of Andre, Lucifer bared his teeth and growled.

Gilmore swiveled the barrel of the pistol in his direction. "Shut that hound up or I'll shoot him!"

He never had the chance. Lucifer sprang high into the air. Gilmore threw up a hand. His eyes widened with fear. Struck squarely in the chest by the hound's not-so-inconsiderable weight, he tumbled to the ground.

It was just enough time for Dominic to wrest the

pistol from him. Directly in front of his face, Lucifer snarled and growled.

Gilmore screamed and covered his head with his hands. "Call him off!" he cried. "Call the beast off, I say!"

By then Andre had darted inside and grabbed the ropes which had bound Olivia. He made quick work of tying Gilmore's hands so he could do no further harm.

Within the hour, a very subdued Robert Gilmore was delivered into the hands of the constable. It was then that Olivia told Dominic and Andre the reason behind Gilmore's twisted plan . . . how it was more than just hatred of the Gypsies—that his father had lain with a Gypsy woman, only to have his wife discover the affair.

"His mother killed herself," Olivia finished somberly, "and his father turned to drink. Gilmore blamed the Gypsies, and his hatred has been festering all these years. How ironic, that in the end, he's hurt no one but himself." She reflected quietly for a moment. "He'll go to prison, won't he?"

"It's no less than what he deserves." Dominic was not inclined to be lenient. "My God, Olivia, he would have killed us—all of us, including the children!"

Olivia's gaze flickered over his shoulder. Andre had remained a short distance away, with Colin and Lucinda. She inclined her head. "Speaking of the children, I think it's time we got them home."

And in very short order, Colin was back with his mother and grandmother, and Lucinda was returned to her family. Lucinda's mother wept openly. She threw her arms around Dominic—and Andre as well, startling them both with her effusiveness. The girl's father, too, clapped both men on the shoulder.

Now they were once again back at Ravenwood. Dominic had already relayed to Olivia that it was Emily who had alerted him that she was missing. They had no sooner stepped inside the entryway than Emily flew down the stairs and threw her arms around her. Both sisters blinked back tears as they drew back from each other—but their smiles were brighter than a thousand suns.

But there was something she didn't know, for Dominic had decided to let her discover for herself the present state of affairs between her sister and Andre.

Andre had looked on with an indulgent expression as the sisters hugged. Emily stepped back and turned. Her gaze sped straight to his.

Wordlessly he held out his hand.

The pair were soon locked fast in a rather amorous—and   distinctly   demonstrative—embrace which left no room for doubt as to their feelings for each other.

From where she stood at Dominic's side, Olivia felt her jaw sag. Dominic gave a raspy chuckle. "Don't stare, my love."

My love. Olivia's pulse beat a little faster. Did that mean what she thought it did . . . what she hoped it did?

Dominic caught her hand and pulled her around to face him. Curling his knuckles beneath her chin, he tilted her face up to his. His eyes searched hers.

"Are you certain you're all right?" he asked.

The tender concern on his face warmed her from deep inside. "I'm fine," she said breathlessly.

His eyes darkened. "Good. Because I don't know what I'd do if I lost you."

The pitch of his voice was very low—it made her quiver inside. Emboldened by it, she placed her fingertips lightly on his chest. She gave a tiny shake of her head.

"You won't lose me, Dominic," she confided softly, "not ever."

The words acted like a wellspring. Dominic made a sound and caught her close. His head came down. His mouth hovered just above hers. Olivia sighed and closed her eyes, eagerly anticipating the warm heat of his kiss . . .

It never came.

The sound of a shocked gasp reached her ears. Olivia's eyes snapped open. Emily and Andre stood just several feet away. Emily's regard was locked fast on the two of them.

Dominic released her. Olivia smothered a smile as she turned toward the pair. She had the feeling Emily looked even more shocked than she herself had just moments earlier. She knew it for certain when her sister spoke.

"Olivia! . . . My lord . . . But how . . . Good heavens, how . . ."

One corner of Dominic's mouth went up. "Fate," was all he said.

Emily glanced between Dominic and Olivia. "So you mean to say that you . . ."

Olivia smiled weakly. "I'm afraid so, Emily. You see, the earl and I . . . the two of us . . . we . . ." It was her turn to be at a loss for words, for what could she say? Things were hardly settled between her and Dominic, though she had high hopes indeed that they would be—and quite soon.

Dominic picked up where she left off, his tone dry. "What your sister is trying to say, Emily, is that the two of us have grown quite close . . . No, I fear *extremely* close is a far more apt description."

Olivia felt her cheeks stain with the heat of a blush. Andre flashed a wide grin and glanced at Emily.

Olivia reached for her sister's hand. "I would have told you," Olivia hastened to assure her, "but the time was never quite right! Emily, you were still so unclear about Andre, and I was so afraid you wouldn't understand!"

Emily squeezed her fingers. "I was rather confused, wasn't I? But no more, thank heaven." The two sisters hugged again, then drew back to smile at each other.

Returning to Andre's side, Emily slipped her hand into the crook of his arm. Andre covered her hand with his. "I think I'll take Emily back to the cottage to rest," he said. "We've all had a long night."

Dominic nodded. "My thoughts precisely. I suspect Olivia could use some rest as well." He transferred his gaze to Emily. "Would you think ill of me if I spare your sister the trip back to the cottage?"

"That depends, my lord." Emily's tone was pert, her eyes dancing. "Are your intentions honorable?"

Dominic's laugh was low and husky. "You may rest assured they are indeed." He reached for Olivia, sliding an arm about her waist and bringing her close against his side.

Andre and Emily started to turn away.

"Oh, and Emily . . ." His tone was light. When

she glanced back over her shoulder, Dominic gave her a wink Olivia couldn't see. "Don't expect her back anytime soon."

"What, good sir, is that supposed to mean?" Olivia tried for an indignant tone and failed miserably.

He reached for her hand. "It means they want privacy, and so do we."

"Do we?"

"We do indeed," Dominic continued, "for I would very much like to continue our conversation from yesterday afternoon. I believe you were saying you were quite fond of me."

"Was I? I'd forgotten." Her tone was airy, her eyes dancing.

"Well then, you leave me no choice but to make you remember." He bent and swung her high in his arms.

Olivia gasped, for he was mounting the stairs. "Dominic! Someone will see."

"So let them see."

She frowned at him good-naturedly. "You are very arrogant."

"And you are ever prim and proper."

He shouldered his way into his bedroom, shutting the door with the heel of his boot. Lowering her to the floor, he kissed her slowly, a kiss so immeasurably sweet it brought tears to her eyes. "Mmmm," he murmured when at last he raised his head. "Do you know how long I've been waiting to do that?"

Slender arms were looped around his neck. With her fingertips she caressed his nape. "As long as I have," she returned, her smile tremulous.

Tender eyes roved her features. Suddenly he released her.

"Wait," he said.

Olivia tipped her head to the side as he removed the gold chain from around his neck. To her surprise, he hung it around her neck. Murmuring something in Romany, he brought the ring to his lips and kissed it.

Almost reverently she touched the ring. "What is this?"

He grinned. "A Gypsy curse?"

She fixed him with a mock glare. "I should hope not!"

"No," he agreed, then paused. "Think of it as— as a Gypsy blessing." He caught her hand and pulled her to the side of the bed and sat, pulling her down beside him.

"It belonged to my mother," he said softly. "She wore it always. And now—now I would like my wife to wear it."

Her heart surely stopped in that instant, then a surge of pure joy shot through her.

"Ah," she said teasingly, "but I am not your wife."

"But you will be."

A slender brow arose. "Will I?"

"You will indeed."

"Soon?"

He laughed at her hopefulness. "Very soon," he assured her. "As soon as it can be arranged. As for now—" His smile was utterly seductive, and utterly wicked. "—now I am going to take you to heaven and back."

"And how will you do that?"

Sliding his fingers down her arms, he began to

ease down the bodice of her gown. "If you'll stop talking, love, I'll show you."

"But I—I could never marry a man who does not love me," she said breathlessly.

His hands stilled. Suddenly they weren't playing anymore. The look he bestowed on her made every part of her go weak inside.

"But this man *does* love you."

Olivia's breath caught. The depth of emotion she heard in his voice made her throat ache. Tears sprang to her eyes, tears she couldn't withhold. With a groan he kissed them away. "Don't cry, sweet. I love you. I do. Don't you know that?"

"I do now." Her heart was so full she could hardly speak. "Oh, Dominic, I love you too. I love you so much!"

Her declaration was like a dam breaking inside them both. Passion flared, hot as a bonfire, a sizzling blaze that consumed them both. Small hands swept the shirt from his shoulders, while his made short work of her gown. But when he would have pressed her back to the bed, she stopped him with a shake of her head and a hand on his naked chest.

Without a word she knelt between his thighs.

Cool fingertips traced an idle pattern in the dense pelt on his chest—then slid slowly down the grid of his belly.

One by one she released the buttons of his breeches.

His manhood sprang taut and free . . . into her hand. Olivia quivered inside, for he was blistering hot and boldly erect.

Her head bowed. Her hair brushed the skin of his thighs . . . just as he'd dreamed. Dainty fingers skimmed the underside of his rigid hardness.

"Olivia—" His breath caught. He could scarcely breathe, let alone talk. "Love, what are you doing?"

Olivia cast back her head and gazed at him. Prim and proper, was she? Well, she would show him. A sultry smile curved her lips.

"Taking *you* to heaven and back."

Lord above, she did. With the tip of her tongue she touched him. She plied him delicately, with wet, heated strokes of fire, a wantonly erotic caress. She pleasured him as he had once pleasured her. Her tongue swirling, she lapped and sucked and tasted, reveling in the shudder that shook his body.

Dominic couldn't have stopped her even if he'd wanted to. The muscles of his belly clenched. His senses awash in an agony of ecstasy, he was naught but a helpless captive to the seductive heat of her mouth and hands.

His hands slid into the unbound glory of her hair. "Stop," he said raggedly. "Olivia, stop, for I can stand no more!"

He caught her and brought her up before him.

Heady with the certainty that she had pleased him, her eyes shone with triumph. "Are you still so convinced I'm prim and proper?" she teased.

"No!" he groaned. "You're a witch!"

Now as naked as she, he rolled to his back and pulled her atop him. His hands at her waist, he lifted her, gently guiding . . . a tilt of his hips, and then he was imbedded tight within her silken channel.

Olivia gasped as she felt herself stretched and

impaled. He was swollen and thick inside her; the sensation was indescribable.

Her hair a wild curtain about them both, she blinked down at him. "I—I dreamed of this!" she confided. "I—I wasn't sure it was possible."

Dominic gave a throaty laugh. "Many things are possible, and it will be my very great pleasure to show you sometime, sweet." His words were hotly possessive yet oddly tender.

Then there was no more talk. There were only whispers and moans, the hushed, provocative sounds of their loving.

Much, much later when passion's fury was spent and peace and quiet settled into their souls, Dominic idly lifted a skein of russet-gold hair that streamed across his chest.

Olivia propped herself up on an elbow so she could see him. With a fingertip she traced the beautiful line of his mouth. "What are you thinking?" she murmured.

He smiled crookedly. "I was thinking about something I once said to you."

"And what was that?"

"That I didn't know if I was a Gypsy who had lost his way—"

"Or a *gadjo* who had lost his way," she finished quietly. "I remember, for I was convinced that you were neither . . . that you were just a man who'd lost his way."

He was silent a moment, and then he said: "Would you like to know a secret?"

"I would indeed."

He rested his forehead against her own. "I'm not lost anymore," he whispered.

Olivia felt her heart turn over. "You're not?"

"I am not, sweet love, for I've found where I belong."

"Ah," she said gravely, "and where is that?"

His arms tightened. He smiled against her lips. "Right here with you."

Epilogue

They were married one year ago today.

It still sent a shiver down Olivia's spine whenever she thought of her wedding day, for it was a day she would never forget. The sun was shining and warm, the skies gloriously bright. Dominic had suggested a private ceremony in the gardens at Ravenwood, but Olivia couldn't imagine being married anywhere but the lovely little stone church in Stonebridge where her father had been vicar.

"Olivia," he had said gently, *"I know there are many in the village who care for you dearly, but remember, you will be marrying an outsider, my love—a Gypsy. I would not have you hurt because few might choose to attend."*

Olivia would not be dissuaded. *"Then I will count the loss as theirs, not ours,"* she said simply. *"I love you, Dominic St. Bride, and I am not ashamed of that love, nor of you."*

And so they had been married by Reverend Holden in the church in the village, with flowers strewn everywhere, their sweet scent perfuming the air.

Dominic's fears were groundless.

The pews were jammed to overflowing. People

crowded everywhere, and there were even well-wishers who stood crammed in the entrance. Every one of the villagers was in attendance, except one . . .

William Dunsport.

William had left for London a week earlier—a permanent move, Olivia had learned from his mother. No, there was nothing to mar their joy, no reminders of the past—even Robert Gilmore was gone. Sadly, he'd died of apoplexy the day after he'd been caught and jailed.

A gurgle at her breast brought Olivia back to the present. Her son's mouth fell away from her nipple. Trevor Michael St. Bride grinned up at her, waving a plump, tiny fist.

Olivia adjusted her gown, then carried him to the window, with Lucifer padding along behind. Cradling Trevor in her elbow, she gazed out into the distance where evening's purple haze had begun to shadow the sky. She pointed toward a brick home that stood behind a stand of stately birch trees.

"Look there, Trevor, on the far side of the pasture. There is your Aunt Emily's and Uncle Andre's house. You know, the one your papa had built for them as a wedding present. He's really quite generous, your dear papa."

Trevor gazed at her as if he understood every word, his eyes as breathtakingly blue as his father's. His hair was lighter than Dominic's, yet darker than her own golden tresses. He really was a sweet-natured babe—though a bit feisty at times when it came to napping.

"Did you know you'll soon have a cousin? Ah, yes, Trevor, your Aunt Emily is due to deliver any day now, and not a moment too soon as far as she's concerned.''

Trevor blew out a milky bubble. He started when the bubble popped, but he didn't cry. Olivia laughed softly.

''That's where your papa is, you know, helping your Uncle Andre deliver Guinevere's foal—though I don't know what good he'll be. He wasn't very helpful when you were born, Trevor. I was the one doing all the work, you know, though by the time you finally made your appearance in the world, I daresay he looked as ghastly as I surely did.''

''So your true opinion of me finally comes out,'' said a voice near her ear. A pair of hard arms slid around her waist, encompassing both mother and child. ''I fear I shall have to look elsewhere for a wife who finds me pleasing.''

Olivia turned in his embrace. ''Don't you dare,'' she teased, ''else I shall look elsewhere for a husband.''

''Well then, I must simply strive to please harder, it seems. How may I serve you, countess?''

Olivia wordlessly lifted her face. Dominic partook of those sweetly upturned lips until the child between them let out a loud squall, reminding them both of his presence.

Dominic took Trevor from her arms, pressing a kiss upon his scalp. He laid him against his shoulder, one big hand rubbing circles on his back as he began to walk back and forth across the length of their chamber.

Within minutes the babe was fast asleep.

Olivia frowned at her husband good-naturedly

from her chair near the fireplace. "How is it that you can get him to sleep so easily?"

He bent and dropped a kiss on her nose. "Just so I don't put *you* to sleep." He left, heading for the nursery across the hall.

By the time he returned, several servants had finished delivering an array of silver dishes to their chamber—including a bottle of champagne.

A smile quirked the corners of his mouth. "What is this? Are we celebrating?"

Olivia thumped him in the chest. "Cad," she accused without heat.

They ate their meal there on the carpet before the hearth. Tonight there was no formality, just the two of them. Olivia queried him about the birth of Guinevere's foal.

Dominic reached for a slice of roast pheasant. "Oh, you should see him, Olivia. He's a beauty, sleek and black. Andre swears he'll be a champion racehorse—and he's probably right."

When Emily and Andre had married, it was Dominic who had suggested that Andre do what he did best—work with horses. Though it had required a bit of talking to convince Andre to swallow his pride and let Dominic stake him in the venture, Andre was willing to try. He'd decided to concentrate on breeding and training racehorses, and Guinevere's colt was the first of his mating attempts.

Olivia wiped her fingers. "So you think Andre's doing well? And people will take him seriously?"

Though Andre had shed his bright Gypsy's clothing for breeches and boots, they were all aware he'd never be comfortable in coat and cravat; it was Dominic who had acted as middleman in several lucrative transactions for him.

Dominic cocked a brow. "Without a doubt. The Duke of Hanford is interested in this colt, so I think they'll be eating quite well for some time to come."

Olivia nodded. She couldn't have been more pleased. While Dominic finished off the last of his meal, Olivia moved to stand near the open window.

By now it had grown dark outside. Just above the horizon, a full moon had begun its ascent in the sapphire sky.

She couldn't help but marvel at how things had changed since they'd met. Emily was no longer blind. She and Andre were together. Dominic was no longer a bitter, tormented man who didn't know where he belonged . . .

He came up behind her and turned her around to face him. Taking possession of both her hands, he gazed down at her. "Do you have any idea how happy you make me, Olivia St. Bride?" His tone was light, but his expression was utterly serious.

"As happy as you make me, Dominic St. Bride." Her answer came without hesitation. Even as she spoke, a shiver of delight coursed through her. She had awoken one night not long after they were married to find him propped on his elbow, staring at her. When she chided him, he merely smiled.

"I do this every night," he confessed.

"Every night?" Olivia was aghast. *"Whatever for?"*

His smile faded. When he spoke, his tone was very quiet, yet utterly intense. *"I lay beside you at night, and I feel humble—humble and proud and so damned lucky. Olivia, I'm not certain I can describe it, but . . . when I'm with you, it's as if there's this tremendous light inside me. I didn't know what it was at first. I was even rather afraid, because I'd never felt it before."*

Gently she touched his cheek. *"And what is it?"*

"Love and hope and . . . and happiness. I didn't recognize it because I—I'd never been happy before . . . Never—" His voice vibrated with the depth of his feelings. *"—until now."*

Olivia was moved to tears by his confession. Indeed, she had only to remember it now and her vision grew misty.

No, there were no shadows in the eyes that lingered upon her. Nothing but love—a love she returned in full measure and more.

Pulling her back before the hearth, Dominic poured champagne into two crystal glasses. He handed one to her, then took the other for himself.

"Do you remember the night we met, sweet?"

Olivia bit back a laugh. "How could I forget? I was convinced Lucifer was about to make me his next meal!" Lucifer was no longer in the room. As usual, he'd taken up his nighttime post outside the nursery.

Dominic's laugh was low and husky. "I remember it as if it were yesterday. Indeed, it seems like we were married only yesterday. It hardly seems a year." He paused, then eyed his glass. "I think a toast is in order, love. Shall we say . . . to the next wonderful year?"

Olivia shook her head.

"What then? To us?"

Again she shook her head.

Dominic sighed. "Of course not. I know, sweet. Of course it could only be one thing . . . Let's start again." He raised his glass high.

"Wait," she said, a smile tugging at her lips. Her eyes sparkling, she let the rim of her glass touch his. "To fate . . . and one moonlit night . . ."

CALLING ALL WOMEN TO THE WORLD OF AVON ROMANCE SUPERLEADERS!

Would you like to be romanced by a knight in shining armor? Rescued by an English earl with a touch of gypsy blood? Or perhaps you dream of an Indian warrior or a rugged rancher.

Then the heroes of Avon's Romance Superleaders are exactly what you're looking for! And our authors know just what kind of women these tough guys need to shake up their lives and fall in love.

So take a deep breath and let the romantic promise of Samantha James, the sexy magic of Christina Skye, the soul-kissed passion of Constance O'Day-Flannery, and the heart-stirring warmth of Catherine Anderson plunge you right in the midst of an explosive love story.

Olivia kissed his forehead. "I know, pet, but I'm afraid we'll have to wait a little longer before we go. First we must find a way out of here."

OCTOBER

*What could be more romantic than an honest-to-goodness **Christmas Knight**, who lives and breathes to rescue damsels in distress? In her truly magical fashion, Christina Skye makes that fantasy come true for a '90's woman, just in time for the holiday season. See why Virginia Henley said, "Christina Skye is superb!" and why this romance should be on your holiday shopping list!*

Hope O'Hara's quaint new Scottish inn is falling down around her ears, but she's determined to get it in tip-top shape for the Christmas crowd. So when she's on the leaky roof one rainy evening, nearly falling off the slippery thatch, her cries for help conjure up a rescuer from across time—knight Ronan MacLeod.

CHRISTMAS KNIGHT
by Christina Skye

Hope screamed.

Thank God the rider had come from the cliffs, answering her call.

He rocked forward into the wind while his anxious bay sidestepped nervously along the narrow trail. A branch swept past his head, and he ducked and called out and at the same moment he saw Hope.

She did not understand, his words lost against

the boom of thunder. Desperately, Hope clawed at the soggy reeds, which shredded at her touch. Her foot sank through a rotting beam and swept her out into cold, empty space.

She pitched down the wet reeds, a captive of the rope lashing down the tarpaulin, her scream drowning out the man's angry shout. As if in a nightmare she plunged toward the ground, spinning blindly.

The great horse neighed shrilly as its rider kneed forward.

Instead of hard earth, Hope felt the impact of warm muscle halting her descent. Her breath shuddered as she toppled forward, clinging to the terrified horse. She was alive.

Breathless, she turned to study the man whom she had to thank for saving her life.

His long, black hair blew about his face, as wet as her own. Darkness veiled his features, permitting only a glimpse of piercing eyes and tense jaw. But the strength of his body was unmistakable. She blushed to feel his thighs strain where she straddled him.

He muttered a low phrase to the horse, the words snatched away by the wind. The sounds seemed to gentle the creature, and Hope, too, felt curiously calmed by the soft rhythm of his speech.

Above their heads the tarpaulin swept free and a four-foot section of packed reeds hurtled toward the ground. The rider cursed and kneed the horse away from the unstable roof, struggling to control the frightened mount.

Hope understood exactly how the horse was feeling. She sat rigid, aware of the stranger's locked thighs and the hard hands clenched around her waist. Dimly she felt the rider's hands circle her shoulders and explore her cheek. Hope swept his hand away, feeling consciousness blur. The cold ate into her, numbing body and mind.

Deeper she slid. Down and down again . . .

Finally, even the rider's callused hands could not hold her back from the darkness.

NOVEMBER

In a rough-and-tumble world, Catherine Anderson always manages to find a refuge of safety and calm, where love conquers all. Publishers Weekly praised her as a "major voice in the romance genre." In Catherine's newest historical romance she shows us that even a former gunslinger can learn to love and **Cherish** a woman.

On the trail to Santa Fe through New Mexico Territory beautiful, sheltered Rebecca Morgan loses everything and everyone she's ever had in the world. She is plucked from danger by rancher Race Spencer, a loner who reminds the young innocent of the wild land. Although she's not ready to trust anyone again, Rebecca is beginning to realize that in this life the love of a good man might be her only salvation.

CHERISH
by Catherine Anderson

"Countin' the stars, darlin'?"

Rebecca jumped so violently at the unexpected sound of his voice that she lost her hold on the quilt. Pressing a hand to her throat, she turned to squint through the wagon spokes at him.

"Mr. Spencer?"

"Who else'd be under your wagon?"

He hooked a big hand over the wheel rim and crawled out. As he settled to sit beside her, he seemed to loom, his breadth of shoulder and length of leg making her feel dwarfed. Drawing up his knees to rest his arm, he turned slightly toward her, his ebony hair glistening in the silvery moonlight, his chiseled features etched with shadows, the collar of his black shirt open to reveal a V of muscular chest. As he studied her his coffee-dark eyes seemed to take on a satisfied gleam, his firm yet mobile mouth tipping up at one corner as if he were secretly amused by something. She had an uncomfortable feeling it had something to do with her.

She expected him to ask what she was doing out there, and she searched her mind for a believable lie. She had just decided to say she had come out for a breath of fresh air, when he said, "You gettin' anxious to go to Denver?"

Her heart caught. Keeping her expression carefully blank, she replied, "I've tried not to count too heavily on it, actually. It could snow, and then I couldn't go until spring."

"Nah." He tipped his head back to study the sky. "Now that we're this close to home, I can take that worry off your mind. We got a good month before the snows'll hit." He settled his gaze back on her face, his eyes still gleaming. "In three days, we'll reach my ranch, and we'll head out straightaway. I'll have you in Denver within five days."

"I'm not in that great a hurry. I'm sure you'll want to get your herd settled in and see to business that's been neglected in your absence. After all you've done for me, being patient is the least I can do."

He shrugged her off. "Pete can handle the herd

and anything else that comes up. Gettin' you settled somewhere is my first concern."

Rebecca gulped, struggled to breathe. *Stay calm. Don't panic.* But it was easier said than done. She dug her nails into the quilt, applying so much pressure they felt as if they were pulling from the quick. *Inhale, exhale. Don't think about his leaving you.* But it was there in her head, a vivid tableau: Race riding away from her on his buckskin, his black outline getting smaller and smaller until he disappeared from sight. She started to shake.

In a thin voice, she said, "Mr. Spencer, what if I were to tell you I don't wish to go to Denver?"

He didn't look in the least surprised. "I'd offer you two other choices." He searched her gaze. "One of 'em would be permanent, though." He shifted his bent leg to better support his arm, then began clenching and relaxing his hand as he turned his head to stare into the darkness. "So you probably wouldn't be interested in that one."

DECEMBER

The dark of night is full of romantic promise and during **One Moonlit Night** *a vicar's daughter had a run-in with a rakish earl. With heart-stopping excitement, Samantha James weaves a beautiful love story that is sure to enchant. As* Romantic Times *said, "Samantha James pulls out all the stops, taking readers on a spectacular roller coaster ride."*

The new Earl of Ravenwood has gypsy blood running through his veins. Half wild, half noble, and completely inscrutable, he is the subject of much speculation. So when the dark lord nearly runs down gently-reared Olivia Sherwood in a carriage accident, she can't help but feel trepidation. Surely there's no other reason for the racing of her heart?

ONE MOONLIT NIGHT
by Samantha James

" 'Tis midnight," he said softly. *"You should not* be about at this hour."

Olivia bristled. "I'm well aware of the hour, sir, and I assure you, I'm quite safe."

"You were not, else we would not be having this discussion."

Olivia blinked. What arrogance! Why, he was insufferable! Her spine straightened. "I am not a sniveling, helpless female, sir."

His only response was to pull a handkerchief from deep in his trouser pocket. Olivia stiffened in shock when he pressed it to her right cheekbone.

"You're bleeding," he said.

Her reaction was instinctive. She gasped, and one hand went to her cheek.

"It's only a scratch." Even as he spoke, he let his hand drop. "It will soon stop."

All at once Olivia felt chastened. Lord, but he was tall! Why, she barely reached his chin. She didn't need the light of day to know that beneath his jacket, his shoulders were wide as the seas.

Her pulse was racing, in a way she liked not at all — in a way that was wholly unfamiliar. Quickly she looked away. Most assuredly, she did not wish to be caught staring again.

To her surprise he stripped off one glove and tucked it beneath his arm. He then proceeded to take her hand.

Two things ran through her mind: for some strange reason she thought his skin would be cold as death; instead it seemed hot as fire. The second was that her hand was completely swallowed by his larger one.

"Allow me take you home, Miss Sherwood."

She tried to remove her hand from within his grasp. His grip tightened ever so slightly.

"Y-you're holding my hand, sir." To her shame her voice came out airy and breathless.

"So I am, Miss Sherwood. So I am." A slight smile curled his lips . . . Oh, a devil's smile surely, for she sensed he was making light of her. "And I would ask again . . . may I take you home?"

"Nay, sir!" A shake of her head accompanied her denial. " 'Tis not necessary," she hastened to add. "Truly. I live there, just over the hill."

He persisted. "You may well have injuries of which you are unaware."

"Nay." She was adamant, or at least she prayed she sounded that way!. "I would know it."

He gazed down at her, so long and so intently she could have sworn he knew she'd lied.

He released her hand just when she feared he never would.

"Very well then." He inclined his head, then spoke very quietly. "I'm very glad you came to no harm, Miss Sherwood."

Three steps and he'd disappeared into the shadows.

JANUARY

Constance O'Day-Flannery changed romance forever with first-ever time-travel romance. Full of passion, fantasy and magic, her novels have delighted millions of readers. Now allow Avon and the Queen of Time-travel to take you back and introduce you to a fantasy lover who will go anyplace and **Anywhere You Are.**

After the War Between the States, Jack Delancy retreats to the tribal lands of his adopted Indian family to ask the Great Spirit for a vision and peace. What he receives instead is a flesh-and-blood woman seeking adventure who dives from the sky, travels through time, and whose soul is as unfulfilled and restless as his.

ANYWHERE YOU ARE
by Constance O'Day-Flannery

"You came."

Hearing the two words, Mairie stopped breathing and lifted the edge of the canopy away from her head. She imagined that, right? Maybe she was starting to hallucinate from the heat and lack of water. Dehydration could do that . . .

"I knew you would. Thank you."

This was too real. She pulled the canopy completely away and looked behind her, just to make sure she wasn't delusional. What she saw didn't help confirm her state of mind.

A man, some kind of man, was staring at her. All he was wearing was heavy jeans and boots. Naked from the waist up, his chest and face were painted in some sort of Indian zigzag decoration that was smeared and his hair hung below his shoulders in a matted mess. He looked . . . wild. Crazy. And he was staring at her as if he'd seen a ghost.

Fear entered her system and made the adrenaline start pumping with amazing speed. She had to stay calm. This guy was definitely not from the skydiving school. He didn't look like he had attended any school. Ever. He looked . . . feral.

"Hi." She tried smiling. "Thank God, you found me. I've . . . ah . . . sorta wandered off course, and I need to get back to civilization. Can you tell me where I am?"

"What are you?" The man's voice was low, as though he might be frightened of her, yet he slowly walked around her to stand in front. He squatted down and simply stared, like she was an exhibit in the zoo.

How do you answer that question? she wondered. He must be like a hermit or something. He wasn't an Indian, not with brown hair, streaked by the sun, and blue eyes. Maybe he was crazy. Really crazy. Damn . . . What kind of luck was this?

Stay calm, she told herself. The best way to deal with crazy people is to stay calm. She had no idea where she'd heard that, but it seemed like good advice considering the person before her. "You see, I was skydiving and, like I said, I must have gotten off course so if you could just point me in the right direction I can—"

"You dived from the sky?" His words were filled with disbelief.

"Well, yes. Actually I jumped from a plane and then dived, but that doesn't matter . . . I just need some help here and then I can—"

"What is a plane?" he again interrupted, tilting his head and staring at her with the intensity of someone examining a bug under a microscope.

She stared back at him wondering if he was messing with her mind. How could he not know what a plane was? "You know . . . an *air*plane." She pointed to the sky and made hand gestures.

"What *are* you?"

Suddenly, she remembered that she was still wearing the helmet, and pulled it off. Of course, he couldn't see her face. That was it.

"I'm a woman. See . . . ?"

He fell back onto the ground in awe.

She couldn't help it. She laughed. How long *had* this guy been out here, if the sight of a woman had that effect on him?

"Are you God, the Great Spirit?" The words were barely audible.

"I'm not God," she said with a grin. "Though I do like the fact that you would consider God might be female. Pretty enlightened." Compliments wouldn't hurt. "However, I'm just a woman who's lost and looking to get back to civilization. So if you could just point me in the right direction, I'll leave you and—"

"You're my gift. I saw you fall from heaven."

FREE TOTE BAG!

Receive a **free tote bag** with the purchase of four of Avon's romance titles:
CHRISTMAS KNIGHT by Christina Skye (on sale September 9th), **CHERISH** by Catherine Anderson (on sale October 7th), **ONE MOONLIGHT NIGHT** by Samantha James (on sale November 11th) and **ANYWHERE YOU ARE** by Constance O'Day-Flannery (on sale December 9th).

Send in your proof-of-purchase (cash register receipts) for all four books, and the coupon below, completely filled out. Offer expires December 31, 1998.

Void where prohibited by law.

- -

Mail to: Avon Books, Dept. TB, P.O. Box 767, Dresden, TN 38225

Name _____

Address _____

City _____

State/Zip _____

BAG 0698